Killer
With
Three
Heads

Thanks to Athina Paris, Editor for your dedication and tireless effort.

Published By

RockHill Publishing LLC
PO Box 62241
Virginia Beach, VA 23466-2241
www.rockhillpublishing.com

Killer

With Three Heads

J L Hill

Dedication

For Roosevelt Hill, a complicated man with a simple view of life;
"Always walk away from a fight.
And if you can't walk away,
Kill the person, so you won't have to fight him twice."

He has set before you fire and water;
to whichever you choose, stretch forth your hand.
Before man are life and death, good and evil,
Whichever he chooses shall be given him.
Immense is the wisdom of the Lord;
he is mighty in power, and all-seeing.
The eyes of God are on those who fear him;
he understands man's every deed.
No one does he command to act unjustly,
to none does he give license to sin.
Book of Sirach

CONTENTS

Head of The Family

Chapter 1

Time to Kill

The sign over the door of the two-story brick building on the corner reads, *Sons of Italy Social Club*. Or at least, that is what it said years ago before five of the letters fell off. But it has been there long enough that the missing letters, the O's and the I's, left their mark on the brick façade. The blackened glass windows look out to the east and north while double steel doors angled between them face the busy intersection. They swing open, letting in the bright morning sun; they are not locked. The *Sons of Italy Social Club* is never closed. The blinding daylight draws everyone's attention to the thigh-high black leather boots, red micro-mini skirt, and rabbit fur jacket that barely clothes a raven-haired ebony Queen. Five men and a barmaid squint to focus on her until the doors shut and the light gives way to a more normal view.

"Marone!" says the old man sitting at the card table facing the woman. The other two middle-aged men nearly snap their necks doing a double take. "You got the wrong place, honey," he continues, slicking back his gray and black dyed hair. "This is a private club. You want the bus depot down the block."

"I think I'm in the right place," she coos and saunters deeper into the room. "I'm here for Benny. It's his birthday and I'm here to make him a man."

A skinny pimply-faced boy standing at the pool table's voice cracks with uneasy arousal, "I'm Benny, but my birthday ain't until next week."

His pool partner, a slightly older boy, slaps him on the back of his head.

The woman stops at a table two feet from the boys, places her foot on the seat of the chair, so they can see right up the skirt, and reveals everything she has to offer. She kicks the chair and it slides across the floor to the pool table. Benny's friend hustles him to the chair and pushes him down onto it. The three card-playing men position their chairs for a better view and one of them calls out, "Red, put on some music."

The barmaid flips a switch and the club fills with Disco sounds, loud and pulsating. The woman starts swaying her hips and shaking her tits, which are now out of the rabbit fur and protruding from her red halter-top. She swings one leg high over Benny's head, giving all the men a preview of what's to come, while spinning around and thrusting her naked butt in his face. She slowly rubs her bare bottom down his chest and onto his lap. Benny already has a hard-on sticking up through his jeans and she is sure the other men have them too. Hands on her knees, she gyrates and bounces on his lap, rotating her cunt so close to his face he can smell her tangy juices and feel the heat that produces them.

The men are spellbound when she leaps up, spins around in the air, and lands on his lap again, wrapping her legs around him, and her ankles lock around the back legs of the chair. His face buried in her ample cleavage, he can feel his pants filling with cum. Ashamed, he tries to stop but his body is out of control, trapped by her overpowering essence. Everything is happening too fast.

The woman runs her hands through her long silky black hair, taking all eyes with them. She reaches down into the back of the rabbit fur jacket, as the men are glued to every move and watch intently as she pulls two .22 revolvers from her back. Hypnotized like rabbits in headlights, they don't even blink when she fires point-blank into the pool player's face. Then with the gun in her right hand, she sweeps across the card table, placing a slug in each man's forehead.

"Sorry Benny, this is as close as you get to being a man," she whispers in his ear before putting a bullet in it. Then pushing him to the floor, she quickly goes to the backroom door and kicks it in with a black thigh-high boot. With disco music blaring behind her and two .22s outstretched before her, she freezes in the inner office's doorway.

"Vicky! I knew it was you I heard getting the boys all worked up," says Nicky Nails with an easy smile. "Haven't seen you in ages. Did you leave any of my guys alive?"

"I told her to kill them all!"

"Goddamn it, MoJo! This is a day for surprises." Nicky's eyes beam at the sight of the man standing behind Vicky in the back office.

She takes another two steps into the room and Morris Johnson slides to the right.

"I go by the name John Morrison now. Morris Johnson has been dead for ten years."

"Worst alias I've ever heard," Nicky laughs while still seated behind his desk.

"And I told you before, call me Clarita Sanchez." Vicky snarls then turns to me. "Why don't you let me kill this guinea prick and we can get on with our business?"

"Because," I sigh heavily as I explain it to her one more time, "This guinea prick is my friend. And he has the drop on us. See he has his hands positioned on the edge of his big metal desk?"

"Yeah... So?"

"He probably has a hand grenade between his knees and is prepared to drop it and flip the desk over for cover."

"That's right," replies Nicky. "This nigger taught me to always keep a hand grenade handy. And I guess you have one in your pocket too. Can we put the pins in now and get down to business?"

"Sure... and Honey can come out of the closet over there," I show Nicky my grenade and thumb the pin back into the handle.

He reaches under the desk and does the same to his. Honey opens a secret panel in the wall behind him and comes out toting a sawed off shotgun. The three of us exchange embraces as Vicky reloads and holsters her guns, still angry that she doesn't get to kill Nicky.

Rozalina brings in a large bottle of Absolute and Nicky pours five shots of vodka, we clink glasses and down the shots. She whispers in his ear and I say, "Come on Cherry Bomb, we are all friends here."

"That's Mrs. Cherry Bomb Rocci to you," Nicky corrects me.

"What? You're kidding, right?"

Rozalina holds up her hand to show off the huge sparkling diamond ring as proof.

"Immigration was trying to deport her," explains Nicky, "I couldn't let my favorite girl go."

"Some guys are out there," Rozalina tells him, "Cleaning up the mess."

"Your friends from Chicago had something to do with my daughter's kidnapping," I let fly a heated accusation. "I intend to find out what. And—"

"Hold on, MoJo," Nicky pours another round, "I don't think Chicago is behind Maria's kidnapping. They have nothing to gain; it's not the way we operate."

I accept the drink sitting on the edge of his desk. Vicky looks nervous and Honey, who had returned the sawed-off back to the hidden closet stares at the two of us, not knowing what to expect next.

I kinda don't blame them; I disappeared for four years and now return to light up the club with Vicky. "As I understand it, you are about to replace your father as head of the New York Mob. Maybe they want to draw me out and discredit your loyalty to the family. After all, you are where you are today because you supposedly had me killed."

"Yeah, but that's ancient history now." Nicky downs his drink and continues, "That all died the day Angelo did as well. Besides, anybody who could stand in my way of taking over from my father is already at the bottom of the East River. Those guys are here... well, were here... because your boys are moving in on their territory back in Chicago. I have been telling your boys to pull back before we end up in a shooting war."

"I have them keeping a close eye up north because you have been asleep at the wheel," I tell him and down my next shot. "Those guys have been muscling in on our drug trade and infiltrating your operations."

"Bullshit!"

"Oh Yeah? How about that little motherfucker, Benny?"

"Benny!" Nicky half laughs, "I had him running for me since he was in the third grade. I was fucking his mother for years," Nicky quickly shoots an apologetic look at Rozalina. "Before I married you, honey."

"That might be so, but his Grandfather is Beniamino Brunello. You know, the Chicago godfather. They have been setting up a power play for years and I think they are going to use Maria as their pawn."

"Look, Maria is my goddaughter," Nicky says, the smile gone from his face. He looks me in the eye with a dead-cold stare. "I have her bodyguards down in the basement, and they've been telling me exactly what happened yesterday. I know they are telling the truth. No one from the north is involved. If I thought for a second they were, bullets would be flying and the streets of Chicago would be flowing with blood."

"You sure about this?"

"Yes, and as soon as those two stunods come to, I'll finish getting the information out of them."

I notice the bruises on his hands. His knuckles are skinned and scraped. Nicky Nails has put on thirty or so pounds since I last saw him, and it's all muscle. Now, he does look like he could chew nails and spit bullets.

"For now, you stay out of sight; I'll handle Chicago and find out where Maria is. Man, I hate to have to tell Benny's mother he's dead. She is gonna be pissed. And if she is connected to Chicago, things are going to get ugly."

"Don't worry about them, call her up and tell her you sent him on a job. My boys will handle the rest. I also got them working the streets, we will find Maria."

"Yeah, we will," he looks down and then back at me with his boyish grin, "You haven't seen Elizabeth yet, have you?"

"No." I say flatly. "I wanted to have some good news to tell her."

"Well, just seeing you're alive will be good news," he tells me. "She is quite sure that you died in Colombia when you didn't return from that last mission. Four years is a long time, MoJo. What the hell happened? Oh, and by the way, I wouldn't just go walking in the front door, the feds are there."

"What?"

"It is a kidnapping case," Nicky says angrily, "It's kinda their thing? And you know they never stopped paying her a little attention. Anyway, you know the guy, he came out of retirement or something to work this case."

A young black man in a red jumpsuit knocks on the door that is hanging half off the hinges. "All done, John," he says.

Nicky looks him over from his paper hair net to his paper booties. He looks like he just stepped out of an operating theatre.

"They are in the van," he continues, "Do you want us to dispose of them in the usual manner?"

"No," I reply as I come to my feet. "We are gonna have to store those guys for a while. I'll be out in a minute."

"Real professional," remarks Nicky then refills my glass and gives it a tap. "Girls, give us a minute."

The three women return to the bar. Rozalina is amazed at the sight, not a drop of blood anywhere, not a chair overturned, the place spotless. When she left minutes previously there were rivers of blood on the floor and flowing from the card table. As precise as Vicky was, shooting five people in the head leaves a mess, but now one can't tell a harsh word had been spoken in the place. The cleanup crew, five husky black guys in red one-piece jumpsuits transformed the place. It looks better than it ever did.

"I'm leaving Vicky here to help you with security," I inform Nicky. He gives me a frown and then resigns himself to the inevitable. "Until we get to the bottom of this, you need someone you can trust watching your back."

"Watching my back," Nicky downs another shot, "She's more likely to put a knife in it. You know she thinks I left you hanging in Colombia. I didn't, you know. I had our people all over the place trying to find you. What the fuck happened down there?"

"I know you did but it's like I told you that night, the government was about to pull a double cross, and did. You saved both of our lives. You didn't tell her, did you?"

Nicky shakes his head, "Not a word, although I don't know why you wanted to keep it from her. Anyway, how many times do I have to tell you? Never work with the government. They'll fuck you every time."

I run a hand across my chest and up to my left shoulder, it's an automatic reaction to the phantom pain that flares up when I think about Colombia. "She knows now. I told her two days ago. She wasn't very happy."

Vicky sits at the bar staring into a half-full glass of vodka. Rozalina and Izolda give her plenty of space; they can tell she wants to be alone. She had slipped on underwear and jeans and sits there barefoot, her mind nowhere near the bar. She is in the Grand Caymans, days ago...

It was 2 a.m. and the only person who could get the drop on her was kneeling by her bedside with his hand over her mouth.

Her eyes snapped open; her fist flew wildly then changed to an embrace midflight. Her arm wrapped around MoJo's neck as he spun and whipped her out of bed without disturbing her sleeping husband, Derrick. His hand went from her mouth to clutching her bare ass and he carried her into the living room.

"My God! You're alive," she whispered then pulled my shirt open, down over my arms, and places her right hand carefully on my chest over the three bullet-hole scars, making sure I was not a ghost. She fell against my chest and I could feel the tears rolling down my body. "I knew you were alive. I told Derrick. I told Nicky. I told them all, it would take more than three bullets to kill you," she said defiantly. "We've got to wake up Derrick; he has to know you are back—"

"Not just yet," I tell her. I notice her eyes are tracing the whiplash welts that crisscross my body. I take her by the hand and lead her out into the night. I hold her tight against my body, searching for the words I must impart. Her body melts into mine, her fingers running along the marks on my back. Finally, I place my hands firmly on her shoulders and hold her at arm's length, "It was Derrick. He set you up. These bullets were meant for you."

"No. No, you're wrong. The Colombians fought back." Tears welled in her eyes, pain and anger collided with confusion and reason in her mind. Her face contorted as thoughts and rehashed events buried for four years but never forgotten resurfaced. "No," she cried. "No. He loves me. He's my husband now; we've been married two years…"

"I know," I said impassively, "And I wouldn't say so if I wasn't sure. I told you he was CIA, not to trust him. He set up the mission; the raid was designed to get you killed. Remember, I wasn't supposed to be there, and that's why I waited until the last minute to show up."

"Half the team got killed that day in the jungle," her voice was hard.

"Yeah, so?"

Vicky turned and walked back into the house. Her slender body stiff, her nightgown fluttered in the gentle island breeze, but she was oblivious to it all, had already switched into killer mode, and from that moment on, she felt nothing, merely focused on the job at hand, moving with precision. Quiet, just as I taught her, she re-entered the bedroom, and slid back between the sheets. Derrick inhaled deeply as if he were asleep. Vicky stretched an arm across his stomach and waited. The minutes passed slowly, both lying in wait for the perfect moment to strike. Vicky turned onto her side, facing him, and her arm went limp across his body. Derrick was lying on his back and thought this was his chance. He flipped over on top of her, clamped his huge hands on her throat, and was about to use his full body weight to break her neck when flames erupted in his abdomen. It coursed through his stomach and exploded into his chest, ripping it way out of his shoulder. And before the first shockwave of pain could be fully realized and reacted to, another fireball cooked his intestines, followed by another, and another.

Within seconds, Derrick's massive weight came down on Vicky's petite frame, wet and bloodied. Vicky lay there with the gun in her left hand and her husband's head cradled to her in her right. She couldn't breathe. She didn't want to. She stared into the dark night, oblivious to everything around her.

Her face in the mirror behind the bar is stone cold and her eyes are empty. I run my hand down the back of her neck, pulling her back from the abyss of self-doubt. I trained her to trust no one but herself, to believe everyone lies all the time. It was the world we lived in, the only way to survive the jungle, and she was a stone wrapped in a façade of humanity. Everyone was a killer, and everyone was expendable. Trust, faith, even love were weapons more deadly than knives, guns, or bombs. I taught Vicky to use each with precision and without a conscious. I taught her to be a weapon.

"I'm heading out to the Island," I say, not certain if she is fully back yet. "Keep your eyes open, if anything jumps off... Well, you know what to do. You know how to reach me."

"I still think your friend knows more than he is telling," she hisses as she watches Nicky in the mirror behind the bar.

"Of course he does," I whisper in her ear, "but all that will come out in due time. I need you here and on point if he is wrong about Chicago. And if he's not, and I believe he's not, then we are in for a nasty fight. Worse than Colombia, and I need you razor sharp and ready to kill."

As I leave the club I take a quick look back and lock eyes with Nicky, he nods and I go. I'm reassured that he'll keep Vicky out of danger, and I hope to hell she doesn't kill him. I hop into the back of a blacked-out Lincoln and tell my three guys there has been a change. We are going to Long Island but not to the mansion as planned, not with the FBI working on Elizabeth. We are rather going to take the indirect approach. And after what Nicky told me in his office, the indirect approach will work on several levels. I will be able to get Elizabeth to a safe place, and then I'll find out how much the FBI knows about the kidnapping. Yeah, the plan has changed, getting Maria back is not going to be as easy as putting a bullet in some asshole's ear.

Chapter 2

Back from The Dead

There are FBI cars a half-mile from either direction of the black iron gate that blocks the half-mile driveway entrance to the mansion. One on the east bound side of the road and another unmarked vehicle on the west bound. They are parked in the ditch just far enough off the road as not to be visible until you are within a few feet of the black Ford Furys. They are recording every car that passes by the mansion, not ordinary procedure for a kidnapping case, but this is no ordinary kidnapping.

A quarter of a mile beyond their position is the eight-foot-high brick wall that runs to the black iron gate, hiding the mansion from all traffic that passes on the road. The driveway snakes and twists through tall hedges and trees that obscure the property. Nicky had the wall built and reshaped the driveway leading up to the house years ago. He is, after all, paranoid about the police eavesdropping on his business. And although the mansion belongs to Elizabeth, part of her inheritance from her uncle, Nicky and the rest of the Mafia bosses still meet there regularly, just like when Angelo Lucerella ran the family.

Now, with much disdain from Nicky, the FBI is in the mansion, setting up wiretaps, going through documents, recording every sight and sound. Nicky still has a dozen men patrolling the grounds, twice as many since Maria went missing, and they are there as protection, and to keep an eye on the FBI. Not a single agent is to go anywhere unescorted. Not a single associate is to speak to an agent, no names, no nothing, not even a good morning is to be exchanged. Elizabeth insisted on letting the FBI in and Nicky couldn't stop her, no matter how hard he tried.

Sam Black showed up at the mansion two hours after Maria Delitanni and her nanny went missing from the Long Island Central Shopping Mall. He is harder looking than Elizabeth remembered, deeper lines cut into his brow and around his mouth, but he still has soft blue eyes buried in thick bags on his face. His hair is all gray now and he has put on weight, not a lot, but noticeable to Elizabeth, whom he had questioned for years after her uncle's death. Sam Black was the first one to concur that Maria had been kidnapped, and that it probably wasn't for money.

He is also there of his own accord, as the Bureau hasn't classified it as a kidnapping, in fact, the pair hasn't been gone long enough to classify them as missing. But Sam Black knows they have been taken, and in her heart, Elizabeth too knows the reason has nothing to do with money. "Let me bring my team in, unofficially of course," he suggests. "And we can start monitoring the situation. I have ten agents I'm training; this will be totally off the radar, so the kidnappers will never know."

"Not on your life, Fed!"

"Shut the fuck up, Nicky! This is my daughter, my little girl, and my house!" Elizabeth stands in the parlor with her arms crossed and a murderous glare — that the other men, all hardened criminals — cannot face. And that settled it, two unmarked cars stationed outside on the road to the mansion and six tech agents busy setting up electronic equipment in the house.

And again, Elizabeth is being questioned about Morris Johnson, Maria's father, who had been declared deceased years previously.

"The last time I spoke with you, you said Morris was dead. But since then you have been to Aruba three times for extended periods. Are you still going to hold to the story that Morris Johnson is dead?" Sam's eyes follow Elizabeth around the room as she paces like a caged lioness.

"That's ten years ago, he wasn't dead then," Elizabeth stops by the window facing the garden, "I believe he is now. I was living with him in Aruba, but something happened, I don't know what." Elizabeth trembles, fighting back tears. She has become hard over the years; is no longer a starry-eyed teenager in love with the bad boy. What she has become is a woman somewhat cold to love and life; what inevitably happens to a young girl when crowned Mafia Queen. She has lost everyone she loved, everyone she hated, and now the only one she has held onto for ten years is gone too.

"What happened?" asks Sam. Then without waiting for an answer, he offers his own solution. "Morris is not dead. He probably grabbed Maria and—"

"No. That is not true." Elizabeth explodes then spins around and is across the room face to face with Sam Black in an instant. "He would never do that. Never take Maria from me. And if he were alive these past four years, he would have found a way to let me know."

"Maybe this is his way," Sam presses harder. "Most kidnappings are done by family members. The only family you have left is your sister, isn't that correct?" Elizabeth nods. "And her father, who was supposed to be dead, but you were living with in Aruba."

Elizabeth shrinks away from the agent, feels the eyes of the six agents in the parlor burrowing into her, and the three bodyguards' quiet condemnations pricking at her mind. She closes her eyes and shuts them out. She wants them all gone. *'Nicky was right, this was a mistake. The FBI is still trying to prove Morris killed my father, mother and uncle; Sam Black isn't trying to find my daughter, he is trying to find MoJo.'* She sits on the sofa and lets out a loud tired sigh.

Cathy, one of the techs, gets up from the table, which holds six phones, removes her headset and sits next to Elizabeth. She also draws a sharp foreboding look from her boss as she places a hand on the young woman's knee. She sucks her teeth, making an audible smack in the otherwise silent parlor. Cathy is barely twenty-two, six years younger than Elizabeth, and the only woman on the team. She is sharply dressed in a black skirt that drops below her knee, a white unadorned blouse slightly open at the neck, and a black blazer with a pistol tucked neatly aside her left breast. Her golden brown hair is tightly wrapped in a bun at the back of her head. She speaks with an accent that suggests a French background, although she is a New Yorker.

"I read the case files," she says softly. "Morris was gone for three years before he made contact with you. Isn't it possible he has been lying low again? Maybe if we knew what he was working on when he disappeared, or who he was working with..."

Elizabeth breaks out laughing in the girl's face then looks around the room with a slow deliberate turn of her head until her gaze locks with Sam's. "This one needs a bit more training. She wants me to name names." Elizabeth shifts her body to look Cathy squarely in the face. "If my daughter was taken by anyone in the Organization, you guys can pack your bags now. You may be too young to remember what happened when some people crossed Morris Johnson before… Tell her Sam, it was not pretty or wise. Anyway, I don't know what Morris was doing, or who he was working with or against for that matter. These guys aren't very talkative… as you can see."

"But you might have picked up on something," Cathy is trying not to look as green as she is. And she feels that Elizabeth's Mafia Queen Act is a thin veil too, and behind it, she is terrified of the situation she and her daughter are in. If it weren't for the eyes and ears surrounding her she might say more.

"I do know he was working for the government."

"The United States of America government," Sam chimes in.

"Yeah, that's the one," Elizabeth replies as sarcastically as she can. "I don't know what he was doing for them, but I do remember him saying, 'Those damn Narcs are assholes.' He said that more than a couple of times."

"You do know your boyfriend was a dope smuggling drug dealer," answers Sam Black just as sarcastically. "Are you sure he was working with them and not running from them?"

"He never said why they were assholes. Just that they were. And that they were going to get him killed someday."

The phone starts ringing.

6:30 pm. It has been fifty hours since Maria Delitanni and her nanny, Akilina Volkov, were last seen and they are now officially listed as missing persons, although no announcements have been made to the press. Usually, if one doesn't hear anything within twenty-four hours of a kidnapping the chances are slim at best of a positive outcome. Sam knows this is no usual kidnapping, but because of who the child is, her age, her lineage, and the fact they took her nanny also, it is both good and bad. Although, he half expected to have found the nanny cut up in an alley somewhere by now, the fact that he hasn't, gives him reason to hope.

Cathy grabs her headgear quickly, Sam holds the phone up to Elizabeth, and waits for the third ring before signalling her to answer.

Elizabeth's hand shakes uncontrollably as she places the receiver to her ear.

"Hey, Sugar Tits."

Elizabeth hits the floor a full second before the receiver.

The three bodyguards rush to the heap of woman on the parlor floor, as Sam begins sweeping her limp body up in his arms with great difficulty. The other techs are also out of their chairs to aid the unconscious woman.

Cathy, still standing by the table with her headset on, says, "Hello."

"Too much for her, huh? Tomorrow, Grand Central Station Clock, at noon. She's alone."

Cathy hears the click that tells her the caller is gone. Sam gives the young agent another look of disapproval. Cathy immediately counters, "What was I supposed to do?"

"You weren't supposed to do anything. You definitely never speak to the kidnapper," Sam is red-faced. "Back to your posts... everyone!"

"At least I got a meeting place out of him. And a little more tape to analyze."

Sam looks at his team and shakes his head. He can't be sure that was Morris on the line, but from the way Elizabeth reacted, he'd bet good money it was. A man coming back from the grave once was a good trick, but returning twice... was trying to outdo Jesus. His team isn't ready for this kind of case. Finally, he says to Cathy, "he would have called back."

Sea spray whipped around the sides of the boat and covered Elizabeth's face with a cooling mist. She sat at the back of the cockpit listening to the drone of the two massive diesel outboards and watched Nicky shovelling coke up his nose. The warmth of the sun on her face periodically interrupted by the cool Caribbean waters felt invigorating compared to the icy winds of a New York winter's day. Nicky had suggested a Florida getaway, and the day after, he had her, Akilina, and Maria on the charter to do some deep-sea fishing. Maria was below in the cabin asleep, and Akilina, who looked and sounded seasick, was in bed with her. Elizabeth didn't know a thing about fishing, deep-sea or any other kind and since Nicky was spending all his time snorting cocaine and doing shots, she didn't think he did either. She sat back with her shades on, relishing the warmth and the wide-open deep blue water around her.

Three men, dark skinned but not black, shirtless and in ragged cut-offs waded out to the boat waist deep in the water. They carried a large long wooden plank with umbrella hooks on the ends, which fit neatly over the gunwale and reached all the way to the beach. One man held her hand and led the women down the gangplank;

the other two held the aft and bow lines to steady the boat.

"Where are we?" Elizabeth asked.

"Your island," answered Nicky then led them up stone steps to the top of the bluff.

Elizabeth looked around; the whole island couldn't be more than a couple hundred feet of sand and grass. A small twin-engine plane sat, propeller spinning, pointing into the wind.

"A plane, Mommy… A plane… We're going on a plane!"

The cabin door shut and the man pulled down the large red handle to lock it in place. He went through the narrow opening in the front and a few seconds later, they were bounding and skipping along the island. A slight roar from the engines and everyone was pinned back in their seat. Blue skies surrounded Elizabeth and the gentle swaying of the aircraft calmed her nerves.

The plane bounced once to the left, then to the right, the tires squealed and the engines groaned in protest. Elizabeth was forced forward against her seatbelt and against her will. Then thankfully, the cabin door opened and dropped down to the tarmac. Elizabeth floated down the steps.

A hand reached out of the blinding Caribbean sunlight, "Welcome to Aruba, Sugar Tits."

"Elizabeth… Elizabeth… Elizabeth, can you hear me?"

Elizabeth can hear the voice, it's not Morris', but it is one she knows. Feeling the cold clammy damp cloth on her forehead, she snatches it away. Water drops run down her face; frightened and confused, she bolts upright and looks for Sam Black.

"It was Morris Johnson on the phone, wasn't it?"

"Yes. No." She barely has time to think. She is home. Maria is gone. The FBI... "I don't know."

"Come on, Elizabeth," Sam huffs. She is vulnerable and he has to take advantage of the moment before she comes to her senses. Before she can put up her defences and avoid letting slip the truth. "How many guys call you Sugar Tits? You don't seem like that kind of girl to me. Stop bullshitting me. Stop kidding yourself. That was Morris and he's got your little girl."

"I don't know," Elizabeth is puzzled, "sounded like him. But if he has Maria, why would he be calling me?"

"Don't know. What happened in Aruba?" Sam's soft blue eyes pierce her mind.

She can feel him inside her head, rummaging through her memories, digging up her past, forcing her to relive those days.

"You'd better tell me before you meet him tomorrow at Grand Central Station; if you want me to help you get Maria back."

She desperately wants to believe Morris has Maria. He is alive, that was him on the phone, but she knows he would never take their child from her. Wherever he has been and whatever happened in Colombia, Maria's kidnapping brought him back. She feels an icy stab in her heart that spreads slowly throughout her body. Maria is in true danger.

Elizabeth slipped back to the sunny beaches of Aruba.

Morris was splashing Maria and pretending to be driven back by her tiny efforts. He ran a few feet then suddenly turned on her swept the four-year-old off her feet, and swirled her in the crystal blue waters. Together, they ran to Elizabeth, who was sitting beneath a beach umbrella. It was just the three of them on their private beach.

Maria giggled uncontrollably as Morris snatched Elizabeth up into his arms.

"No… Wait… What are you doing?" She asked, startled.

"Daddy's gonna swirl you. Daddy is going to swirl you in the water, Mommy," Maria said jumping and clapping with excitement.

"No. Don't… my hair, Morris," Elizabeth protested as he took off running to the surf.

"Don't worry, I won't mess your hair," I assured her as the water splashed up my legs. I got waist deep and dove into the oncoming wave. For seconds we were suspended motionless in an embrace, and then the water pushed us back and up to the surface. I stood up and she clung to my neck, her wet hair plastered to her face, anger welling inside her and pouring from her eyes. Like the sea, it dripped from her body. "What? I tripped. Honest."

"You are such a jerk. I told you not to mess my hair. Let me go."

I smiled at her, "OK."

"Nooo."

I tossed her high up in the air and into the next oncoming wave a few feet in front of me. She tumbled gently in the surf and was returned to my waiting arms. I swept her up and turned towards the beach, "don't be mad at me, this was your daughter's idea; she said you didn't look like you were having fun."

"Don't you hide behind a little girl, Morris Johnson," Elizabeth said smiling, "you are going to pay for this."

"But you are having fun, aren't you?"

"Yes. I couldn't be happier," she admitted.

We sat in the shallows and let the waves wash over our legs. Maria was dancing and kicking at the incoming waves. I ran my hands through Elizabeth's hair, pulling and straightening it down her back. We waited until the tide came in and Maria was waist deep, then it was time to go back to the house.

The Aruba house sat ten-yards from the beach, its sandy white exterior just slightly darker than the sands of Blue Mountain Beach. The three-story colonial had balconies on each floor that ran the length of the building along the ocean side and connected to each of the seven bedrooms by French bay doors. The house accommodated its fifteen occupants in luxurious style.

Nicky and three of his men, stayed three months, conducting business with Morris in the first level corner office then returned to New York in the spring of '77. Elizabeth, Maria, and Akilina remained another three years. Morris, Clarita, and various other men, came and went.

The house was mostly hidden from view by palm trees along the roadside and Elizabeth couldn't help but feel that as nice as it was the place was a hideout. Morris assured her this was home, her home, that except for the conversations between him and Nicky, the bulk of his business was conducted far from there. It was a safe haven for the three women. As she watched pink sunsets above a pale blue Caribbean Sea from the balcony, she was happy.

"He bought you a home in the Caribbean. He must really love you," Cathy practically whispers in her ear.

Elizabeth is back at the window, having been there motionless for nearly an hour already. The other techs left the parlor under the guise of getting more surveillance equipment for tomorrow. They drew all but one of the mobsters with them. Trying to get Elizabeth to open up, Cathy repeats her observation, "Morris must really love you."

"You know he doesn't, Rita," she responds, still lost in another place and time.

Rita was what she called Clarita, Morris' second in command, and sometimes bed partner. At first, she was jealous of her and worried about what they did when they left on missions. Then she became envious, for they shared a bond she could never have with him. Morris took care of her, provided for her, made love to her, but it was different from the way he looked out for Rita. But eventually she felt sad for her too because Rita loved him, the same as she did, but he didn't love either of them. "Morris loves his Little Maria, not us."

It was late August. Morris was sleeping deeply in their master bedroom suite but Elizabeth could hear the rattle of a wine bottle in a bucket of ice through the open bay doors. Wrapping a white floral silk robe around herself, she went in search of the noise. Rita sat alone on the balcony that summer evening. Elizabeth pulled up a deckchair. They had been gone a month this time and Rita always seemed miserable when they returned. The longer the mission the more cheering up she needed.

"Is he finally asleep?" Rita asked.

"Been asleep for hours," Elizabeth said as she stretched out on the deck chair. Rita handed her the other glass of red wine. She shifted sideways to face Rita and pulled her robe tighter at the chest. "He always comes back so beat from your so-called missions. What do you do? Does he get any sleep?"

Elizabeth regretted asking the questions as soon as they came out her mouth. Morris had told her numerous times not to ask about what they did or where they went, gently but sternly. Besides, she did not want to know what Morris and Rita did when they were alone. It was bad enough she had to put up with him sleeping with her at the house, she certainly didn't need to hear about it when they weren't there.

"He only really sleeps when he's here with you," Rita assured her. "When we are on a mission, he is up three, four days in a row. When he does sleep, it's only for a couple of hours and never very deep, he's up at the crack of a twig." Seeing horror etched on Elizabeth's face, Rita reached out and took her hand, "oh no! It's not from danger or anything like that, he's only... relaxed with you and Little Maria."

Rita saw the tension drain from Elizabeth and her features return to their peaceful repose. Even in the moonlight Elizabeth was radiant, Rita envied that, as she never got that satisfied feeling from being with Morris. Never. Elizabeth seemed to have the contented family life. "At first I thought you were a conniving bitch. I mean... you named your daughter after his murdered girlfriend, that's some fucked up way to keep a man."

Elizabeth sipped the wine and took the statement without offense. "When I had her, I didn't even know if Morris was aware I was pregnant. I named her Maria because..." Elizabeth took a big gulp of wine, appearing to struggle to find the words to continue, "Ok, I never told Morris this so please, don't. This is going to sound crazy..."

'Crazier than naming your baby after your boyfriend's dead girlfriend?' Rita couldn't image how.

"I believe I gave birth to Maria's child... or a reincarnation of Maria... or something like that."

Elizabeth's dead stare sent shivers up her spine, "Yeah, girl, that sounds crazy. I wouldn't mention it to anyone either, especially not to Morris."

"Did you ever meet Maria? Little Maria is her spitting image."

She had seen her once and it was true that the little girl looked exactly like her namesake. Rita wanted out of this conversation, "well, you know, all you white chicks look alike. Anyway, I've known Morris since we were kids, and it's you he loves. Don't worry about me because when he is with me, it's more like he's teaching me, another kind of training, more than making love to me."

"He's not in love with me either," Elizabeth said sadly and poured wine into both of their glasses. They clinked them softly and she continued, "He is in love with someone, I'm not sure who, but unfortunately, it's neither of us."

Elizabeth wasn't sure when it happened or even how it did, probably after they emptied the bottle of wine, but they found themselves on the bed kissing, caressing, and consoling each other. Rita's hand gently circled her nipples, ran down her body between her thighs, her fingers softly peeling her open and making the trip back to her breasts, while her tongue circled inside her mouth. She made the trip repeatedly, and each time spent a little more time massaging her clit. And each time, Elizabeth felt waves of heat rush over her body. She found herself mimicking Rita's actions, her hand gliding through the rough hair and into the soft smooth folds of Rita's vagina.

Rita moaned low and arched her body up, willing giving herself to Elizabeth's penetrating fingers. Elizabeth clutched Rita's silky black hair at the back of her neck as her partner sunk her two middle fingers in and up her pussy. The women gripped each other tighter as their fingers rhythmically rolled in and out of their wet holes, each woman's body quivering with an unknown delight.

Elizabeth had never been with anyone other than Morris and Rita had never considered this as a possibility. But it felt right, good, and pumped harder in response to the other's motions, their bodies writhing wilder towards climax. Perceptive fingers caressed tender erogenous areas of breasts and crotches, sending electric sparks to the other, each holding back as long as she could to milk as much pleasure from her partner as she could. A brush of cool night air ran across their fever-hot skins, releasing rivers of vaginal fluids down their legs. Rita's body pulsed with pleasure and Elizabeth's stiffened in sensual ecstasies. They let out a long guttural exhausted and satisfied moan that carried them into sleep.

Morris stood in the doorway amidst the flowing curtains. He was a ghost, a phantom of the night watching over the women. Their shield, protecting them from dangers they could not imagine. Not even Vicky who had been in the jungle fighting by his side knew what forces moved against them that night. He watched them sleep, taking comfort in each other's arms, comfort in a shared life, and comfort in a common purpose. A purpose that they would never see fulfilled. He would be gone before dawn.

Chapter 3

I Declare War

Agent Sam Black is briefing his team on the operation. He broke them up into three teams, Alpha team, consisting of Cathy and Jonathan – they will remain close to Elizabeth in case she is diverted into a ladies' room in Grand Central Station. The Beta team of Benjamin and Dean will back them up on foot, they are the bird dogs taking a wide angle and watching for anyone approaching Elizabeth. Finally, Robert and Pierre, Charlie team, will be mobile, remaining a block away to give chase or cut off the kidnapper's escape route. Sam is in the command van with the two agents from the cars stationed in front of the mansion. Elizabeth is with him. "Give me a sound check," he orders her.

"What do you want me to say?" Elizabeth is shaking, "testing 1...2...3."

"Yeah, that's fine," Sam says in a soothing voice then holds her hands between his, "that mike is also a transponder, so we will be able to track you no matter what. Don't worry, Cathy and Jonathan will be real close at all times."

"Where are they?"

"They are in disguise, so you won't inadvertently tip off the kidnappers. The most important thing is for you to convince Morris to talk to me. Together we can get your daughter back."

"Why do you insist he has Maria? If he had her, he wouldn't need to contact me, would he?"

"I can see your point," Sam says, "I'm just covering all the bases. If he doesn't have her, he'll need to work with us to get her back." Elizabeth nods in agreement. Sam flips a switch on the wall unit in the van and a row of green lights come to life. "Mike check, Alpha."

"Alpha One," replies Cathy.

"Alpha Two," Jonathan responds, "ready."

Sam gives the command to the other teams and they acknowledge. "We are green," Sam says to all units. He opens the side door of the black van and lets Elizabeth out a block east of Grand Central Station. The plan is for her to walk to the main entrance, wait a moment and then proceed to the clock above the information booth. The streets are crowded; Grand Central Station will be crowded too.

'This is Friday afternoon, there will be a sea of people in there. Morris picked a great time for this,' she thinks, and doesn't believe for a second that Agent Black's people will be able to pick out Morris or anybody else in this crowd. She stands at the top of the stairs looking at the masses, "suppose that wasn't Morris on the phone... Suppose this is a ransom demand."

"Just stay cool," Sam coaches, "Morris may not come himself anyway. Whoever approaches you just let them do the talking. Don't get too close to them either. Try to stay out of reach. Don't worry, we've got your back."

Elizabeth takes slow steady steps down the stairs, sure she is about to fall as she searches for Morris. When she reaches the bottom, she can tell he's nowhere. Slowly and carefully, she makes her way through the crowd and stands a foot away from the information desk. She looks around the station again, trying to pick out the one familiar face from the hundreds that swirl around her. She fights back the feeling that she is going to throw up, or worse. Minutes pass, that feel like hours, while the big black hand of the clock steadily advances with loud clicks.

"Can I help you, miss?" asks a voice out of the crowd.

Elizabeth spins around searching for its owner.

"Over here, miss," the voice is a little louder, coming from the information booth.

Elizabeth locks in on the old gray haired man in the transit uniform behind the information booth and lets out a deep lung empting breath; it feels like the first one she has taken in hours. "No. No, I'm fine," she tells him and starts walking around the booth, her attention pulled away from the dizzying parade of people to the train schedules and maps of the booth. She circles it and returning to her original spot, notices a schedule with red marker writing, '3 p.m. Pittsburgh.'

She grabs the train schedule from its holder, on the bottom is written, 'NOT A WORD. OPEN.' Elizabeth opens the schedule to the middle page.

"Hold it a little higher and turn to your right," Sam instructs her.

Elizabeth complies with both instructions. There is a red zigzagging line drawn across the pages. At the left end of the line is GCS, at the other end US, and the words 'START WALKING'.

"Teams, he's sending her walking to Union Square," Elizabeth hears in her earpiece. Good thing because she didn't know what it meant. Looking at the map a little closer she notices numbers denoting where she is supposed to turn. "There is no time marked on the map so take your time getting there," Sam instructs her.

He presses down a large red switch on the equipment panel and says to his teams, "keep a sharp eye on her. I think he is going to try to contact her on the way to Union Square. Did anyone see who left the map?"

"Too many people," answers Cathy, as she watches Elizabeth pass her and ascend the stairs to street level. Jonathan walks out the station seconds before her and starts heading downtown. "I think the schedule was there before she got here. And as people took the ones in front it was exposed."

"Keep a forward and rear position on her," commands Sam Black to his team. "At the first turn, Beta team takes the hand off, get in position. Charlie team, you head straight down Fifth Avenue, and stay a block behind the others. I'll take Park and get ahead of her. From the picture of the map you sent me, Dean, he has her walking against traffic so the mobiles won't be able to stay on her."

Elizabeth walks down Madison Avenue then turns east on 37th Street again against the flow of traffic. She walks over to Third Avenue and turns onto it. She realizes the directions are designed to shake her tail and she feels afraid once more. She gets to 30th Street and turns west on the eastbound street. She hears a squeal in her earpiece and her hand instinctively grabs for it then she lets it drop as she recalls Agent Black telling her, "no matter what... do not touch that receiver."

Cathy and Jonathan pick up the tail and hear the same high-pitched squeal. Sam hears it too. Someone is trying to ping her tail. He orders everyone to turn off their transmitters. He will be able to direct them, but they cannot reply. Elizabeth enters the park on Broadway and walks from the northwest corner to the southeast. Sam orders Charlie team to follow her down Broadway, while he pulls over on the northeast end.

It's a chilly day out but there are plenty of people in the park, drug dealers, push cart vendors, uniformed police, business suits, and the visibly unemployed. Elizabeth is getting the usual "Hey baby, where you going?" and "Oooh mamasita te estan calientes!" She ignores them all and passes the subway entrance to the N, Q, R trains.

A minute later, Cathy and Jonathan pass the entrance. A crowd comes up out of the station and they have to push through them, trying to keep up with Elizabeth. Jonathan feels a sharp pin prick in the back of his neck and cries out, "Arrgh my neck! Somebody stabbed me." He stumbles and Cathy catches him before he hits the ground.

The crowd stops and surrounds them, staring curiously "Is he drunk?" "I think he's having a heart attack."

Jonathan starts convulsing in Cathy's arms, as she tries to cradle his head in her lap and reactivate her radio with her free hand. Then she hears Pierre call in, "This is Charlie team, Alpha team is down. Repeat. Alpha team is down."

"Beta team, do you have eyes on target?" Sam calls outs. He waits three seconds and repeats the call. "Beta team do you have eyes on target? Open your mikes and respond Beta." There is no answer. "Close in Charlie. Get Elizabeth out of there!"

"If you want to see your daughter, get in the van," a strange voice comes from Elizabeth's mike.

"I see Elizabeth," Robert calls in, "she is getting in an unmarked white van at 14th Street."

"Go hot," shouts Sam Black to the only team members still responding. His van pulls out into traffic with sirens and lights flashing and can hear the sirens of Charlie team from across the park.

"The van turned west on 14th. Get out the way. Get the fuck out the way. Goddamnit." The black Ford turns onto 14th just in time to see the white van turn into an alley in the next block. They are crossing the intersection when a delivery truck slams into the car, flipping it onto its side. Sam can hear the sounds of breaking glass and twisting metal, but he hasn't reached 14th Street yet.

He is on the scene seconds later. A crowd of shocked bystanders stands on the corner but none dare approach the vehicles. Sam Black jumps out of the van, his FBI badge swinging from his neck, the big white FBI letters on the back of his jacket announcing who he is. He rushes to the vehicles with gun drawn and pointed at the truck.

Someone from the crowd yells out, "You're too late! They're gone."

The bystander is right. Sam sees the windshield of the black Ford has been pulled off and a short blood trail is all that remains of the two agents inside. He looks around frantically and the crowd starts to walk away just as eagerly. He holsters the gun and pulls his radio from his belt, "Alpha team come in… Alpha, come in… Beta, do you copy… Beta respond!"

One of the agents from his command van puts a hand on his shoulder. "Elizabeth Delitanni's transponder has gone dead. Edward is calling it in."

Sam sits patiently at the glass table in a conference room on the 23rd floor of 26 Federal Plaza, the FBI Field Office in New York City. The magnificent view of the canyons of Manhattan could just as well be a blank wall to him. His thoughts and concern is on his team of recruits, now missing for six hours. And although the police flooded into the park quickly when the call of 'officers down' was broadcasted, there was no sign of the six agents, or any reliable witnesses to relay what had happened to them. Those who did know something was amiss fled the park just as quickly as the police entered it, and those who remained, gave vague accounts of a man having a heart attack and being taken by an ambulance with a woman. The problem was; there was no record of an ambulance being dispatched to the area.

The witnesses to the car crash, or Charlie Team's abduction, reported four men in black overalls and ski masks ripping the windshield from the overturned car and dragging the injured agents to another awaiting van, which sped off down 14th street and rounded the first corner it came to. There were no fingerprints or trace evidence at the scene. The witnesses gave conflicting license plate numbers, leading the police to conclude the plates were mismatched and stolen. As was the ramming vehicle used.

Officers canvassed the park with pictures of Benjamin and Dean, mainly concentrating on the street vendors, but none could say they either saw or heard anything that would indicate they were forcibly taken. Beta team simply vanished without a trace.

The door to the conference room opens, S.A.C.'s Rose Peppers and Jim Garnett enter, followed by Joe Cox, the Assistant Director in Charge.

"What the hell were you thinking?" Cox starts before he is fully through the door. "This is one fucking ball of shit that's flying around, and someone is going to get it square in the face. You know you should have cleared this with the office."

"It's in my report," Sam says confidently, trying to counter the Director's incriminations. "She wouldn't have come to the Bureau. She barely cooperated with me and my men."

"Trainees," interjects Special Agent in Charge, Peppers. "Not fully qualified for an operation of this sort."

"An operation woefully understaffed," adds S.A.C. Garnett.

Sam knows where this is going, the Bureau is going to hang him by the thumbs. Not that he doesn't deserve it, but he isn't going down without getting in a shot or two, "I had more than enough manpower for a ransom demand. This was something else; Morris Johnson wanted to grab Elizabeth Delitanni."

"Yes, I read your report" Cox says with the growl of swallowing rusty nails, "in the decade since the Banoa-Rocci War, Morris Johnson has not been sighted once in New York or anywhere else for that matter. Your obsession with this two-bit hoodlum has led you to make some very bad career choices, the worst one today. I'll have your badge now... pending criminal investigation..."

"I can't leave my men out there—"

"YOUR MEN," Cox slams his fist thunderously down on the table, "THEY ARE FBI AGENTS. Agents whose lives you have thoughtlessly put in danger. Agents who might very well be dead at this moment, and if so, whose deaths YOU WILL BE CHARGED WITH. Leave your badge on the table and be available for further questioning."

Cox turns and storms out the room, Peppers and Garnett begin setting papers on the table before Sam. He signs them without another word and drops his badge on top of the pile. *'As crucifixions go,'* he thinks, *'this wasn't so painful.'*

Sam arrives at his lower eastside apartment, after spending a considerable amount of time and money in his neighborhood bar. He places his gun in a locked box besides his bed and starts to unbutton his shirt in the dark. Scorching white light smacks him back against the headboard as he puts his hands up to shield his eyes.

"'Bout time you got here. I was getting tired of sitting around this rat's nest waiting for you."

Sam is shocked back to sobriety by the voice in the dark. He thinks about going for the gun between the mattress and the headboard but waits to see if the voice belongs to who he thinks it does. "Morris Johnson?"

"Morris Johnson?" enquires the invisible voice. "That guy died years ago. You need to keep up with the times. I'm John Morrison. I am here because someone kidnapped a little girl and you are going to find them."

"First off, get that fucking light out of my face," snarls Sam. He gives second thoughts to the gun. "And second, that is the worst alias I have ever heard."

I click off the flashlight and the room returns to the gloom of a broken life. In a moment, our eyes adjust to the light of the streetlamp illumination. I'm leaning against the wall with the flashlight tucked in my belt. He has risen to his feet in a boxer stance. I laugh, he is well into his sixties and although he is tall and still muscular, a well-placed kick will break him in two. "I get that a lot these days. But you'd be surprised how many people don't question the obvious. Like those guys following you around all night."

"If you want me to help you find your daughter," Sam stammers, "you should have thought about that before you kidnapped my agents and got me kicked off the case."

"You're not listening. I said you are going to find the people who kidnapped my daughter. I'll find Maria, you can bet on that. And I didn't get you kicked off the case," I correct him. "They will never let you investigate the real crime. So I freed you, now you can go after them."

"I'm not doing anything until you release my agents."

"This... This is not a negotiation," I tell him with venom in my words. His eyes widen and he stiffens as I approach. "Your agent kidnapped my daughter. I kidnapped your agents. You get them back when you deliver him."

"Are you crazy?" Sam protests. "The FBI doesn't kidnap little girls."

"Well, this one did," I shove a VCR tape in his chest, "I think you'll know who I'm talking about when you see him. Find him and do it quickly, the clock is ticking."

"How am I supposed to do that? You got me cut off from all my resources," Sam complains.

"You have been in the Bureau a long time, don't tell me you don't have any hidden assets. But you don't want to fail this time, that pretty little recruit is counting on you," I warn him as I walk out the apartment door.

Sam grabs the gun from between the mattress and headboard but immediately throws it onto the bed. The missing clip makes going after Morris Johnson, or John Morrison, or whomever he is a futile effort. Instead, he puts the video tape in his player and begins to watch. It's two minute clips, all taken from approximately the same vantage point across the mall from the women's bathroom. He sees Maria and her Russian nanny coming and going, sometimes stopping at the restroom, other times just passing by the camera. In each clip, they are being watched and followed by Tom Green, an FBI agent. The FBI agent his partner, Willie White and he had brought in to infiltrate the Banoa crime family.

The operation was a bust. The Rocci's won the war and Tom Green was sent packing. He remained in the Organized Crime Unit, but like him, Tom was reassigned after it became obvious they were not going to get evidence on Nicky Rocci for either of the Joe Banoas' murders. The father was gunned down by a pair of masked gunmen inside his bar, the Bella Rosa, and his son died shortly thereafter, in what was described as a hunting accident, his body cremated. When Elizabeth's mother and uncle – the godfather of a New York family – died mysteriously a few years later, Sam tried to launch an investigation but was turned down repeatedly.

He had lost track of Tom Green, but from the tape, Tom Green had remained as interested in the family business as had he. He doesn't believe Tom kidnapped the girl, but he probably knows something about it. He has to find him, and in a hurry.

It's 2 a.m. and I'm back in the basement of the *Sons of Italy* with Nicky and Maria's two bodyguards. They had been stripped to their underwear and are tied to chairs with their hands behind their backs; they have stopped bleeding and turned black and blue. The older mobster's head is hanging limply towards the floor, probably staring into the Hell he knows he will soon be going to. The younger man is following us intently with hope in his swollen eyes.

"I don't know who is worse," Nicky shouts and waves his .45 in a circle above his head. "These two marrones who can't tell they are being tailed by the fucking Feds or you... You crazy son of a bitch... Kidnapping a bunch of Feds!"

I watch Nicky pace back and forth, mumbling, stopping, looking at the pair, and back to pacing again. This is the Nicky I know, always worrying about the little things. "You are going to give yourself a heart attack if you keep this up. I have things well under control."

"UNDER CONTROL... UNDER CONTROL," Nicky explodes. "This is not under control. I have these two, I should blow their fucking brains out, but he's one of my father's best men..." Nicky sticks the .45 to the older man's forehead. "And this moron is my top soldier. Oh, and come morning, the Feds are going to be crawling up my ass looking for their missing agents, no, all our asses... that is not gonna sit well with the other families. Do you know why we don't fuck with the Feds?"

I let out a long exasperated sigh, "the Feds are not going to come looking for you. By morning, they will have another rabbit to chase, and he will lead them far from anything that even smells Italian. As for these two, cut them loose, you worked them over pretty good. I am sure they will keep their eyes open next time."

The younger guy's head bobs up and down like it's on a spring. I'm sure he'd be swearing to Jesus if he didn't have a rag stuffed in his mouth. The older man's head drops back down after Nicky pulled the gun away and he has not looked up since. "You kill them!"

"Me," I ask, "Why me? They're your guys."

"My father will understand if you kill them," he reasons, "she's your daughter and they fucked up royally."

"Look, I'm just glad the manager at Radio Shack was such a perv he recorded women going into the ladies' room. But somebody knocked out the security cameras," I add. "That was no accident. You took care of the manager, right?"

"Yeah," Nicky assures me. "And we grabbed every piece of video in that store. Ever since the Kohl's job, there have been security cameras in every mall. For them to go out on that day…"

"If I'm right, I got a lot more to worry about than your dad and a couple of Feds." I pick up a .22 from a small table between the two bound men. I nonchalantly swing the gun back and forth firing a shot into the back each of their heads. They slump over.

Sam hears the call on his car radio at 6 a.m. while he is watching his tail watch him. He peels out of the parking lot and heads uptown. He runs through several red lights and almost broadsides a taxi before putting on his siren and lights. He slams on the breaks and skids to a hard stop behind a dozen other cars from every branch of law enforcement in the city. He hops out of the car and with a couple of steps and a leap that he couldn't have made when he joined the Bureau he is on the loading dock of the meat warehouse.

Just as quickly as he gets to the massive opening, he stops dead in his tracks, "For God's sake, get him down from there!"

Two FBI agents look at him momentarily then continue taking pictures. Each time the flash lights up the warehouse it is like a scene from a 'B' horror movie. Two other agents grab Sam and try half-heartily to hold him back.

Sam busts through, yelling, "That's enough, I said get him down from there. He's one of our own."

"I thought I made myself clear," A.D. Cox barks from the shadows, "you were to stay at home until I summoned you." He motions to a man by the control panel and the hook starts down slowly with Agent Dean Jones' body dangling fifteen feet in the air. Three agents in haz-mat yellow suits straddle the pool of blood and carefully cradled the dead man's legs. "Hold right there. Get more pictures."

"Is that really necessary?"

"He's one of ours," Cox says in a demurred tone, "we are not going to miss a single piece of evidence. We ARE going to get the bastard who did this, come Hell or high water. Now get out of here, your presence is contaminating my crime scene. It's hard enough for them to do their job without having to look over their shoulders at you."

As he leaves the warehouse, he hears the sucking sound as the hook is pulled from Agent Dean Jones' back. He thinks back to last night; he should have made a move on Morris Johnson in his apartment. Jones would probably be alive had he done something... anything. He waits by the coroner's vehicle for Jones to be brought out. It is a long wait. When his body does finally make it to the back of the vehicle, Sam stops them and unzips the body bag. He sees the hole in the middle of his forehead; it is odd, not like any gunshot wound he has ever seen. "What's this?"

"Best I can tell," answers the Chief Coroner, "someone drilled a hole in his head."

"Was he…"

"He only has the two wounds. Both received while he was alive. I'll know more when I examine him at the morgue."

Sam jumps into his car, takes off, and beats the coroner back. He is waiting in the exam room.

Despite the coroner's objections, and with one blatant threat to kick the shit out of him, he watches the autopsy performed. Yes, Jones was alive when he was picked up and slammed down on the hook. Yes, he was alive when someone took a drill to his head and bored halfway through his brain. The coroner retrieves a bullet, casing and all from the wound. Sam again threatens the doctor not to mention or make any note of the bullet. He places it in an evidence bag and leaves. He knows it won't be long before the other agents are finished at the scene and Cox will be coming in for a full report.

Sam clutches the bullet in his hand, he has to find Tom Green, and the next time he is face to face with Morris Johnson or John Morrison, he promises himself to put a bullet in his head, the old fashion way. But to find Tom, he needs help, and the only one he can reach out to is his old partner Willie White, now retired and living back in Texas. Sam races for Long Island; he has to get to Trusty Trudy before Cox can speak to the coroner. He can't be sure if the doctor feels sufficiently threatened or not.

Trudy is a twin engine Cessna Golden Eagle, which had once belonged to a smuggler, who had been killed in a shootout with him and Willie. It was such a beautiful plane they couldn't bear to turn it over as evidence, and felt justified, as it didn't have any drugs onboard anyway.

What it does have is a programmable transponder that can send out a signal mimicking any plane he wants, and makes tracking it nearly impossible. If it hadn't been for a hot tip from a rival smuggler, they would have never known the plane was landing on Long Island.

Sam flies behind and below some small jets and copies their signals. To them, he appears as echo, to ground control he'll be practically invisible. He is safe while in the air, but if the doctor talks, the Bureau could be waiting for him at Willie's ranch, because where else would he go? He's quite sure Cox will hold him liable for Jones' murder, and stealing evidence that just screams, *'lock me up.'*

It is nearing noon locally when Sam drops out of the skies over Willie's ranch. Willie lives so far out that he doesn't have to worry about air traffic control; the only things in the skies around here are crop dusters. Still, Sam has to be cautious, working narcotics for so many years one learns the trade tricks well, like buzzing the drop zone before coming in for a landing. He circles low over the house once then makes a run straight at the house, as if he was landing but with the wheels up. He watches the porch light; if it starts blinking on the next pass, he will land, but if it goes on and stays on, he will have to keep flying. He checks the fuel gauge, almost empty, he won't be flying for long.

The porch light between the second and third pillars comes on and stays on for a moment. Just as he is about to pull back on the yoke, it starts flickering like crazy. Sam waggles the wings as he climbs over the house. He makes one more run out to the edge of the field and comes in slow. He puts Trusty Trudy down softly and rolls her all the way to the porch steps. Sam comes down the steps with a worried look on his face, still not sure if the Bureau got to Willie or not.

Willie White comes out onto the porch with a heavy double barrel shotgun in his hands. He watches his partner approach the steps. When Sam gets to the top, Willie drops the barrel down and says, "How did that go again, 'On long and you're gone. Lights a-flicker put her down quicker.'"

"Yeah, something like that," Sam says, "so you just gave both signals and let me choose which one suited me?"

"I remembered that old Trudy wouldn't have enough left in her to make it past the trees, so you'd be putting her down like it or not." Willie leans the shotgun against the wall and sits down in the chair on the porch with great effort. He shakes the arm of the chair next to him and Sam takes a seat. "What kind of trouble are we talking here? My phone hasn't rung so much in one day since I shot the kid robbing my bank back in '79. And they were reporters. What got the Bureau pissing in their pants?"

"So they have contacted you?"

"Unlike you, I still have friends in the Bureau," Willie jokes.

"Good because we are going to need them."

"Hold on cowboy! We?"

Sam takes a deep breath. "Just hear me out. You remember that boy you trained from 'Nam, Tom Green? Seems like he is mixed up in the Delitanni kidnapping case. And I mean deep in the mix. I don't think the Bureau knows he's involved but he is all over this tape. You have a VCR?"

The two old men get up and go into the house. Sam picks up the shotgun by the barrel as he enters, "Is this thing loaded?"

"Would be of no use if it wasn't," Willie holds out his bony hand, "let's see this tape of yours. Where did you get it?"

"From the girl's father."

"The dead black kid," Willie cocks his head to one side and looks off into the distance. "What was his name again? Morris Johnson, that's right, his friends killed him. He finally made his way back from the dead, huh?"

"That's right and he killed Dean Jones."

"Who?"

"One of my new recruits. He says I have to find Tom Green or he'll kill the others too."

Willie White scratches at his scraggily beard, "he said that."

"Not in so many words," Sam admits, "but with Jones hanging from a meat hook, I'm sure that's what he meant."

"Are you sure it was him who hanged Jones up there?" asks Willie. "I never really liked that boy, too sneaky if you ask me." Seeing Sam's puzzled look, he clarifies. "Tom Green that is, I never met Morris Johnson. But if he's back, that could be real trouble for New York. Yes... I suppose he could have put your agent on that hook, that boy was as mean as a wet cat. But like I was saying, I wouldn't put it past ol' Tom, if he got something to hide. Let's see what's on this tape."

After they watch, Sam asks flat out, "do you suppose some of your friends at the Bureau can help track down Green?"

"He sure is tracking that girl. I guess I can ask around, kind of quiet like," Willie says with a voice that falls to a whisper. "Have you shown this to anyone at the Bureau? Maybe he is on assignment."

"Didn't have a chance," Sam tells him, "they kicked me out of there faster than if I had been glowing green with radiation. Besides, I got the tape last night and Jones was found dead today. Didn't think it would sit well for me to come up with new evidence of this nature. And speaking of evidence, what do you make of this?" Sam holds the bullet in a bag before Willie eyes.

Willie takes the bag, turning it on all angles, "hmmm, copper pointed tip, no machine markings, a little longer than a .22 rifle shot, yet the casing is not a rifle casing. I'd say it's a sniper's round, handmade for a close range shot. Where did you get this, from your mysterious Mr. Johnson?"

"No. Out of Jones' head," Sam replies with bitter pain in his voice. Jones was a ripped 240-pound black man from the notorious Robert Taylor Homes in Bronzeville, Chicago's South Side. The scars on his face spoke of gang fights. The scars on his arms of gang tats he had removed in the Marine Corp. He joined the team late, only a month ago, by special directive. *No way did Morris get that hook in him alone.* "Someone drilled a hole in his head and placed it in there."

"Ah, gangs," Willie says with confidence, "it is one gang, letting the other gang know, they are coming for them."

"Are you serious? He is declaring war on the FBI. He said we took his daughter…"

"No," corrects Willie, "he said Tom Green took his daughter. He is declaring war on Tom Green, and whoever he is working for. Let's hope it is not the FBI, and frankly, I don't think it is. You're going to have to speak to Jake Justice, up in Montana. He's the one who brought Tom in and I always thought he held back a little on the details. Let's hope he's more talkative these days. I'll let him know you are coming. If you drop in unannounced at his place, he'll blow you out of the sky with something much bigger than a double barrel. And I'll find a safe way to get this tape into the Bureau, maybe they'll be able to confirm Tom is on the job, or if he's gone rogue."

Chapter 4

On Angel's Wings

Willie White calls a friend to bring over his special shine and they fill Trudy's tanks. According to Willie, his friend is more into making explosives and stockpiling weapons for the coming apocalypse than making whiskey. The two men have lunch while Willie contacts Jake on his ham radio. He doesn't tell Sam who Jake is or which agency he worked for, but he doesn't have to, only NSA guys live that far out in the sticks, and only an Agency guy would have an anti-aircraft gun in his attic. When Willie gets him using his code handle for November and tells him to expect a visitor, Jake replies with a single short message, "315. 425."

Sam finds himself fighting a vicious headwind, but Trudy is humming along on what he assumes is the best jet fuel money can buy. *3:45, 'only 40 minutes to get to Harve, or the mountains just south of Harve on the 315-degree heading, or this Justice guy is going to slice us up, Trudy.'* He has dealt with NSA guys before; they are a breed apart, as edgy as squirrels on acid. *'Don't know who is worse, Agency guys or Company men, don't like either of them much.'* Sam throttles up the Cessna a little more, he can't afford to be late; this guy can easily shoot him down and be across the border in Canada before anyone sees the smoke.

There is to be no radio communications. Sam checks his coordinates, his heading, and his time; he is where he is supposed to be on the northeast side of Bear Paw Mountains. He begins his descent. Nestled between the evergreens in a valley between two sharp peaks is a patch of brown dirt a hundred and thirty feet long. As he gets closer to the ground, he can see a log cabin at the end of the dirt road, which is his runway. Fifty feet above the dirt road, he spies a large sliding barn door in the attic of the log cabin. *No doubt, Jake Justice is sitting behind them, finger on the trigger, deciding if he really wants company.*

White steam slips from his mouth on this frigid Montana afternoon his snow-white hair framing a darkly tanned and sun-beaten face absent of any signs of emotion. Jake stands in the doorway of the huge cabin, waiting for Sam to make his way up the road. He studies his walk, his demeanor, analyzing every aspect of the FBI man more out of habit than concern for his safety. He has his .45 at his side and an M-16 just inside the door for that. "There's a lot of chatter about your disappearance back East."

Sam assumes that's his way of saying hello; they get right down to business then, "I am on a tight schedule, and a lot of people's lives are at stake here. I need to know who Tom Green is working for, to know where he might be hiding, and if he has the girl with him."

"You need to know who you are working for," Jake cautions him then steps aside and lets Sam in from the cold.

"I work for the Bureau," Sam says with attitude, "whether they like it or not. Who do you work for if you don't mind me asking?"

"I'm retired," Jake replies as he sets the safety on the M-16 mounted on the vertical gun rack for easy access. "I guess the correct question is... do you know who you are working with? John Morrison is either completely insane or the devil. I really could never figure that out." Jake leads the way through the living room, where a roaring fire burns in the fireplace, then down a hall decorated with army pictures dating back to World War II. They are arranged in chronological order, starting with him as a private in the army in Europe, a sergeant in the Philippines, onwards as a captain and major in Korea, and then they reached an inner office.

Sam takes note of the memorabilia around the spacious log cabin. Bayonets, swords, pistols, guns, rifles, flags and banners hung and displayed everywhere. The place is a war museum. *Every single weapon is probably locked and loaded. No family pictures though, typical Agency guy.* "So, what can you tell me about Tom Green?"

"Not much," Jake answers flatly, "he was a decorated Nam soldier. Smart, a get the job done type person. You know... followed orders. The type of guy the Bureau could work with."

This guy is blowing agency smoke up my butt. If he wasn't going to give me any information, why did he have me fly all the way up here?

"Your man, John Morrison, he's a different story all together." Jake takes up a stance by a smaller fireplace; a crackle and hiss accent his words.

Sam settles back on the sofa and lets the sixty-something-year-old man spin his tale. *This is why he wanted me here.*

"He was already working in Colombia when I got orders to recruit him. Was making a name for himself as a tough trader in the Cocaine business, and that's saying something. I don't have to tell you what a cutthroat business it is."

"Why the hell would the Agency or the Company want to train someone like Morris Johnson? I'm sure you didn't trust him."

"You got it flipped around," Jake laughs, "we didn't want to train him. Oh no, we wanted him to train our guys. America isn't a very good loser, in fact, we are the worst. Nam left a bitter taste on a lot of people's tongues, tongues that had a lot to say about how we wage war. Nam taught us we couldn't draft the type of people we needed to fight these wars." Jake looks fondly at a photo from WWII, and gently runs his hand over the gold frame on the mantle. These guys, even if dead, are his family. "We needed dedicated, motivated, men willing to take the fight to our enemies. We needed someone who could train them to fight the type of fight that would eat away at a man's soul. We needed a man who didn't have a soul to speak of, and could train others to put their souls in their pockets and get the job done. When the President declared the war on drugs, we found our general sitting smack dab in the middle of it."

"But he was a dealer," Sam objects, "You couldn't have trusted him to fight against himself."

"On the contrary," Jake Justice smiles, "he was more than willing. As long as we didn't go after his business, he was fine. In fact, it was a win-win for both of us, he knocks off the competition with our help, and we got invaluable training in urban warfare. The type he had been waging all his life. As he put it, 'it doesn't matter if your battleground is a ghetto or a jungle, you must annihilate your enemy so completely, no other will want to take his place.'"

Bogota was hot, humid, and horrifically violent. At any given moment, gunshots would erupt and the people would dive for cover. When the silence returned, three or four people lay dead in the street and the living would simply go back to their daily routines. Some quickly crossed themselves, thanking God it was not their time yet. I never bothered to make the sign of the cross; God had nothing to do with the business there.

I sat at the bar drinking my beer; Vicky sat two stools to my right.

Philippe returns from the commotion in the street and sits between us, "A couple of Medellin boys in the wrong place at the wrong time."

"No doubt," I say as I let the obvious disgust roll out with the words. "We need to get a handle on this thing. There is plenty of money to go around, but all you cowboys wanting to be the top dog is dragging the whole thing through the mud. Take a clue from America in the twenties and thirties, people are going to get tired of the shit, and then you are going to have a real problem on your hands."

Philippe orders another round of rum and beers, "what are you suggesting?"

"Let me reach out to the other players. I'll set terms that will be beneficial to all concerned."

"That's OK with me," Philippe downs his shot and then his beer.

He's a thin man, twenty years my senior, but is hanging on my every word like a schoolboy in the principal's office. He keeps flinching and nervously checking Vicky's actions in the mirror behind the bar. I told Vicky before the meeting not to speak, to not even say hello when I introduced her. That she was to sit behind him and apply the pressure of uncertainty. She isn't up to killing anyone yet, but he doesn't know that. As for me, I have already picked out who is in his organization and the order in which I will kill them, if needed. He is number one, and he knows it.

"What if they don't want to come to terms?"

"They will." We leave Bogota and head south-west to Cali, where I had sent an advance team to scout the major cartel members for weeks.

Killings in the States are turning up the heat and Nicky and I know it won't be long before coke, the harmless plaything of the rich, becomes the dangerous drug peddled by ruthless murderers. *We worked too hard cultivating our image to let a bunch of yahoos ruin the show for us. This is the type of thing you have to control at the source.*

We fly over the mountains and land in a little town just east of Cali. There, I meet with Jose, a representative from the Cali Cartel. The setup is a little different, even if still a small cantina. We sit at a table in the middle, but this time, Vicky is behind me at the bar facing Jose, and his men sit at tables surrounding us.

"Let me just say, thank you for meeting me, although, I was hoping to meet with your bosses."

"The Italians send their gopher," he grins, "and they send me."

"Oh," I am surprised by his assumption, "I see. My friends thought it would look better to others if they met with me, so it wouldn't look like they were taking orders from my partners. I came myself because I didn't want the message getting misinterpreted."

It is hotter in this bar than in all of Colombia. I picked the town of Candelaria because we aren't doing business with the Cali Cartel and even though we are in their region, we are not in their stronghold. It makes for better movement for my guys, and keeping track of who is who a lot easier.

"I was sent with a message for you and your partners," Jose says with venom in his voice, "we do not care what your plans are. Here in Cali we run our business our way. We are not afraid of your Mafia friends, your United States D.E.A., or you." He points to my left and I hear the quick shuffling of feet and a short shrill shriek from Vicky.

There is a large oval mirror across the room and in its dirty reflection, I can see one of Jose's men with a handful of Vicky's hair, pulling her head back, exposing her neck to a Bowie knife. A pair of men quickly come to their feet on either side of me and draw their weapons. They stand with Uzis trained and ready to fire.

I wait a moment for it to get very quiet then say in a low and deliberate tone, "I would believe that if not for the fear in your eyes. My Mafia friends are thousands of miles away, hoping you are a reasonable man. The D.E.A. has not been giving orders to act yet, but I think it won't be long before those orders are signed. But that is not the fear I see in your eyes, you are afraid that I am about to blow your dick off with my .45, and you are right."

The man with the Bowie knife to Vicky's throat head explodes in a bloody shower across the bar and the knife drops to the floor. The four men with machine guns in hand, heads split open like melons left too long in the noon sun. They too drop to the floor. The heads of two more of Jose's men spray blood across the table where they sit. There is only Jose and two more men behind him, their eyes wide with fear. The snipers stationed around the outside of the cantina await their orders.

"When I said to meet Clarita and me at this cantina, did I say we would be alone?"

"I was not told—"

"But you were told to kill my friend and I," I cut his answer short.

"No. No. Not to kill you," he quickly corrects me, pleading for his life. "I was just to warn you. Not to kill you, we don't want trouble…"

The loud bang from my .45 under the table drowns out the rest of his words. Jose is knocked from his seat writhing in pain and blood pouring from his groin. He twitches for three minutes and twelve seconds on the bar floor in front of the last two men as he bleeds out from his femoral artery. When he finally lies still, I stand with my gun in hand and look the pair dead in the eyes, "tell your boss to stop the violence, it's bad for business." Then I fire one shot into the head of one of the men seated at the table. I turn, walk to the door, and wait for Vicky, who gingerly steps around the bloody corpses on the floor. The last man is sitting frozen in his chair next to his partner who is staring up at the ceiling, blood pouring from the back of his head. I take Vicky by the arm and tell her,

"What the hell, they will get the message." I fire over my shoulder; the blast conceals the thud of the last man hitting the floor.

By day, I train Vicky to shoot, like in the cowboy movies, starting with shooting bottles off of posts. The only difference is that I stand in front of one of the posts, the one she is supposed to miss. As the days go by, the posts get closer together and she moves farther away. Although I plan to keep her close to me, I want to be certain she will be effective from a distance.

By night, I train her to use her body as a weapon. "Sex is the deadliest weapon you can wield. You must be able to make a man's mind go blank in a second with a single touch. Must be able to blind him, draw him into your eyes, your body, so the world around him goes dark and you are his only light."

Vicky is atop me, her hips grinding down slowly, engulfing my dick. Her hands slide up and down my chest in time to the motion of her moist strokes. I run my hands around the small firm butt cheeks and up her sides to latch onto her breasts. Our bodies glisten with sweat from the heat of passion, her eyes slowly roll up towards heaven. I reach up and slap her cheek softly but firmly to bring her back to the moment. "Concentrate, I'm the one who is supposed to be losing myself in you. Focus, work your body, not your imagination."

She thrusts her hips hard and forcefully forward. I grip her by the waist and toss her over onto her side. *This lesson is over, I can teach her to shoot like a pro, but it is more important that she learns to fuck like one.* "Go practice on one of the guys."

"Which one?" she fumes with her back to me and legs tightly crossed at the ankles.

"I don't care. Pick one of the snipers and fuck his brains out. Maybe Miguel, he let that guy from Cali put a knife to your neck. You need to show him what his job is, let him know what he is really working for." I know she loves me and will do anything to save my life, and that is the problem. What I want her to do is learn how to make someone, anyone, fall in love with her. To be willing to do anything, kill and die for her, without a moment's hesitation. It is the only way she will survive this life.

Vicky grabs the white cotton sheet from the foot of the bed and swirls it around her body like a tempest. She storms out of the bedroom into the dark hallway of the ranch house trailing the fabric like a bridal gown wrapped across her breasts and flowing out behind her. Moonlight paints alternating squares of black and white on the cold marble floor through the windows that give views of the courtyard below. Sounds of the Colombian night play softly through the corridors. Moments ago, they serenaded her, accentuating the pleasures that only the night can reveal. Now, they are screams of tortured souls, her soul. *How can he treat me like this? Sending me off like a common whore. He thinks I don't know how much he needs me. How much he wants me. Why won't he let me love him?*

She flings open the door to a room far down the hall, a thunderclap of moonlight shocking the inhabitant. Miguel spins out of bed and lands on his feet with both hands clasped around his Colt 45 Automatic. His eyes quickly adjust, as his training has conditioned him, to the vision of an angel bathed in the purest of light and robes. "Clarita?" he asks in disbelief.

"Si," she replies, her voice a sweet whisper that matches her appearance. "I know I am only another soldier to you, covered in armor, but I bruise so…" Miguel drops the gun to his side and she lets the sheet fall to her waist. She steps forward out of the bright light revealing her creamy chestnut torso and burnt bronze breast in the dark heated night. Miguel's eyes widen, he's speechless, not sure if he is awake or caught in an erotic dream. Vicky slowly walks to him and at arm's length reaches a hand to his chest and silently drops the sheet to the floor. Her fingers spread and contract, interlacing with his chest hairs, as streams run down from her golden eyes, "I have been so afraid since—"

"Ssshhh, mi encantadora Clarita," he says softly as he takes her hand, afraid if he reaches out she will disappear as quickly as she appeared. "I will protect you. Voy a matar a cualquier hombre que te toca."

Vicky continues pushing him down onto the bed then slides her hand inside his white boxers, softly squeezing and releasing. Miguel inhales deeply and exhales with each massaging stroke. He wiggles free of his boxers and Vicky freely runs her hand up and down his pulsing penis, while still taking time to gently squeeze his balls and run his pubic hairs through her fingers. The night has fallen silent, except for the sound of Miguel's groans of pleasure and anticipation.

Her free hand runs through his chest hairs and grabs hold as she climbs onto the bed and guides his thick pink head into her body. His feet are planted on the floor and his back is held to the bed as she rides slowly up and down, lifting her hips with an arching back. His eyes follow every movement of her breasts as they rise and fall away from his face. He reaches up for them and sheepishly strokes her protruding nipples. She quickens her pace.

Miguel latches onto her breasts and she feels him thrusting hard in time with her, as his breathing becomes labored and struggling. She leans forward, digging her nails into his sweaty chest and he pounds his dick upward, producing a squishy sloppy sound from her pussy. He grabs her hips with both hands and freezes all motions in the room. Then he contorts in ecstasy and she feels his dick pumping its fluid into her. Her vagina contracts involuntarily to the intrusion of hot semen, sucking up his cum and gushing forth a waterfall of her own orgasmic fluids. "Te amo Clarita, te doy mi corazon, mi alma, mi vida."

Vicky collapses on top of him, confused and betrayed by her body. This man lies in the heat of passion, caressing and professing his undying love for her, while in her mind she is still cold and thinking of Morris. *Is this what Morris wants, for me to turn his killers into schoolboys? This is nothing special.*

I meet Nicky at the airport in Nassau. It is a place where we can talk freely. There are no Feds here. The Bahamian police are busy looking for smugglers among the droves of tourists. We arrive with fake passports and the usual assortment of swimming trunks and beachwear. They don't give us a second look.

"You need to bring the girls to me," I tell him over rums in the airport bar.

"It's too soon," Nicky objects, "Angelo has been dead less than a year. It will raise suspicions."

"I couldn't care less what the mob thinks."

"I'm talking about the F.B.I.," Nicky looks around nervously, "they are still watching the house. They came by about a month ago, to question Elizabeth about the Aruba house."

"What did she say?"

"What could she says? She knows nothing about her uncle's business," Nicky smiles.

I know that smile; it's his look of satisfaction of putting one over on the cops. He's a consummate criminal.

"As far as she knows, it's just another one of his properties she inherited."

"That's perfect," I tell him. "And you don't have to tell her where she is going. Just get her and the girls out of there, there is a war coming."

"If we are going to war, don't you think they will be safer on Long Island?"

"They will be safer with me," I insist. "I won't make the same mistake twice."

Fifteen days after the Cali meeting, an incident takes place at a Miami shopping center. A couple of Cocaine Cowboys open fire in broad daylight on a rival gang. Four drug dealers are dead, two others are in the hospital and heading for jail, but the worst part is that an innocent bystander also dies in the crossfire. Not just any old shopper, they kill a well-to-do, white housewife and mother of three. No one in the government gives a rat's ass when drug violence kills some pauper, Black, White, Hispanic; it happens every day and does not even get mentioned on the evening news. But this is a big deal, something has to be done. Three days later the President declares a war on drugs...

"I got orders to start an operation in Colombia," Jake concludes, as he returns to the present, "with or without Bogota's cooperation." Jake shifts position. He sits on the edge of his desk, and leans back, letting the memories of the past campaign flood his mind. Rewinding the movie that is memory and replaying it for Sam. "I heard of this American, a black guy, who was setting himself up as an enforcer for the Mafia."

"Morris, I presume," Sam says with a smile.

"Yes. Your friend Morris Johnson," Jake lights up a cigarette and holds the pack out to Sam, who declines with a wave of his hand. Jake moves a picture to the edge of the desk and flicks the ashes into an ashtray made from a Civil War cannon ball. "The Company knew he wasn't dead. They did a DNA test on the body and his brother's corpse. They couldn't even have been from the same part of the planet. I sent one of my operatives to make contact."

Vicky comes into the parlor at the Bogota ranch around 4 pm, she just got out of the shower but the sweat has already returned. I am cleaning guns and drinking rum and coke with plenty of ice in the glass. I tell her to help me assemble the weapons. I can see in her eyes she is still pissed off about the other night when I threw her out of bed. But she has done the job on Miguel; he can't take his eyes off of her. Although the others don't know what transpired, they see the change in him whenever she is near. They ride him hard.

"I have a job for you," I say, while casually putting the .38 revolver I just assembled in its box. "I need you to go to Nassau and meet a man. He's been asking questions."

"And what do you want me to do with this man?" Her tone is as hard and icy as the look in her eyes.

"That depends on what he asks you," I reply, ignoring the animosity radiating in my direction. "If he wants to buy you a Sex on the Beach, kill him. If he wants sex on the beach, then you decide what you want to do with him."

Vicky just finished a 9mm. She pulls the slide back, cocking the hammer then extends her arm and places the weapon inches from my forehead.

I watch her finger flinch slightly and hear the hammer fall, making a faint click.

"You're not coming with me?"

"No, I have other business to attend to. I'm sending Miguel." Her eyes light up. I can't tell if she is glad or wishes she had a bullet in the gun. "Be careful. He's either C.I.A., D.E.A., or from some other government agency with initials that spell trouble."

"Why should I kill him if he just wants to buy me a drink?"

"It will probably be drugged." I hand her the box with the .38 revolver. "No matter what he wants, don't trust him."

Vicky arrives at the hotel bar at exactly 3:20 pm and surveys the nearly empty room; there is the bartender, of course, a couple sitting in the shade in the corner, a bus boy with his wipe rag draped over his shoulder leaning against the kitchen door, and Derrick Patterson. She watches him watch her cross the room to his table. She can't blame him; she is purposely wearing a head-turning silk floral waist wrap and bikini top. He stands up by the table when she is halfway through the almost empty room.

He is tall, muscular and looks like he's carved from a solid piece of obsidian. He crosses his arms, showing biceps bugling out of his white short-sleeve polo shirt. Vicky will swear he is flexing his pectorals beneath the sport top. With the crystal blue sea behind him, he looks like a god.

"I was told to expect your boss, Morris. I'm glad my people were mistaken."

"Who?"

"I'm sorry, I guess he goes by John Morrison now," Derrick says with just a hint of sarcasm. His eyes hide behind black shades.

Vicky takes the remark as the opening salvo to battle. She instantly forgets how handsome he is and concentrates on the true motive for this meeting. "You've made two mistakes," she hisses, "John is not my boss."

"Then, boyfriend, Miss Harris," Derrick sits back down and places his sunglasses on the table. He looks up at her with dark brown eyes, lifeless pools that dare her to take the seat across the table.

"My name is Clarita Rosario," Vicky corrects him, "and I'm here as Mr. Morrison's liaison. Who are you representing?"

"Let's just say I'm here in the interest of peace." Derrick smiles a little and takes a sip from his drink. "Oh, forgive me, Miss Rosario, would you like a drink? And may I call you Rita? I hear that's what your friends in Colombia call you."

"That is what my friends call me, Mr. Patterson." Vicky pushes her sunglasses up, locking down her wavy black hair. Her golden eyes shoot out at Derrick, piercing his armor, drawing first blood.

Derrick can't hold back the spreading grin taking over his face.

"You can call me Ms. Rosario, and no thank you to that drink. We are not on a date. Why don't you just deliver the message, your bosses… sent you with and we can *both* get on with our day."

"Mr. Morrison knew what he was doing sending you," Derrick holds up two fingers and waits for the bartender to acknowledge his drink order. He turns his attention back to the stunning beauty, who is everything his intel had made her out to be. She is hotter than a summer breeze, yet cold and hard as a bullet waiting to be fired. "Well, it is like I said, certain people in the United States recognize the work Mr. Morrison is doing to police the Colombians. We just want to show our support. Supply him with manpower and equipment to get the job done. Things are heating up in the States and in Colombia; it appears to be heading towards an all-out war. The President has already declared war on the cartels; we would like him to be on our side in this one."

Just then the bartender arrives with two tall glasses of rum and coke on the rocks, "Miss Rita, good to see you again."

"Thanks, Robby, anything special going on tonight?" Vicky asks.

"It's always a special night when you are around." He clasps her four fingers in his hand and departs.

"He gets to call you Rita?" Derrick tries one more time to pour on the charm. "So you are going to be around tonight?"

"I might," Vicky gets up from the table and slides her sunglasses back down over her eyes. Locks of black waves stream down her face curling carefree around her cheeks. "The food is really good here. The kingfish is to die for. And they have a pretty good calypso band. Enjoy your drinks."

Derrick watches as she exits the bar onto the beach, the flowers of her wrap dancing to her music. He waves to the sailboats and yachts anchored off the beach, wondering if the sniper on one of them has relaxed his trigger finger yet. He also wonders if Rita is going to give him an answer tonight, or if she is leaving the door open for something more.

Derrick returns to the table that night decked out in a colorful Island shirt, open to within an inch of his abs, white slacks with a navy crease, and bright shining loafers reflecting the moonlight streaming in from the beach. He eats a plate of freshly caught kingfish and coconut rice with peas then drinks several rum and cokes on the rocks. And he listens to hours of steel drum music from the band. The place is packed with vacationers and locals alike. By midnight, it seems as if the entire population of Nassau has found their way into the bar, except for Rita. By 2 a.m. it's obvious she isn't coming. Several other lovely ladies try to get his attention, some with a direct request, because who was the idiot that let a hunk like him slip away? But Derrick is on assignment, two in fact, one to enlist Mr. Morrison into the war on drugs, and now a personal mission to bed his mistress.

I arrive at the house of Juan Jimenez in Medellin alone. It is a three-story colonial with huge white wooden columns all around the exterior. It is more like four houses laid out in a rectangular pattern. The two side houses are two-story tall and twice as long as the main house to the front. Six columns hold up the porch of the main house and through the two-story glass doors I can see across the inner courtyard to the mirrored rear house. It looks like something out of ancient Rome and plonked down in the middle of the jungle.

Jimenez' men drove me from the city to this hidden palace in the foothills. They pull up to the steps, my host rises from his wicker fan back peacock chair, and gives me a great big smile. Obviously, he heard about Cali and is going out of his way to make a good impression. From the looks of it, his entire family is sitting in the shade of the porch. His wife is on a peacock wicker chair of her own on the right of the glass doors sipping tea and fanning herself. His two sons, probably about my age, are to his left. One had been leaning against the white railing, but quickly snapped to attention when the car pulled up. His daughter had been on the floor at her mother's feet. She quickly got up, smoothed her floral and lace dress down with both hands, and disappeared into the main house as I got out the car. I just caught a glimpse of her as she twirled to leave, possibly in her mid-teens, and flawless.

"Welcome to my humble hacienda, Mr. Morrison. Is it just you then?"

"I would hardly describe this place as humble," I say with a warm smile. "Yes, I came alone, although, it does look like you could house an army here."

Juan holds his hand out for his wife and she joins him at the top to the stairs, "Well, it is mainly me and my family here. A couple of, how do you say… groundskeepers. This is my lovely wife, Selena, and my two boys, Juan Jr. and Carlos."

I give them a nod, climb the stairs, take his wife's hand and bow my head, "lovely is such an inadequate description for one as beautiful as you. Surely, this house was built as a temple to a goddess."

"Didn't I tell you dear, this New Yorker has the tongue of the devil; I think he comes to steal you away." Juan laughs a little too loud at his own joke and then shakes my hand vigorously.

The door opens behind him and a woman steps out onto the porch. She is twice Selena's size, with a colorful makeup job designed to hide her age. Her sharp dark eyes lock in on me. "Even if he is the Devil, we should invite him in out of the heat."

Juan and Selena step aside and I walk forward to the door. The painted lady swoops my arm up in hers and presses it close to her breast. Although, I don't think she could have avoided that even if she wanted to and leads me into the main house.

"I am Lila," she whispers in my ear then says louder for everyone to hear, "worry not my dear brother, I'll keep his mind off your wife."

Inside, are maids in uniform, one just by the door holding a tray of iced drinks, Lila grabs one and fills my free hand. She grabs another for herself and continues through the foyer with me in tow. We pass several groundskeepers at each exit as we make our way to the main parlor deep inside the main house.

This is going to be some business trip, Juan is making sure to display. For the number two guy in Medellin, he is a serious force not to be taken lightly. And Lila, the tiger he intends to feed me to if I get out of line.

Soon, the women excuse themselves and it is just me, Juan, his two sons, and several groundskeepers left to talk business. I begin, "I've come to make you an offer. How you receive this offer will decide if I am to have a short stay at your lovely home, or if I will be leaving before dinner?"

"Before you make your offer, may I ask, why me?"

"That's a fair question," I shift in my chair to direct my answer to Juan alone, also to show that I am not concerned with the others in the room, that this is between him and me. "You don't go to the king and ask if he wants to be a prince. And you don't approach a pauper and ask if he would like to be king. In both cases, the answer is obvious, and not likely to turn out the way you want. The king is not going to take a step back, he has already said as much with the incident in Miami. And although there are a couple of others around who would jump at the chance to dethrone him, they lack what it takes to be effective in that endeavor. That's what brings me here. You have the organization and with the right amount of backing you can step into the number one spot."

"Or, I could lose everything I have built for my family so far if these endeavors you speak of go bad." Juan's face is hard. He looks for a sign of weakness or fear while showing he has none, of me, or Pablo, the so-called king. "How do I know you can deliver on your end?"

"Back in New York," I tell him, "when I recruit a new member for the gang, there is a ceremony to test the person's resolve. We call it a jump in, where the new member must fight the other members and in the end all of them at once. If he proves his mettle, he lives and becomes a blood brother, having spilled blood with us. The Mafia has similar procedures to assure their partners are up to the task. They have their candidate murder someone beneficial to the organization to assure their loyalty to them."

Juan's attention is focused on my every word and move. The others in the room are equally spellbound by the conversation.

I continue, "Naturally, I didn't come here looking for a fight and a murder would prove nothing to either of us. What I propose is a hit on the king's operation. Nothing big, just enough to prove our worth to each other and move forward."

Juan looks around the room, first to the groundskeepers and then to his sons. He turns back to me and nods for me to continue.

"I have information where, when, and how the king moves his shipments of coke. Your men are going to steal one of those shipments."

"De ninguna manera!" shouts Juan Jr.

"This American is loco, Papa," adds Carlos.

"Deberiamos matar ahora y teminar con esto, antes de que nos maten a todos llega," says one of the groundskeepers with a smile on his pox-marked face.

"Un simple no le interesa lo haria," I reply.

"You do realize such an operation would bring Pablo to my door," Juan says calmly, weighing my proposal.

"Not if we take the shipment to Cali," I confide, "I have no holdings there and neither do you. The ensuing war between Pablo and the Cali cartel will weaken him and we can move you in."

"Let me think about this."

"I guess I'm staying for dinner."

The dinner table is dressed in a fine white linen cloth; on it is a full-bodied roasted hog. Around the hog are bowls and trays of side dishes, some of them I recognize, like the rice, black beans, and croquettes, others, I have no clue about their names or taste. Around the table sits Juan's entire family, some I met earlier; Lila, who positioned herself next to me on my right and the pox-faced man who is two seats from me on the left. Juan's oldest brother Ramon is seated next to Juan, who is at the head of the table, Selena on his right and across from her brother-in-law. The children sit across the table from the rest of the adults, starting with Selena's two sons next to her, ranked by age, followed by her daughter, Valentina, then followed by Ramon's three sons and two daughters, then Andres – Selena's oldest brother sitting next to Ramon – three girls and two boys. All the other children are younger than Selena's. And lastly, both Juan and Selena's parents at the end. Beyond Lila are the wives of the other men at the table. Diego, Selena's other brother, who was in the parlor earlier is to my immediate left, which means I can't avoid the penetrating stare of Valentina's sea green eyes, as the seventeen-year-old seems to have become infatuated with me.

"So how would we proceed with this plan of yours?" Asks Diego as soon as prayers are said and the food starts being passed around.

At first, I let the question hang in the air as I scoop some unknown food onto my plate, as Valentina had done, covering my rice before topping it off with black beans. I notice Juan stopped filling his plate and is expecting an answer. "I find the dinner table to be an inappropriate place for a business discussion."

"No confias en mi familia!" Juan's voice is just a tad harsh. Then in a softer tone he says, "forgive me, you are not fluent in Spanish, are you?"

"I understand it a little," I joke with a smile to ease the building tension, "I speak it even worse." I let the words filter through the room and then continue when the head bobbing ceases, "it's not a matter of trust, it is a matter of exposing your family to unnecessary risk." I purposely let my gaze run down the table at the children across from me before returning to Juan. "There will be time to talk about business after this fine meal."

"Usted debe ser muy importante para Juan para preparer su major cerdo," comments one of the mothers, who probably understands English but is more comfortable speaking Spanish.

I catch the gist of what she said and reply, "The honor is all mine. Anyway, I'm in no hurry to go back to New York."

"What is it like in New York?" Valentina takes the opportunity to join the conversation.

"Right now it is winter. So I would say cold and probably snowing."

"I would love to see snow. What is it like?" she asks with mounting enthusiasm. "I have seen it in the movies, of course, but I'd love to see it in real life."

"Well..." I pause trying to come up with a good description for someone who doesn't know what cold is. "It is beautiful, clean and pure at first, all bright and shiny and soft."

"At first?"

Those eyes are doing a number on me. I wonder if she knows how powerful her gaze is, the innocence and the unknown. "Yes, like a virgin, once touched it is never the same." *Probably shouldn't have said that.* "The first day of a snowfall, the city looks like it is built in a cloud, but then as you touch it, shovel it, it compacts down, becoming hard, icy, dirty gray slush. Its beauty is gone."

"I was in New York once," Lila breaks in, releasing me from the spell of those green eyes, "it was loud, dirty, and smelled really bad."

"You were there in the winter?" Valentina asks.

"No... the summer."

"Yeah. That's New York for ya," I chuckle, "It is like that in the winter too, except when it snows."

"You have family waiting for your return," Juan asks, "a wife, a kid, no?"

This is a loaded question, because not only does he want to take his daughter's attention off of me and divert mine from her, that's for sure, but he is also looking for leverage. Something he can use in case our deal goes sour. It is no secret cocaine dealers use family members against you when necessary.

"My wife died." With those three little words, a flood of emotions races back to me from a deep dark emptiness where I had buried that part of my life, and a single image is my solace... Maria standing in the moonlight before three weathered angels vowing her undying love. It's the only image I allow my memory to keep.

"How did she die?"

Valentina's voice is ethereal, and it echoes in my head as if she asked it a thousand times at once. I hear the others admonish her for asking, but I feel the empathy in her voice. A sadness that should not be there, but she cannot hide. A new image invades my mind, one I tried hard to destroy but know it can never be erased. Maria's head lying in my lap, a blood stain spreading from her waist across her dress, blue eyes slowly growing dim. "She died in my arms," I reply nearly inaudibly to everyone except Valentina.

"How beautiful!"

"You don't look old enough to be a widower," Lila blurts out and stuffs a piece of meat into her mouth. "When my first husband died I was twenty-five, luckily I didn't have any kids. You have kids?"

"Don't invite death to your dinner table," I say exasperatedly, "my mother says He will always show up."

Once again the dinner stops. People stopped chewing, the children stopped poking each other, and time stood at a standstill. It is up to Juan to restart the afternoon, "your mother sounds superstitious and interesting. Are you a superstitious person too? I would like to meet your mother. Maybe you bring her here for a vacation from the cold."

"Don't know about that," I smile. "My mom is a winter baby; she really likes the snow, especially on the first day."

The conversation moves on, jumping from topic to topic, with Juan trying to slip in a query or two about my family and those closest to me. He asks about Clarita and that sets Lila off on another rant about ex-husbands and boyfriends. That is good because I didn't answer how close she is to me. I give him enough information about myself to make sure the deal will get done. But it really doesn't matter how much I reveal, because as I look around the table I know everyone here will soon be dead. Everyone!

Miguel knocks on Derrick's door at sun up. He tells the blurry-eyed agent to get dressed and meet him downstairs. He only has to say that Clarita wants him to meet her to gain his full cooperation. Derrick doesn't know who Miguel is, but he wastes no time in getting dressed. He almost leaves the room without his .22, then turns back and grabs the clip holster and shoves it into his back. Then thinking about the look on Miguel's face when he mentioned Clarita's name, he grabs his .38, then the shoulder holster, puts it on, and throws a jacket on to conceal it.

Miguel drives the agent to a marina and takes him aboard a sixty-foot Hunter sailboat. Miguel and two other men quickly untie the lines and the captain fires up the twin diesels pushing the white single mast yacht slowly out and away from the island. Miguel and the other deck hands stow the lines without a word to Derrick as to where they are heading. They untie the main sail cover and when the sleek vessel turns into the wind, they begin hoisting the main sail. It flaps, shakes and rattles in protest to the breeze. Each man pulls a full arm's length of the main halyard, stretching the sail up the mast and out along the boom until the sail is its full size. Then the sound of the engines ceases and with a snap, the main sail billows to life, pulling the boat to a steep angle, cutting through the water.

Derrick sits in the cockpit admiring how efficiently the three men get the ship under way. The marina is a good distance behind him now and Miguel slides open the teak cabin door and descends into the darkness. The other two sailors take positions at the front of the cockpit and work the sheets to trim the sail. The captain is barely visible inside the cabin at the wheel. Moments later, Miguel returns to the cockpit with a bucket of beers on ice and places it on the console table in the middle of the cockpit.

Finally, Derrick asks, "Where is Clarita? I thought you said she wanted to see me."

"She will be up," Miguel answers and opens a beer for himself.

Derrick looks back, the marina is just about gone from view. The island takes on a lush green appearance, speckled with multi-colored clumps of civilization. Derrick reaches forward and grabs a beer, twists off the top, and takes a long deep swig. *Nothing wrong with a beer for breakfast, and I could think of worse ways to die. Miguel is probably packing; these other guys look like they come with the charter. If he thinks I'm taking a dive today, he should have taken my guns.*

"Smile a little," Clarita says, stepping out into the sunshine. "This has got to be better than sitting around that bar running up a tab, even if the government is paying for it."

"That it is," Derrick says with a big silly grin on his face as he sees her in a white mini sailor's outfit. *Ok, control yourself, she might still be taking you to a shark feeding ground.* "So, has your... Friend... decided to take me up on my offer?"

"Don't know," she says sitting between Derrick and Miguel. Both return to their seats; they had sprung from the bench as if it were on fire when she appeared in the cabin door. Derrick pulls a beer from the ice and holds it up to her. "No thanks. It is a little too early for that. I just want to enjoy the breeze for a while."

"Mr. Morrison..."

"Relax. He is away on business. Your proposal is in proper hands." Clarita unties the blue bow in front of her neck and opens her sailor top, revealing the blue bikini top beneath. "When I know something, you'll know something. You are a man of the sea, so I thought it would be nice for you to get back out on the water again."

Derrick finishes his beer and twists the cap off the next. "You've been checking up on me. Is everything in good order?"

"As far as I know things check out OK," she smiles, "you are not on a one-way cruise. Sit back, enjoy the beer, and the cook will bring up some food shortly. Me, I'm going to soak up some rays before it gets too hot." She places a hand on his leg and glides out of the seat.

One of the sailors hands her a beach towel as she passes him on her way out. Clarita stands at the bow facing forward, sheds her sailor dress, and lets it drop to the deck. All eyes are upon her as the morning sun decides to play along and silhouettes her tight round ass. Next, her arms reach back and unclasp her bikini top and it too drops to the deck. She bends over, putting on quite a show for the crew and Agent Patterson, as she fans out the towel and lies on top, mercifully out of view. The five men can pretend all they want they are not thinking what they are thinking. Well, four of them can try; she is still in plain view of the captain at the wheel hidden in the cabin.

"She doesn't have any suntan oil," Derrick turns to Miguel, "you think I should take her some? I wouldn't want that... cute little body to get a nasty burn." Derrick tips his beer up and begins downing the cold liquid in big gulps.

"You no need to worry about her," Miguel warns him, "I take care of her. And when the time comes, Mr. Five Years Naval Intelligence Officer, I take care of you too. You won't hear me. You won't see me. I will put a bullet right down the neck of that beer bottle. Make only a little hole in its base."

Derrick holds up one finger as he swallows the last two gulps. "AAHHH... That's not really all that difficult to do." *Every man on this boat would make the shot if she just winks at him, including me. What is Morris up to? It's a simple yes or no proposal. Why does he have his girl twisting his boys' balls up in knots? Why is she twisting mine?*

I lay my plan out for Jimenez, his brothers, and sons after dinner. We are going to set an ambush for Pablo's drivers on the road to the port. Exactly when and where I keep to myself, all he needs to know is that I have an inside guy back in New York who will give me the signal. The signal came tonight; Pablo is moving five hundred kilos in institutional sized cans of fruit. One truckload is leaving his warehouse about an hour from the port. "...so, it is me, Juan Jr. and two of your men in three trucks. I will lead the way."

Juan Sr. grabs his oldest son by the arm, "I told you I don't like this plan. It's too risky. We never kept the cocaine here."

"That is exactly why it is the safest place to keep it. Besides, where else are you going to hide eleven hundred pounds of coke at such short notice? In about two hours, Pablo is going to know he's been ripped off. He'll hit every spot in Medellin, including yours, before his guys turn up in Cali. It will take an army to take on this place, and he won't commit to that unless he is sure you have his product here. Junior, that is why your part is critical, not a drop of his men's blood is to be spilled until you are at the drop off in Cali. Then you slit their throats fast and clean, from right to left. Understand?"

"Si. Yes, Senior Morrison," the young man replies while patting the ten inch hunting knife at his side.

"Before morning, Pablo will think his men betrayed him, and the Cali cartel double-crossed them. We sit tight on the coke here for a while, repackage it, and move it while Pablo and Gustavo are beating each other into the ground." I place a hand on Juan's shoulder and give him a reassuring shake. "This is going to go like clockwork. We've got to move, my men are already at the ambush point setting up."

A beat-up wood-sided flatbed rumbles through and down the hill towards the lights of the port miles below. The driver slows to a stop, shouting profanities at the fallen tree blocking the road. The two men sitting on the ten-gallon drums of fruit grab a heavy coil of rope and hop off the truck. The young passenger is shoved from his seat by his father, the driver, to assist in the removal of the blockage. This is a familiar routine for the men, also a good time for a cigarette break and a piss. The driver yells more obscenities at the young men before giving in to nature's call.

When the four men turn to the tree trunk, they see four strangers with Uzis trained on them. Another four emerge from the brush and force them to their knees with pistols at their heads. The four men start praying and calling, "Madonna, Maria. Madonna, Maria."

I hold an Uzi on the four while the rest transfer the load to two of the trucks. When done, the four men are tied to the wood rails in the back of their truck and Juan Jr. climbs in with them.

"Let some of the air out of those tires. The tracks have to look like it's still carrying a heavy load," I instruct the driver.

Two of my men pick up the hollowed out tree trunk and carry it into the woods. We split up. Juan, another driver in their truck, and one of his soldiers, head towards Cali with the four men to their death at a Gustavo hideaway, while I and Jimenez's other soldiers and the other two trucks loaded with the cocaine, head back to his fort outside of Medellin to await war.

As one of the soldiers of the second truckload of cocaine is about to climb into the cab he asks his partner, "¿Crees que podemos fiarnos?"

His partner replies looking back at me. "Esto le llegó muy fácil. Me pregunto qué viene fácil para él?"

So many things come easy these days, but trust is not one of them. If Juan Jr. weren't riding to the drop-off point with my men, one of these guys would be putting a bullet in me instead of wondering when I am going to put one in them. It won't be long now.

The war starts on time. Like clockwork, Pablo hits some of his Medellin cartel rivals with machine guns and bombs before dawn. He hit two of Jimenez's warehouses by the port, but of course, they are empty. By dawn, his truck and men are found twenty miles outside of Cali, throats cut from right to left, the signature of Alejandro Ortiz, the enforcer for Gustavo's Cali cartel, a lefty. Pablo's full attention, anger, and armament turns to his rival to the west. And what a glorious war it is shaping up to be. Everyone is a target, cartel members, police, and politicians, anyone with any ties to the drug lords are under fire.

Jimenez calls in all his men to protect the house from invasion. In all, thirty-eight family members and hired guns fill the four buildings, and me. The two long houses hold the guards, who patrol twenty-four hours a day. They work in three shifts with men on the roofs of the front and back houses. As long as his barn is filled with cocaine, Juan will be on alert and on edge. And I have so far convinced him he needs to keep it off the market for a while, "you don't want it to get around that you are moving an unusual amount of product after such a loss."

"You are absolutely right," he agrees, "we will repack it in smaller quantities and fly it to Panama. We can sell it from there with fewer eyes on us. We are safe here. No one will get past my men."

No number of men can save you when you invite the Devil to dinner!

The party starts immediately after Juan Jr. returns from Cali. Drinking. Dancing. Drugging. Day and night, night and day, we are at a non-stop Mardi Gras. As the guards get off duty, they join the party. Their replacements take their positions blurry-eyed and burnt-out. No one notices. Except me, I noticed everything. I notice the eyes like snakes ready to strike, Jimenez and his brothers waiting for the moment to make the kill and silence the last outsider to their deed. I notice the angel's eyes piercing my heart and giving rise to my salvation from this unholy crusade, green eyes that follow me through the haze and heat, longing for me to rescue her from this graveyard. I also notice the jealousy that pours out from Lila whenever my attention is drawn to my Angel. I notice the pawing and prodding of fat fingers in search of some trophy she needs to prove herself the Queen of the Duped. I realize a week has passed and it is time for this war to go worldwide.

I have been avoiding Lila's overt advances like a man trapped in a cage with a tiger. She asks me time and again to escort her to her room. On two occasions, I did then carefully slid my arm from her grasp and said goodnight. Tonight, I whisper in her ear to escort me to my room on the third floor of the main house. She loudly accepts. The angel's eyes fall to the parlor floor in deep disappointment as she leaves for her room on the second floor.

It is very late and the week of partying has taken its toll on all in the house. The guards can barely make their rounds, those who are not on duty sleep heavily where they fall, and the young children have already been sent to their beds. Everyone partook in the drunken orgy, except for Valentina and Selena. I overhear Selena plead with her husband to send the devil on his way, before it is too late. I feel Valentina's desire to accompany me to my room, my world, my New York in the snow. Tonight will be the night.

Lila is even louder in accepting my dick, she is screaming, "Oi Dios Mio! Oh my God!" It couldn't be called making love what we were doing; it was more like a naked wrestling match. She is trying to prove she can fuck me harder than any woman ever did, and I am trying to keep her busy until everyone else falls asleep, which I know is going to take even longer with her yells and screams of fake pleasure.

In the darkness, I sense my Angel's pain and distress. The tears roll down her face, drowning her soul. But eventually, I feel her force sleep into her mind to escape the bellowing of the beast on the third floor. Finally, 3 a.m. comes and only a few guards still walk the grounds. 3 a.m., the bewitching hour, when evil has a free reign.

I roll Lila over onto her stomach, slap my cock on her behind, and she laughs. She shakes her ass and giggles like a schoolgirl, thinking she has broken my resistance and

I want her as much as she wants to prove she can have anything she sees. She giggles at the thought that her silly little niece could possibly win the affection of someone she desires. She raises her hips, grabs her ass cheeks and spreads them wide, revealing her dirty brown hole like it is the ultimate prize, that I am lucky she is offering it to me.

I place my hand on the back of her head and her body quivers with anticipation. Beads of sweat from excitement and expectation run down her butt and pool in the small of her back. A sharp burning sensation spreads from one thigh up her back and forces its way out her mouth in the loudest yell of the night. Selena says a prayer, hoping this is the last night. Another flash of fire erupts in Lila's other thigh and she screams louder than before.

She has done anal before but somehow this doesn't feel right. She tries to lift her head and I shove it back down into the pillow. She twists and tries to pull away, but I have a fistful of hair. She manages to get her head turned to the side and I stab the bloody blade into the pillow inches from her eye. Lila watches a single drop of blood roll down the blade and spread out onto the pillow. Her legs now ache with the realization that she is bleeding from her inner thighs and her struggle weakens as the blood pours out onto the sheets.

I kneel in a red fountain as her body goes limp, then lifeless and finally still. I remain kneeling over her as the rolls of fat in her flesh sink onto the bed and bloat outwards. I listen to the silence that fills the room. I listen as the silence rolls out and fills the house. It rolls down the stairs through the halls and throughout all quarters.

When the silence like the darkness fills the night, I climb off the bed covered in Lila's blood and sexual stench.

I pull out my other knives from beneath the mattress and strap two to each leg, two form an 'x' across my back, and I have one on each forearm. Leaving the room wearing nothing but the blood of the first dead, I head for the roof.

The first two guards are sitting and laughing. They say something about Lila, which I can't quite translate, but it's likely they are glad she is finally silent. They don't see me when I stand before them with a bowie knife in each hand. I have to order them to stand up before I thrust the blades up through their diaphragms. They drop on the rooftop when I quickly pull the blades out.

I climb down the ladder to the long house and run to the back house. I clamber onto its roof and find the guards there sleeping in their chairs. The party went on too long. I cut the throat of one of the men and grab the other by the mouth and arm. Twisting his arm to near breaking point, I usher him to the edge of the roof then shifting my hands from his mouth and arm to his neck and balls in a single move, I lift him over my head. I toss him over the roof and down onto the guard below. I flee down the stairs and out the side door of the rear house just in time to meet another guard responding to the thud of the falling body. I slash his throat.

Back in the rear house, is the electrical generator. I take the hoses I cut days earlier from the shelf in the room – where the 500 kg's of coke are being stored – and feed them into the exhaust pipe of the generator. The other ends I place into the air ducts of the two side houses. All those asleep on the ground floor will never wake up.

I walk across the courtyard, the blood has dried and is cracking on my skin. I slash the throats of the next guards, who don't seem surprised at all to see me. Then again, by this time, anyone who is awake would be naked.

I reach the two-story glass doors at the back of the main house and stop for a moment to regain my focus then I enter.

I go back up to the third floor and pass the room where Lila lies with her legs cut open to the bone. Down at the other end of the hallway are the large golden double doors of Juan and Selena's bedroom. Juan is asleep in the outer bedroom with two women. I take one of the machetes from my back and position the blade across their necks. I raise the blade above my head and arch my back. There is a swoosh, the faint crackle of bones, and the three heads roll down the pillows, Juan's and the black haired woman nestle together on her shoulder, the redhead drops to the side by her arm. A sea of red engulfs them.

Beyond the outer bedroom, behind a single white door, Selena sleeps. She watches me approach from her dreams, and I watch her in the wall size mirror. She is regal in her satin nightgown. I take a small knife from my forearm holster and gently make a tiny slice just below her ear. So swift is the cut, she barely stirs in her sleep, and willing slips into eternity.

I continue onto the second floor and into each of the children's rooms. I use the same blade to slice their windpipes. I had worked my way from the youngest to the eldest son on purpose, none saw me. Then I came to the last room. I had passed it twice already.

I push the door open extremely slowly, expecting God Himself to be standing guard. She lies on her back, I stand watching. The silence roars in my head, as her breast rises and falls in slow motion, time slows down. An eternity passes between each inhalation, her nipples covered in lace lifting, then receding, then rising again.

Hypnotized, I draw closer and hear her breathe. I don't know how I am standing over the Angel. My dagger is silver, reflecting pure light in utter darkness. It lifts her gown and peels it to either side. Wings spread around an immaculate body, it is unblemished, perfectly formed, golden and radiant, beaming its beauty up past me to heaven.

I see the tip of the blade gently touch the Angel's breast, I see my hand gripping its handle, my left hand on top. A tear moistens the blade's tip and my Angel's green eyes set the night ablaze. The blade plunges down, her body arches up, levitated by God's hand, drawing her back to Him. She expels her soul. I exhale mine in an all-emptying breath of death, letting the Angel take my soul, my sins, and my life as I offer her up to Him. I drop.

The sun burns my face. I wrap the Angel in the sheet then carry her out of the palace of death and into the hills.

Chapter 5

Lies, Spies, and Setups

Elizabeth is surprised to see Rita in the park holding a small sign, which reads: "I know you are wired. Don't say a word." Another woman quickly steps in front of her and Rita shoves Elizabeth onto the bench. The woman is dressed exactly like her. Elizabeth watches in silence as the switch is made and the agents scramble to catch the white van. She hears the car crash, sees Cathy and Jonathan go down, and are suspiciously taken away in an ambulance. It all happens so quickly, so methodically, she knows Morris is back.

The door of a black Lincoln opens and Elizabeth feels herself being drawn inside. The door closes.

"Hey Sugar Tits, you look good."

"Where the hell have you been?" screams Elizabeth, relief, anger and outrage exploding in the one question.

"I've been tied up," I say and wipe away the sole tear rolling down her cheek. I reach inside her blouse, pull out the microphone, and toss it out the window. We draw together like our lips are made of magnets; I savor her taste for as long as I can.

She pushes me away. "It's been four fucking years," her eyes race across my body, "Rita said you were shot. I thought you were dead! Again! Why do you keep doing this to me?"

"You know me," I give her a half smile; "I'm bulletproof."

Those words transport Elizabeth back across the years. Back to her bedroom, back to the day she lost her virginity, the night she lost her ignorance of her family's business, back to when her father lost his life to the man she loves.

"Do you remember what I told you on the tarmac in Aruba?"

"Yes. You said we would never be alone. That no matter where Maria and I were, you would always be there. Then three years later, you disappeared in the jungles of Colombia with three bullets in your chest. That's what Rita told me." Elizabeth has hardened once more. "Did she lie?"

"No, it's the truth," I confess then wrap my arm around her shoulder and pull her close, "things happen in this life. You know that, Liz. But I came back the minute Maria went dark."

Elizabeth is used to Morris speaking in code to Nicky, saying things in half sentences and in ways that only makes sense to them. Nicky hated discussing mob business in front of her, Morris didn't care. At that time, she ignored them, didn't really want to know what dirt the boys were playing in. Since his second death, she has become more involved in the business, and more adept at reading between the lines, but this is about her daughter and she needs him to say exactly what he means and what he knows. "Went DARK? What the hell does that mean? Where is my daughter? What the fuck have you done?"

"I don't know exactly," I admit. Her eyes are on fire, rage boiling under her skin. She is on the verge of going nuclear and I have to pull her back, for both our sakes. "She is safe. The people who took her won't dare harm her. Of that I am sure."

"Who took her? Why her? What do they want?"

"I know who took her. I don't know what they want," *that is a lie,* "but I do know they took her to get to me. Do you remember an FBI agent, called Tom Green? He was hanging around when your uncle was alive."

"Yeah, I remember him," Elizabeth is already reliving those days. "He didn't strike me as a cop. I didn't know much about the police or FBI at the time, but he didn't seem to act like one. Nicky got rid of him."

"Unfortunately, he didn't go very far."

Maria came bouncing out the doors of Sacred Heart Academy shortly after the final bell. It's an all-girls catholic school for the rich and elite of New York. Daughters of CEOs from the financial world, political world, and in a few never-spoken-of cases – criminal world, attend the private school in the heart of Manhattan. Police block off the streets so the long lines of limos have exclusive access to the school.

As usual, Akilina is waiting in the back of one of the big limos and one of Maria's three uncles holds the door open for her. Her other uncle, Frankie, is standing on the other side of the car, scanning the rooftops and sidewalks for trouble.

Maria is excited. She is always excited on the second Wednesday of the month. They stop at the Long Island Central mall for some shopping. Then when she gets home, Uncle Frankie, Uncle Dom, and if she is luckily,

Uncle Nicky, her only real uncle – although she isn't completely certain about that – will take her into the range in the basement for target practice. Maria is sure, almost positive, that she is the only ten-years-old at Sacred Heart who has a shooting range in her basement. But she is absolutely sure she is the only student who has regular shooting lessons. Uncle Nicky says it's a precaution... just in case something bad happens. But she will also swear she has more uncles than anyone else, who all make sure nothing bad does happen.

Uncle Frankie and Uncle Dom sit on a mall bench with six bags each, while Maria and Akilina go into the third floor ladies' room across from the Radio Shack. They wait ten minutes, fifteen, then half an hour... for Maria and her nanny to return.

When Maria and Akilina walked into the bathroom, a cleaning lady was busy wiping down the counter. Maria went into a stall, Akilina checked her reflection in the mirror. The cleaning lady swiped the countertop next to Akilina then pulling out her spray bottle, she pumped two misty squirts into Akilina's face. She dropped into her arms. Then she waited outside Maria's stall and sprayed her as she stepped out.

Locking the door, she strapped harnesses onto the young woman and child. She carried Maria's limp body to the utility closest at the back of the bathroom and lowered her down the hole in the floor. Next, she lowered Akilina from the third floor to the first behind the locked Utility room doors. Two men dressed as plumbers placed the young women in heavy black body bags and zipped them up. At that moment, Maria went dark.

The third floor cleaning lady unlocked the door and left, and the pair of plumbers two floors below wheeled their utility carts out a service exit. Tom Green relaxed his grip on the pistol in his pocket and left the mall. In the span of five minutes, Maria and her nanny disappeared from the face of the earth.

Elizabeth finally asks Morris, "Where are we going?"

"To an airfield Upstate," I tell her, "I can't risk you being a target too."

"No, I need to be here when Maria and Akilina are found," she objects.

"When I find her we will be together again," I promise, "and I'll make those who took her regret that foolish move."

The fog rolls back, and seeing Akilina's blurred smile inches away, brings her comfort and familiarity. The lamp on the nightstand casts eerie lights and shadows onto the small twin bed and wall. This is not her room, she is not home, and fear replaces the throbbing headache. "Lina... Lina, wake up," Maria whispers, afraid of what monsters might lurk nearby. When Akilina does not respond, Maria grabs her by one shoulder and shakes her violently, "LINA..."

Akilina's lips peel apart, the pain in her throat matches the dull burning sensation in her head, and the memory of a strange woman grabbing her by the hair flashes out of the blackness. She scans the plain white room with the slightest of motions, and then pulls the ten-year-old to her, "are you OK?"

"I think so. Where are we? What happened?"

"You are safe." The rough voice of a man speaks and the two look down past the foot of the bed. He sits, like a reclining sentinel in an armchair in front of the door. He is big, with a big empty smile, and a big bald eagle perched on a sword tattooed on his left bicep. The eagle's beak drips blood, its talons staining the sword's blade with crimson rivulets that continue down the man's arm to his elbow. Both voice and tattoo tell the girls they are anything but safe.

Akilina bolts upright and Maria scrambles around behind her for protection. Together they are but a fraction of the man's size blocking the only exit from the room. No one needs to tell them they have been kidnapped.

"Let us go. My mother has money. She'll pay you anything you want, just please… let us go."

"Don't worry, I won't keep you here long. And I am not after any money."

"Don't hurt her," Akilina commands, "she is only a child!"

The big man with the eagle tattoo chuckles and says, "I am under strict orders not to let any harm come to her. I'm like her guardian angel. And as soon as her father agrees to our terms, the sooner you go home."

Maria, kneeling behind her nanny, locks her steel blue eyes on the big tattooed man's cold grey ones, "My father!? My father is DEAD. He died in a plane crash four years ago."

"Ah, if only that was true," he can feel the hatred burning inside her, she really is Morris' daughter. "I know your father, we worked together briefly… and he is very much alive. As soon as he agrees to… let's just say he has something that belongs to us. Make yourselves at home, there is food in the fridge. A warning first, you can't leave the house, so don't try. If all goes according to plan, you will be out of here in a couple of days."

"Who are you? When did you work with my Dad?"

"You can call me John." The tattooed man stands up and opens the door. He is almost as big as the opening. "There are cameras everywhere, so behave yourselves, and this will all go smoothly."

John, the eagle tattooed man, if that is his name and they both doubt it, departs, leaving the door open. They hear another door shut. They sit there just the same, afraid to move.

Finally, Akilina speaks, "We can't just do nothing. Even if your father is alive, we saw his face. He's not going to let us go."

John, the eagle tattooed man enters the control room; two men with smaller versions of the same tattoo on their forearms monitor two rows of six screens. He puts a hand on one of their shoulders and says, "Do not take your eyes off that girl."

"Yes sir, Sgt. Warren."

Sergeant Warren picks up the phone and waits for the voice on the other end to answer. "The canary is in the cage."

"Good. Then I'll put the plan in motion," says a smooth voiced man.

"I hear there is another player at the table," Warren says with displeasure.

"He will not be a problem," assures the man. "That is why I had you plant one of your men on his team. You just make sure the girl is unharmed, and off the radar for a few days."

In the quiet of Trudy's cockpit, Sam replays the conversation with Jake. His reluctance to speak about Tom Green nags at him. His willingness to recruit someone like

Morris, even after the Medellin Massacre, makes him wonder how far he is willing to go to protect his secrets.

Jake told him it was simpler with the FBI, "you are on this side of the law and the bad guys are over there on the other side of the law. In my world, the monsters are all around you. Some of them you create, some of them you destroy, and some you feed the other monsters to, just to keep them from devouring you."

Then it hit him, the reason for his trip; the picture, and something was puzzling right now. The picture was on Jake's desk, and it was of Tom Green's Vietnam Unit. Only, in this rendition, Tom wore the golden eagle insignia of a Specialist. There was however, a tall, six-foot maybe six-two blond man, the First Lieutenant of the outfit. When Tom first came to the FBI, he was the war hero First Lieutenant, who had seemingly saved his unit, or at least, the six who survived the ambush. Sam radios Willie White a coded message; requesting him to track down the survivors of the five-two ninety-seventh, Tom Green's old Unit.

Sam checks into a motel in Lanham, Maryland, a few miles outside of Washington D.C., one of Sam and Willie's safe houses. Working in the drug task force for years provided them many lives that only the two know about. It was necessary to hide an asset, or to lay low when an undercover OP went bad. Likewise, it is now essential to run this operation behind the FBI's back. There is an envelope waiting at front desk and a bottle of Kentucky bourbon.

The records hold one glaring inconsistency; Tom Green graduated high school six-one and two-hundred-and-seven pounds. He joined the FBI six years later at five-nine and one-eighty-five. Sam has heard of people having a late growth spurt, but never retrogression. To their credit, somebody went to a lot of trouble changing Tom's service records, and to Willie's better credit, he dug even deeper. The question that a bottle of bourbon will help answer is, "who is Tom Green?" But the bigger question is, "why the cover up?" Included in the envelope is a second report, one that promises to shed some light on the mystery. It contains the name and address of the last survivor from Tom Green's unit, Peter St. Claire.

Sam pulls up to the building in the very poor black section of D.C. The streets are still covered in snow from two days ago, and when he steps out of the car, a number of young men disappear from their appointed positions. Sam smiles to himself, recalling what a dime-bag once told him, "You look like a cop and smell like a fed." *I guess that informant was right. Good thing this guy lives on the first floor, this place doesn't look like it has an elevator.*

Sam knocks on the door politely and waits. Minutes pass, and he knocks again a little harder. He waits some more. *This guy has got to be home with all this snow and ice on the ground.* He knocks again, this time pounding on the flimsy wooden door with his fist. The distinct sound of a pump-action shotgun comes from the other side. Sam quickly pulls out his badge and holds it up to the peephole, "FBI, Mister St. Claire. Can I talk to you for a minute?"

"If you are holding a badge up to the peephole I can't see it. Down here."

A hole about the size of a can top below and to the right of the doorknob projects a circle of light on Sam's crotch. He lowers his badge to the circle then hears the three door locks unlatch.

"What you waiting for? Come on in."

Sam opens the door slowly. Peter St. Claire is sitting in a wheelchair, pump-action shotgun across his lap, and a dingy yellow smile painted on his scraggy bearded face. He sits there in silence, letting Sam absorb the full visual, from the graying tattered wife beater to the faded blue jeans sown off below the knees.

St. Claire waits a good minute before he spins his wheelchair around in the hallway and with a single thrust of his oak-like arms sails off into the living room. "Well, what the hell do you want?" he shouts back. "And lock that door! Crack-heads will rob you blind before you can turn around."

Sam had read the file. He knows St. Claire lost both legs in Vietnam, but the picture in the file is of a much slimmer, fitter man, cleaner too. The man in the wheelchair today has been ravaged by time and despair. He also knows why Willie sent along the bourbon. He needs him to remember Vietnam, and the alcohol might just make him want to relive those days. Although, he has his doubts, "I'm with the FBI, but I am here on unofficial business."

"Oh, really," Peter peeks out the window, "that sounds like more trouble than I care to get into. That's your ride out there?"

"Don't worry, it's a rental."

"Hope you took out the insurance on it," Peter turns his gaze and attention to the brown paper bag, "that's for me, incentive for me to talk... unofficial."

"I was hoping to join you," Sam pulls the bottle from the bag and hands it to St. Claire. "You know... one old warhorse to another."

Peter pours two drinks in glasses that were on the coffee table. The two men clink them and down the liquor quickly. Peter pours another round and rests the shotgun on the sofa. "So, you want to talk about Lt. Tom Green. Which one, good ol' Lt. Green, or the bastard that cost me my legs?"

Sam sits in the armchair across from the sofa in the tiny living room with dark red drapes and carpeting that is worn to an undistinguishable color and style. "Who do you think I'm here to talk about? What happened in Nam that turned a specialist into a lieutenant? And who was that specialist before he became the war hero?"

"WAR HERO," Peter cries out, "he was no war hero. He was an evil man. He enjoyed killing the Cong. Would come back off of patrol with our unit and go right back out with someone else's. He even went out alone, called it clipping gooks."

"He hated the Viet Cong that much?"

Peter laughs and pours himself another drink, "he didn't give a damn about the Viet Cong. He came to Vietnam for one reason and one reason only, because he loved to kill, and there they were paying him for it. He used to say, 'Back home this many jobs would bring serious heat.'"

Sam asks bluntly, "Where is back home? Who is Tom Green?"

Peter St. Claire looks off into the distance, the moon-yellow grin gone. A shine covers his face as beads of sweat roll from his nappy head. He pours another drink, "Hey, you need another?"

"Come on St. Claire, you gone this far," Sam chides and holds out his glass. "A lot of guys went into the service as somebody and came out as someone else. You've been in that chair for a dozen years, don't you think it's time to tell who put you in it?"

"War hero," the smile returns, "you are gonna love this story." Peter checks the window again. "Our platoon went out on patrol with 39 men. We were humping deep into the jungle looking for the rat holes. By this time, we knew about the North Vietnamese tunnels and were on seek and destroy missions. Franco, that's his real name, Franco Benzoni…"

Sam's eyebrows arch and he leans forward to hear better.

"Oh, you know that name, don't you, Mr. FBI? He used to say he was connected, in the family business. Other guys thought he was bullshitting. You know, every Italian said they were in the Mob. But I knew he was the real deal. He was walking point; why not said Lt. Green, he knew that country better than any of us. That sick bastard led us right down into Hell…"

. . . Peter St. Claire heard the first explosion, and the scream of a soldier. The sound of the jungle was drowned out by the blare of gunfire and the anguished cries of those caught in it. He was scrambling for cover when a grenade went off. The platoon was spread across a football field patch of jungle and the enemy was all around them. They were taking fire on two flanks and there may have been a minefield ahead of them.

Snipers sat in the trees and he figured at least two rat's nests were nearby, maybe three, from where the Cong were popping out of to lay down fire. The platoon was pulling together to concentrate their fire power, and that was when he saw Franco darting across the line. A couple of seconds later the left flank erupted in explosions and machinegun fire. The Cong was coming in heavy and they started falling back . . .

"Two of the guys covering our rear took hits, one was the radioman. The machinegun burst tore him and his equipment to shreds. There must have been more rat holes than I thought. I fired my M-16 into the ground all around me, just hoping to hit something. We divided into smaller groups about thirty yard apart. There were nine guys with me, I don't know how many in the others. We were pinned down, except for Franco. That crazy fucker was scurrying through the jungle having a good time."

. . . The fire-fight lasted for what seemed an eternity. The VC would charge and be cut down. Small bands of men like waves on the ocean rose up and were thrown forward, splashed down in a sea of crimson, and withdrew into the greater body. All afternoon they continued the attack. All afternoon the soldiers repelled the enemy. They had followed their training when they broke into smaller squads, some forward, others further back, so they could keep the other squads to their right and left in the cross fire. St. Claire's squad was third from the left and forward . . .

"Nightfall came and it was a good thing. The VC had come en mass. They knew Franco was part of our platoon, and I think they were intent on killing him at any cost. So intent, they advanced too far from their rat holes. Explosions shook the earth, three of them in rapid succession, but there was very little fire to mark their positions. I imagined that Franco had slipped behind them and booby-trapped their rat holes. The VC were trapped between the minefield to their rear and our platoon, and they were angry, charging headlong into our ranks. We returned fire and fell back, returned fire and fell back some more. The lieutenant was making his way down the line, giving the order to bug out. We were hopelessly outnumbered and it was only a matter of time before we would be overrun. That's when Lt. Tom Green took a headshot. Several of the other guys, who had started to retreat were also cut down by sniper shots. We had already cleared the trees of VC. I knew it was Franco. He wasn't going to let us leave. I could hear him zipping around above in the trees, cutting down anything that moved.

"At dawn, the Viet Cong regrouped and made a last attempt to break the soldier's line. A solid black cloud of screaming, shooting, machete-waving VC enveloped the trees ahead. The soldiers lobbed a steady stream of grenades, but they kept coming. Machineguns blazed and a torrent of bullets rained in both directions. With less than ten yards to go, the Viet Cong's advance was halted by a line of well-placed claymore mines. Their thunderous retorts hurled the bodies of the enemy back and broke their spirits for good. As they retreated, sniper fire further thinned their ranks until those that were left found a safe hiding place.

"We once again started to pull out, but I didn't get very far. I stepped on a trip wire and a grenade sent shrapnel through both my legs. We were trapped just like the Viet Cong. It took another day before the Viet Cong radio pleas to surrender were answered. Two platoons of Marines and an Army Ranger team finally arrived and got us out. A kid named Johnny told me in a MASH unit that he saw Franco killed the Lieutenant. He too died from his injuries, even though they weren't life threatening. I was in Germany, in my hospital bed when a pair of army big brass pinned some medals to my pillow and told me Lt. Tom Green was getting the highest medals of honor for bringing his platoon out alive. All six of us."

"Why didn't you report what really happened?" asks Sam. "Why would the military cover up such a horrendous act?"

"Why indeed," replies Peter St. Claire, back from the war in his head. "They knew what happened. Maybe they didn't want to award the Medal of Honor to a certified psychopath. Maybe after going over the battlefield and the plan he devised, he took down hundreds of the VC with only a handful of men, they wanted him for something bigger. Anyway, I never walked again and I never saw Franco Benzoni or Tom Green again. You can leave the bottle and see yourself out FBI."

Sam sits in his car and lets it warm up. *The grandson of a Chicago Don! No wonder he wanted to get into the Bureau's Organized Crime Division. All this time, the fox has been living it up in the henhouse. I've got to get to Chicago before this kidnapping turns into another bloody war.* Sam pulls off down the icy street.

"Good man, that Sam Black is," I say to St. Claire, "glad you didn't make me kill him."

"You heard everything I told the FBI, I don't know anything else about Franco Benzoni," Peter says as he rolls over to the sofa and eyes the shotgun.

"What are you going to do with that thing, club me to death? I have the shells." I look back at the television in the corner, A Christmas Carol is still playing, its volume turned all the way down. "The FBI agent who just left is the Ghost of Christmas Past, you told him everything he wanted to know. I'm the Ghost of Christmas Present; I want to know where I can find Franco now."

"I told you the guy hardly spoke to anybody."

"Ah, hardly you say," I am thumbing through his Playboy magazine I found in the bedroom while Sam was here. "That means he did talk to somebody. Who was it and what did they talk about?"

"I don't know," Peter retorts. "It's been over ten years. And what do you think you are going to do to me? I've been waiting for death to come walking through that door ever since Nam. If you are not going to kill me, put my damn Playboy down and get the hell out. I ain't afraid of the likes of you."

"Really," I sneer. "You think the last ten years have been bad sitting in that chair? What has it really been like? Once a month some crack bitch comes over and polishes your wood when the VA check arrives. The rest of the time you have to jerk it yourself to these pussy mags." I throw the magazine in his face like a fastball. I grab his arms and spin the chair around in a full circle, then stop it with my foot in his groin; I send the chair flying back against the wall. The recoil almost throws him out. "Kill you! I am not going to kill you, War Hero. No, I'm going to tie those big oak tree arms of yours to that chair and then I'm going to cut off both your hands. I'll turn you to face that blank wall, you won't be able to move, and you won't be able to jerk off while you sit there and starve to death. I think it will be a long time before one of those crack-head bitches gets hungry for your VA money. What'ya think?"

"I've met some demons in this life," Peter weighs the threat carefully. He outweighs this guy by a hundred pounds, easy and could probably break him in two if he could get his hands on him. Even beat him to death with the shotgun, but it is now out of reach. He finally replies, "How deep was the pit in Hell that you crawled out of?"

"Who said I crawled out," I respond. "Stop wasting my time. What do you know?"

"OK. There was one guy who passed through a couple of months before. They knew each other back in Chicago."

"Who? What was his name?"

"Don't remember, that's not important, this is. He told Frankie, that's what he called him, Frankie Boy. He told him he had hooked up with this Creole gal down in Mississippi. Frankie Boy got all upset that he was with a black chick. Then he tells him, he's running a disposal service for the boys back home. You know, he takes the guys they want to make disappear down to Alligator Alley and feeds them to the gators."

"How did you find this out?"

"I was sitting right there when he said it," Peter says, "they talked about all kinds of Mob shit like I was deaf or not even there. I don't know where that guy's place is at but I do know where Alligator Alley is. And he told him if he ever needed a place to lay low the door was always open."

After he gives me some landmarks to look out for I am ready to leave. The movie is nearing the end and I warn him, "You know how that story goes. Scrooge is visited by three ghosts, the past and present have already found you. The Ghost of Christmas Future knows where you live, so he won't be far behind me. If I were you, I'd stay out of the light; it is safer here in the dark."

Peter is still sitting in the living room as night begins to fall when the apartment door opens and closes silently. A tall man in a black wool overcoat and hat stands in the doorway between the hall and the living room. He glances at the shotgun on the sofa and then back at Peter, "you've had company today."

"Seems like I'm very popular for some reason, you want to know about Tom Green too?"

"I know all about Tom," the man informs him. "I want to know what you told the FBI and the Gangster."

"I told them what they wanted to know," Peter says. "The FBI wanted to know what Tom Green's real name was. So I told him Franco Benzoni. The black guy wanted to know where he could find him. I told him I didn't know."

"Come on Pete, no need to lie to me," cajoles the man in the black coat, "I'm not here to hurt you, I'm here to make sure there are no slipups; like your vet benefits don't get cut off. I know this guy, Morris Johnson, if you didn't tell him something that pleased him you wouldn't be sitting there right now. So, come on… what did you tell him?"

"I told him when I was in the VA Hospital I got a letter from Tom telling me to keep my mouth shut. I told him I threw the letter away, and gave him a phony address so he would leave. I lied; the letter is in my bedroom, in my dresser drawer."

"In there," the man says pointing to the bedroom, "stay right there. I'll just take that letter for safekeeping. You don't mind, do you?"

The man walks into the bedroom and clicks the light switch on the wall. An ungodly roar fills the apartment. Peter waits a moment until the familiar smell of gunpowder reaches him. He rolls to the bedroom; sees the walls sprayed with blood, and the window blown out, letting in the moonlight through the tattered shade. The man in the black wool coat is sitting on the floor propped up against the dresser; he has one sleeve torn off midway up his forearm and one side of his body is an undistinguishable bloody mess. Peter looks up at the crater where the light switch used to be. Now he knows what happened to his shotgun shells.

Peter St. Claire calls his buddy with one arm to come get him. After explaining his odd day and the visit by the three Christmas ghost, Peter walks down the stairs of his apartment building on his hands, throws his backpack filled with his life savings, which are substantial, onto the back seat, and tells his friend from the VA Hospital to drive west.

Chapter 6

Sold Down the River

June 18, 1978

I watch the plane land with the first group of team members and a cloud of dust kicks up as it comes to a stop on the makeshift runway. Thirty people from various backgrounds line up before me, twenty-six men and four women.

I start right in on them, "I don't know what you were promised that got you on that plane. Some of you probably think since Nam is over you missed your chance to get in on the action, and jumped at the first war that came along."

"I wouldn't have got on that plane if I was told this thing was led by a nigger General Patton wanna-be," interrupts a muscular dirty cowboy with jailhouse tats. He pulls a pack of Marlboros out of his rolled up sleeve and jerks his hand upward. A single cigarette flips just high enough for him to catch it between his lips, his favorite move. "Boy, you got a light?"

I instantly pull out and fire my .45. The cowboy convict falls backwards with a huge bloody cavern where his nose used to be. The cigarette drops, smouldering on the dirt at his feet. "I didn't shoot that fucker because of what he said, I have been called worse by my friends. There are only two things you can be on this team, you can be an asset, or you can be a liability like that asshole." I holster my gun and grind out the cigarette. No one looks at me, or the dead cowboy. I continue speaking directly into the ear of the man standing to the right of the corpse. "If you're a liability, you will be leaving here through Hell's Gate. If you are an asset and follow your training, you might survive the next two years."

I step back in line with Vicky on my right and Miguel on my immediate left. "I'm John, I head up this team. This young lady is Clarita, my second in command. To my left are my technical instructors, T.I.1 and T.I.2, they will teach you to be snipers and killers, and I will teach you to do it without a second thought. How many of you heard of the Geneva Convention?"

Three of the men and the four women raise their hands.

I look at them hard and then scan the other twenty-two. "At least you're not all a bunch of illiterate assholes. Well, you seven can forget it; it doesn't apply to what we're doing here. We are not soldiers. This is not the army, the marines, or any other sanctioned military outfit. I guess some of you are here because some GOVERNMENT MAN got you out of jail like that dirt bag lying there. But I suspect most of you are here for the two-hundred-thousand you were promised. Did that GOVERNMENT MAN tell you that you have to survive the two years to collect? If the training doesn't kill you, then what we are training you for probably will."

I walk down the line and back. The sun is just above my head and the people are squinting to keep track of me. I stop at the middle of the line before a kid who is barely eighteen. He's tan, Mexican and White, bandanna, and a red chequered shirt. I pull him from the line. Fear is swelling up in his eyes. I look down the line to my left and point to another Californian boy, a surfer type, "You! Larry, step forward."

He steps forward, "my name ain't Larry, Bro."

"Everybody standing to your left is named Larry," I inform him. "Everybody to your right is Reggie. The person in front of you is Frankie and the person to your aft is Allie. You got that!" I don't wait for an answer. "Get over here." Larry, the surfer boy, quickly stands next to Reggie, the half Mexican. "You were instructed not to speak to anyone before you got here. Did you?"

Both shake their heads emphatically, NO. I drop an eight by ten glossy of them at the airport bar on the ground between them. Their eyes stay glued to the photo because they are afraid to look at me. "Hey, it's OK, this isn't high school. And I'm not the principal. Larry, what's his name?"

"Reggie, you said his name is Reggie," Larry, the surfer boy, says fearfully.

"No," I correct him, "What is his real name? He must have told you over drinks while you two were getting all buddy-buddy. You know… both from California… different neighborhoods, no doubt, but neither of you ever saw two hundred G's, and that probably gave you a lot to talk about. Come on, what's his name? What were y'all planning to do when you got paid?"

"Umm…"

"Look, I'll make it easy for you," I sympathize, "I'll give you a million… right now… cash. You can go home right now with five times the money promised and none of this G.I. Joe bullshit for the next two years. Just tell me his name."

"You're serious, aren't you?"

I hold up my hand and Mark, the other T.I. brings over a briefcase. He holds it up and opens it for all to see. I pick up one bundle of bills, "Fifty stacks... one thousand twenty dollar bills in each stack... one million dollars for just his name."

"His name is Carlos Rodriquez."

I close the case and hand it to him. I tell him to go wait by the plane, which has taxied to the other end of the runway for takeoff. I wait until he is a few yards away then I begin again, "You have no friends here. What you are here for is to do a job, survive the two years, and go home. Once home, you will never see or speak to anyone you worked with. You will never mention what you did while you were out here. Everyone is either a Larry, Reggie, Frankie, or Allie because anyone can sell you out just that easily." I take the rifle from Mark's shoulder and hand it to Reggie, the half Mexican. "Shoot him. And don't you hit my plane!"

"Hell No! I'm not going to shoot him."

"Oh, you're not!" I mock his indignation. I lean into him but speak loud enough for all to hear. "Ok, it's two years from now. No, make that five years, and you're just getting home from work. You walk into the kitchen to see what your lovely wife has for dinner, but what is this? There's a guy holding a gun to her head. She has obviously been beaten, and her eyes tell you she's been raped and sodomized, and they plead with you to end this. You hear your two little ones in the bedroom crying. You cannot imagine what has happened to them."

Tears well in his eyes, as he fills with rage for me. His hand grips the butt and rifle stock tighter.

I continue the story, "the man says he will kill you and let your family go if you give him the name of the man who led your team, my name. He says you cost him billions in drug money and he's been hunting you for years. He says if you don't tell him, he will force you to watch your wife and kids go through even more torture before they die, before you die. He tells you one more time, he will kill you so you never have to know what horrors your family has suffered because of you, just give him the name of your team leader."

"John," Carlos sobs, "Just John, I don't know his last name."

"Exactly." I place a hand on his shoulder. "Because you will never know my name, Reggie. The man tells you that sorry *sonofabitch,* Larry, was in a bar bragging about how he made a million dollars for just giving out your name. Then he shoots your wife in her head and you hear two more gunshots from the bedroom."

"What? No! Why? I told you what you wanted to know."

"Yeah, but he was a drug dealing scumbag. So he kills your family and leaves you alive to suffer with the pain. I know, because that's what I would do. I'm a drug dealing scumbag. And I'm telling you, it is better to kill that sorry *sonofabitch* Larry right now, than wish you had five years from now. He just became a liability to you."

Carlos swings the rifle up, looks through the scope at the back of Larry's head and fires. A pop then a wisp of a blood cloud hangs in the air around Larry's head. He drops to his knees then face down into the dirt beneath the plane's wing.

"Just so you know," I announce, "a million dollars is less than I make in one day. To track you down, the drug czars you are going to war against will pay ten times that amount. That is the first lesson for today, don't become a liability. In that house behind you is where we will live, breakfast waiting."

"All of us in that one barracks?" asks one of the women.

"We will sleep, shower, and shit together," I inform her. "So if you are shy, get over it."

The twenty-eight people murmur as they slowly walk to the wood plank long house. I tell Mark and Miguel to take the two bodies to the bay and make sure the sharks are hungry before throwing them in.

Vicky grabs my arm. "What the hell was that? That's no way to build a gang. You can't build trust by telling them they can't trust each other."

"First of all, we are not building a gang, we are building..." I think hard for the right words to describe what we are doing here. I give up, "I'm not sure what this is, but don't trust any of them. As long as they get the job done that is all that matters."

"That is another thing," Vicky scolds me, "this job. Why are we doing it? You don't care about the government or their war on drugs."

"I don't think the government gives a rat's ass about cocaine dealers in Colombia either. And as soon as we train enough of these guys, they are going to come after us too. What I do know is if you want to know what's cooking, you got to be in the kitchen."

The next four weeks go by quickly, we lose eight more in live fire exercises. The first, one of the women Larrys, throws her first grenade. She makes two mistakes, tossed it too high, and doesn't take cover afterwards. A single bit of shrapnel hit her in the heart. Two Frankies are killed while advancing on targets. "Three seconds bursts," I yell at a male Reggie who cut down a Frankie ahead of him. The other Frankie jumped up when he came upon a snake's nest. I warn them, "If you land on a snake in the grass, cut its head off. It is better than getting shot in yours." Three more disappear in the night. I heard their plan to swim to a fishing boat not far from the island. I also know that trying to swim a mile in shark-infested waters is impossible, and serves as a good lesson to the others. Two more are killed by police on a neighboring island, during a botched practice kidnapping.

The remaining twenty are split into two teams based on who worked well with each other, and how their strengths and weaknesses would complement missions. The teams comprise of 3 Larrys; 3 Reggies; 2 Frankies; 2 Allies; 1 Leader, and 1 Second. The first exercise is a two-part affair; the first team is going to kidnap Pablo's Lieutenant on his way to California and convince him to reveal their factory locations. The second will hit multiple sites before Pablo knows his man is missing.

Colombia has turned into a warzone since the Medellin Massacre, even though I sent word to Pablo to let him know where his missing cocaine was, and suggested his need of my services to regulate all the warring factions. But the attack on the Cali Cartel could not be undone and an all-out war between the three cartels has been going on ever since. I lead the first team, as the kidnapping needs to be flawless and is key to a successful mission. I don't know if Pablo has eyes on his Lieutenant so the grab has to be made quickly, quietly, and a duplicate must board the flight to California in his place.

A small landmine in a rut blows out the tire of the Lieutenant's car in his motorcade in a relatively quiet part of town. A shabby garage on the side of the road serves as the ambush location. My men take out the four bodyguards and I convince the Lieutenant to join me in the back room for a talk. Reggie, the half Mexican, and four of my men take their places and continue on to the airport. Reggie is a close enough match to double as the lieutenant from a distance, but if Pablo has someone on the plane, it could be trouble. We make sure Reggie boards the plane seconds before takeoff, which prevents potential slipups, and gives us a six-hour window to accomplish our mission.

The last crack of the bat flings blood from Antonio Rivera's head to mine. I wipe my face before helping the drug czar's lieutenant back into his chair. I have my two huskiest Larrys work on him for an hour with bats and chains.

"I think he's been softened enough, guys. Besides, we are running out of time. Antonio, can you hear me?"

Blood flows freely from his ear, but he nods wearily. "I hear you. Doesn't matter though... I will tell you nothing. You might as well... kill me and get it over with, because what Pablo will do to me, will be ten times worse than this."

"No doubt. And do not worry, we are going to kill you," I assure him. "But first, you will show me on this map where all of Pablo's drug camps are. You know who I am, don't you?"

"You are the Medellin Monster," he smiles through swollen lips. "You killed Juan Jimenez's family, and kidnapped his daughter. Some say you kept her as a trophy, a sex slave... as a warning to the other cartel bosses."

"Good," I smile back. "Then you know I will kill yours too, starting with your little girl." I hold up a Polaroid picture of a school building with a beat-up white Chevy parked in front. Antonio focuses his one good eye on the picture. "You know the deal. It's the same as you did to that judge. When your daughter walks out of that school in…" I glance at my watch. "Ten minutes. My man will set off a trunk full of dynamite. Your little girl, her friends, the nuns, they are all gonna be gone."

"If I tell you anything, do you not think Pablo will kill my family just the same?" Antonio drops his head into his hands.

"No. No, he won't. You are his brother-in-law. She is his niece. His sister won't let him harm her," I reason, "When he finds your body, he will know you fought the good fight. You didn't give in easily. That is why I had these guys do such a good job on you. A person can only hold out for so long, he knows in the end a person will talk. That end is here, you point out where the camps are and I call my man and tell him to let your daughter go home to her mom."

Antonio is unresponsive, his face still buried in his hands. I nudge him on his broken collarbone, he barely twitches. After a while, the body feels no pain, shock sets in and the mind wanders. He looks at me with a vacant smile. *Thinking about the good times, he had with his daughter no doubt. Or thinking he will be united with her in Heaven soon. Foolishness, I have no time for this.*

"Look, we are both going to Hell when this life is over, you sooner than me. Don't face the Lord on Judgment Day and tell him I blew up a school full of little girls and nuns, and you let me do it."

"Let me see that map," he says with a renewed spirit. "It is not really going to help you. The minute your friend gets off the plane in California, he's a dead man. Pablo will know something is up; he will strengthen the guards at the camps, the warehouses, everywhere."

"We are running out of time," I caution, "better start marking off places."

He circles five areas on the map and I X them with his blood. I nod and one of the husky Larrys makes the call. "You did the right thing today. But if I show up at these places, and they are not what I expect to find, that car will be parked at your house tonight. What do you think happened to Valentina?"

"You sacrificed her to the Devil to become invincible," he answers coldly as if he is stating a well-known fact.

"Well, whatever happened to her will happen to your daughter. And don't worry about my man on the plane; he's going to have a heart attack just before landing. An ambulance will be there to take him straight to the hospital. That should buy us a couple more hours."

I leave Antonio Rivera with the two husky Larrys and head for a makeshift helicopter pad just outside of town. The other team is waiting. Of the five camps, we figure we can make two before it turns dark. I tell the team the plan is to drop a mile away from the first camp, destroy it, and then cut through the jungle to the second. I give the pilot the coordinates where to make the drop off and pick up. The pilot and co-pilot come straight from Derrick; they don't know who we are or what we plan to do.

The jungle is a raucous place. Birds, insects, and animals large and small cry out their objections to our presence. The team is nervous and spooked by their surroundings. *I should have taken these scary-cats out once or twice to get them used to this. Oh well, too late now.*

We walk in two rows about twenty yards apart. I'm leading one group with a Frankie, and Reggies behind followed by an Allie. Clarita has the other group; she is following her Allie, covering our rear. The sounds of the jungle are suddenly silenced and replaced by music and human voices. We drop to the ground. We have reached the first cocaine processing camp.

It is a small place, maybe thirty yards across. Two houses sit at the right end of the clearing; less than half the size of our long house, barely wooden shacks. I espy about fifty women and children working under a ten-yard-long 'A' roof held up by four posts and mosquito netting for walls. A few men with machine guns are supposedly guarding the area, but some are engaged in a fierce dominoes game, while two others appear to be sleeping in the shade against one of the houses.

The Frankies setup on the edge of the jungle, their sniper rifles trained on the sleeping guards. I pass the word down the line, "no one leaves the camp alive." The Frankies fire and the sleeping guards' shake is nearly invisible from here. The Larrys have the best angle on the dominoes table and fire a short burst, shattering the calm of the camp. The Reggies fire a continuous sweeping spray of bullets at the ground ahead of our charge, testing for land mines in our path. Three more guards come running from behind the other shack, I drop one and Clarita kills the other two. Two small boys dart between the trees and disappear into the jungle.

"Fuck. Frankie, did you not have a shot at those kids?" I yell into my headset.

"They were only children," replies one of the snipers.

"They are runners, YOU ASSHOLE! They have gone to alert more guards. We have about twenty, maybe a half-hour before they show up. Fuck people. Let's get to work."

The women and other children are still working at the vats and tables like nothing has happened. The men push them outside and sat them down on the ground. One of the Larrys tells them to put their heads down in Spanish and that gets them praying.

"Check the houses for more people... and be careful," I warn, "start pumping that diesel fuel on everything that's not hot, we don't want to be sending up smoke signals. Douse the place good." I walk over to the Larry who speaks Spanish. He's from New Jersey, a black kid who grew up in a Puerto Rican neighborhood. "Ok, let's finish this."

"Finish what?"

"You're kidding, right?"

The three Larrys are looking at me wide-eyed, agape.

"Remember before we left base I said, quote, 'We may have to kill some women and children in this raid.' And you all said, again I quote, 'That's Ok.' And just a few minutes ago I said, 'No one leaves alive.' So tell me. What the fuck did you think I meant?"

"I thought you meant some women and children might get killed in the crossfire," volunteers Black Larry from New Jersey. "I didn't think you meant we were going to execute people."

"What difference does it make? Dead is dead," I am astounded.

"We don't really have to kill them," Clarita advocates, "They have nothing. They can't do us any harm."

"No, they can't do us any harm," I agree, "but when the guys with guns show up, they will point which way we went. You are right, they have nothing, just this job in this cocaine factory, which we are about to blow up. You do realize we are not their liberators; we are the ones taking the food out of their mouths. And since they have very little to live for, I say we end their lives right now."

"How about if we send them off into the jungle, the same direction the other kids went? That way they won't know which way we go."

"Is that good with all of you?" I give a snide look at the team. "But they go that way." I point to the south. "So when the other guards show up, they have two trails to follow. Let's hope they don't pick ours. Larry, tell them to start running, and if they so much as slow down or turn their heads..."

He doesn't wait a second longer to give the orders. The women grab the children who are too small to run and trot into the jungle.

I walk over to one of the guards who had come from behind the house. "Clarita, this is your kill."

She walks over.

I kick the body and it rolls onto its back, revealing the face of a boy in his mid-teens, at most. "All these people are going to be poor, young, and doing whatever they are told to survive. You'd better start doing the same. That goes for all of you. Reggie, rig me a tripwire and disguise it well, we can still get a head-start on the others."

We are a few minutes into the jungle when a loud boom resonates through the trees. I look up and back towards the camp but only see faint wisps of black smoke through the canopy. *That will slow their pursuit.* "Let's pick up the pace people, we have another camp to hit."

The next camp is not far at all, a dozen miles from where we were at, and thankfully downhill. It is a bit larger and much more active. From the tree line above the site, I spot three jeeps with mounted machineguns, 50 calibres, I'm sure, parked on the roads leading to the camp. There are also as many guards as workers, and no one is sleeping or playing dominoes. The guards are dispersed in groups of threes, some behind defensive blockades of oil drums, others patrol the perimeter. I signal the team to fall back into the jungle.

"We are going to fan out along the tree line. One click when you are in position, understand? When I give the signal, we open fire and do not stop until there is no one left standing. Am I clear on this?"

There is a sombre and collective 'Yes' from the team. We ease into position, 2 Larrys on the left, myself, the 2 Frankies, then Clarita, and finally 2 Reggies, each of us about ten yards apart. The two Allies and a Larry and Reggie cover our rear fifteen yards behind the line. I warn them there may be squads patrolling the jungle, since they have obviously been radioed about our prior attack. I count off the clicks in my earpiece. *Eight, nine, ten, and that is eleven.* "Fire! Fire! Fire!"

The birds above flap noisily from their perches as the low rattle of suppressed automatic gunfire disturbs their peace. The two Frankies and I concentrate fire on the three 50 calibre machineguns on the jeeps. They can do real damage if they manage to return fire on our position. We take out the gunners first and then the jeeps, turning them into burning wrecks. We have LMGs, and Stoner 63s, that we modified for silencer and explosive ammo. The rest of the team sweeps the camp. The exploding rounds cause panic and death, rendering any form of defensive positioning useless.

I hear a couple of pops behind me and the anguish cries of a patrol taken down by the Allies. I radio the Frankies, "let fly the mortars. Take out the generator, the buildings, and the processing hut. Level everything down there."

A couple of seconds later, explosions one by one, shatter everything before us. Three minutes and the camp is a burning pit of death. The gunfire ceases and an eerie silence fills the jungle. "Larrys, Reggies, cover our flanks. We are pulling out."

The ride out of Colombia is sombre. The team waits for night to radio in for the pickup. The helicopter flies to a commercial fishing vessel in international waters and offloads the crew. The vessel is a floating cocaine processing plant, owned by Morris, and operated by Nicky Rocci. The team leaves by speedboats for their base once the helicopter is out of range. Vicky watches Morris the entire trip but he never looks her way, although she can tell he is very much aware of her interest in him.

T.I.1, Miguel, gets the radio message that the mission is completed and he can wrap up his operation. The two husky Larrys deposit two bullets in Antonio Rivera's head and leave him in the trunk of his car at the local police station. They take a speedboat back to base the same night.

Next morning, Reggie, the half Mexican, T.I.2 Mark, and the rest of the kidnapping team arrive at base and gathers in the dining room of the long house. They are jubilant, having completed their first successful mission.

Clarita, at the head of the table, sits subdued, awaiting John's arrival in trepidation. She sees the door at the far end of the long house open.

He enters and keeps a steady determined pace from his quarters, through the men's section, past the curtains that mark the women's quarters and finally into the dining room. The teams are so enveloped in recanting their exploits they don't notice him standing at the end of the table.

"I'm glad to see everyone made it back."

A hush descends over the room. Smiles quickly fade from view as the usually stern leader has a look about him of crazed contempt. He seems to be looking into each of their eyes at the same time, and his gaze scorches their souls. Their eyes lower, as if they are being accused, and rightfully so, for stealing his most prized possession. The only one who manages to keep her head up and lock horns with him is Clarita. She refuses to be chastised, and her glare is as fiery and fierce as his.

"If ANYONE… EVER… fails to carry out an order again," he pauses for a long moment before finishing, "I'll be coming back alone." John waits as those on the kidnapping team look quizzically at the others.

Miguel glances at Clarita. She notices his neck and face muscles twitch and shoots him a *don't be stupid* scowl that keeps him in his place.

"T.I.s, there are plans in my quarters and supplies on the way; erect two more buildings by day and train these assholes for night assaults. Be ready on my return. CLARITA!"

John turns and leaves. Vicky gets up from the table immediately and follows. The rest sit in stunned silence, contemplating if they have actually received a death threat instead of a *job well done*. Each in their own mind reasons they have, those on the kidnapping team don't know why, those on the assault team do. Minutes later they hear the roar of the plane pass angrily overhead.

The seaplane splashes down and slowly motors forward to the dock. Two of the men from the house tie down the pontoons as Morris and Vicky exit onto the dock. Vicky quickly passes by Elizabeth and Maria at the end of the pier, running her hand through the little girl's black curly hair in response to her greeting of, "Hi Auntie Clarita!"

Maria, arms and legs flailing in all directions, races down excitedly and leaps into her daddy's arms. "What did you bring me?"

"Is that a proper greeting from my Little Princess, whom I haven't seen in weeks?"

"No, Daddy," Maria giggles with a lack of remorse, "Hello Daddy. How are you? Did you bring me a present?"

"That's a little better... But you still need to work on your manners, these are not at all fitting of a princess," I smirk and spin her around at a dizzying speed on the dock then place her down, wobbly-legged at her mother's side. I fan eight-by-ten glossies before her eyes with my right hand, and sweep my left around Liz's waist, gripping the lower curve of her butt. "And what kind of greeting do I get from the Queen?"

"You've been gone too long," she sighs, "I hope you brought me something nicer than pictures."

"I brought you my love. And this..." I reach into my pocket and produce a necklace. A pair of diamond studded golden three-inch wings joined in the middle to an enormous round emerald hanging from a fine gold chain. "It took a while to wrestle them from an angel, but you are worth the fight."

"Oh, that's so pretty Mommy," exclaims Maria. "How come you didn't bring me something pretty like Mommy's?"

"Women," I say with a deep sigh as I watch Vicky's dark figure disappear into the house. "Look closely my Little Princess, there are secrets of the jungle in those pictures."

Maria studies the top picture, scanning from left to right and back again. Then she locks onto the golden eyes staring back at her, "it's a cat. There's a big cat in the tree, right Daddy?"

I nod, "show Mommy."

Elizabeth takes the photo and examines it. *No markings. This is a real picture of a real panther.* "Where did you get this?"

"It was slightly harder than wrestling with angels," I quip and lead them back to the Aruba House. It doesn't take long for Maria to become completely absorbed by the pictures of jungle cats, crocodiles, birds, and monkeys. I slip away from Elizabeth and her questioning eyes as she points out the animals buried in the jungle scenes. I go upstairs to the bedroom and close the thick oak door behind me.

"So, now you don't even knock," screams Vicky.

"This is not a social call," I yell back, the six-inch concrete walls muffling the verbal battle. I built the house to withstand an assault by anything less than a tank round. There are no tanks in Aruba. The walls and heavy doors also keep in what I don't want getting out. "What the hell did you think you were doing out there? You gave our enemies valuable tactical information and could have cost us our lives."

"I don't want to be some kind of executioner. And I don't think those boys and girls can handle COLD BLOODED MURDER the way you do." Her voice climbs in intensity and volume.

Elizabeth's head jerks toward the second floor. The indistinguishable sound can only be the major fight she sensed looming at the dock. Morris is good at hiding his feelings from others, but not so at hiding them from her. She noticed the way he looked past her at the dock and his eyes followed Clarita. They were full of anger, even as he smiled sweetly at her and Maria.

"I told you once before, YOU BECOME WHAT YOU DO. We are assassins, enforcers, executioners, and now MERCENARIES." I inform her, to her displeasure. "You can only hope your boyfriend works for the right government. Did you notice that in the second raid, we came upon a much more heavily defended camp? Why do you think that was?" I am inches from her face, but still just as loud, "they radioed our strength, the number of people we had... how we overran the camp... they were expecting us to do the same thing again. And they were ready."

Most of what Morris says falls on deaf ears; Vicky fixates on the word 'boyfriend' in reference to Derrick Patterson. *How dare he accuse me of being... What? ... Unfaithful. That sonofabitch pushed me to meet him month after month. Made me his 'go between' to keep his identity a secret. The nerve of this... this bastard!* "Maybe Derrick was right. Maybe you are nothing more than a two-bit hoodlum pretending to be a great leader. I've followed you around all these years like a stupid lovesick schoolgirl, hoping you would love me back. But you don't! You don't even care about me. You are incapable of any human feeling whatsoever! You're not jealous of Derrick, you just want to see everything around you burn."

I place a hand on her cheek, she slaps it away, but I can feel the heat burning inside her. "I am jealous. I'm jealous of Patterson. I'm jealous of Miguel, and I don't trust either of them around you. We have been friends since childhood and at times I do wish we could be lovers too." I put my hand back on her cheek, and this time when she tries to free herself, I hook the back of her neck. "I wish we could be more than 'fuck buddies'. I wish I could give you more." I pull her close to me but she resists. "And you are wrong! I do love you. As much as I could allow myself to and still keep you safe. When you helped me fake my death, you made me promise to take you with me. I knew that was a mistake, and since then I have tried to force myself to send you away, for your own sake, for your own good, but I could not. I can't love you and protect you, because the person I need to protect you from most of all… is me."

Elizabeth has been watching Clarita's door intently since the fight began and discovers that she has drifted from being beside Maria to sitting in a chair in the corner of the living room with a direct line of sight. The thunderstorm in the room seems to have subsided but no one has emerged yet. Akilina had since taken Maria for dinner, bathed her, and put her to bed. She also set a plate on the table next to Elizabeth, who absentmindedly thanked her.

Day turned to night; Uncle Dom asks if she needs him to stay up, or if she is going to retire. Receiving no response, he gathers up the plate of untouched food and murmurs, "Fucking prick."

That brakes the trance, Elizabeth finally says, "Something terrible has happened." She stands zombie-fied, walks upstairs, and slows her step outside Clarita's door. She reaches out then withdraws her hand, as if touching a hot stove. She quickly goes down the hall and slams her bedroom door shut.

Uncle Dom adjusts his shoulder holster and reiterates, "Motherfucking Prick."

Elizabeth lies motionless in bed, clutching her daughter and the golden angel wings. Her head aches from the swirling images of Morris and Clarita torturing her. She imagines them in the throes of passion, mocking her. She imagines Morris' hands around Clarita's throat, wringing the last breath from her body. She imagines Clarita stabbing Morris' lifeless body until it is nothing more than a hunk of bloody flesh. But mostly, she imagines the two entwined.

Elizabeth shudders when Morris slides into bed behind her, repulsed by the scent of Clarita and sex that clings to his body. She shifts away from his touch and grips her daughter tighter, "Don't. Maria is in bed, you'll wake her."

I run my fingers through Maria's thick curly black hair, "She's fast asleep. She won't wake up."

Elizabeth drags my hand away, "don't touch her. Do you think... What are we doing here? Why did you bring me here? To this prison... What am I, your slave?"

I can hear the tears in her voice. I curl a lock of blonde hair around my index finger and gently let it slip through my fingers. "This is not a prison; I brought you here to keep you safe."

"Safe from what? From whom?" Her words crack as she fights to keep her voice down and under control. "We were perfectly safe in New York. And how are you supposedly keeping us safe? You're gone more than you are here. And whatever you and Clarita are into must be much worse than the usual mob business between you and Nicky. What is going on with you and her?"

"You know I don't keep secrets from you. It drives Nicky nuts that I tell you so much about our business. But it would be unwise for me to involve you in what I'm doing now. And unsafe," I prop myself up on one elbow to look down on her face. Liz turns face down into the pillow and I have to pry her head back to face me. "You are safer here because nobody knows you. Nobody knows me. The people I'm... involved with are not the run of the mill drug lords and such. I can handle those without breaking a sweat. These people have a greater reach, more resources at their disposal, and are capable of greater evil than you can imagine. I couldn't do what I have to do, if I didn't know you were safe here."

Her eyes glisten and I lower to kiss her moist lips, but she breaks free of my hold, and flips her face back to the pillow. I am content to kiss her ear, run my hand down her body to her thigh, and up the inside of her nightie, stopping when I feel hair.

She trembles. "No."

I kiss her ear again and rest my hand on her pubic mound. I lower off my elbow and slide my arm under her neck, across her body, and cup her breast, sliding her nipple between my fingers. Stinging pain on the back of my hand forces me to roll her back towards me. She is digging the wing of the necklace into my hand. I keep a firm grip on her and she resorts to biting my arm now trapped around her chest. I feel the trickle of blood from the back of my hand and the burning in my bicep that tells me she has drawn blood there too. I kiss her ear gently and wait.

My arm throbs in rhythm to my dick against her soft behind. Her body softens and a flush of heat from between her legs warms my hand. I tenderly massage her, letting my fingers comb, separate, and search for the source of heat. My middle finger at last finds her tiny dewy opening and I rub my fingertip gently around it, soaking up her fluids, and then running that same finger up her soft slit to the lump of flesh hiding her clit. She moans and licks the blood from my arm then arches her back, driving her ass into my groin and pinning my dick between her cheeks.

Simultaneously circling her nipple and clit slowly, I shift her body back towards me. Still holding the angel wing necklace, she grips my hand tighter to her breast then rubs her ass up and down my dick, pumping semen onto her backside. I shift again, position my dick between her legs, letting my engorged head stroke the soft folds of her vagina. My index finger now firmly on her clitoris, works it in ever quickening circles.

Her breath is hot against my bicep and her pussy contracts and releases as she writhes back and forth on my dick. Gentle nibbles on her earlobe give way to hard bites at the sweet sweaty area between her shoulder and neck. Another louder and prolonged moan is followed by clutching and grasping at my hand between her legs. I spread my fingers out and dive the two middle fingers in and up her wet hole. Her body stiffens against mine, her breathing halts in mid inhalation, her legs clench around me.

Cool liquid delight runs down my fingers and I lift her up by those same two fingers. I slide them out and my dick in as she exhales a low throaty, "Ooooh, Baby." I respond with the same and continue slowly pumping her. I squeeze her tit and roll her nipple in time to her vaginal contractions, milking as much pleasure out of her as I can. She hisses and sucks the blood from my arm. I replace the taste of blood with her cum as I finger her panting mouth. She licks my fingers and kisses my hand eagerly. I roll her onto her stomach and lift her hips in my hands. She stretches out and arches up to accept me as I drive harder and deeper into her body with each thrust. My pace quickens and I run one hand up her back to grab her golden head. She orgasms again as I pull back on her silken reigns. Her pelvic convulsions are so strong I explode in one long stream, followed by another and another, before collapsing onto my forearms sparing her the full weight of my exhausted body.

Elizabeth wakes in an empty bed in an empty room, and the bright streaks across the walls tell her it is late morning. She walks through the empty house, out onto the ocean side porch, and the sound of waves gently washing up on shore instantly soothe her spirit. She sees Morris sitting in a chair, leaning back on its two hind legs against the house, his muscular legs elevated by a small circular table, asleep.

"Didn't your mother ever tell you it is bad manners to rear back in a chair like that? And your feet don't belong on the table!"

"I have lots of bad habits," I reply, looking up at her with one open eye.

"Like not knowing when NO means no," she scoffs while running her fingers across the welted teeth marks on my arm. "And look at what you did to my neck! Everyone will be staring at this hickey for days."

"Not if you are wearing that nightie," I say grinning boldly. "I'm sure the guys' attentions will be much lower."

"Don't worry, I am going to change," Elizabeth slaps my hand away from the pink silk lace hem of the nightgown. "Where is everybody?"

"Maria and I had a lovely breakfast then Akilina took her into town to do some shopping. The guys went with them, of course."

"And Clarita, is she still asleep?"

"No. She's gone."

"What did you do to her?" Elizabeth asks in wide-eyed amazement. "You didn't kill her last night, did you?"

"What?" I ask, equally amazed. "No. She left this morning on business. What kind of monster do you think I am?"

"I don't know; but not a very nice one at times. You kill people for a living, I know that."

"I can be nice sometimes. And I don't kill people for a living, it's more of a hobby," I tell her, running my hand up and down the back of her leg. The joke gets no response, "You have the prison to yourself for a few hours. What would you like to do, Sugar Tits?"

She straddles my lap and slaps my face, "I told you not to call me that."

"But they are so sweet." I peel off the straps of her nightie and suck her stiffening nipple into my mouth. I suck hard, pulling in a mouthful of creamy white breast and dark pink studded areola. Sloppily and noisily working on her, my dick comes to full attention in my shorts beneath her.

"Suck all you want, you missed your opportunity to get anything out of them years ago," she says, cradling my head to her breast.

"I can fix that," I inform her as I switch a breast then massage her swollen nipple with my fingertips.

"FUCK THAT!" Elizabeth leaps up and grabs a handful of throbbing cock, "I'll cut it off before I let you put another baby in me."

I grab her by the ass and pull her back down, "How do you know I didn't already?"

"I'll cut your prick off anyway, you prick." Elizabeth forces her tongue into my mouth, furiously darting it about, her hand just as forcefully pulling my cock above the waistband and shoving it into her fiery pit. She hisses long and deep as I fill her to breaking point.

Morris and Maria are down on the beach early in the morning. Both are staring up at the sky, even as Maria turns in circles, her arms outstretched, and giggling gleefully.

Elizabeth walks down to them and asks, "Why didn't you wake me? What do you have there?"

"Daddy got me a string-less kite," Maria says and increases her circle to encompass her mother.

"What? There is no such thing as a string-less kite, Dear."

"Up there, Mommy," Maria stops long enough to point.

Elizabeth shields her eyes from the sun and spots a bird high overhead. Before she can grasp what she is looking at, Morris holds up the black and silver radio control. "Oh, it's a radio controlled plane. Why did you tell her it's a kite?"

"Because it is a kite," I inform her. I push one of the two joysticks forward and the bird makes a long arching swoop over the water and heads towards us. It sails quietly a few feet over our heads then soars skyward again. "See, no engine. It flies on the wind; I control the angle of the wings and tail. Want to give it a try Sugar… Liz?"

"No. I'd probably crash it," she says. She watches the intensity on Morris' face as the bird swoops and dives, rises and circles out over the ocean, comes sweeping in low and fast at them, then races back up to dizzying heights. "Why did you buy that?"

"It's relaxing."

"You don't look relaxed," she remarks then rubs my cheek and my chest. "Did you two have breakfast?"

"We're waiting on you, Honey."

"You sleep too long Mommy," Maria complains, latching onto Elizabeth's leg. The mention of breakfast makes her stomach growl loudly.

"Mommy stays up too late," I explain.

"Daddy keeps me awake all night," Elizabeth counters.

"Doing what Mommy?"

"Yeah, doing what Mommy?" I echo the question immediately.

"Your Daddy is a bad… bad… boy. OK, it is time for breakfast. You want strawberry waffles?" Elizabeth redirects the conversation and flashes me a whimsical scowl.

I bring the kite in for a landing on the beach; its wheels catch in the sand, the beak nosedives, and buries itself in the wet softness.

Elizabeth picks it up by the plastic wing; it's light for such a big kite. Its wingspan is longer than her extended arms and half her height. A bird is painted on clear plastic and the frame is made from what appears to be umbrella tubing.

I work the controls, flipping the tiny arms, wiggling the kite in her hands.

"Where did you get this?" she asks curiously.

"I made it."

"Hmm, boys and their toys," she hands me the kite, "speaking of which, are you going to be here for you know who's... you know what?"

"I wouldn't miss it," I say proudly.

Elizabeth throws me a scornful look, "Really? You missed all her other ones."

"All my other ones what?" Maria is hopping along the sand between the two of us.

"Your birthday my Little Princess," I wink, and her face lights up with the news, "Your Mommy says I missed all your other birthdays, but I was there for your first one, remember? That is the most important one... and this one. You're turning five, that's a very important age in a princess' life."

"Really! What happens when I turn five?" Maria's big blue eyes grow larger and brighter with anticipation.

"That's the age when a little princess gets her first pony!"

"What! No. Oh HELL NO. Are you crazy? What are we going to do with a pony?"

"Oh Mommy, a pony! Yes, that will be the bestest birthday present ever. Oh, yes. Please. Please… Please… Please." Maria jumps up and down with joy, energy radiating out of her golden cinnamon face towards her mother.

"Your father is a very bad boy," she says sternly while looking me square in the face, "who exactly is going to take care of a pony? Couldn't you have promised her a dog, like someone normal?"

Clarita sits on the outside deck at the beachside bar. The palm trees rustle in the gentle Bahamans breeze, carrying with it the fragrance of hibiscus, red, white, and yellow. She lounges comfortably against the bar with her feet stretched out on the neighboring stool and sips a peach and pineapple flavored concoction the bartender said he made just for her. Letting her mind drift aimlessly across the white sands, she watches the children playing in the water, lovers snuggled on the beach, and listens absent-mindedly to the steel band music. She imagines a normal life of vacationing in the sun.

"Thinking about me, I hope," Derrick's husky voice interrupts her daydream.

"I'm thinking you're late," she replies annoyed.

Derrick taps her feet and she takes her time repositioning herself to allow him access to the stool. "I was out to sea, didn't get your message until an hour ago. I had to shower off the sea water first."

"If you had taken any longer," Clarita pulls a cigarette from her pack of Newports, "I would have been gone."

"More like asleep," he smiles and flexes his broad dark shoulders then pulls a lighter from his shorts and lights her cigarette. "I didn't know you smoked."

"Why should you? You don't know anything about me," she states.

"I know you're here alone this time."

"Spying on me, Mr. Spy?"

"No. I can feel when someone is watching me," he replies sincerely, "I don't feel any eyes on me. I guess your friend, John, trust me now."

"Guess again," she quips.

"Then I guess it's you who trusts me."

Clarita laughs and runs her slender manicured finger down his t-shirt. "What's this? You've gone native."

"I've started a scuba shop," Derrick stretches out the logo of a yellow cartoon fish wearing a diving mask and snorkel. "You like it?"

"It's OK. But shouldn't the fish be wearing a scuba tank?" Clarita takes another sip from her drink. "What's the matter, the spy business not paying well these days?"

"The spy business is paying for the scuba shop. I can't be on vacation forever, people would start asking questions, and that is bad in the spy business." Derrick takes the cigarette from her lips and takes a drag. He studies her long smooth creamy Hershey legs for a few moments and continues, "You never answered my question. Do you trust me?"

"No." Clarita takes her cigarette back and drags hard on it. She blows a long stream of smoke back at his face. "But I'm a big girl, I can handle myself. And before you get too ahead of yourself, do you have my intel?"

"Of course, but not here, can't exactly pull out satellite photos and such at the bar," he chuckles.

"Ok, then let's go up to your room."

"I don't stay here anymore. Like I said, can't be on a permanent vacation," he winks at her, "I live above the scuba shop about a mile down the beach. My car's out front."

"Let's go." Clarita hops off the bar stool, grabs her purse, and pack of Newports. She runs her hand across his chest and gold-tipped nails across his bare shoulder. Her sundress falls to her knees and Derrick takes a minute to study her taunt ass as she exits the bar.

He tries to engage her in conversation on the short drive down the street to his place, but she just watches the colorful houses of palm greens, salmon pinks, and sunny yellows passing by the window. They are mostly two-story houses of sandstone, the bottom floor contains little boutiques, and most likely their owners' dwellings above. Between them, momentary glimpses of pure white sand and bright blue ocean catch her eyes. She imagines his place will be like this, quaint and humble, non-assuming.

He turns off the street between two towering palms and drives slowly down a long narrow cobblestone driveway. He watches with a wide grin as the four-story mini fort, made from gigantic granite stone splays before her. He drives through the cavernous archway into the courtyard and circles around the fountain embedded in flowers to the main door. There are window boxes of flowers at every window. Pale blue shutters open to the sides. On the ground floor, large bay windows display mannequins dressed in various swimwear and diving equipment. He kills the Mercedes motor, waits for a moment to let Clarita soak in the grandeur, and says, "The spy business is doing very well."

"I see," she can't help but flash him a smile, "you have been keeping busy. I take it you are not alone here."

"I have a couple of guys to run the boats, extra instructors to help give scuba lessons to the tourist, and of course, a few girls to run the shop. But at night it's just me," he pouts.

"Poor King Midas, all alone on your throne."

Derrick quickly races around the car, opens the door, helps her out, and leads her to a small door to the right of the shop windows. He reaches up and pulls a string, dimly illuminating a narrow steep stairwell running along the wall. "This way, my Queen!"

He watches her ascend, and when she turns around he quickly follows. On the landing, three stories up, an old oak door bars the way. Derrick slips his hand around her waist and twists the knob, flinging the door wide open. The glistening Caribbean Sea dazzles her senses. The room is filled with crystal and silver furnishings, reflecting and enhancing the incredible view.

Clarita slowly lowers his hand from around her waist and steps forward onto the marble floor. She nods as she moves across the room to the balcony. "Not bad, King Midas," she says as she turns back to him. "I wonder what your boss is going to say when he gets the bill."

He follows her out onto the balcony and slips both hands around her waist. She pulls back a little and feels his hand slide down her backside, cupping the bottom of her cheeks. "Like I said, the spy business is doing very well." He leans in to kiss her.

She runs her hand up his chest and catches his Adam's apple between thumb and index finger. She applies a little pressure and drives him back. "Intel first."

He grips her firmly and notices she has no panties on. "What's second?"

"That depends on how good your intel is," she smiles, gives him a peck on the cheek, moves around him, and back inside.

He stands there with the sun sinking into the ocean, casting a golden aura around his muscular black body.

"I'm sure the other... ladies, just melted out of their clothes at the... view. But I am still here on business."

Derrick smiles as he watches her parade around the room running her fingers over the silver globes of the table lamp. Her creamy white satin dress hugs every curve, delicately detailing the tiny peaks atop her breast mounts, flowing like rivulet over her flat tummy and cascading into a waterfall over her swaying hips. *Sure you're here on business, but it's not my intelligence you're after today. But we'll play your game.* "Make yourself at home. The bar is over there," he points to a mirrored wall, "fully stocked. I just have to go upstairs to the office."

When Derrick returns with a manila envelope in hand, he sees Clarita has her sandals off, legs curled beneath her on the sofa, and a pitcher of drinks on the glass table.

"I hope you like sex on the beach."

"I'd like sex with you anywhere."

"Yeah, I'm sure you would," Clarita coos sultrily.

"Now, who's bragging?" Derrick laughs. He slides in next to her, drops the envelope on her lap and an arm around her shoulder, hooking her strap with his thumb. "Intel, as promised. Pablo has moved his operations deeper into the jungle. The camps are smaller too, harder to pinpoint and easier to defend."

Clarita pulls the photos and reports out. She studies them, ignoring Derrick's hand rubbing little circles between her shoulder blades. She rocks forward, reaches for her purse, pulls out her pack of cigarettes and offers him one.

But his mind is absent, enraptured by the flawless line of her spine running down to the hollow of her lower back.

"I said... I need a light," she demands, shaking off his huge paw. "And I thought you were going to get us information on the Callie Cartel as well."

"Don't shoot me. Like you, I'm just the messenger." Derrick pulls the lighter from his pants' pocket and flicks it for her.

"I'm no messenger." She lights the cigarette. "We have to make sure they think that the attacks are from one another. Or our asses will be hunted all across Colombia. You don't want that, do you?"

"Wait a minute, John has you going on these raids too?" Derrick questions. "He must be crazy. I would never expose you to such a risk." His eyes become dark, reaching a semblance of compassion.

Vicky doesn't know what is worse, Morris pretending not to care, or this man pretending that he does. His eyes lock on her and his breath is deep and powerful. "Like I said, I can take care of myself. Ashtray?"

Derrick picks up his glass and empties it in one large gulp, then holds it up to the end of her cigarette. She flicks the ashes and swallows her drink. She uncurls herself, and walks to the bar for another glass.

Derrick's eyes follow her every move.

When she returns, she pours two more drinks, and without so much as batting an eyelid, she folds herself into his rock solid body, her head resting on his chest and her legs stretched out on the sofa. She looks up into his dark eyes, "If this is all you got for me then I guess business is over."

They skip on their drinks and watch the last of the sun disappear into the ocean. The moon shimmers off the water but is not visible in the picturesque window. Derrick's hand goes exploring again, this time down the front of her dress. Her skin on his palm is softer than the satin against his knuckles. She offers no resistance as he runs his fingers slowly down her breast and one by one over a nipple. Her nipples thicken and her breast heaves as she draws a deeply sensual sip of air. She snakes her arm up and around his neck, drawing his face to hers. She parts her lips slightly and her tongue licks his before sliding into the warmth of his mouth.

One strap slips off her shoulder and the dress drapes her like a Greek Goddess. Derrick's hand continues its slow exploration southward, his fingers becoming entangled in the boscage of coarse hair that is hidden from view. He gently grooms and strokes his newfound pet with one hand and cradles the silky locks at the back of her head with the other. Her mouth moves wildly over and around his, sucking in his tongue. Her legs spread under his hand and warm ripples of flesh invite his fingers in.

Derrick glances down at the dress that is now a thin veil wrapped around her waist. He marvels at the deep reddish inner lips nestled in the black curly blanket of hair. A small stream has already begun to flow from the mouth of her tiny volcano. "We can take this to the bedroom," the bass in his voice reverberates in her ear.

He won't own me. He can't control me. Not in his bed, I'm not going to be another bitch to feed his ego. She grabs the back of his head, kicks and twists, and lands on top of him on the floor, his head just missing the edge of the glass table. She rises up, straddles his waist and pulls madly at the yellow fish, until he raises his arms and gives up the shirt. Her fingers quickly go to work on the belt buckle.

"The bed would be more comfortable, you know."

"Shut up and do me," she commands.

Derrick effortlessly lifts her up with his hips and with both hands pulls his pants down to his thighs. He fumbles in his pocket for a moment then holds up a condom package. "Mind if we take time for one of these?" He can't tell if the she is angry or annoyed. "I've been in the navy a long time and we never send a diver down without a wetsuit. It is as much for your protection as mine."

"So what! You think I'm some diseased whore?"

That face is definitely angry. "No, that's not what I meant at all. The Company will pay for all of this, but babies... that comes out of my paycheck. Not what they consider the cost of doing business. And you are way too gorgeous to be somebody's mother just yet."

"Give me that," she snatches the package with one hand and grasps his hard-on with the other. His dick is stiff, strong and a handful. She strokes it roughly four times up and down making it glisten. Then she bites the corner of the condom package and savagely rips it in two. Derrick's mouth hangs open, gasping like a fish out of water. She loosens her grip and gently rolls the condom down his shaft, letting him breathe again.

Clarita rises up onto her knees and holding Derrick with both hands descends on him. His head penetrates her, forcing its way into her. "Hssssss." She inhales loudly and sinks a little lower.

"Whooooos." This time it's Derrick who struggles for air, as the tightness of her pussy painfully squeezes him.

She falls forward, braces her hands on his solid torso, and begins flexing her back, hips, and thighs, working his dick further into her. She feels every inch of her vagina fill with his thick rigid flesh and takes her time to savor its size and firmness. When she is all the way down on him, she digs into his chest and begins the slow ascent back up his pole.

Derrick stares into her eyes, which are electric golden brown. Her breasts are heaving from her heavy breathing. And her two black nipples are tiny, compact, erect, tantalizing. Her face twists between a mask of pain and pleasure then she drops down to his chest and whispers, "fuck me."

Derrick responds immediately to the command. He lifts her, spins her over beneath him, and pins her to the floor. He stops for a moment and her eyes go wild, wanting him to continue. He pulls a cushion from the sofa, lifts her by the small of her back, the area that a few minutes ago enchanted him so, and lowers her butt onto the pillow. He raises himself up and thrusts down as hard as he can. Then he grabs a second cushion and places it under her head. "Better?"

"Yessss."

He begins pounding away at her, and to his surprise, she humps back with equal ferocity. He can feel the head of his dick striking her cervix. Her eyes glisten and she takes tiny sips of air each time he hits a dead end inside her. He eases up and slows his thrust, but that only makes her coo, "Harder. More."

Derrick slips back to his days in the gangs of Philly, to the GG's, the Gang Girls, those who had to go through a gangbang initiation. The girls who wanted to join the gang took on five or ten gang members, one after another, each trying to inflict as much pain as possible. If the girl did not cry out or called it quits before each gang member had a turn, she was a GG, there to serve whichever gang member wanted her at any specific moment.

He was known as the Pussy Popper back in those days. His massive size could make any girl scream in agony if he so desired. But Clarita is no GG. She can take a lot and wants more. She is a tiger. If she had been in a gang, she would had been somebody's Main Piece. A gang leader's girl. John's girl. Now she will be his.

He kneels, raises her slender sweet legs up, and she instinctively hooks her feet around his neck. Tenderly, he plants kisses up and down the backs of her legs then lifts her hips, his hands gripping her butt. Positioning her vagina before him, he stares for a moment down the black hole. It looks so small yet so wide open. He goes at it like a mad man. Pulling her to him as he stabs her harder and harder, with each retraction his condom-covered cock growing whiter from her scum. Each insertion a slap of thighs and squishing of fluid, he is lost in his mission to pop her pussy. Sweat runs down his brawny arms and his hefty chest shines like armor. Clarita locks her hands and digs her nails deep into his beefy wrists. His dick grows and twitches then jerks crazily inside her, but she does not cry out. She bites her bottom lip and enjoys the moment. Breathing heavy and hard he can take no more and spastically comes.

Derrick studies the stunning figure lying motionless on his living room floor. He takes another cigarette from her pack but doesn't light it. *I haven't smoked in two years but one day with this woman and I'm a chain smoker again. God help me, she'd gonna be the death of me.* He looks in the bar, on the bottom shelf, way in the back and retrieves a hand sized black plastic box. It has an on/off switch on the side and a red LED on its face. He switches it on and the LED flashes three times then goes black again. He walks over to the glass table and slowly waves the device over the pack of cigarettes. Nothing. Then he waves it over Clarita's purse, again nothing happens. He starts back to the bar then stops. Gazing down at the nude Nubian beauty, he kneels beside her and runs the device up and down just inches from the curvaceous creature. The device does not react, but he can feel his device coming to life once again. *Thank God no one tampered with perfection like this.*

She murmurs agreement through her dreams. Derrick gets up and tosses the device onto the sofa. He returns to the bar and studies his naked physique in the mirrored wall. *We'd make a good-looking couple. But back to work.* He picks up the cigarette on the bar and lights it. The device on the sofa flashes red and stays that way. Derrick picks up the receiver, taps the plunger rapidly three times and waits for the faint beep. "Derrick Patterson 1248596," he says softly as not to wake his sleeping beauty.

A cold and dispassionate voice replies, "Yes. What can I do for you?"

"I need infrared and high resolution satellite photographs of everything from the Valle Del Cauca south to Suarez sent it to my usual location," he tells the unidentified female on the other end. "Also, who is working in that region?"

"I'll need a moment to check," she replies and the phone goes silent. Derrick drags on the cigarette and taps on the bar impatiently. The woman speaks again, "Fernando Alvarez."

"Yeah, he'll do. Get him on the line."

"Hold please."

A half a cigarette later, "Derrick, you old son of a bitch, I hear you landed a sweet spot in the Company."

"Yeah, can't complain. But I know you Druggies, aren't exactly slumming it down there either," Derrick whispers. "Look, I need all the intel you have on the Cali Cartel. Manpower, time schedules, firepower... and definitely let me know what they are armed with..."

"Things have gotten really hot down here lately," Alvarez replies, "wouldn't be any of your doing, would it?"

"Look Alvarez, all I can say is, we are throwing the party, but outsiders are running the show. Can't really say what they are capable of."

"Hey," Alvarez shouts, "you got one of them in your bed right now... don't you?"

"Not in my bed," Derrick smiles, "you know the business. I need this stuff like yesterday. And keep your head down, these people are real wild. No telling who they are going after."

"Don't worry about me, you better watch your back, it's always the women who are the deadliest."

"Look who you're telling," Derrick laughs a little too loud, hangs up, and snuffs out the cigarette. The red LED on the black device goes dark. He gently picks up Clarita and lays her on the sofa, getting the black device wedged behind her and the cushions. He leaves the room and returns within a few seconds with a silk sheet. He takes one last long look and drapes the white cloth over her. *Who the hell screwed you up so bad?* He takes the pack of cigarettes upstairs to wait for the intelligence reports to come in. He is too wound up to sleep and it will be daylight in a couple of hours.

When daylight comes, Clarita is up and dressed before Derrick returns with a new envelope. "What is this?" she asks.

"It's the intel on Cali you wanted. The elves were working all night while—"

"No. I mean what is THIS." She holds out the black box.

"Oh that, nothing," He stalls for a plausible answer, "it's a diver's apparatus, warns you when you are going too deep." He takes it from her hand and switches it off. "Do you want to go out with me?" He quickly changes the subject as he looks for a place to stash the device then throws it back onto the couch.

"Go out with you," she snorts, "what are we, in high school?"

"I meant... go out diving with me today. I have a group coming in later. We can have breakfast and spend the day together."

"Oh... Yeah... would love to, but it's back to work for me." She feels like a fool, like a silly schoolgirl with a crush on the handsome jock. "I've got to get this information—"

"That will keep. It's not like these guys go and change things every other day," Derrick is trying to be cool, trying not to sound like he's begging for her company, which he is, "OK, then let's at least have breakfast and I can go over the information with you."

Clarita straps up her sandals, grabs the envelopes and sticks them under her arm with her purse. She stretches up to meet his lips. He doesn't tilt down, he is not going to make it easy for her to go. "Look, when I get wet, I prefer to be on dry land." *Oh God, that sounds asinine. And high-school-ish.* But it works.

Derrick smiles and plants a soft kiss on her lips. "I've got time, let me drop you off."

"No need," she says, backing towards the door. "I'll catch a cab. I've got to make a few stops and you have a business to run. Next time... we'll do the whole scuba thing."

Clarita is out the door and doesn't look back. She manages two blocks of brisk walking before the pain between her legs becomes unbearable. *Breakfast my ass. That bull wanted to break my choochie. Another ride like last night and I won't be able to walk at all.* She sees a group of tourists getting out of a cab and waves frantically to catch his attention. She gets in and sits down gingerly in the back seat. *Damn, he's also got my cigarettes.*

Elizabeth rolls in bed and tries to shake off the heavy headiness she's feeling. She looks at the empty wine bottle and glasses on the nightstand next to the bed. She shakes Morris' shoulder, "wake up. What time did you get back last night?"

"What? Go back to sleep. One... Two... Late."

She shakes him again, harder, and he rolls over to face her. "Did we do it last night?"

"That's not ego crushing at all," I rub the sleep out of my eyes, half sit up and my head feels like lead.

"Remember? You took Maria to her room because you said, 'It's not going to be a quiet fucking tonight.' And that was before we opened the wine."

"I don't remember much after we opened the wine," she pushes herself up into a sitting position, "OW! My ass hurts. What did you do to me last night?"

"Well, I didn't do that. It didn't get that wild in here."

"No, my ass hurts, not my asshole. YOU ASSHOLE!" Elizabeth has her left hand on her forehead and rubs her right cheek with the other. "I have a lump or something on my ass. Did you bite me?"

"Let me see," I say and push her over. I lift the sheet and run my fingers over an inch-long red welt in the middle of her cheek. "Hmm... That's not a human bite, probably a mosquito or spider."

"Let me see, liar." She stands up, wobbling in the middle of the bed and looks over her shoulder at the mirror. "That's fucking huge. It's no mosquito bite. What did you do to me?"

"It's not a human bite," I assure her, "and I'll prove it." I grab her legs and pull them out from under her. She falls face down onto the bed and I pin her down. I bite down hard and then ease up on her left cheek. "See, that's a human bite. It looks nothing like the one on the right. Take my word for it."

Elizabeth is rubbing her left cheek now, "asshole."

"You probably had an allergic reaction to an insect bite." I straddle her, "let me rub something on it."

She flips over and elbows me in the gut as the door swings open. She grabs the sheet and throws it over us just as Maria climbs onto the bed. "Didn't lock the door... AGAIN... last night. Did you?"

"You took her to her room last night. No more wine for you after midnight. You are cranky in the morning."

Maria pulls at the sheet and we pull back, "Aunt Rita is back! Come on, let's go say hi!"

"You go say hi, dear. Daddy's going back to sleep for another twelve hours," I growl.

"We will be down in a minute. Let Mommy and Daddy get dressed," Liz says sweetly.

Maria sits back on the bed, crosses her arms, and gives us a stern look. "You don't have on any clothes again."

"That's none of your business. Beat it, Shorty."

"We have clothes on," Liz defends with one arm holding the sheet tight to her chest, "just not the kind we can go downstairs in."

"Let me see!" Maria commands with a condemning tone.

"Out!" I yell and turn over on my side.

Maria runs off the bed with a big leap, giggling all the way down the hall.

"Hey! Shut the door!" But I'm too late and she is long gone.

"You are still mad at Clarita," Liz says, poking me in the back.

"No, I'm not," I protest.

"Liar."

"My head is pounding," I confess, getting out of bed. *Next time, I drug just her wine instead of the bottle.*

"Where are you going?" She asks.

"To shut the door, and lock it. I can still rub a little cream on the insect bite for you," I tell her, waving my dick at her.

"I thought you had a headache," she responds, purposely looking away.

"That's the difference between men and women," I tell her returning to the bed, door closed and locked. "We have two heads and this one never has a bad day."

"Yeah, well, with two heads you'd think you would be able to come up with one good story." She turns over rubbing her butt.

I can't tell which side hurts her more now. "I thought you were going to welcome Rita back."

"Later, my head is killing me too. And so is my ass. Insect bite... you fucking liar."

If you had drunk the wine faster, then I wouldn't have been so stoned when I injected the RF tag in that sweet little ass. Oh well, I've got to find another place to inject Maria, because if she sees a mark like that on her she'll fucking kill me. I'd better find a spot where neither Liz nor Akilina will find it. My Little Princess doesn't have much fat, so maybe her armpit or inner thigh. But first, I've got to see what the range on the radio tag is, make sure it's strong enough. Then I need to get her away from her two mothers for a day.

I watch the green dot on the radar screen approaching slowly from the right. The red dot at the top of the scope displays 1.5 mi beneath it. *Pretty good range so far.* I nudge the joystick and the mileage display increases slowly, 1.6... 1.75... 1.8. Liz is calling for Maria as she approaches. "Shhh, your puppy is asleep in the pup tent," I call out when she is within earshot.

"Asleep?" Liz peeks in the little dome tent on the beach. Maria is lying motionless on blankets out of the sun. "Is she ok? Why didn't you bring her in?"

"She had a busy day," I smile to ease the concern of a worried mother. "We went for our morning swim; you know she is developing quite a powerful stroke. She launched the plane and flew nice tight circles around the house, I'm sure she will make a fine pilot one day. We had our lunch. Now she is taking her nap and I promised her she can bring it in for the landing on the dock."

"She is only four," Liz looks over the control panel in my lap, "Do you think it's okay to let her play with such an expensive gadget? She might crash it."

"It's just a toy."

Elizabeth is perplexed by the lap size display with the multiple joysticks, knobs and buttons, then remarks, "it looks very complicated for a toy."

"Big boys like big toys, what can I say." I hold the control panel up to her, "want to give it a try?"

Elizabeth looks up and slowly turns in a complete circle. "Where is it?"

I point towards the ocean, "it's two and a half miles that way."

"How can you fly it if you can even see it?"

"That's what the radar scope is for… and cameras!" I flip a switch and the displays turns to a multi-display of three video screens. One across the top half and two split the bottom half of the display. "That's the forward view," I say pointing to the top half, which displays blue skies and white cloud formations. "The bottom left is the rear view, and the bottom right is the belly camera."

Liz slides into my lap and takes the controls. "Doesn't look like there is much to see."

"It's flying at about a thousand feet, too high to interfere with parasailing and too low to interfere with aircraft. Right now, I'm testing the range. It's actually flying on autopilot."

"Oh, it has an autopilot too." She is amazed. "Where did you buy this?"

"The plane is a kit, you put it together," I nuzzle her neck, "the electronics, which are mostly in your hands, I built. You know, radio circuit boards, that kind of stuff, pretty standard."

"You are so smart, you can be anything you want," Elizabeth leans back in the comfort of my arms.

"I have a daughter… a wife, I'm just what I want to be… a good family man."

A cold chill runs up Elizabeth's spine and she shudders at those words. *A good family man. How many times did Uncle Angelo tell her father the same thing? Just be patient… be a good family man… As a little girl, she didn't know what they were talking about. Now she knows all too well. Morris isn't Italian so he can't actually be in the Mafia, but he is in deeper than anyone she has ever known. But above all things, she wants out, for her, her daughter, and Morris too.*

"Are you ok?" I ask as she quickly scrambles to her feet.

"I'm fine," Liz replies, not looking back, "I'll just take Maria in the house now. You can play with your toy."

Something struck a nerve, so I change the subject and pull her back by the other end of the control panel we both have a hold of, "Maria is fine and I'll bring her in shortly. Don't you and Akilina have a plane of your own to catch? I thought you were going to New York for Italian food for this party."

"Yes, but I have some time," Liz is struggling with the fear those words have dredged up, "Maybe I should take Maria with us..."

"Not a chance," I rebuke her jokingly, "the next two days will be Daddy Daughter time. Now you run along..."

"But..."

"Oh no," I wag a finger at her, "no buts, we agreed. Besides, what do you think? I'm smart enough to build robotic planes, but too stupid to take care of a five-year-old?"

"No... Ok... But come in soon."

"I already turned the plane around," I tell her with a big smile.

Liz turns and walks quickly up the beach.

I watch her ass sashaying beneath the wrap. *Three and a half miles is more than a good reading on the radio frequency tag. I'll tell one of the guys to monitor her in New York. See how it does in a city environment. But so far, this is good.*

I walk in the house with Maria sleeping, head on my shoulder and feet dangling at my knees. Akilina rushes to take her from my arms. I twist away, "I got her. Really, you women!"

"No, it's nothing like that, Mr. John. There are some men out front in a truck, they say you hired them," she apologises and holds out her arms for Maria.

"Oh Ok, take her," I reluctantly give up my precious cargo. I go to the front door and push Uncle Frankie aside.

Liz is questioning the leader, as his men are unloading wood from the truck.

Vicky catches me by the arm before I get to the porch steps, "What's all this?"

"While you were out, umm, shopping, I hired these guys to build a stable for Maria's pony." I step behind Liz and slip my arm around her waist, "What's all the commotion about?"

Vicky shouts from the porch, "You are actually buying the girl a pony for her birthday?"

"Bought it!" I turn Liz around toward me and point the men to the east side of the house. "Honey, I told you the builders were coming today to start working on the stable."

"But it's so late."

"They've got a couple of good hours of daylight ahead of them," I assure her.

Manny, a tall lanky dark Jamaican adds, "No worries, Ma'am. We just unload the truck and dig the holes for the main beams today. No worries."

"So, you really bought her a pony," Vicky says standing next to us on the front lawn. "Who's gonna walk it? Do you know what to feed it? How much?"

"Walk her?" I quiz her. "She's a pony not a dog. We are going to fence off a couple of hundred yards on the east side of the house as a pasture. And as for taking care of her, I hired the boy who was with her from birth to come here and take care of her."

"A boy! What boy?" Vicky demands.

"The man who I bought Rachelle from, his son, he's eighteen, I think. When I asked if he would like to come to Aruba instead of staying in Staten Island... well, let's just say he was more than happy to take the job."

"And his father was ok with him working for you," Vicky sneers. "Knowing what you do and all."

"What he knows is that I'm a manufacturer and importer of fertilizers," I state coldly, "that's what everyone knows about John Morrison. And the fertilizer business pays well. Don't you have some business you need to take care of?" I give her a cold hard stare and she turns back towards the house.

Liz separates from me and reaches out to Vicky, "Clarita, wait, I'll go in with you." She gives me a bitter look. "Sorry, we've been a little busy and haven't had a chance to welcome you back properly. You are going to be here next week for Maria's birthday, aren't you?"

"Of course, she will," I interject, "it wouldn't be a party without her."

Both women shoot me a dirty look and continue into the house. They exchange a short conversation that I can only imagine is about what kind of bastard I am.

An hour later, the three women gather in the living room with more suitcases than I thought they had. Uncle Frankie loads the car and Maria starts whining about her mother and Akilina going without her. With three cars laden with bags and passengers, we drive to the airport. There, we all wish Vicky a successful trip before she departs on her plane for Texas.

More tears and "Don't go Mommy" from Maria, and I have to pry them apart to get the two women, Uncle Frankie, and Uncle Vinnie onto the plane to headed for New York. I pick up my teary-eyed distraught daughter and carry her to one of the cars. "What do you say to a big bowl of ice cream for dinner, hmmm?"

"We can't have ice cream for dinner, can we?"

"For the next three days, we are going to do all kinds of fun things," I wink, "just you and me. OK?"

"Ok Daddy. But I miss Mommy and Lina," she pouts.

"I know you do," I whisper, "don't tell Mommy, but I miss her too."

"And Lina?"

"Of course… Akilina too."

We eat pizza for breakfast, something Mommy would not allow, and instead of going down to the beach for a swim, Maria wants to watch the stable being built. Actually, she wants to help build the stable. Manny obliges by giving her a spray paint can and letting her do the line for the corral fence. We carefully follow the marker line east from the stable area then turn south, stopping a hundred feet from the bluff. We head back west to an area south of the stable construction and turn north until we reach the men again. I explain all the way around how a white four rail post fence will keep her pony safe while she rides around the corral. The walk tires her out and we have a normal lunch of peanut butter and jelly sandwiches and milk. I have beer.

After lunch, we sit in the living room, and I drop a Polaroid in her lap of a shiny chestnut brown pony with one black stocking and a black mane.

"That's Rachelle," she beams in delight, "I promise to brush her hair every day so she stays pretty, Daddy. When is she going to be here? Is Mommy bringing her back with her?"

"No honey, she'll be here next week, on your birthday. I promise."

Maria sits in my lap and stares at the picture until her milk takes effect. I pinch her arm hard and she doesn't move. I grab the phone and call Russell Mills in New York. "Have you got somebody on her?"

"Yes. We picked her up at the airport; I got a mobile team tracking her from about five miles behind, and another at ten. The signals are strong, no problem at all. I just talked to another stationary team on the observation deck of the Empire State Building; they were able to pick her up all the way in Jersey. Only glitch was when she went through the Lincoln Tunnel."

"Understandable, and I'll see what can be done about that." I hang up the phone. I pinch Maria's underarm softly between my thumb and forefinger, probing for fat. *My Little Princess, you are all skin and bones. Luckily, this microwave transponder is tiny.* I squeeze as much flesh as I can under her armpit and slowly stick the tip of the needle in. I push the needle into position between her upper ribs towards her back ever so carefully. The radio tag is only the size of a postage stamp when laid out flat, and just as thick. It comes rolled up inside a plastic sleeve and encased in a green biodegradable gel, which I inject with a smooth steady push on the syringe's plunger. The gel and sleeve will dissolve in a day, and once gone, her body heat will power the tag and I'll be able to test its output. It doesn't put out a steady signal, it will only transmit a reply when pinged with a specific frequency, and then only for two seconds. Just long enough for a microwave receiver to pinpoint its location. *Everything will be back to normal long before Mommy returns. And I'm glad this went much smoother than your Mommy's tagging. But just to make sure you don't feel any pain, my Little Princess, I'll keep you asleep until tomorrow.*

Nicky arrives early for Maria's birthday party. As is the case with so many kids' parties there are more adults than children present, although, I am surprised that a dozen kids are running around. Apparently, Liz has made friends in my absences, which I admit are frequent. Rachelle arrived late the night before with Anthony. He explained that travelling at night was less stressful for the young pony, and there would be no need to sedate her. It suited me fine, because she was in her stable whinnying when Maria woke up. All the children are in the stable petting and rubbing Rachelle under Anthony's watchful eye. He had also told me that he had brought some of the neighborhood kids into the barn back home to get Rachelle used to children. Still, we had to limit their playtime because the pony was sure to miss her mother.

Elizabeth pulls Nicky aside and asks him to walk her down to the dock. Out on the beach, she reveals what had been troubling her when she met him in New York. "Is there any way you can convince Morris to get out of this life with you? You know what life in the Mafia can do to a person. We both know it destroyed my family, and I just want out. But I can't get out if Morris is still in business with you. He has a child, a family, and I'm sure more money than he'll ever need."

"Morris isn't in this for the money, Elizabeth. For him, for me, it is part of who we are," Nicky takes her hand, pulls her down to the sand, and draws a circle, "this is my world, the Mafia. Sorry, Morris can't be part of it, Italians only, you know that." He draws another circle, which intersects the first. "This is Morris' world, the world of street gangs. When I met him, we were what... Fifteen, I guess, and he was already ruling his world, a major warlord. Our worlds play the same games, but we play by different rules. See this part here?" Nicky zigzags his finger through the intersecting part of the circles, "this is where we are the safest. He's got my back, and I watch his. Every place else, we are on our own. Don't worry about the business he does with me, it's all the shit over here that should worry you. That is the stuff we were born into and there is no getting out. He is running twelve gangs across the country, that I know about, and I don't know how many more. But like I said, Morris has been at this shit a long time, so if anybody can handle it, it's him. Ok, let's go get that stuff you need from the dock."

"It's ok, we can go back," Elizabeth despairs.

"One more thing," Nicky lifts her chin. "He loves you and that little girl; he won't let anything happen to you. You may not know this, and don't you tell him I told you, but half a mile on either side of your place are gang houses. No one can get close to this place. I guarantee it."

There is no smile on Elizabeth face, no look of relief in her eyes; and her response is flat and monotone. "It's not my life I'm concerned about."

After Maria's birthday party, which lasted longer than a week, Vicky and I are back to work. I have a new plan and put it into effect as soon as we meet with the team. We brake the two teams into four-men groups. One group attacks the processing camps. Two people enter covertly from one direction and toss grenades into the buildings; the other two enter perpendicular to them and spray the place with bullets. It is very effective. It is very thorough. It is very deadly.

The attack on the camps is lightning-fast, and over before the smoke from the fires can be located. And that's when the second four-man squad goes into action. They wait on the roads to the camps and ambush the security forces as they rush to their defence. We attack at night and use the robotic planes equipped with infrared cameras, to pinpoint the camps and the security forces.

In the jungle, at night, the only true heat sources are manmade. The cartels don't stand a chance. We sweep through a couple of camps, knock off their security forces, and are out by dawn. We are a killing machine. The camps are becoming smaller and smaller, and have started moving around nightly. But they still can't hide, and after several months of night raids it looks like the war on drugs might amount to something after all. But like all other wars, politics have taken over.

Vicky returns from one of her weeklong recruiting trips with Derrick. She is beaming, and it isn't from the news she brings, which to me is all bad. Both the US and Colombian governments agree that we've had a significant effect on the drug cartels' businesses, but they are haemorrhaging money and manpower. In turn, the cartels are also desperate and striking back at Colombian officials, not just the corrupt ones from each other's organizations, but legitimate judges, cops, and mayors, as they realize the attacks are coming from a central force. Emboldened by our attacks, officials trying to fight the overwhelming power of the drug lords have pressed for arrests and trials. It is all becoming very public.

The Colombians want to say they are behind the attacks on the drug cartels, but they have one big problem, how to explain Colombian deaths. It doesn't look good, because no matter how bad the drug lords are, it is the poor workers who are being killed in the hundreds. The drug lords, with wealth, means of evasion, and protection are near impossible to touch, and in their local communities, are viewed as heroes. The government, Colombian and US, are seen as bad guys in the streets.

Vicky tells me, "Our new objective is to destroy the camps but leave the people alive." She had never liked the idea of total annihilation anyway. "We can defend ourselves against the security forces, but the unarmed workers are to be left alone. Only equipment, products, and buildings must be targeted."

"I don't know why you are so happy," I seethe, "the workers are already reduced to the bare minimum needed to process the cocaine. The drug lords are going to beef up these paramilitary security forces and attempt to wipe us out. They are already chasing our helicopters into the jungle every time we enter the country. We are going to hit a camp and they are going to rain down on us like ants at a picnic."

"Yes, that's why Derrick suggested we still use a four to six-man team to destroy the camps, and increase our security forces to say, 'twenty' to ring them."

"I guess Derrick is now running the show," I balk. "I don't know what these guys are up to, but this is no longer a war on drugs, if it ever really was one. It is more like a skirmish on drugs. And do you know what happens in a skirmish?"

"NO." She is irate.

"Not a damn thing. A lot of people die and nothing is accomplished." I storm off.

I was right, and operations slow to a pathetic crawl. Since the cartels have begun tracking our birds, we have also started fast-boating in and only use copters for extractions. We spend a lot of time trekking through the jungles from camp to camp, knocking them over, and then engaging in hours long gun battles to get out. *Thanks, Derrick Patterson.*

To further complicate matters, Nicky pays me a visit at the Aruba house one weekend between raids. Seems the Mafia is convinced the whole War On Drugs campaign the President is championing is a setup by Nicky's family to monopolize the cocaine business. Families from east to west coast are feeling the sting of our operations, except us. Nicky is in the office when I arrive and I am indeed surprised to see him. He's not alone either, four guidos have tagged along.

He sends them out before he begins to speak. "MoJo, this thing you got going with the government has got to stop. You are taking food off a lot of tables and word is getting back that a Black American... a gangster, is behind it all. It was different when everyone was dying; now, even in your black ops outfits... people are talking. And because our flow hasn't dwindled the other bosses are... upset."

I know the four musclemen are there at the other families' request, to show he talked to me, not as a show of force. But still, it doesn't sit well with me, "What the fuck, Nicky, bringing a bunch of goombahs to my house. Are you crazy?" I am having a hard time controlling my temper and my volume. "I worked hard to keep the girls out of this, and you roll up here with a fucking hit squad."

"Come on, you know this isn't that," Nicky is taken aback, "we've been friends and partners for years. I had to bring those assholes to convince the other members of the board..."

"I don't give a fuck about the Board. Those old fucks can kiss my ass. But if you wanted to talk, why didn't you meet me in Nassau?"

"Too many Feds getting a tan these days," he laughs, "but those old fucks still run the Mafia. Which means, I still have to answer to them, and they don't like it when profits drop. I keep telling you to hit a couple of our guys too; especially since you are out of the killing business, makes it look good."

"And I keep telling you, I'm not taking food off our table," I reiterate, "not to appease anybody. You can tell them—"

"I told you before," Nicky becomes stern, "we operate by one rule; no one is bigger than the organization. Don't push back on this; you'll get us both killed."

"Ok, I get the point," I concede. "But it's not that I'm protecting our business, it's that I've had the foresight to move our processing plants into the cities. I knew the US government would never send us into the cities on raids. Way too risky, and too many civilians. Tell your friends to get their businesses out of the jungles, no protection there. Hell, they might as well put up neon signs saying, 'Come and get it.'"

And just like that, the tension is over. We are back to joking around and making half-hearted threats to dismember each other. We leave the four men outside for a long while and do lines of pure powder and fire up fatties. It's like the old days back in the Bronx. *God, how I miss those times!* "It's a good thing you dropped in anyway," I say. "I have something for you. Call it an insurance policy, in case our friends in Washington get funny ideas." I hand Nicky an envelope.

He opens it and pulls out several typed pages. He peruses through them and then looks at each one again carefully. "Is this what I think it is? A list of DEA agents?"

"The 'A' list of government agents," I acknowledge, "DEA, FBI, CIA, and others I didn't even know existed. The whole fucking spy network, all around the world. And not just our spies, other countries too."

"How the hell did you get this?" he's amazed.

"It was like a big ball of string," I tell him. "I started pulling and before I knew it the whole thing unravelled. These fuckers are so busy spying on each other, once you get inside it's like a candy shop, goodies everywhere."

"And you want me to start crossing people off the list if something should happen to you?"

"No. Not at all," I shake my head in disbelief. "If you kill them the list is worthless. You once told me that when a guy owes you money, you don't kill him, you break his arm, the non-check writing arm. So if anything should happen, you show it to the guy at the top of that list and make sure he understands that nothing bad ever happens to Vicky, or every name and whereabouts will be made public. It takes years for these guys to get people into places; they can't afford to have the whole thing come crashing down."

Nicky goes back to studying the list of names, addresses, aliases, and other contact information. He points out one name in the middle of a page. "Hey, this guy works for me. Can I at least kill him?"

I take the list back, "he works for you and Interpol. He is also my tie-in to some guys in the Middle East. So... HELL NO. I need him alive and unaware that we are onto him... For now, you just show the list to Jake Justice."

"Sounds like you are about to jump out of the plane without a parachute. Why?"

"I don't know what the government has been up to," I do another long line of coke to collect my thoughts, "but this whole war on drugs thing has been bullshit from the start. We've been corralling these guys for about two years, but we are not trying to put them out of business, just move them around. Tell your friends to get out of the jungles if they want to stay in business. And whatever you do, don't let anyone know you have that list until you have to. Keep it in a safe place, they WILL come after it."

Nicky hangs out the rest of the weekend, without his four friends. They are gone before the coke and reefer runs low. But I was a gracious host and invited them back in for a couple of blows before their long trip back home, to show I had no hard feelings about the unannounced visit. I also used the time to get one of my boys to get a line on who they worked for, just in case.

Nicky leaves, glad we didn't have a big blow out. Some of our conversations have ended badly because that's the way it is with friends. But in our case, it could be deadly. We are tight, but we both want to stay alive. And Nicky did express his feelings loud and clear, that he suspects the government's plan is to drive a wedge between the families, and that I am that wedge. I tell him it is a valid observation, a sickening possibility.

I get back to base just in time to see Vicky loading up a helicopter with a dozen commandoes, some new and some veterans. We are constantly running operations, but this one wasn't scheduled, at least not by me. "Where are you taking the boys?"

"I didn't know you would be back so soon," she says. "I just got intel on a big shipment moving through the jungle near the Venezuelan boarder and was asked to make an intercept. Should be easy."

"Yeah, sure," I agree. "Got room in there for one more?"

"Huh, yeah, if you want in on this."

"It will give me something to do," I tell her and look over the men already onboard, "and it'll give me a chance to see how these new guys handle themselves." *I will tell Vicky later there is no such thing as an easy job in our line of work. We have lost fifteen men in fire-fights in the past two months...* Something else starts eating at me. Attacking a mule train is not our modus operandi. We trained to hit stationary targets or ambush cartel security at fixed positions. *This is more complicated than she realizes.*

I take a seat next to a big fella; dirty blond crew cut, eagle tattoo on his shoulder, hard steel eyes. Ex-military, for sure. I have told Vicky to dump any mercenary types, but Patterson keeps sending us more and more. "How long have you been out?" I ask him.

"Two months and three weeks, Sir," he snaps out his answer.

"You can drop the Sir," I reprimand, "What did you get kicked out for?"

"Sir?"

"Marines, army, you got booted out of one of the armed forces. Why?"

"Conduct unbecoming an officer," he answers proudly. "We were taking down a warlord in the Middle East, classified of course."

"Of course."

"We took heavy fire and when we finally broke through... Well, I didn't see any reason to take prisoners."

I don't respond. Instead, I study the eagle flying with a sword in its talons on his shoulder. It's large and colorful. Finally, I say, "Make sure that is completely covered. It's the kind of thing that will come back to haunt you." I give Vicky a 'what the fuck' look.

She shrugs.

This is a daytime op and we have to drop in even further from the target. The way Vicky had planned it; we drop in twenty-miles from their last known position. Hike ten to a cut-off point and engage there. The plan has some glaring problems: no time to set a proper ambush, next to no intel on how many in the mule train, they can change their route at any time and we'll miss them completely, and the biggest concern, mule trains are heavily guarded.

We just manage to deploy in groups of fours along the road when the first mule team appears. We let them go by and the second follows five minutes later. We hold our fire. A jeep and a beat-up truck rumble down the road. This is it. I open fire on the jeep and Vicky takes the truck driver out. Men pour out of the back of the truck like roaches, screaming and shooting wildly. I toss a grenade into their midst and the explosion fells a bunch. I hear gunfire ahead of me and to my rear. The others have engaged the mules.

The mules, unarmed men with large sacks of cocaine on their backs, don't stand a chance. The militiamen however, take position behind the truck and jeep and do their best to hold us off, some even reach the trees and lay down cover fire. The sound of another jeep approaches angrily. It has a .50 calibre machinegun, which blazes a trail on either side of the road. The bullets explode and blow off big chunks of trees. Smaller ones are cut in two.

The men have marked our position with their gunfire. I grab Vicky by one shoulder and pull her back from the road. We have to change position before that .50 calibre gets here. I toss another grenade under the truck and when it explodes we make a run for it through the jungle. We are low to the ground but still moving quickly towards the oncoming .50 cal. The safest place to be is behind the approaching rain of death. A shell hits a tree and showers us with burning splinters. We hit the ground and lay motionless.

I start laughing and she says, "What's so funny?"

"Should be easy, huh?"

The jeep with the .50 cal. is almost on top of us and I side-arm a grenade through the trees. It bounces off one tree and rolls out onto the road. The jeep driver never saw it. The explosion flips the jeep up and backwards, landing on top of its occupants. The .50 calibre machinegun doesn't stop firing until it runs out of bullets, although, I believe the gunner was already dead. After a couple of minutes, the shooting is dying down.

Vicky gets to one knee, surveys the area, and starts towards the road. I see a sharp red dot cutting across the trees in front of me, slowly tracking towards her. I scramble to my feet, run, and jump over the debris. I bump her into a tree and she rolls behind it to the ground. Sledgehammers strike my chest out of nowhere; they pick me up and body-slam me into the ground. I can't breathe, there is a ton of force holding me down and squeezing the air out of me.

"Morris. MORRIS…" Vicky has me by the collar of the vest and pulls hard.

I catch a breath, kick frantically, and instinctively spray an arc of bullets before me.

"Morris, you're shot. You've got to get up. Got to get you out of here!"

My chest is on fire, the bullets penetrated the bulletproof vest. I sit up painfully and rip off another barrage of bullets. I can't see who fired the shots but I know from which direction they came. They will be shifting position, trying to outflank us. I have to get Vicky out of here. "You got to go," I say through the pain, "we have been betrayed. I'll cover you. Get to the extraction point… take no one with you… trust no one. Go, now."

Vicky tries to object but I open fire on a much wider arc and she knows I'm right. She runs low into the jungle and I make a dash across the road. I draw some return fire but the other side of the road drops off a steep hill, and I am out of sight. I roll, bounce, and slide a hundred feet down the rough terrain, but my momentum is interrupted by a Colombian's body. I pull the pin from a grenade and tuck it in his armpit. I hear voices and slither further down the hillside.

There is another drop off, steeper than the one I just rolled down from and I can hear a river below. I also hear voices above again. I can make it to the river and escape, but first I have to draw the traitors my way. I can see three men on the road above, but luckily, they can't see me – not at this distance anyway – but they sure are searching hard. I look at my chest and count three holes, all oozing blood and pain. Those motherfuckers… I need to get one good shot before they split up, but my rifle is gone, lost in the tumble down the hill.

I reach down my leg and pull out my .45, roll onto my stomach, and fight back the pain. I steady my right hand on my left, slow down my breathing, zero in on the man closest to the edge of the road, and squeeze the trigger. The shot rings out loud and clear, and he falls. I hear shouts, "this way" and "down there".

I roll over the edge, slide down the hillside on my back, and break through some trees onto the bank of Rio Orinoco. I start stripping off my vest, as I know it will sink me to the bottom of the river in my condition in no time. It's agonizing and slow, and the only thing that gives me reason to smile is the sound of a hand grenade going off up the hill. I wade into the water and start up-river near the bank. *Getting weak and dizzy, got to find a log to keep me afloat. Have to get away from the shoreline before I come upon an alligator... or is it crocodiles in South America? No matter, got to keep moving up river, they won't look for me there. Assholes.*

Head of The Business

Chapter 7

Just Lucky

Akilina is awake and waiting for Maria to open her eyes. She immediately clasps her hand over the girl's mouth and pulls the covers over their heads in the pitch-black bedroom. "Are you hungry?" she whispers.

"Yes," Maria is frightened by her actions.

"Don't worry," Akilina strokes her hair to calm her down, "everything is ok. What do you want to eat?"

"I don't know," Maria is still confused, "cereal, I guess."

"Breakfast, good, me too, I estimate it is the morning of our second... or maybe third day. I cannot be sure of that, since we were unconscious. I'm glad your dad taught me some survival skills when we lived in Aruba, and one of the things he told me is that your biological clock will reset after a day or two of regular sleep, then you can judge what time it is by your stomach."

Maria giggles. "Is the tattoo man here? Why are we hiding?"

Akilina says, "I don't want to take any chances, so it is better we hide from the cameras. I have a plan, but first, we must find out how we are being held. All the windows are boarded from the outside…"

"Yeah, so we can't call for help."

"Probably," Akilina agrees, "but I want to try something. We are going to leave the lights off for now. I want you to put your ear against the wall and listen."

"Listen for what?"

"You'll see." Akilina hops out of the bed.

Maria kneels up and places her face against the wall.

Akilina makes her way down the dark hall to the other end of the trailer. She pounds her fist three times on a wall, which is perpendicular to the one Maria's ear is pressed against. She waits for a reaction from Maria and when none comes, she repeats her pounding. Then she does it one more time for good measure. She returns to the bedroom, climbs back under the covers, and asks softly, "What did you hear?"

"I didn't hear anything," Maria responds, "what was I supposed to hear?"

"I was banging on the kitchen wall. You couldn't hear it?"

"No. Is that bad?"

Akilina can hear the fear rising in Maria's voice. She holds the girl close to her and chooses her words carefully. "It's a good thing. It means we are being held somewhere out in the open, maybe the woods or an abandoned lot." Maria's breathing quickens and Akilina feels tears moistening her arm. "No. No. It's okay, it means we have a chance of getting out of here. You see, sound travels really good through the ground. If you heard me pound on the wall, then… well… Sometimes, a kidnapper takes a trailer like this and buries it. That makes escaping almost impossible. Your father told me about listening for sounds, like in the western movies when they listened for the rumble of the train approaching. No sound means my banging on the wall was escaping into the open air."

"But we don't know where we are."

Akilina wipes the tears from Maria's face. "But this is a big trailer, so wherever we are, there has to be a road. When we get out that door, we are going to run and run and run until we find someone to help us. And we are going to do it tonight. Now, let's go have breakfast."

Vicky ran through the jungle faster than she had ever done, her feet seeming to know just where to plant themselves to keep her upright and moving forward. She radioed the pilot to meet her at the emergency egress point, a small clearing in a shallow part of the riverbed. She couldn't be certain if the copter would be there, as Morris said they were betrayed and hoped instead they had rather walked into an ambush, but surely... The mule train could have been a Columbian setup. Or perhaps there had been a second team shadowing the train...

She heard the blast of the grenade and it gave her hope that Morris had made his escape too then she lay in the underbrush until she heard the sound of the helicopter overhead. As it touched down, she quickly ran for the open door, jumped onto the landing skid and flipped into the belly of the bird. "Let's go. Get the hell out of here!"

"Where's the rest of the team?" asked Carlos, the half-Mexican pilot.

"Dead or dying," she shouted, "we need to go now."

"The plan is we wait five minutes for the others to make it to the emergency extractions point."

"Plans changed. We walked into an ambush, or a setup."

"Where's John, Clarita?" pressed Carlos. "I'm sure you don't want to leave him behind."

"You know the rules, you walk out, are carried out, or leave through Hell's gate. John is taking the long way home. May God have mercy on the Devil! He covered me so I could get out; now get us in the air. NOW."

Carlos sees another man running out of the jungle into the river. He is waving frantically and shouting to them. "Look, one of our guys made it."

"Take no one with you. Trust no one." Morris' commands echo in her head. Vicky raises her rifle and fires. The man falls backwards into the river and the current sweeps him slowly away. "Take off," she orders.

The base was in an uproar when Carlos told the others of Clarita's actions. She didn't return with him, she first went to Derrick for help, and then to Elizabeth to tell her what had transpired. It was a week before she returned to base and discovered that six of the team had made it back, and none knew who had fired on her and John; they had been too far up the road when it happened.

The news Clarita gave them were all bad, Derrick had been given orders to cease operations, everyone was to be paid then told to pack up and leave. Clarita got Miguel, Mark, and Carlos to go to Aruba with her. Nicky Rocci sent some men from New York and she got another six from the Notorious Niggas, one of Morris' gangs in the South Bronx to join her. Altogether, fifteen people comprised the rescue team that returned to Colombia to search for Morris. She could have had a hundred men searching; it would not have made a difference. Morris was gone.

First light. A time for fishermen to prepare boats, a time for women to gather water from the river's edge, and a time for children toying with secret discoveries. They push and jostle each other in the universal game of chicken, daring to see who is brave enough to touch the body floating face down at the shore. Their squeals of excitement soon bring concerned mothers to the encirclement. One look and the women know this is nothing to be toyed with, also sensing the inherent danger the figure embodies.

"Vaya llaman a doctor," orders one of the women.

The oldest boy takes off like a bullet yelling, "Giselle! Giselle! Ven rapida!"

The young woman arrives with the village men. The women had already pulled the body up onto the shore and Giselle instructs the men to turn the body over slowly. They all recognize the signs of bullet wounds on the camouflage shirt. Some of the women cross themselves quickly and mutter a prayer, as much for their own protection as for the sake of the stranger in their midst. Giselle places two fingers on his neck but finds no sign of life. She pulls a pair of scissors from her lab coat pocket and cuts the shirt down the center. His chest has a thick patch of mud. She starts performing CPR. After a few moments, one of the men takes over. He has no success either. Giselle tells the crowd, which now comprises of the entire village, that the man is dead but instructs the men to take him to her house anyway.

The man who was performing CPR sits the body up and grabs it under the armpits from behind. With a jerk and a lift, he stands and pulls the body up to its feet. Water vomits forth, its eyes open, and loud gasp of air is heard by the crowd. The man drops the body. There rises a chorus of, "Oi Dios Mio!" and the sign of the cross furiously covers every head.

Giselle falls to her knees again, "Respire. Tómelo lento."

"What?" I gasp and the pain burns through my chest.

Giselle looks to the crowd now backing away, "Ayúdeme a conseguirlo a mi casa."

One man grabs my legs and two others take hold of my arms and slide their own under my back. I'm too weak to resist. They hoist me into the air and the sea of faces – hands rapidly blessing themselves – part. I'm carried along on the voices of angels singing, "My God. My God."

One angel hovers close. Shimmering darkness flits around bright ambers and soft tender tendrils caress my face. They soothe the fire as a yielding void overtakes me.

I open my eyes to the flowing black shinny hair that covers most of the woman's white lab coat. I groan loudly as pain fills my body, forcing it back down on the bed. She turns and sparks of amber light up the night.

She places a hand on my bandaged chest. "You can't get up. Lie still or you will rip the stitches."

"You speak English." My voice is hoarse and feeble. The pain subsides as I sink back on the bed. Fire still smoulders under my bandages.

"Yes, you spoke a few words while I operated on you," she smiles, "I guess you are American?"

"Op... per... rated?" It's incredibly hard to speak.

"Yes," she lifts my head and wets my lips with a cup of water. "Little sips. You are lucky to be alive. I removed three large bullets from your chest. One nicked your heart. Although, from the size of them... I don't know why they didn't go right through you."

"Luck," I cough painfully, "key." I try to keep my eyes open, fighting hard against the drugs to remain conscious, but the doctor's gentle strokes sap my willpower and back into the silent blackness I go. I float in the river of nothingness. I bob up to the surface momentarily to strange voices and faces, then back down into silence and blackness. Over and over it repeats itself. Sometimes it is bright; sometimes I emerge to the night, but always to the angel with long flowing sable locks and burning amber eyes.

I finally awaken for good to a commotion outside. "What is happening?"

"Shhh. The soldiers are back," she whispers.

"They are here for me," I struggle to get off the floor.

"No, they come for the men in the village. They don't know you are here, so lie still and be quiet."

Another few minutes pass and the activity outside dies down. Footsteps above us and the creaking of floorboards alert me to danger. I reach for my guns at my side. My hands come up empty as bright daylight rains down upon us. My eyes slowly adjust and I see two women removing and placing floorboard planks to the side. They help the doctor from the shallow hole and then me. She speaks with them briefly; concern and worry are plainly visible on the three.

"What's going on here?"

"The soldiers took the rest of the men and some of the boys this time," she explains.

"This time... How long have they been coming here? Where are my guns? I can help."

"Guns won't help, there are too many of them. And you are far too weak," she grabs my arm. "You can barely stand and your wounds are still infected. Putting mud in the bullet holes stopped you from bleeding to death, but it gave you a bad infection. And I'm out of medicine to fight it."

"Do you have liquor?" I ask as the fire starts to flare again in my chest. "And my guns."

"Americans... You think guns can solve everything. If they find you here, they will kill you. If they find me, they will do worse. Doctors are hard to find in this part of Venezuela."

"Then what brings you here?"

"This is my birthplace. How about you? How did you come to be in the river with three bullets?"

"Just lucky I guess." My eyes have been scanning the one room shack for my guns the whole time. I see the women outside the door and window; they are keeping a safe distance and a watchful eye over me.

"Lucky?"

"You said I was lucky to be alive." I don't see my guns. "Why are the women staring at me?"

"They say you bring bad luck, or worse."

"Why? Is it because the soldiers showed up and started taking their men away?" I ask jokingly.

"Yes, there is that," she laughs, "but they have been raiding the villages around here for months. But it is because you were in the river and not eaten by the crocodiles. Care to explain how you did that?"

"I taste bad." I laugh.

"That is what they think. You are bad... how do you say? Oh. You got the Devil inside of you."

Two weeks pass, I haven't found my guns. But I do recall a dream, dark eyes coming at me. I lift my .45 out of the water. Drops of moonlight drip silently between us. The flash lit up the river. The recoil of my revolver tossed it over my head. There is splashing and crunching all around me. That explains what happened to my revolver, it is at the bottom of the river. I must have lost my pistol before I went into the water.

Giselle has been fighting my infection with moonshine, at least that's what I call it. The women make a pretty powerful batch. She dabs it on my wounds. I take a big swallow when I can. It burns my throat, but it also kills the burning in my chest. And I sleep without dreams.

The soldiers return in the middle of the night. They kick in Giselle's door and are on me before I know what is happening. They drag her and me to an awaiting jeep. The other women are undisturbed. It is obvious someone talked.

We are forced to kneel, heads on the floor, as the jeep bounces through the jungle. Giselle tries to lift her head a couple of times and gets it shoved back to the floorboards. It is useless for me to try take a look at where we are going, so I just keep my head down. I reach out to Giselle and stroke her hand. She understands.

When we reach the camp, she is dragged one way and I in the opposite direction. There are a couple of long wooden houses and a very small one, where I'm being led to. I prepare myself for what might await inside. It can only be bad.

Two of the men tie my hands and feet, then take a gaff and hook the rope between my ankles. A quick jerk slams me to the dirt and then I'm hoisted into the air. A third man enters the cabin, orders the others to hang me higher, because they pull the rope again, and I'm another two feet off the ground. He says something else and the two men leave. Now it is just the big guy and me, and he is huge.

He starts talking as he spins me around.

"No comprehender," I say, but I don't think he cares. He is trying to intimidate not inform me. This is going to be a long night. The first blow is delivered right in the middle of my back. A classic move; strike where and when I can't see it coming. I feel all four of his knuckles against my spine and I swing forward. I'm sure the next blow will come on the return trip. Of course it does, and this time in my rib cage. As I spin around, I catch a glimpse of his face, a twisted smile buried in a thick black beard. Although both punches send shockwaves of pain throughout my body, I remain silent.

Instead of crying out, I retreat into my head, slipping away from the here and now. Away from the hulk and to my old stomping grounds. It's funny how the mind works, in order to escape the pain, I go to a place and time where I was dishing out the punishment. I smile the same sadistic and twisted smile as the hulk.

"Russell, you can fight better than that," I tell the lanky boy on his knees spitting out blood. I grab him by the thick woolly afro and yank his head back almost hard enough to snap his neck. His eyes are watery and full of rage. His lip is swollen and bleeding. I told the others no face shots, body blows only, but in the frenzy, one boy's foot made contact. I didn't want him to go home with any visible signs of a beating, not yet. I wipe the blood from his bottom lip, "tomorrow, it's just you and me. And you better put up a better fight than you did today."

"I don't give a fuck what you do," he twists out of my grasp. "I'm not joining your gang."

"Tomorrow, you either win the fight, or die trying. You'll be part of the gang or you'll be no more."

"Don't try hiding or running away, we will find you," adds Bone Crusher, as he holds the door to the basement coal room open. As Russell Mills walks into the courtyard between the apartment buildings holding his side, as if his guts are about to spill out, he receives a lump of coal to the back of his head from Bone Crusher. He stumbles but regains his step quickly and runs for the stairs that lead back to the street level.

"What are you doing? The last thing we need is for his parents to call the cops," I tell Bone Crusher. He gives me a look, like he doesn't care. Bone Crusher is six inches taller and has fifty or sixty pounds on me but size never stopped me. I jump and drive the heel of my foot down on the top of his and grab him by his balls. He hollers loud but does nothing. "You are the leader of the Double Ns because I say you are. When I decide the Notorious Niggas are in need of new leadership, you better hope I like the look on your face, because you don't have the balls to stand against me. Understand?"

Bone Crusher sheepishly shakes his head in agreement and I release him. The four other gang members look away, avoiding eye contact with either of us. Bone Crusher adjusts his cut-off denim jacket, making sure the red Ns are properly over his heart, then shoves his hand down his jeans to take assessment of his manhood. He leaves and the four, in their colors, follow, stepping carefully past me.

The next morning I'm sitting on a steel garbage can in the courtyard, it's early, 8:00 a.m. on a summer day. Bone Crusher and his four followers are across the yard; they are talking low but I can hear what they are saying. "Don't worry, he'll be here. Russell's not afraid," I call out. And as if summoned, Russell Mills appears in the alleyway that leads to the street.

He walks to the middle of the courtyard, away from me and the five Double Ns. "I don't want to fight you," he shouts. "You are right, I'm not afraid, I just don't want to join your stupid gang."

Bone Crusher makes a move towards him but stops when I leap to my feet. I walk over to the boy; we are evenly matched in size and build. "It doesn't really matter if you want to fight or not, you have to." I throw a swift right to his eye and send him to the ground then follow with a kick to his jaw. The five Double Ns start jeering and shouting.

Russell realizes the fight is on regardless and springs forward. He wraps his arms around my legs and tackles me. My back hits hard on the cement and I kick furiously to get free from his grip. We roll over and come to our feet. I smile at him. He looks back stern and angry. His eye is already starting to swell and I'm sure I reopened the cut on his lip. He charges.

I throw a right and then a left, which he blocks, but then I catch him with a knee to the stomach. He slows for a moment but continues the charge. He throws punches in combination and I block all but one. It lands on my cheekbone. I am dazed but not long enough for him to get a second shot in. I grab him in a headlock and spin us around then I throw him to the ground. But he has a firm grip on my leather jacket and pulls me down with him. He lands on his side and shoulder, while I tumble over him and hit my head.

Russell makes it to his feet first. He kicks me in the side and back as I roll away from him. He continues after me, trying to kick and stomp on me. One of the Notorious Niggas stops cheering and makes a break toward us. Bone Crusher grabs him by the collar and yanks him back, smiling at me. I hear voices from the apartment windows above.

"Hey, you boys cut it out!"

"I'm calling the cops!"

"Get the hell out of here before I throw this boiling water on your asses!"

It all means nothing to us, Russell is fully engaged in the battle. I avoid another kick and punch him in a hamstring. His next step causes him to topple over and I jump on his back. I get him in another chokehold but can't keep him from twisting loose. The next thing I know, we both have each other by the throat and we are becoming lightheaded. We both release and I grab his ear and slam his head on the ground. And as if to say, "Oh yeah, take that," he does the same to me.

We roll a foot away and lie on our backs staring up at the bright blue sky, the angry faces in the windows, and a flock of pigeons swishing back and forth.

I laugh, "You fought really good for a change."

"Does not matter, I'm still not joining your gang."

"Who said I want you to join the gang?" I tell him and get to my feet. I hold out my hand to help him up. "I want you to be the gang's leader."

"What?"

"Yeah, what the fuck did you say?" Bone Crusher and the other gang members join us, now that the fight is over.

"I said give him your jacket," I give Bone Crusher a scowl and his four followers take a step back. "I'm not sure if I like that look on your face."

"What look?" says Bone Crusher as he takes off his colors and throws them at Russell, who lets them fall to the ground. "See. He doesn't even want it."

"Doesn't matter," I tell Bone Crusher and give Russell the same look I gave Bone Crusher. "Pick it up. The Notorious Niggas are now your gang; they answer to you. And you answer to no one, save me. Understand?"

Russell Mills reaches down and puts on the cut-off denim jacket with the two large red Ns stitched on the left chest, the words NOTORIOUS NIGGAS in red letters slanted down the back, and a length of chain (detachable) weaving through the waist hem. It fits him more like a cape rather than a jacket.

Warm smelly pissy water returns me to the hot little shack in the jungle. A moment later, I drop to the dirt. I hurt. I try to turn over but the pain is intense, just as if someone reached inside me and ripped my ribs out. The big guy sits on a chair enjoying a drink. Giselle gently turns me onto my back and straightens out my body. She is yelling at the big guy and he laughs at her. Her face is bruised and swollen, and has one black eye.

"Stupid over there doesn't understand English," I say to her quietly, but am not positive that he doesn't. "Just blink once for yes."

She blinks.

I inhale and it hurts like hell, "my ribs are broken, aren't they?"

She pokes around on my left side and blinks twice; she pokes around my right and blinks once.

"Is the guy who did that to you coming?"

She does not blink.

"I guess I'm in for round two."

She blinks again. The big guy gets up and leaves the shack. Giselle whispers, "He is going to get bandages. The Commander wants to know who you are and why you are here. He thinks you are a spy. He doesn't know I speak English."

"Don't you let him find out then," I warn her. "Your face... but that is not the worst thing he has done to you..."

"No." Her head drops.

I try to reach out but the pain is overpowering, "Don't worry, I will make him pay."

"He will kill you once he finds out what he wants to know," she is even more disturbed to deliver this news. There is a strange look on her face.

"What?"

"Santiago has been beating you for hours. We can hear the beating, even over the men working outside. But you did not make a sound. Do you truly have no feeling left? Are you really dead?"

"I don't think so," I attempt a smile, but know it's a grimace. "Pain is physical. Hurt is psychological. Remove the hurt and you will feel no pain."

I hear Santiago and others approaching, I stop talking. I hope she gets the message and can hold out. A couple of the men, workers from the looks of them, help Giselle wrap my broken ribs with bandages from dirty sheets and tree limbs. They sit me in a chair, tie my neck to the back and legs to the chair's legs.

Giselle hurries to the door. I can't blame her; I too would like to get out of here before round two starts. But the big guy grabs her by the arm and says, "No has terminado todavia."

He drags her over to a small table then pulls it over next to the chair. He grabs my arm and slams it down on the table. Santiago pulls a hammer out from behind his back and pounds my hand into the table. Giselle turns her head quickly, but not fast enough to save her from the sight. Santiago looks at me and smiles. I smile back. He grabs Giselle by the neck and pushes her into me, "Fijar que!"

He leaves the shack mad. The workers are in shock. I whisper to Giselle, "See. Think happy thoughts."

I was tied naked to the chair in the shack for another week and my hand throbs between the two wooden boards Giselle used to make a splint. I went round three and four with the big guy for two days then, thankfully, he was sent away and the beatings stopped. Giselle has been changing my bandages and sneaking me food and water. It's not much but it keeps me alive. I can tell she is still being abused.

I managed to turn the chair around and now have a good view of the camp through the cracks in the shack's wall. Giselle leaves and is taken to the Commander's quarters. She is definitely in for another treatment.

Commander Perez stands before a table full of food. He is not in his usual khakis, his uniform is pressed and decorated with medals. He has an air of honor about him that Giselle has not been treated to so far. "Come, sit down. Have some dinner and let's talk." He says in English.

Giselle does not respond, she is frozen with fear, wondering what new forms of savagery the commander is planning tonight.

"You can stop pretending not to understand," he says in a soft sympathetic voice, "I know you speak English better than I do." He pulls out a chair. "Sit down and tell me what you know about the American, unless you prefer our other arrangement."

She hasn't eaten much since she got there, just bread and meal, and the bread she has been splitting with John. She sits down, grabs a handful of meat, and quickly shoves it into her mouth. She chews fast to guard against him taking the food away before she has a chance to squelch the pain in her stomach. "I don't know anything about him."

"The others from your village tell me he was in your care for weeks. Surely, he must have told you something about why he is here."

"Most of the time he was unconscious," she says, while not slowing down on the food. She knows he will turn on her at any moment, and the brutal assaults will begin again.

"Then in his dreams, did he say anything?" his voice is becoming harsher.

"He was heavily sedated, but he spoke some names a couple of times." She tries to eat faster and chokes on the water she swallows to wash down the food.

"That's good, no need to worry," he cooes and picks up a rib. He sucks the meat off the bone and uses it as a pointer. "No need to fear me. We can be friends. I can be quite the generous lover too, you know." Commander

Umberto Perez positions himself behind her and drops the bone on the table before her. He places his hands on the edges of her shoulders. Giselle shudders and twitches. The commander chuckles at her reaction and rubs her shoulders gently, "What were the names? Take your time; I don't want you to make any mistakes."

Giselle thinks back to the days and nights when John was in the worst part of fever. He had mumbled Maria several times, Elizabeth, and Lizzie, whom she figured was the same person. He had thrashed about violently when he called out Nicky Nails. He called for Vicky and Clarita when he was calm. Giselle picks up a glass of wine and gulps it down. Her stomach hurts even more from eating so much so fast. She pours another glass, thinks for a moment that it might be drugged, then drinks it anyway. "I remember him calling for somebody named David. Yes, David, he called his name several times. And Sara, could be his girlfriend or wife. There was another woman too, a Martha or Margarita, I'm not sure. He slurred a lot from the drugs."

"This is good. See, we can work together you and me." Commander Perez starts unbuttoning his shirt. He tosses it on the chair across the table from Giselle so she understands dinner is over. He isn't big, only five-five, but he is big enough to manhandle her with ease.

She looks around the table, but there are no forks or knives. The only weapon she can think of using is the wine bottle. She picks it up and slowly pours another glass. "Can I have a little more wine first?" she pleads.

"Of course, my dear."

Before she could swing the bottle, he whipped his belt from his pants, wrapped it around her neck, and pulled her up and away from the table. Then unfurling it, he flung her across the room and into the wall. The wine bottle tumbling harmlessly to the floorboards. He grabs her hair, just like he had done before, and likewise, she scratches, kicks, and grabs the doorframe to the bedroom and tries to hold on. But he's much stronger and she loses her grip when he slams her face into the wall. He lifts her off the floor and tosses her toward the bed.

The room spins even as she is trying to crawl away. The commander sweeps her off the floor with one arm and body slams her onto her back again. The floorboards crack and tossed her back up towards him in his twisted game. He catches her by the throat, cutting off her air. His eyes, mouth, and face distort and churn as it comes closer. Feeling his hot thin lips press against hers, she clamps her mouth shut. Commander Umberto Perez throws her back against the wall and her head hits it with a loud thud.

She lies on the bed, barely conscious but aware of his presence over her. He pulls the flimsy dress down her body and discards it on the floor. He grabs her legs and rips them apart. Although she has no strength left to fight, he spread her legs until they hurt. *Remove the hurt and feel no pain.* She thinks. *Close your eyes. Be nothing.*

He pushes and shoves his limp dick into her with great difficulty, while grabbing the back of her knees and jerking against her body as hard as he can. He continues for minutes, trying to force his way into her flesh. Her body flails lifeless beneath him. Finally, he clutches her neck with both hands and squeezes until she rattles for air. Just before she passes out, he releases her, pulls his flaccid lump of meat from her and slaps her across the face with all his might. He then throws her limp body to the floor.

Giselle awakes on the floor. Her eyes dart around for a few seconds, looking for the beast then she grabs the tattered rag that is her dress and painfully pulls it up over her bruised body. The commander is back in his uniform eating at the table. She can barely get her balance, probably has a concussion. The commander hears her stumbling about in the bedroom and when she appears in the doorway, he holds up a shining sharp steak knife and cuts a hunk of meat. He then stabs it viciously with a fork and holds it up to admire the dripping juice. Giselle limps from the cabin across the swathe of barren jungle to the long wooden shack, where the other captives are held.

Next morning, I am awakened by nasty piss water thrown in my face, Santiago is back. He also has a new toy. He pulls the ripcord three hard times before the machine roars to life. The generator instantly fouls the air in the tiny shack. He holds the red and black wires up to my face and touches them together. A loud pop and hiss accompanies a bright flash, "I get it. The vacation is over."

A man in uniform pushes him aside. He is much smaller than Santiago; he's smaller than me, stocky though. Not fat, short, stout and muscular like a Venezuelan Napoleon. I shake my head, throwing piss water on his uniform. Santiago quickly touches the bare wires to my chest. I hear the hum in my head and my teeth clench. The commander slaps Santiago's hands away. Funny, the electric shock didn't really hurt. "There will be plenty of time for that later, first we talk."

"It's about time you showed up. I only talk to the head torturer," I quip.

"Ok, I'm here. Why don't you tell me why you are here?"

"Excuse me! Wasn't it your soldiers who dragged me out of a very nice house and dumped me in this shithole, General?" I am truly annoyed.

"Not general," he pumps up his chest, "I am Commander Umberto Perez. I want to know what brings you to Venezuela."

"Oh," I say shaking my head, as if clearing my mind, but tossing what's left of the piss water on his clean starched uniform. "Well, you see, I'm a freelance photographer for that Geographic magazine and was out shooting wildlife pictures in the jungle—"

"You expect me to believe you are a photographer with three large bullet wounds in your chest."

"Sometimes the wildlife shoots back."

"No. I think you are the Negro Americano D.E.A. that has been fighting in Colombia. And now you are here to what… destroy my operation?"

I take a long slow breath in and blow it out in a loud exasperated sigh. "Once again, I was nowhere near your base. You came and got me. As we say in America, let's lay our cards on the table, shall we, General?"

Commander Perez is visibly annoyed by my disregard for his rank. Military men are sticklers for titles, but after regaining his composure, he says, "Go on… what have you to say for yourself. I'm listening."

"First of all, you are no more a drug smuggler than I am a photographer. The runway you are building out there is not for drug planes. It is too wide and already long enough for that, yet, those men are still cutting down trees. I believe you are building yourself a little jetfighter base here. Am I right?"

"Why would I be doing that?" Commander Perez says surprised.

"Since you ask; looks like you are planning a coup." I watch Perez's face. He is back to stone. "My guess is, you are planning to strike that jet base that's not too far from here. I can hear the planes high overhead. You want them to think the attack is coming from Colombia. That's why the men are cutting down the trees by hand and the women are making camouflage netting. Am I right?"

"Know what I think? I think you are a spy—"

"Hold that thought," I interrupt, "This whole secret attack base thing you got going here is going to fail. Unless, you are planning on a one shot coup, which, believe me more often than not fails miserably."

"And what makes you think launching a coup from here will fail?"

"You may be able to hide this place from a high flying pilot, but that is World War II thinking. The government uses radar and high resolution satellite photos. Your base is going to stick out like cat at a dogfight. And you won't have a second shot if the first attack fails."

The commander is pissed off that I guessed his secret. "Let me tell you what I know. You are the American working for the D.E.A. Your friends are going through Colombia trying to find you, because they don't know you are in Venezuela. Your other friends would like for me to bury you deep in the jungle somewhere. They are done with you. And the Colombian Cartels are willing to exchange two hundred men for your head. Three hundred if it is still attached to your body and breathing. With three hundred men in the right position, added to the force I already command, my first strike will be overwhelming."

"Sure," I concede, "but I can help you build a base that will be invisible to radar. And maybe you might not get your ass blown up."

"And what would you want in return?"

"You let my friends know where they can find me. The ones who want me alive," I tell him.

"You are forgetting about the three hundred soldiers for your head," Commander Perez laughs. "What about my army?"

"Not everyone in Colombia hates me," I confess, "I can get you three hundred soldiers. Hell, I can get you a thousand if you like."

Commander Perez smiles and kills the generator. He paces back and forth in the tiny confines of the wooden shack. He stops and pokes a finger in the bullet scar in the middle of my chest. "I still have a problem with you. The people think you are here to free them. They are superstitious and think because you have not cried out in all this time, you have been sent by God or the Devil to save them. I can't have you undermining me."

"I totally understand," I try to convince him I'm not a threat, "I'll go out and make sure the people know you are the boss. That you are making me work for you."

"Yes. Yes, you will. And I know just how to show these people who is the boss."

Santiago takes a chain with handcuffs on the ends and clamps one side to my wrist. He cuts the ropes holding me to the chair and without hesitation drags me from the shack. He is walking so fast I can't get to my feet. The three feet of chain rattle and kick up dust from the freshly dug runway. The workers have been gathered around the stump of the last tree cut down this morning. They look down and away, there is shame and sorrow in their eyes, disappointment too. Here is who they imagined their savior being dragged naked to his death.

I see Giselle in the crowd. She is bruised and battered badly. Fire flares up inside me. The last few feet to the tree I manage to get to my feet and walk proudly, even defiantly to the stump. I throw my arms around it and Santiago clicks the other handcuff onto my other wrist. I do not know if the camp's captives have any idea what is about to happen, but I do. The Commander wants them to see me fall; instead, I will show them I cannot be broken. Whether it is by the heavenly fires of Sodom and Gomorrah, or that which flows in the river Phlegethon, I will see this Commander burn.

I start humming "Whipping Post" by the Allman Brothers Band as the first lash cuts its way through my skin. Bum, bum, bum, bum bid-bum, bum, bum, bum, bid-bum. CRACK. Then even louder... BUM, BUM, BUM, BUM BID-BUM, BUM, BUM, BUM, BID-BUM. CRACK. And as the commander continues to crack the whip across my back, fanning the flames already raging inside me, I sing loudly, *"SOMETIMES I FEEL, SOMETIMES I FEEL, LIKE I'D BEEN TIED TO THE WHIPPING POST, I'D BEEN TIED TO THE WHIPPING POST."* The last thing I remember is that the commander is not keeping time to the music. I don't think he knows the song.

Commander Perez' attempt to humiliate the American fails as he sings to the crowd. This infuriates the commander and he swings the whip wildly, twisting and turning the man until he lies in a bloody heap at the foot of the stump. The commander is exhausted, sweat pours down his body and he walks wearily from the crowd, looking as though he has been the one beaten. Giselle waits until the commander is in his cabin before going to

John. He is not breathing. Again. She looks up at Santiago; he walks away, leaving John the American chained to the tree.

Giselle looks to the crowd and one man steps forward with an axe. It takes him several swings to chop through the chain. Then more men come forward to pick up the body and carry it to the long cabin. They place him on Giselle's mat at one end of the cabin. The workers gather at the other end, having been locked in by the guards. Giselle works on John.

"How long have I been out?" I ask groggily.

"This time you were dead for twelve minutes."

"This time?"

"Yeah, you were quite dead when we found you in the river," Giselle tells me.

I don't know why she didn't tell me this before, but now she looks quite shocked that I am alive. I hear the murmurs of the others in the room. "What's with them? I guess they've never seen anyone beat to death."

"They are terrified of you," she replies.

I reach up through the pain and touch her face, softly stroking her swollen cheek, "tell them to have no fear, all my vengeance shall be on the commander. You are some doctor, bringing me back to life twice."

"I can't take all the credit," she says, "Carmelita gave you mouth to mouth. She breathed life back into you. She was the only one not afraid to touch you."

I glance over to the crowd and a woman three hundred pounds, at least, with few teeth that have yellowed to gold, steps from the crowd. "Carmelita?"

"Yes," says Giselle.

"Next time, you give me mouth to mouth or just let me stay dead." I smile at the woman, "thank you. I'm gonna kill that bastard twice for putting me through this."

Giselle tells me it's three days since the whipping, and no one has left the cabin. All work on the airstrip has stopped until I am well enough to direct the new efforts. She is supposed to alert the commander when I regain consciousness. We plan to keep it to ourselves for as long as possible, as it is the first break these people have had in over a year. They are in no hurry to return to the backbreaking work either, even if it means being locked in with the Diablo Negro. I need a couple of days rest anyway, I'm just about broken and falling apart. And as long as Giselle is tending to me, she too is safe from the commander.

Chapter 8

Scout's Honor

Two weeks is all the time I am given to heal. Two weeks is all the vacation time the workers get. Two weeks is Giselle's respite from the sadistic torment of Commander Perez. Two weeks and Santiago finally unlocks the cabin doors, and marches us out into the blazing sun.

Commander Perez is standing in his jeep, bullwhip coiled in his hand, "So, tell me, how do you plan to hide my airfield from sight?"

"I'm glad you are ready for a ride," I say cheerfully, "because on my way here I am sure we crossed Rio Orinoco not too far from here. Am I right?"

"The river is approximately a half kilometer east of here."

"Yes. We drove along it for a mile or two before we crossed at a low point. Can you take me there? I'll need to do some surveying," I request.

"You would not be trying to escape?" questions the commander suspiciously.

"You are holding the whip."

I get into the back seat with the commander. There is a driver and another man riding shotgun and Santiago in the back. I am still badly cut up and bandaged, it's not likely I'd be able to make a run, or swim for it. We drive down a winding slope through the jungle a few minutes and then arrive at a large clearing. The river is wide and slow moving here. I tell the commander to head up river until we reach a narrow bottleneck that feeds the river's pool. "We need to build a floodgate here," I say, "and a drainage channel to the other end of the pool."

"What are you talking about?" asks Commander Perez.

"The river bed will be your runway," I announce. "We will use the gate to control and divert the water around the pool. It is long and wide enough to launch and land jets. And when not in use, the water will conceal the runway."

"This is your plan," challenges the commander, "you are loco, Americano. The jets will sink in the mud."

"Not after we lay cement blocks in the bed. Big long concrete slabs will make up the runway. We make them in the camp and then use a system of rollers to get them down to the river. Still think I'm crazy?"

"Yes. But it could work," agrees Commander Perez.

He immediately gives orders to split the workers into three groups. One to work on the floodgate; it has to lay flat in the river and be able to rise quickly to cut off the water. Another team will work on digging the drainage channel because not only does it need to be excavated but also lined with mud-fired bricks and then buried, so as not to be detected by any casual passerby. And the last group gets to hollow out a cement pit twenty by ten by six-feet, where the cement molds will be made. They dig eight of them to make as many blocks as possible without attracting unwanted attention. They also make the rollers, from the trees they had cut down building the first runway. They bury them in mud pits on the winding path to the river. While the cement blocks set, the team helps dig the drainage channel.

There is no wasting time – it will all take long enough anyway – and the commander has everyone working from sun up to sundown. I am left to supervise the work. Once the blocks get to the river we flip them into place on tracks dug into the riverbed, then let their weight level them off.

I convince the commander I need Giselle during the day to translate my instructions to the workers, but he sure takes delight in taking her to his cabin at night. I pretend not to care, but drop subtle hints that I need her mind clear and hands steady, since she still tends to my wounds and those of the workers. It seems to work, or he is getting bored with beating her. She's returning each morning with no fresh bruises.

We sit in the jeep, like so many other days, weeks, months... watching the men and women latching together wooden logs for the gate.

"Why do you help him? Perez is going to kill you as soon as you finish his runway," Giselle confides in me.

"Of course he is," I agree. "But this runway is keeping us alive, and it will be our way out of here."

"It's not the only way," she argues, "We are many, we can overpower the guards. Take off through the jungle."

"We would not get very far on foot, and a lot of these people will die unnecessarily."

"They are dying every day. Drowning, cave-ins, being crushed by the cement blocks... this work is worse than cutting down the trees." She is becoming desperate. The beatings may have ended but the sexual assaults are still going on.

"We are getting close to finishing," I try to cheer her up, "What would you like to do when we are free?"

"We are never going to be free."

"Of course we are. I have a plan for that too. So, what would cheer you up? What do you want most in this world?"

"Ice cream. Strawberry ice cream. I used to eat bowls and bowls of it when I was in school in the city. I haven't had any since returning to the jungle," her spirits drop even lower.

"Then that is what I will get you," I smile. "You will be eating the biggest bowl of strawberry ice cream you ever saw by the end of the month."

"That soon," she is amazed.

"What soon? We have been working on this runway for over a year. As soon as the gate is in place we can stop the water and expose the runway." I lean in close but am careful not to touch her. She jumps now at the slightest touch. *I'm going to enjoy killing that bastard, Perez.* "I'm going to tell the commander to fly in a jet, in two weeks… maybe three… I'm going to tell him it needs to be fully loaded to test the weight capacity of the runway. Then we are going to fly it out of here."

"You can fly a jet?" Giselle asks in disbelief.

"Flying it is easy," I tell her. "It's the landing that may not go too well. Not a word of this to anyone, absolutely no one."

"What about the workers?" she objects, "we may escape, but he will kill all of them."

"When I leave a place," I whisper, "I don't leave a single person behind who could be a threat. Your people will be able to walk out of here and return to their villages.

I promise. By the way, strawberry is my favorite flavor too."

Commander Perez arranges for a jet to make a secret pre-dawn landing. The commander, myself, and of course, Santiago wait in his jeep alongside the river's pool. Flashing lights appear in the sky. Santiago radios the floodgate team to raise the gate. They are the only other ones not locked up this morning. Even Giselle is locked in the commander's cabin for the test.

The river water swirls slowly, causing tiny whirlpools along the edges then it washes away from the banks. Hearing the sound of the approaching jet growing in the sky, the commander turns to me, "the water is not draining fast enough. I have to call off the landing."

"Patience, General, this is a tidal pool not a bathtub. We still have plenty of time. And see, the water is draining faster now that the supply has completely stopped."

Another five minutes and the cement blocks are clearly visible through a few inches of murky water. When the jet lines up over the riverbed, a slimy dark film of mud is all that covers the runway. The jet hit the cement hard, slid twenty yards and twists to a stop. The commander smiles confidently at Santiago.

Santiago caresses the sidearm lovingly in its holster and stands up in the back of the jeep. And just as the sun is beginning to pour gold and orange rays through the trees, the dying whine of the jet engine is smothered by a growl coming from the south, up river. A roar like that of a hungry jaguar deafens the jungle. The sudden rush of wind topples Santiago out the back of the jeep as a three-foot high wall of water tumbles down the riverbed and catches the pilot half out of his plane. It spins the jet around, slams it into the muddy banks, the pilot is tossed into the turbulent waters, and swept away.

"What the fuck happen?" Perez demands.

"They must have lowered the floodgate," I answer, fighting back a smirk at the lie offered.

Santiago dusts himself off and the commander eyes him with scorn. "Averigua quien es el responsible de esto. Voy a matar al burro."

As Santiago radios the other team, and they respond with fear and shock, I offer another possible explanation. "It could also be that the shockwave from the weight of the jet hitting the runway caused the floodgate to shift position. You know, like a mini earthquake."

"So this is your fault," Perez hisses. "Your plan is a failure. You've wasted a year of my time. Santiago, kill him!"

It is a good thing for me that Santiago is extremely slow at interpreting even the simplest of English. Before he can obey the order I say, "THIS is why it is called a test run, General."

"COMMANDER PEREZ!"

"Yes, Commander Perez. We need to work out the kinks. I'm sure it is just a minor glitch, like the gate not weighting enough."

"You call this a minor glitch," he seethes. His face is blood red and the veins in his neck throb angrily. "The jet is buried in the mud and the pilot is lost down river. Probably drowned."

"Come on, it's an F-14, I'm sure a little muddy water ain't going to break it. And I do hope that pilot could swim. Or at least was wearing an automatic life vest." I smile. "I'll get the guys to pull the plane out the river, and

I'll survey the damage to the floodgate. You need to calm down; you're heading for a stroke."

The commander floors the gas, leaving Santiago standing at the riverbank. I look back at the F-14 tilted on its side in the river; the water is up to the belly of the fuselage. *Plan 'A' accomplished. We have our jet.*

Giselle is shoved into the cabin dishevelled and worried. "What happened this morning? Perez is going crazy over there."

"He didn't hurt you, did he?"

"No. He is too busy cursing you and panicking over his plane."

I laugh. "That's what he gets for bringing us a plane with dummies. Like, I wouldn't think he'd deliver dummies instead of real bombs."

"What are you talking about?" She is totally lost.

"The floodgate gave way. The General's plane is sitting in the river. Swamped!" I laugh even harder.

"That's terrible. How are we going to..." Giselle catches her words and looks around at the others in the cabin.

"First, some of our friends here are going to remove the fake weapons from the jet so they can tow it up here to do whatever maintenance is needed. Then I'm sure the General is going to arm it with real weapons."

"So you knew the floodgate wouldn't hold," she whispers.

"I designed it," I wink.

"But if the runway is no good, how are you going to fly the jet out of here?"

I lean in and kiss her forehead. I feel a shiver run through her body and she recoils slightly. I withdraw. "There is a perfectly good runway right outside the door."

Later in the day, I inform the commander that we will need six small cement blocks to anchor the floodgate, three at the bottom, that will drop into a trench in the riverbed and three at the top to keep the gate from rising up. I tell him also that we have to dig another drainage ditch at the other end of the pool, to speed up emptying the water. I give him two weeks to completion. He gives me one. A week it is. I request Giselle's presence day and night, so I can go over any problems the men have during the day. He agrees. *Clearly, he no longer gives a damn about her.*

He reports the F-14 lost over the ocean. It was supposed to be on a training flight but became separated from its squadron... It sits on the runway under camouflage. I don't think the pilot survived. Two days after they pulled the jet from the river I hear the engines roar to life, and today a truck arrived with live ammo. His ground crew fit the F-14 with Sidewinder missiles and a five-hundred-pound bomb, and of course, bullets for its cannon. Now the dragon has teeth. I tell Giselle, "Tomorrow we take off."

Morning comes and I give the order to raise the floodgate, a much harder task to accomplish with three half-ton blocks having to be hoisted twelve-feet into the air. Even using two jeeps and a complex system of pulleys takes five minutes before the gate drops into place and the waters divert from the river. The second drainage ditch empties the river pool quickly and the runway is much cleaner this time. From his cabin, the commander gives the order to start up the F-14. He also gives Santiago another order, Giselle and I are back in the jeep heading towards camp.

As we pull into camp, the jeep turns left, past the F-14, where two pilots stand donning their flight suits, and head toward my old home, the little shack at the far end of the camp. I guess either success or failure wouldn't have mattered for me, my time is up. Santiago clutches my arm and leads me into the building. Giselle is left in the jeep with the driver. She will be next.

"Santiago, I hope you learned a little English since I met you," I tell him.

"Si, I learned little," he replies, grinning like the sadistic bastard he is.

"Good, because I want to tell you, I'm about to FUCK YOU UP!" I grab a dirty combat knife from the table, whip around, kick his leg out from under him, and pin his hand to the table with the knife. "I noticed you favored your left leg, so it's probably an old wound that healed badly, right?"

"Que?" He doesn't cry out. Wants to show he is as tough as I am.

"I don't have time to translate," I say as I seize his other hand and nail it to the table. I take my time pounding the six-inch iron spike through the back of his hand. With each blow, he grinds his teeth harder and pushes the heavy wood table an inch across the room. An inch of spike is exposed above his right outstretched hand and the metal hilt of the combat knife shines brightly over his left; I connect the teeth of the generator leads to them. "Oh, Buddy Boy, this is really gonna hurt."

I pull the ripcord on the generator and it noisily sends a current down the lines, through Santiago's hands and across his chest. I slowly turn the knob, increasing the current until Santiago is banging his head uncontrollably against the thick wood, blood sputtering onto the wall before him as I walk out the shack. *Wonder what will give out first, his heart or his skull. No matter, he's a dead man now.*

I walk up behind the jeep's driver and toss him out by his head, breaking his neck in the process. I take his pistol and climb into the driver's seat, "We got to get moving, if we are going to catch our ride out of here."

Giselle smiles, the first time I've seen her do so in more than a year. When we reach the F-14, one man is already in the plane and the other is about to climb the ladder. I step out the jeep, the gun in my left hand. Giselle had done a good job setting the bones in my right hand, but thanks to Santiago, it is still much too stiff for rapid fire. Like any good gunslinger, I taught myself to be equally good as a lefty. I shoot him and the two other grounds men. I climb the ladder, stick the gun in the pilot's face, and tell him to get out. When he stands up, I fire up under the helmet and he tumbles onto the wing. I help Giselle into the front seat.

"Why did you shoot him? He was agreeing to give you the plane."

"I find people are much more agreeable when they are dead."

So far, the jet engines had masked the sound of gunfire in the camp. Most of the guards are still in their cabin and all but a few prisoners are locked up. Those who aren't in the cabins are at the floodgate. Commander Perez sits in his. The campgrounds are deserted. I buckle Giselle in, place the helmet and face mask on her, and tell her. "No matter what, you keep that mask on, it will feed you oxygen."

She nods. I take the other helmet and shake the blood out, put it on, climb into the pilot's seat, and turn on the intercom, "Can you hear me?"

"Yes," replies Giselle. I can tell she is scared to death.

"It will be ok. Take off is going to be really fast, not like an airliner," I tell her. "More like going on a rollercoaster, only we will go up. After that it will be like any other plane ride." *I wish we had time to put on the flight suits, but a guard could emerge from the cabin at any moment and won't hesitate to shoot.* I manoeuvre the jet to the left and activate the first sparrow missile. Although it's an air-to-air missile, I guess it will take out the guard's cabin from this range. I press the fire button and the missile drops to the ground before igniting its rocket. Then it bounces along the ground and smashes through the wall. Seconds later, amid screams, the missile explodes, engulfing the cabin in a fireball. I push forward on the stick and roll the jet to the right. I activate the 20 mm cannon and begin firing.

"What are you doing?" Giselle screams. "Our people are locked in there."

"I know, I'm opening a door for them." The five second burst is enough to shear off a corner of the cabin. As the smoke clears, the prisoners run through the hole and disappear straight into the jungle. "Hang on."

I push the throttle all the way forward and as the jet shakes in protest, I release the brake. We are pinned back in our seats and the trees rush towards us. With all my strength, I yank back on the joystick and we rocket into pure blue. My sight dims and I get dizzy. *I really wish I had that flight suit.* I ease the stick forward and throttle back the engines. We level off over the jungle. "Giselle, are you ok up there?"

"You lied, this is not like any rollercoaster I have ever been on. I think I'm going to be sick."

"Me too, but hang in there a little longer. I need you to do something for me," I tell her as I gently bank the jet to the left. I spot the river and its empty tidal pool, and running parallel to it, the break in the trees which almost undetectable from our altitude. I dip the nose and slow the jet even more. A brown ribbon meanders through the jungle greenery. I know Commander Perez will be on that jungle path fleeing his secret base, because he knows I'll never leave without him. I light up the radar panels in the front compartment for Giselle. "You see that red square on your weapons' display? That's our friend the General. When it turns green, I want you to press the little red button on the joystick and send him to Hell."

Commander Perez is gunning the jeep through the trees, but can hear the low rumble of the jet behind him. He tilts the rear view mirror upwards, looking for the F-14 on his tail. The jeep bounces off a tree and he is almost thrown out. The jet makes its appearance above the trees and races ahead of him.

"OK. Now!" She screams with true glee.

Seconds later the jungle erupts with a multitude of fireballs shooting out behind the jet, and the MK 20 sets ablaze a quarter mile of forest. Thick black smoke appears in the rear view mirrors of the F-14.

"Wow! All of that from one bomb. But are you sure we got him? How can you be sure he was in the jeep?"

"At this very moment, Commander Perez, is taking it up the ass from Satan," I assure her. I hear a sound in my ear that is barely audible, I can't tell if she giggled or grimaced at the image. *Poor choice of words after what she's been through.* "He was the only one left at the camp. He's definitely dead. Now we've got to hightail for the coast."

"Where are we going?"

"I know a place or two in the Caribbean where we can ditch the jet."

"What do you mean by 'ditch'," she asks with real concern in her voice.

"This is a military plane," I reply, "We can't just land it at any old airport. As a matter of fact, we are going to have to try and stay off radar until we are out to sea." I push forward on the throttle and we are again pinned back in our seats.

"I'm going to throw up," screams Giselle in response.

We are cruising over a sea of green towards the blue ocean ahead. I would like to push the throttle forward even more, but I know the G's will be too much to bear. I also know that the nearby airbase must have heard the bombing in the jungle. If Perez didn't alert them, then that surely did. An hour in the air and still nothing, but the closer we get to the coast the more our odds are bound to drop. *That is what I would do; deploy my air force west along the Colombian border and north to the coast.*

Giselle's comforting deep breathing in my ear is interrupted by the aircraft's warning system. She awakes in a panic as voices crackle over the radio. She announces, "They want us to identify ourselves."

"Yeah, I know."

"What should I tell them?"

"Nothing... What can we tell them? We stole their jet, blew up a secret base, and killed their commander. See ya later?"

Giselle cries out, "They are saying turn around or they are going to shoot us down."

"Honey, I hate to do this to you, but I'm going to have to really step on the gas now."

The F-14's wings sweep back as the plane leaps forwards, leaving a vapor trail behind. Giselle screams in agony. The warning system is going crazy and I am losing sight again. Two sparks above to my left are the cause of all this turmoil. I throttle back with the shoreline in sight, deploy counter measures and dive closer to the water. Two thunderous shockwaves hit us.

Giselle yells, "They are shooting at us."

"Yeah, but they are too far away. We might be able to outrun them. But it is going to be painful."

The display shows something on the water ahead. The code looks like it might be a British aircraft carrier. I tell Giselle we might be in luck if we can ditch close to them. I radio the carrier, "HMS Bulldog... HMS Bulldog... This is a LBS. Repeat. This is a Lost Boy Scout requesting assistance."

"Venezuelan aircraft say again."

"HMS Bulldog, this is a LBS, this is a Lost Boy Scout requesting assistance."

"Boy Scout, be advised you must make international water before assistance can be given. You have two Venezuelan F-14s closing fast. Increase speed Mach 2. Now!"

"I can't do that Bulldog; we are flying naked. No G-suits. Had to leave town in a hurry," I laugh.

A young officer on the bridge relays a message to the captain, "Those F-14s are going to overtake him in five minutes. They will be in missile range in less than two."

"Radio those planes. Tell them to hold fire. Tell them that any missile launches this close to our ship will trigger our automatic defences. That will give that bloody maniac a little time."

"The Venezuelan has acknowledged our status and increased speed. They say he stole their plane and attacked a base and they intend to shoot him down," the officer informs his captain.

"What the bloody hell are the Yanks up to now? Get command on the line, inform them of our situation." The captain then opens the radio mike, "Boy Scout, your friends are going to do you serious harm. We have a fix on your position, bailout... bailout... bailout NOW."

"We are still in their waters, you won't be able to come get us," I reply, "look, this is just a big misunderstanding. I'm going to have a talk with them boys."

"Boy Scout, do not fire on those planes; we will not be able to grant you asylum. Repeat, do not fire, you will not be able to land on this ship."

"Don't worry about that, I don't think I can land this thing on your ship or anywhere else anyway. Not in one piece, that is. I'll be right back."

I pull back hard on the stick and push the throttle to full force. The jet whips up just in time as the two F-14s open fire on a crossing pattern. I flip the jet over as everything goes from sky blue to sea blue in an instance. I roll right, squeezing the trigger for the cannon. The familiar sound of gunfire fills the cockpit. I can't see the jet, but one of the F-14s passes right below us and through our stream of bullets. Giselle yells out, "You got one. He radioed he is damaged and heading back to base."

I pull out of the dive moments from crashing into the sea. My eyes play tricks on me, black spots and red curtains cloud the instruments but somehow, I manage to get a fix on the other jet, who is closing fast on my tail. I go into dive, roll the jet over and pull up hard. I am ahead of him, but heading in the opposite direction, back to shore. "Giselle, tell him he wins. Ask him where he want us to land?"

"No. We can't go back..."

"We can't out-fly him without flight suits either; we will crash or be shot down. Tell him. Quickly, before he fires on us again."

She radios the message and receives instructions. The F-14 crew is surprised to hear a woman's voice on the radio and pull ahead to look in our cockpit. *As I knew they would.* I hit the airbrakes, fall behind them, and immediately lay on the cannon, riddling the jet with bullets until it explodes. I pull up and away, heading back out to sea.

As the carrier grows in the blue water, I slow down and let the jet drop in altitude. By the time we get within a mile of the carrier we are on the verge of stalling. I tell Giselle to look down and without warning eject her from the plane. I go next. I don't see any sign of the jet when I hit the water but I do see Giselle's parachute. Divers are already in the water, strapping her into a helicopter's harness then two men grab me, and the three of us are hoisted out of the water.

I hear the rustling of keys outside our detention cell door. As far as cells go, it is a very nice one. Like a small suite on a cruise ship. No window, of course, but a nice twin bed, desk, dining table and a roomy bathroom with a shower. The door opens out into the corridor, and a naval officer steps in with a hand on his side arm, followed by Captain Emery Charles.

"What the hell is she doing in there? What am I running here, a brothel?"

"She wouldn't stop screaming until we put the bloke in with her," responds the officer, "Doc says she is probably suffering from severe trauma. It's in the Report of the Day."

Giselle clings tighter to me, and I run my hand through her hair before gently turning her to the wall. I get out of the bed in the white jumpsuit provided me. Giselle huddles in the corner in hers. "Which day's report? We've been in this cell for two days now."

"Come with me," orders the captain.

Giselle springs to her feet and locks onto my arm like a lobster.

"Not her, just you, Mr. Morrison."

Giselle grips my arm tighter.

"Either she comes with us, or you can just say what you have to say, right here and now."

"Oh Father Christmas, bring her along," the captain concedes. "She is going to see the doctor anyway. Your girlfriend is in need of help, lots of it. Let me tell you, I haven't seen anyone in your condition... not alive anyhow."

We follow the captain down the corridor to a large room at the end. There are television screens, tables and chairs, – bolted to the floor in small groups of four, and a large service bar along the back wall – a kind of mess hall or recreation room for the crew. The captain swings one of the chairs around on its pole and holds out his hand towards Giselle. I nod and she sits down. I sit next to her. The captain sits across from us and his security officer remains standing.

"If she wants, she can go over to the mess window and get some breakfast," the captain suggests charmingly.

"Do you have strawberry ice cream?" I ask the captain and smile at Giselle.

"Yes. But for breakfast?"

"Go ahead," I say encouragingly. "This is as good a time as any to enjoy that ice cream I promised you."

She gets up slowly then hurries across the room to the food service wall.

I wait until she is out of earshot and whisper to the captain, "she had a worse time of it than me."

"I read your medical report," says the captain sympathetically, "that's hard to believe."

"Not all injuries can be easily seen. She hasn't said a word since we boarded your ship, and she hasn't stopped shaking."

"She is suffering from PTS," the captain offers, "Post Traumatic Shock Syndrome, shell-shocked. What happened to you two in Venezuela? But more importantly, who the hell are you? The call sign you gave, LBS, Lost Boy Scout, was disavowed two years ago by the CIA, during a security shake up. For the last two days, my government has been in contact with every diplomatic and intelligence channel in your government. No one will acknowledge you. The closest we came was a NSA chap who said he'd be happy if we dropped you back in the ocean where we found you. She is obliviously Venezuelan... You... You are a man without a country. The Queen doesn't want you and you do look like a lot of trouble just waiting to happen. So my question to you is... What do you want me to do with you?"

Giselle returns with two large bowls of pink strawberry ice cream and one spoon. She sits down and digs in. After several large spoonsful, she shoves one in my mouth without warning.

I spot a newspaper on a table behind the captain. More accurately, I spot a picture of Yana on the front page. "Is that a current newspaper? Can I see it?"

Captain Charles reaches back and grabs the paper. He looks it over and hands it to me, "it's today's. You want to know the date?"

"Yeah, I've been away a long time." I wait for Giselle to go for another bowl of ice cream. "Can you drop me off in California?"

"Don't tell me you know Yana?" asks the security officer in disbelief. The captain shoots him a disapproving look.

"Yeah, I know her," I smile.

"This is not a Hanson Cab," interjects the captain.

"It says here; she is getting married tomorrow. I would really appreciate it if I could be at that wedding."

"You are going to stop her wedding," the security officer chimes in again, "good luck. She's marring her producer, the guy is rich, and he owns the studio that makes all her movies."

"You guys seem to be pretty interested in her," I tell them, "I'll get her to sign a nice photo for you. How would you like to see what that snake's head is doing?" I slap the paper down in front of the captain with my finger on the tattoo of the snake wrapped around her midriff. It disappears under her blouse.

"Nobody knows what the snake's head looks like," says the captain, "she never shows that much in her films. A real classy lady she is."

"I know what it's doing," I brag, "I'm the one who drew it on her."

"You want us to violate American waters, with you on board," objects the captain. "You want to start up the Old Quarrel again, over a woman. Her Majesty is right, you are trouble."

"Captain Charles, how would you like to know where that snake comes from? Trust me, she is not as classy as you imagine after a night of tequila. You get me back to the States and I'll send you a private movie. You'll really want to see her make it dance."

"We are in the Caribbean Sea, the best I can do is get you to the British Virgin Islands by nightfall," agrees the captain.

"BVI is good enough for me. I can make my way to California from there."

"Huh hem," the security officer clears his throat as Giselle is making her way back to the table with another huge bowl of ice cream, "what are you going to do with her?"

"I guess I'll set her up with a nice ice cream parlor on the island."

Captain Charles, the Chief Security Officer, the Chief Medical Officer, and two others identified only as security personnel, a man and a woman, disembark from HMS Bulldog dressed in pressed white uniforms at 11:00 pm at the naval port in Road Town, Tortola. The captain signs the group through customs and they are about to part company when the doctor takes John's arm, "Mr.

Morrison, if you care anything about this girl you will check her into a medical facility for treatment."

"You're a doctor, she's a doctor... you two work something out. You'll be around for a while; I heard the Queen gave you an extended shore leave. I, on the other hand, have to make some calls, get an ice cream shop and a jet."

Giselle pulls me away from the doctor, "you are not really planning on buying me an ice cream shop, are you?"

"I was, if it will make you happy."

"I'm a doctor, John." She smiles and lights up the night.

"I'll buy you an ice cream shop and an obesity clinic," I jest. "Are you going to be OK? I can't take you with me."

"I don't want to go with you," the smile is gone. "I don't want to have to bring you back from the dead a third time."

"I'll check you into the hotel. By morning somebody will be there to help you start your clinic, ice cream shop, or whatever you want."

"You don't have to do this."

"Are you kidding, you brought me back to life twice. The least I can do is come back once for you." I turn to the doctor as she is getting in the car, "Nobody touches her, understand me?"

The captain hands me a piece of paper.

"What's this?"

"It's the secure communication channel for the Bulldog. Are you really coming back for her?"

"Of course I am. Look at her."

12 am. I'm on a private jet heading for California. I have a beer in one hand and a phone in the other. After several rings, a man answers, "Let me speak to Mr. Gordon."

"Whom may I say is calling?"

"Tell him I'm a friend of his fiancée's, with a wedding gift for him."

There is a long silence then there is a click, before I hear, "the Gangster, I was wondering when I was going to hear from you."

"You have lousy bugging equipment, but I'll fix that for you."

"And what do I have to do for you to fix my equipment, agree not to marry Yana? I dealt with your kind before. You are nothing new to me..."

"You dealt with mobsters before, I'm something completely different," I tell him. "If Yana wants to marry you and it makes her happy, then go ahead and do so. But I have a proposition for you; and it's entirely on another level."

"And if I decide I'm not interested in your proposition?" he asks with as much bravado as a sixty-three-year-old man can muster.

"Then Yana will be a bride and widow at the same time. I'll be there before sunrise; get some sleep, we have a busy day ahead of us."

The wedding is a lavish Hollywood affair. Hundreds pack the country club grounds, movie stars, politicians, press, and throngs of fans rich enough to be able to afford entry to the club. This is Yana Kerchovich's first marriage and Guy Gordon's fourth. Except for his first marriage, all had been to actresses he produced. His first marriage ended thirty years ago, after his first blockbuster movie and his first academy award-winning starlet and soon to be bride. He has had a new wife every ten or fifteen years.

Yana walks down the aisle in the garden in a white satin dress of her own design, and at Guy's insistence, he, would not marry a woman not dressed in white. Her dress is a mini halter-top of crushed roses with diamonds in the center. The front rises up just past her ample areolas, showing plenty of creamy tan flesh and cleavage before sweeping down her sides and exposing her all the way down to the small of her back. A silk mesh diamond sprinkled train fans out from her waist and trails behind her. She appears to float through the garden as glittering white roses mystically grow out of the ground to engulf her. Three rows of black diamonds spring from her eastern diamondback rattlesnake and writhe magically in and out of her rose garden across her back. She is an enchanting sight that at once hushes the crowds.

Guy, at the altar, is looking about nervously like a preacher in a cathouse in his black tuxedo. A few years shy of doubling her age, when they stand together before the priest, he looks like her father rather than her groom. They exchange vows and rings in a simple ceremony and then the party resumes.

They spend the next few hours in true Hollywood style, taking pictures with celebrities and wannabes, drinking champagne that flows from the many fountains inside and out of the club. They cut the cake. Yana tosses the bouquet to Izolda, the only one of her Russian Dolls left to be married. Guy takes the garter, which was visible the whole time in a dress that short, from her leg and tosses it over his head. A ten-minute riot follows as men and women battle for the star's sacred item. He walks her to the limo, stopping a few feet from the open door and awaiting usher, "there's a jet waiting at the airport, I'll be along in a couple of days, I have some business to wrap up here."

"This is supposed to be our honeymoon," she pouts. "You'd better not spend it working."

Yana climbs into the car, the usher quickly seals her in, and the driver speeds away. It may have been the champagne, or the dimness of the blacked out limo, but she is unaware of the other passenger in the back. Until she hears,

"You look like God's first Angel."

Yana bats her eyes several times as if to clear away the champagne haze. She looks hard and shock sets in, "Morris... It can't be you. Not here. Not today."

"Yeah, it's me. Back among the living."

"You no-good, lousy, muthafucking scumbag... it's been ten years and not a word. I waited for you. I even prayed for you. And you, YOU PRICK... you show up today." Yana grabs a champagne bottle from the bar and swings violently at my head. She swings two more times before throwing it. The bottle flies through the confined space, makes contact with the limousine's window, flies a few more feet, and smashes the windshield of the car in the next lane. It swerves into the car next to it and a chain reaction pileup starts forming on the LA freeway. The driver prepares to pull over.

"Keep going," I yell at him through the partition glass.

"HELL NO. Stop this car. Stop it now," Yana yells at the driver as the window slowly lowers. "You're getting out. Right here... Right now."

"Sir?" questions the driver. "The accident, I could lose my job."

"Don't worry," I assure him. "Between her husband and me, you won't have to worry about finding a job. Keep going to the airport." I raise the window.

"Guy. What did you do to Guy?" Yana is frantically looking around the car.

I grab the other bottle of champagne. "I didn't do anything to him. I simply made a business deal with him. He gets to marry you, and I get to take you on your honeymoon. It's a win, win, win."

"So you still think I am some cheap whore you can buy and sell," Yana thunders. Then she launches herself across the car, ripping my shirt and skin from my chest. Six long bloody streaks sink and burn into my flesh. She shoots back across the seat and stares. She keeps staring at the three large scars around my heart. Her eyes flood with tears as she surveys the damage the years have done. "Where the fuck have you been?"

"It hasn't been as bad as you think," I laugh.

"Oh no, it looks like you should be dead," she chokes on the words. The tears are rolling down her checks in lavender lines.

"I was. Twice. Hahaha. Stop crying, you're messing your face."

"How can you sit there and joke about it?" She wipes her cheeks with the back of her hand, smearing the makeup even more.

"I came back to life," I say a bit more seriously, "there's no sense in crying about it now. Anyway, I only got free yesterday, and then heard you were getting married... well, I'm here now."

"Why? Why did you come here?"

"Because I love you."

She launches herself across the back seat of the car again, pinning me down and locking her mouth to mine. We kiss long and hard, trying to erase ten years of separation. I suck her in and allow her to take me into her like I have never been able to do before. My hands go wild over her body, grabbing her hair, ripping her breasts from her wedding dress, running down around her bare ass to the hotspot between her legs. "I see you still like to go alfresco."

"Shut up and fuck me," she demands, clawing at my pants.

"In a moment, but first…" I lift her up and out the roof of the car and dig my face into her pussy. Her golden-red bush scratches my nose and tongue as I manoeuvre her around until she unfolds like a sweet tangy rose. I lick noisily, greedily, sticking my tongue into her tiny hole as far I can. The blaring horns of cars passing on the highway do not deter me from what I waited an eternity to do. The top half of her naked body, her breasts through the moon roof, draw cheers. Through the busted out window, it is clearly visible why she is so happy and carefree. I continue alternating thumb and tongue on her growing clit protruding from its tender fleshy hood. I run one finger into her, feeling for her G-spot, then a second as I milk her creamy pussy. I work a third in, extracting a scream and pounding on the limo roof, and I mercilessly suck in her flushed pink clit. When she starts convulsing in my hands, I plunge my tongue into her crimson gaping pussy, fulfilling ten years of desires.

As we arrive at the tiny airfield, I instruct the driver to pull up to the stairs of my waiting jet. We run naked into the cabin. The co-pilot pulls the door shut and the stewardess turns her head and cast her eyes down. I sweep Yana up into my arm and she wraps her legs around my back. I split her open and stick my dick up her juicy hole as I make my way back to the bedroom, pausing momentarily to grab a bottle of champagne from an ice bucket. I kick the door shut and dive onto the bed. She screams.

Chapter 9
Redemption

They landed on the bed and Morris was driven deep inside her. Yana cried out in pain even as an overwhelming wave of pleasure warmed her from inside out, replacing the sting of him striking her cervix. He was wild and savage in his taking of her, stabbing at her with furious fervor. He pulled, bit, and mauled her like a starving man at a banquet. She accepted his intensity, and invited his uncontrolled passion with equal animalistic actions.

Yana dug her nails into his back, tore at his neck, and drew her knees to her chest then slamming her feet into the bed thrust her pelvis and Morris up and over. She straddled him, pinned him between her hips, and slammed herself up and down on his black rock. She rose so high that the tip of his massive head was momentarily freed. Then she drove it back into her engorged vagina, riding it all the way down until their hips collided. Ever greater waves of pain and pleasure ran up her spine and stiffened her nipples as they bounced. The friction of raw flesh caused a fire that engulfed and swelled his manhood to the point of bursting. Unbridled sensations rippled through their bodies from one to the other.

The diamondback wiggled out of her fiery bush, crossed her left thigh, coiled around her midriff, and rose between her breasts. Its head swayed back and forth from each meaty mound and its tongue flicked at the tight nickel-sized darkened nipple just out of its reach.

Morris' hands struggled to control the coils of snake as he pulled her closer. Yana's legs were spread wide across his body almost reaching 180 degrees. Their bodies slid across each other on a film of sweat, the river of passion flowing from every pore. Morris' mouth tugged on the button of flesh that eluded the snake's forked tongue, its eyes jealously peering into his with its hypnotic power. Her body quivered and her breath expelled deep-throated moans. "Not yet. There's more to come," he breathed into her ear.

He rolled her over, twisting and folding her legs until without leaving her body he rammed his throbbing iron rod into her from behind. She was hissing, seething, squirting, and biting into the pillow between blows to the deepest regions in her. His hands lifted her lower half from the bed to meet his thrust. A scorching sea erupted all over her body, spreading in all directions at once. Yana splayed out on the bed as the all-consuming orgasm blotted out the world, oblivious to everything except the electricity coursing through her and the lightning bolt in her core. An eternity passed then a second sensation exploded, filling her with overpowering hammer strikes in her palpitating pussy.

The hum of the jet engines plays a subtle lullaby as we glide along at thirty thousand feet. I can always tell how well a plane is put together by the hum of her engines. The quieter the better; and this Whisper Jet is one of the best. The two engines are mounted just behind the bedroom wall, and unless you have your ear against it, you'd never know it.

I feel them as I sit up in the king size bed with my back against the mounted headboard. I sip what little champagne is left from the bottle, as the majority had poured out onto the bed. The bed is drenched with champagne, sweat, and sex. I look down, satisfied at my flaccid dick, "you outdid yourself today, Mr. MoJo."

Mr. MoJo nods twice, and his throbbing painfully shifts him on my thigh. "What, You're ready for more? No, I understand, we waited a long time for her… And yes, it was all my fault. We could have been nailing it in Florida. I don't know… I wasn't ready. I know you were ready but the time wasn't right. Yeah, now is a good time. Let me see if we can get her up."

Yana is laying on her stomach motionless, her left leg straight and her right bent at a right angle. I look over her silky smooth skin; the rounds of her bottom are firm and toned. Her thighs and calves have strong defined curves. Every inch of her tanned body is sculpted to perfection by years of workouts. The tangled mass of auburn curls shrouds her face.

"She looks so peaceful. Maybe we should let her sleep… I know ten years is a long time, but it's not like she's gonna get up and walk out at thirty thousand feet." My dick throbs in protest. "I know… ten years!"

I rub her ass. She does not move. I run my hand over the firm flesh letting my two middle fingers guide the way through the crack of Yana's ass to the soft bristles between her legs. The heat from her vagina warm the palm of my hand and Mr. MoJo stiffens even more. I gently squeeze the puffy mound in my hand and she moans sweetly in her sleep. Mr. MoJo pulses with eager anticipation. "We are going to take it slow and easy this time. I think she might be a little swollen and sore. And so are you my friend."

I cuddle up behind her then rub my head tenderly up and down her slit. She murmurs and slowly unfolds her lips. I eased into her. She sighs but remains asleep. I let out a long puff of air like blowing on hot soup as Mr. MoJo catches fire. *Yeah I fucked us raw.* I slowly push in and past the pain until I am completely in her again. Yana wiggles and snuggles back into me. I gently gyrate in tiny circles inside her until the pain dissipates and I drift off to sleep.

Yana opens the bedroom door and watches Morris snort a long thick line of coke from a silver tray in the lap of the stewardess. She wraps the floor-length white silk robe around her and clears her throat, "ahem! Am I interrupting?"

"Just getting started, Sweetheart." I shake off the burn and hold out my hand to her. "We have about another three hours before we land. Do you still like to party?"

"Not so much anymore," she chuckles. "I have to stay in shape for my career." Yana takes the tray and sits opposite me in the other plush recliner.

"The last two movies, Russian Roulette and that cop one..."

"Red, White, and True Blue," Yana smiles.

"Yeah, that's the one, where you are a fed helping the New York City police take down a rogue KGB spy." I respond excitedly. "Kind of a true story... don't you think?"

"Not at all," she contests, "How much of that stuff have you done?"

"Not much. I have been off it for a while myself." I sense my enthusiasm is disturbing her. "Alicia, get some champagne, dear."

The stewardess goes to the front of the cabin and returns with a cart holding champagne bottles and glasses in ice. "In Russian Roulette you were the spy, deadly, but good," she says, "I liked that."

Yana bends over the silver tray, takes the glass straw and inhales a good amount of the white powder. She shivers, "still don't believe in cut. Svetlana and I were doing okay with our production company, but we didn't get really good scripts until we partnered with Guy." She takes a glass of champagne from the cart and sips. A drop falls from the glass between her breast and she adjust the silk robe that is slipping from her shoulders. "Oh, and speaking of Guy, my husband, this little escapade violates my pre-nup... so thanks a million or more like half a billion, Morris."

"You don't have to worry about that... He had a change of heart," I laugh.

"What did you do? Make him an offer he couldn't refuse," scolds Yana.

"What is that supposed to mean?" I enquire.

"Nothing," she replies.

"Guy is not such a bad dude for a snake," I muse, "but that worm of a lawyer, him, I did not like. Guy was more than happy to burn your pre-nup, it wasn't any good after Wormy ate the signature pages. Man, there were a lot of signatures on that thing. Anyway, I convinced him that starting a marriage with plans on how to end it was bad business."

"What is this business you keep talking about?"

"You say he's worth a half billion now," I pass the silver tray to Alicia and she takes a hit. "By this time next year, He'll be worth several billion. And so will you." Alicia's eyes widen as much from the conversation as the pure cocaine she is snorting. "You are welcome, Sweetheart."

Alicia passes the tray across the aisle to me and I hand it directly to Yana, who is in shock.

"You're not getting him mixed up in your drug smuggling..." she begins.

"No, totally legit," I boast. "You are about to become a communications giant. Satellite TV is the next big thing, and you and that snake are going to be at the forefront. Take another hit." I reach into a bag on the floor between us and pull out a video camera. "And while we're on the subject of snakes, you know that dance you used to do in Florida?"

"Oh no..."

"Come on, Baby, it's your honeymoon, live a little," I coax her as I start the recorder. "Besides, I kinda owe it to the British Navy for saving my life." Not exactly the truth but it is close enough for her to tell Alicia to put on some music. It's not long before her snake is visibly tempting my snake.

"Why a snake?" asks Alicia, captivated by Yana's naked gyrations.

"She is forbidden fruit," I answer from behind the camera, "the snake is her protection."

"So, you are the snake," Alicia says.

Yana slithers around the cabin for a while naked. She enjoys turning Morris on and slapping him away. After the workout, she climbs back onto the recliner, pulls her knees up and crosses her legs in front of her at the ankles.

"This is a nice plane, must've cost a fortune. You must be doing well for yourself, despite the setback." She is referring to the scars, which she had examined with tender care in the bedroom.

"I don't own it, it's a rental."

"You mean a charter."

"Yes, a charter," I stand corrected. "I got it from a small company in the Caribbean. They cater to rock stars, movie stars, diplomats, and corporate heads; they will fly anyone anywhere and supply the crew, all very discreet." *I don't own the plane, but I do own the charter company. It's the perfect way to move merchandise around the world. With high-ranking clients onboard, we rarely land at commercial airports and never get checked by customs. The passengers have no knowledge of what's hidden in the cargo hulls.* "But not to worry, I can still afford it."

The seatbelt sign comes on and I tell Yana we should dress warmly. We go to the bedroom to put on jeans and sweaters. I put on a jacket to cover the two shoulder holsters I'm wearing and the .45 Smith and Western pistols in them.

"Expecting trouble?" she teases.

"Always," I reply. "Remember, when we are in public, I'm your bodyguard, John Morrison. You are a big star and need one."

"That's the best alias you could come up with," Yana laughs, "did they beat you in the head too?"

We return to our seats. Alicia has cleaned up the cabin and buckled in. "Why are we dressed like this? Greece never gets too cold, not even at night."

I ask Yana, "When was the last time you've been home?"

"Never. I have never gone back. There's nothing there for me, you know that," she laments.

"But you're a big star now, a national treasure," I say cheerfully, "don't you think it's time you see your folks? You're in movies, married, and a fucking icon; all that dead girl shit is a forgotten past."

"I don't know," she worries, "You don't know Russians, they hold grudges. Besides, I'm a newlywed, returning with my lover. How is that going to look to my father?"

"With your personal bodyguard," I correct. "And there will be a team waiting when we land. But if your father gives you any grief, I'll be glad to shoot him in the head."

"Please... Try not to shoot my father. I think this is going to be a very short honeymoon, but thanks anyway. Maybe I'll get to introduce you to my Mom. She will like you."

We land at a tiny airfield with one runway and a two-story building that is smaller than my two-bedroom apartment was in the Bronx. A chain-link fence runs the length of the runway behind the building, on the opposite side are thick dense woods, and a dirt road cuts straight through the forest. Out the other side of the plane window is a vast wheat field. Four black Lincolns are waiting in front of the building.

The co-pilot opens the door and unfolds the stairs to the tarmac. Four of the Russian security men approach and wait at the bottom of the steps. I emerge from the cabin and start down.

Yana grabs my arm and pulls me back.

"What's the matter?" I ask.

"Are you fucking kidding me?" she vents. She had caught sight of the tattoos on the men's necks, and that poked out from their jacket sleeves. "You hired fucking Bratvas after all I've been through?"

"These are not the same guys from the past. And not all mobsters are alike, you know." I try to give her a reassuring smile as she shrinks back into the plane.

"Aren't they?" Yana sees the smile vanish from Morris' face and realizes he was not speaking of the Russians but referring to himself. She feels terrible. She has just inflicted a wound more painful than any that had left behind the scars on his body. She is about to apologize when the clamor of car horns rises from the dust cloud on the road outside the fence. Morris turns and watches as people, too excited to wait for the cars to reach the fence, jump out and rush the fence. The Russian security squad, the four at the plane, and the eight by the cars, swing their Uzis to the ready position.

"Hey, hold it! Don't Fire!" I call out. Yana translates into Russian even louder.

The crowd at the fence is calling out, "We love you, Yana!" In English and I suppose in Russian too.

"Is this your doing?" She emerges from the cabin radiant and with a revitalized spirit.

"Not I." I follow her down the stairs and to the fence. "I would guess your snake for a husband told people you were coming. I told you, he's not such a bad guy."

Yana doesn't hear or acknowledge what I said; she is busy signing pictures, scraps of papers, whatever her fans shove through the fence. She rattles off 'Thank You's' in both Russian and English. She writes 'YANA' on some guy's arm, he had pressed against the fence, one letter in each diamond.

She pulls up her sweater and rolls her stomach, making the snake dance in response to what some guy calls out. The crowd erupts. "I should go out there! I could sign more autographs."

"You are a huge star and they love you. But they would tear you to pieces trying to prove how much they do," I caution.

After she has been up and down the line for a third time, I say it's time to go. Two of the security men prepare to open the gates as we climb into the cars. When the motorcade reaches the gate, they swing it open, and begin firing wildly over the heads of the crowd. Everyone runs to the side of the road and crouches down for safety. The first three Lincolns roar through the gate and barrel up the road in a cloud of dust. The fourth Lincoln stops outside the gate, waits for the security guards to lock up, then proceeds slowly up the road, giving the motorcade time to distance themselves.

"What the fuck, Morris!" Yana yells, as she's gawking out the rear window, the growing dust cloud obscuring the scene. "They could have killed someone back there."

"Hardly," I soothe her, "they were firing blanks. We would never have gotten out of there any other way."

Yana goes silent, watching the fall colors whiz past her. There is a slight chill from the open windows, but she doesn't seem to care. Memories come rushing back as fast and jumbled as the kaleidoscope of greens, reds, oranges, and browns of the leaves. She can barely believe she is on the road to Koviskhan. The smell of the Black Sea fills her lungs. The squeals of her girlfriends on the beaches invade her mind. She smiles. A satisfied and content feeling warms her. It feels strange and foreign and at the same time familiar and inviting. She had travelled this route countless times with her family on holiday. Travelling back from the resorts on the Black Sea always made her melancholic, but not this time, she is filled with excitement. This feeling of anticipation surprise her; she has always dreaded the thought of returning home. In fact, in twenty years she never considered it. Now that it is happening, the growing exhilaration is almost too much to contain.

The dirt road had turned to highway long ago. We could be anywhere in the world, only the cryptic lettering on the billboards hints that we are in Russia, and the radiant reflection of Yana in the window. I rub her thigh, "You good?"

"I'm good," she answers in a daze. "There are airports much closer to my home town than where we landed. Why did you choose to land there?"

"I remembered how much you said you missed the drive to the sea, on the way back you can enjoy it one more time." *I also feel it would have put her in the proper frame of mind to face her father. He disowned her after she was kidnapped and raped by Ivan the Terrible, like it was her fault for not getting shot or killed or something. She was a sixteen-year-old girl and he ran her off with a shotgun, back to the men who raped and abused her. Maybe this drive is more for my benefit. If I'd stepped off the plane and saw her father standing there, I'd have shot him in the head. Fuck, I might still do it, BAM right between the eyes. Thanks for nothing, Dad.*

I see the tension grow in Yana as we turn off the highway heading for her family's farm. "Oh My!" she exclaims.

"What's the matter?" I ask as we drive down towards a huge white walled gated entrance.

"The farm, it has changed!"

There is a massive white brick house, three stories high, with more than a dozen windows looking at us. There is a second house, slightly smaller, but not by much, off to the left. Fields of wheat stretch out behind them like a golden sea. Waves of gold and brown ripple through the field, driven by the gentle afternoon breeze. The low guttural sounds of cows rise from the valley, although I can't see any.

"Not quite how you remembered the old place?"

"It's nothing like the place where I grew up," she says in shocked disbelief. "I have been sending money to my brother since I've been gone, they must have bought out three or four of the neighbors, and completely rebuilt the houses. This place is bigger than South Fork on Dallas."

Yana didn't just send money home. When she worked for Ivan, she sent a Russian year's pay every month, cashing in the gifts his rich client's gave her. When she went into the movie business, she sent ten times that amount. And in the last four years, working with Guy, it was ten times greater still. Even with all the government corruption and skimming off the top, her family is the wealthiest for miles around.

Her brothers not only took care of the farm, but made sure the money helped improved the community as well. They built roads, school, and processing plants; especially after Ivan the Terrible and his people were gone. Life is good here and they owe it all to the local girl turned movie star named Yana. Like Cher and Madonna, she goes by a single name, but everyone here knows exactly where she came from and how she got her start. But it wasn't until after Ivan's demise that any girl he promised to make a star actually turned out to be one. And he never made her that promise.

The motorcade pulls up in front of the house. The front passenger opens my door and I step out. Two other men, one from the lead car and one from the rear, get out and stand guard, Uzis carefully tucked beneath suit jackets. I extend my hand and help Yana exit the Lincoln.

The main doors fly open and a tidal wave of people flow down the stairs and engulf us. Everyone is speaking to Yana and each other all at once. I can't understand anything being said, but from the multitude of people, I gather the entire town has shown up to welcome her home. As we are swept inside by the receding wave I say, "See... you're a big star." I doubt she heard me.

Inside it is loud. Music blares from the stereo and people break out in off key renditions of their favorite songs. It is crowded. Wall to wall people jammed into the great room. Yana is whisked away from me and is surrounded by young girls, none older than thirteen. I fade back into a corner by a bowl of chips. Amazing, everyone eats some sort of chips at these affairs. The men hoist drinks in riotous cheers. I have the feeling this party was going on long before we got here.

I keep an eye on Yana as she drifts through the crowd like a cork in the sea. She is safe here. I also keep an eye on a black-haired stone-faced man who is intent on following my every move. He gave Yana a kiss when she arrived and embraced her tightly but separated quickly. Since then he's been studying me, and I him.

He is tall and strongly built, weathered and streaked with silver veins running through his head. Late forties or early fifties, too young to be her father, her father sits quietly in an armchair diagonal from my position, watching her and casting a steely eye stare at me.

I chose my position to be furthest away from the old man and keep him in my sights. If he causes one teardrop to fall... "So, you are the bodyguard," the weathered man finally speaks in excellent English, pulling my attention away from their father momentarily.

"Yes, and you are Peter, her oldest brother?"

"Pyotr," he corrects me with a thick Russian accent. "She is safe here. You need not worry about our father; he loves her more than any of us."

"I worry about everything, Pyotr." I match his pronunciation. "It's my job."

"You watch my little sister, but not with eyes that are bought," he snickers and hands me a shot. He taps my glass and says, "In America you call them puppy dog eyes, no? Welcome to the family, Killer." We drink.

He heads straight to Yana, sweeps his arm around her waist and clears a wide circle as they begin to waltz around the floor. Cheers and salutes ring out as another shot is shoved into my hand by a young lady. I drink and go back to studying the old man. There is much pride but no joy in his face. I know the look; Yana is back but his daughter has not returned home.

Pyotr bangs on a huge soup pot by a wall of glass doors. Another riotous roar erupts from the crowd. The four pairs of white curtained doors swing back, revealing the banquet hall. Chandeliers hang in rows between the columns of marbles, an immense table dominates the center of the room. Large circular tables flank either side of it. A white-haired lady in a well-worn smock stands at the far end of the room by the door to the kitchen. Even at such a distance, she is beaming beauty and refinement of a simple life.

Yana's knees weaken, as if Heaven's Gates opened before her and there appeared a Saint. No one moves. The room falls silent, as if spellbound. Her father walks proudly to her, takes her by the hand, and guides his little girl to her mother.

I am too far away to hear Yana's words to her mother, or the reply, not that I would have understood, but I do understand the outpouring of tears the reunion produces. There is not a dry eye in the place, not even mine. The young lady who handed me the shot earlier takes hold of my arm, "Come, we have a special place for you."

She leads me into the dining hall before all others. She seated me on the right of Yana's father, who is at the head of the table, between Yana and her mother. "By the way, I'm Valeria, Yana's younger sister, whose life you saved," she whispers in flawless English. The crowd flows in, boisterous but a bit more subdued.

Halfway through dinner Yana stands up, raises her glass, and makes a statement, ending with, "Killer with a heart."

The whole room rises and cheers. Even her father slowly comes to his feet and holds his glass towards me, then drinks. There is a broad smile smoothing the deep etched lines of time. The first time I see him smile.

"What was that all about?" I enquire when she sat down.

"I just introduced you as the hero of Koviskhan, the man who rid the world of Ivan the Terrible, the Killer with a heart." She laughs.

"You should not have done that," I admonish her. "Remember, I am supposed to be your personal bodyguard."

"You can guard my body all night, Morris MoJo Johnson." I realize all the vodka has gone to her head. She is giddy and says, "They all know who you are. Everyone has seen my movie."

"Red, White, and True Blue."

"No, Svetlana and my original version, 'Killer With A Heart'. Everyone has seen it," she boasts, "except father."

"Even he has agreed to watch it," shouts Pyotr from across the table, "Now that you are here, Morris."

I didn't fully realize it before, too focused on the old man, the people have been eyeing me with great curiosity and admiration all night. A number of times, girls shyly stole a peek, and men pounded my shoulders or grabbed me in an unexpected embrace. Now I understand the fascination of the little kids who tapped my hand and quickly ran away. I thought they had never seen a black man before, at least not in person. Now I know it is something altogether different.

Rows of chairs are set up in the great room after dinner. Yana's mother and father sit front row center, she sits next to them and I sit next to her. Pyotr and Valeria sit on the other side of their parents with her other brothers and sisters and their families. The rest of the town fills the room. The movie plays on the wall that doubles as a screen, with English subtitles.

I don't need the subtitles as the story unfolds the way I remember it. The girls kidnapped, their lives as strippers and hookers in the Dollhouse, her father's pain clearly displayed as he grips her hand, the young teenage gangster who arrives in Florida with a soul darker than his skin. Then the story takes an unexpected turn, Yana, Svetlana, and Morris, *yes they used my real name*, chase Ivan back to Russia after blowing up his den of inequities. In the woods of Koviskhan, Svetlana shoots Ivan in the leg. Yana manages to cut his face from ear to chin before he fights them both off. Standing over them preparing to deliver fatal shots, Ivan asks, "Where is your hero of the night now?"

I step into the clearing, and fire an arrow, pinning his hand and gun to a tree, an impossible feat. I say, "I am always here to protect them." As I help the women out of the blood soaked snow, gray wolves close in on Ivan and devour him.

"You know that is not how he died."

"Of course not," Yana whispers, "you poisoned him with the crystal somehow. This is a much better ending. The three wounds in Russian folklore symbolize you cannot run from justice, you cannot hide from justice, and you cannot fight justice."

"And being eaten by wolves is justice I suppose."

"Yes, around here it is," she hugs me, "I kind of like the idea of him being torn to pieces. Payback for the many lives he ripped apart."

"I like your version of the story better, but did you have to use my name?" I quip.

"Only your first name," she replies unapologetically. "Besides, how was I to know you would bring me here?"

"True, I didn't know I was bringing you here until yesterday either. But still, it is dangerous. Ivan had friends as well as enemies," I emphasize.

With the movie over, the party resumes, going well into the next day. We spend the next three days visiting places in the area and Yana does publicity shots whenever asked. Finally, we drive back down to the Black Sea and spend a couple of days relaxing at one of the seaside resorts. We get a message from Moscow; Guy has arranged a film festival at a theatre in her honor. We board our jet and take off for the Russian Capital.

Chapter 10

Their Own Worst Enemy

Lines are around the block for a theatre that holds 1500. Yana is at the hotel window watching the crowd, most of who will not get into the movie festival, milling around, hoping to catch a glimpse of her. She steps out onto the tenth floor balcony. A roar rises to her ears and a steady stream of flashes from the street below. She leans over the edge to see the marquee announcing her four most popular films.

A knock on the door draws her attention away from the crowd. A General and a dozen soldiers enter; he orders her bodyguards out. Yana closes the balcony door, shutting out the adoration from below. She takes a seat on the sofa. The solders line the room as the General takes a seat across the table from Morris. This is standard Soviet intimidation. She folds her legs and reclines on the sofa in her short white lace dress.

"Welcome home, Comrade Yana," the General greets her in English, "and welcome to our country, Mr. Morrison."

"Thank You," replies Yana.

"I'm honored to be here," I remark.

"Do not mind the soldiers," General Stanovich cajoles, "it is standard for a man in my position."

"And what is your position?" Yana asks politely.

"He's the Communications Minister," I tell her.

"That is accurate," agrees the General. "I am here to discuss satellite communications with your husband's representative."

"So this is not about me at all," pouts Yana.

"On the contrary, it is all about you. The theatre is already filled to capacity with all dignitaries," General Stanovich counters. "But before we go down to the show, or I agree to let your husband's company put satellites over the Soviet Union, I hear there is a special dance you do."

Yana rolls her eyes and sits up straight, more businesslike. "I don't know what you have heard..."

"Naturally, this will be a private show. My men will leave the room, Mr. Morrison will, of course, remain," the General explains.

"Let's lay our cards on the table," I say looking dead into the General's eyes. I pull my .45's out so fast no one has a chance to react then set them on the table facing the General. "I have enough bullets to kill everyone in this room for you just thinking what you have in mind. And are you really going to go back to the Kremlin and tell your bosses you blew a billion-dollar deal over a T&A show? Do they still send people to Siberia, General?"

"T&A?" questions the General.

"Tits and ass," Yana says disgusted. "And what would your wife say about all this?"

"My wife would understand," the General insists, "she was once a beauty queen herself. But that was so many years ago."

"Then do what men of your position do," I order, my tone is calm but my eyes burn their way through his head. He cannot look away. "Go home and fuck your daughter."

Moments pass without motion. There is no sound; not even breathing can be heard. He smiles, "Alas, my wife blessed me with only sons. I know all about you Mr. Johnson, and if your paperwork gets lost, you could end up in the gulag as a spy, a drug dealer, any number of charges, in Siberia."

"So now you would attempt to take us out of here in handcuffs, with that crowd out there."

"Not Comrade Yana," says General Stanovich smiling brazenly. "She is a national treasure. You on the other hand are nothing but a common criminal."

"Criminal... Yes... Common, not at all. If you had plans of doing anything more than escorting Ms. Yana to the movies, you should have brought more men. Because, instead of being the man who brought the World Cup to Soviet TV; you and your men will be the ones who were massacred at the Yana Film Festival."

"Boys... Boys... Boys," Yana is on her feet at the table. "General; you want to see me dance. My husband wants this deal with Russia. And Morris would rather not see all your men's lives wasted on such a trivial matter."

"And what would you like, Comrade Yana?"

"I'd like to see Baikonur Cosmodrome."

"Then perhaps we can all get what we want," the General carefully backs away from the table. He kisses Yana's hand and he orders his men out. He says he will wait for us in the lobby.

Before going into the theatre, Yana climbs onto the roof of the limo and sings a Russian lullaby to the crowd.

Morris' jet arrives in Kazakhstan at the Baikonur Cosmodrome two days before the launch and six months after Moscow. There is the usual fanfare Yana is now accustomed to awaiting them. She is photographed with cosmonauts, beside a Soyuz rocket, and alongside one of the satellites.

Behind the scenes, Morris works the technicalities of the deal to get the satellites into space. The minister of Defence and the minister of Science are not supportive of the idea of an American taking part in the Soviet Space program. Mistrust and pride being the main obstacles. General Gorgi, the defence minister insists, "We will have to take the satellites apart and rebuild them before any can be launched. We will need full specs and all codes controlling the satellites."

"You have twenty-four satellites, all are identical," I assure him. "Six will be in a geo-stationary orbit over the Soviet Union, and twelve will orbit every ninety minutes. That leaves you six to tinker with to your heart's content. But do not break them; they are your backups in case any fails."

"Not good enough," shouts General Gorgi.

"General, you do not honestly believe I will let you monkey around with the satellite I am going to put in orbit in two days?"

"How do I know that your so-called communication satellites are not just spy satellites for your American CIA?"

"Because we both know the CIA already has spy satellites over the Soviet Union. They don't need mine." I can only speculate that this is true, but all the others in the conference room nod in agreement. "With this communication program, there will be a satellite over Langley every five minutes. One of the twelve will be going out of range; one will be overhead, and another just coming into range. And since all the satellites are in continuous communication with each other, you will have twenty-four-hour real time ears on the CIA."

"We do not need the American spy help," objects General Abranoff, the science minister. "The Soviet Union was the first to put satellite in orbit."

"Sputnik was a great achievement," I agree, "but your more recent endeavors have not gone so well. One crashed in Canada, costing the Soviet Union six million in damages, and cleanup. Another in the Sea of Japan, I can't wait to see the bill on that one."

The room fills with bickering among the dozen generals and civilian ministers. There is a voice from the intercom on the table and all go quiet. The big dog had barked.

Finally, I say to the science minister, "you have done well in getting them up. It is keeping them there that seem to be your problem."

General Abranoff counters, "I studied your flight plan. We only need six to orbit at sixty-minute revolution to achieve the same coverage. We could keep twelve here to study."

"Yes. But that is why you are failing and your spacecraft keep falling out of the sky."

There is more arguing throughout the room before the voice from Moscow bellows. All sit frozen in their seats as he chastises them for five long minutes. Then it is settled, my plan will be implemented.

The day before the launch, a forklift driver watching Yana instead of where he is going runs into one of the six geo-stationary satellites. There is pandemonium in the facility. I tell General Gorgi, "You have your guinea pig. Bring out one of the backups."

He does not want to make the change, having done at least a cursory check of the six. However, even General Abranoff says not to send up a satellite that might already be damaged, especially if it is to remain over the Soviet Union.

Launch day, Yana sits front row center in the viewing stand surrounded by the ministers. I sit several rows behind her out of the camera's eye. I would have preferred to be in the control center safely underground, knowing the propensity for disaster, but the generals convinced Yana that 20 kilometers is more than a safe distance to watch the spectacle of a triple launch at dawn.

The three rockets stand in a line before us blowing a ceaseless white cloud behind them. They look small and benign from this vantage point. Having stood beneath one of the gigantic engines two days prior I am not fooled.

A fifty-piece military band plays the Russian National Anthem. The loudspeaker comes to life with what I assume is the countdown. Yana places her hands over her mouth to contain her excitement. The white cloud turns fire red and grows exponentially. A roar fills the air and the ground rumbles beneath us, threatening to open up and swallow the grand stand. Then one by one, the rockets start slowly upwards.

Within a minute, the whole skyline is ablaze, orange, yellow, red, and purple. Yana is on her feet, her scarf and dress fluttering wildly among the starched uniforms. The rockets are bright balls of white light atop of fluffy smoky pillars arching away from us. A few more minutes and they are new stars in the dawn sky.

Yana turns to me with a look of a child on Christmas morning discovering a new bike. She yells "Amazing!"

I scream back, "Yeah, fucking awesome!"

We are driven to the control center to monitor the mission. Each rocket carries six satellites in its nosecone. The satellites are the size of large refrigerators packed with electronic equipment, rocket propellant, and nuclear cores, and sit on two levels in the nosecones. When the nosecones reach the designated orbit, they will release a satellite. There is a team of controllers for each nosecone and a team for each satellite. A roar goes up each time a satellite exits the nosecone on the screens.

The six geo-stationary satellites are in place within two hours and tracking 100. The other dozen takes until late afternoon to get the last one in orbit. There are six on one track moving northeast to southwest, and crossing the equator somewhere over the Pacific. The other six are on an opposite track from southeast to northwest crossing the equator over the Atlantic.

There is a huge celebration when the last satellite leaves the nosecone and climbs into position. Then, very quickly, the control room emptied, leaving only a skeleton crew behind to monitor the satellites' condition. Another facility called in to report they were receiving data.

Yana and I follow the twelve generals down a hallway to the conference room where I had fought hard to make this happen. Yana and I sit at the middle of the huge glass covered elongated table. Fourteen buckets of ice and champagne wait for us, one beside each seat.

Yana's expression goes from giddiness to dread as she sees the lustful looks on the generals' faces. They pop champagne corks and say, "What a glorious day for Mother Russia," but their eyes and attention are trained on her.

She recalls every moment of being passed around like a trophy to some official. Every second, dancing and pleasuring some man in the Dollhouse. She recalls every man's touch that burned her skin and left its scar deep within her. It's reflected on her face for anyone who bothers to look.

"You don't have to do this, you know," I whisper in her ear. "I can kill every one of these old bastards in this room."

"You don't have a weapon."

"I am a weapon."

She runs her hand down my cheek, "sure you can kill these twelve, but what about the thousand armed troop outside this room. How are we going to get out of here alive?"

I kiss her cheek, "we won't. But you will leave with your dignity intact."

"My dignity," Yana laughs. "I surrendered that to you a long time ago when I let you talk me into getting this tattoo, along with my heart. Do you remember what I said to you the next morning?"

"Yeah, no good decisions are ever made after you open the tequila," I laugh.

"Well, yes, and, this tattoo is going to get me in a lot of trouble." She holds out her hand and I help her step onto her chair then up onto the table.

I stand up and glare at the men seated around the conference table with champagne glasses in their hands. "Gentlemen, a deal's a deal, I present YANA. And the dance that cost many men their lives."

Yana saunters to the middle of the table, her heels clicking seductively on the glass top. She isn't sure if Morris had given her an introduction or the generals a prophecy. One of the Generals grabs the intercom from the table, presses a button, and slow melodramatic music flows from its speaker. He looks at her for approval, she smiles, and he quickly put the box on the floor.

Yana begins to sway to the music that is slowly filling her head, and erasing any thoughts that lingers in her mind. She had once told Morris that when she danced she let the music take her out of the present space and transport her to a place where only it existed. No eyes, no hands, no men groping her... in that place, she didn't exist either, just the music.

Yana grabs the hem of her red and yellow silk Daylily dress and crumples the lower petal up to her crotch. The other two petals, pulled taunt across her breast, reveal her nipples reacting to the pulse of sound coursing through her body. She twirls on her heels down one side of the table and up the other. Her left hand hides her most precious treasure as her right sets free her fiery mane.

She spins like a top flashing reds, yellows, and gold throughout the room, her hair whipping wildly through the air. Without warning the two yellow petals drop to her waist. Her snake's sinister black and gold eyes transfix the men. She folds herself down in the center of the table like the fine silk she wears then laying on her back, it changes, becoming menacing as it coils around her, sending her body into convulsions before them.

Yana rolls and rises to her knees, the colorful silk now wrapped tightly around her ass and tucked between her legs. She slowly turns and dips, making the snake's head appear then disappear between her golden supple breasts. She rises on one leg, crossing the other over her thigh, locking the red heel behind her calf. She twists her body, slowly tightening the snake's coils around her torso.

Yana and the snake are one. The snake and music are one. A horn blares and it strikes with blinding speed as she spins, and it's fangs shower the men with sweaty venom. The dress whips around on her heel, driving all the men back in their chairs, all except Morris. His eyes look through her, lock onto the men, his intensity matching hers. And throughout the performance, her eyes had been locked on his. As she spun, twirled, and slithered on the smooth glass she was intently aware of his presence. She danced for him.

Her dress leaves her foot and sails into his lap. The generals roar with delight. He doesn't flinch. Not a muscle in his body twitches. He is a rattler, silent and coiled, prepared to strike. She had seen his eyes darken as she danced, and in her trance-like state, she also saw the true nature of the man. He shone like an angel sent from Heaven to watch over her. A demon rose from Hell to kill the evil that surrounded her. A warrior, born of impenetrable armor, invincible and unfaltering formed to guard her. And she danced to keep this weapon from detonating. For surely, if she wished it; if she commanded it; he would destroy the whole place.

"Comrade Morris, she is worth betraying your country, no?" asks General Stanovich, sitting on Morris' left.

"Watch the show while you still have eyes to enjoy it." The words register not in Stanovich's ears but in his heart, like venom spreading through his skeletal frame, drying his blood and darkening his vision.

Yana finally comes to rest on her stomach, her legs wrapped around themselves and folded up to her ass. She covers her breasts with one arm and reaches with the other hand out to Morris. She pants slow and heavy, her body glistens. Morris holds out her dress and takes her hand. As she rises, the red and yellow Daylily drapes her like a falling curtain. He stands and assists her off the table. He is the only man who can stand at that moment. The others are paralyzed by her rattler's venom.

Yana sits holding Morris' arm to the chair and drinking champagne from the bottle. The Generals slowly come out of their trance and laud over her in Russian. Some kiss her hand, holding on to it for a moment too long. Most are too embarrassed to stand.

"This was worth a billion dollars, right?" She whispers in my ear.

"More, much, much more," I assure her. "Gentlemen, we thank you for your business, your champagne, and your overwhelming hospitality. I must get Yana to her plane now."

They protest like schoolboys at bedtime, but finally, a military motorcade is arranged and we are at our jet on the other side of the Cosmodrome.

Once in the air, Yana asks, "are we finally going to Naxos? I would like to enjoy my honeymoon, even if my husband will not be there."

"Yes, of course, just as soon as we make a stop in Cairo."

"Morris," she pouts.

"Come on, Honey," I plead, "We'll see a camel race or two, some other old crumbly ruins, and be on our way. And I swear, no more dancing."

"Oh sure, like that matters now, the entire British navy has already seen me, and a couple of those Generals probably died from a heart attack by now." Yana Jokes.

The jet lands at Cairo International Airport and they pass through customs without any trouble. A few Egyptians recognize the movie star and she draws a small crowd, but mainly, it's younger boys hustling for a buck. Morris draws more attention being a black American.

The hotel was once an 18th century palace. Two massive towers rise on either side of the original wing and they occupy the top floor. The towers shade the courtyard side and the top of the royal seal of the French monarchy forms the windows on the front façade. At the Nile Palace Hotel, Yana receives the star treatment as an entire floor has been reserved by Morris. She comes to the conclusion that whatever Morris' plans are in Cairo, her husband has not been informed of it. Only one elevator goes to the ninth floor, beyond two guard stations on the mezzanine. The pair remain secluded, moving from room to room, not even room service sees them when they are called to clean or deliver food at all hours of the day and night.

They spend most of their time in the rooms overlooking the palm tree lined courtyard and pool. Occasionally, one or both appear on a balcony naked, to enjoy the cool night breeze and watch as the pool lights turn the water from emerald to sapphire to ruby and back again. The courtyard is a beautiful mosaic of white and clay bricks that meander through the lush gardens around centuries old fountains and modern restaurants. Yana relaxes and enjoys the calm after the hectic months in Russia. Even the morning calls to prayer from the dozens of minarets in view from their windows have a strange soothing effect. She relishes hours in bed, seeing a tender gentle side of him that she knew existed but had never experienced. He tells her the seclusion is for her security, but she knows he wants her all to himself. He wants to stop the world for her, and does.

Their second week is full of sightseeing. They visit the Citadel, an old fort turned into a mosque. They marvel at the exquisite artwork on the columns, the great chandelier, and stained glass ringing the vaulted ceilings. They get a private viewing of the tomb of Mohammed Ali. Yana's stardom has caught up with her as the Egyptians are in love with everything Russian, due to their financing the Aswan Damn. Her coming out of America, from Hollywood, doubles her popularity.

They spend the late afternoon and early evening on the Giza plateau, home of the Sphinx and the three Pyramids. They enjoy a camel ride around the plateau and pictures on and in the Pyramids. And as the sun sets behind the Pyramids, the camel jockeys put on a special race for their star guest and her Nubian guardian.

The following day, they leave before dawn, fly to Luxor, and their guide drives them from the small airport to the Valley of the Kings. According to him, they are trying to beat the desert sun. According to Morris, they fail. They crawl down the narrow tunnel carved in the rock and into the colorfully decorated tombs. Inside, mercifully, they escape the blistering heat of the morning; the same heat that has preserved the reds, greens, yellows, and oranges of the hieroglyphics that adorn every inch of the tomb from the entrance to the deepest walls. Yana is dressed like a 1940's archaeologist in a white blouse, khakis, and a pith helmet. Morris wears his usual blue jeans and tee shirt.

They wait out the afternoon's 100 plus temperatures in what passes for a gift shop, drinking slightly cool Cokes. Yana doles out hundreds in Egyptian pounds to the young boys selling souvenirs, obviously sent by the older men. It is late afternoon when they move on to the Valley of the Queens a couple of miles away, and their tombs. Like the kings' tombs, every inch is covered with hieroglyphics detailing the aspects of their lives. The pictures came alive in vibrant colors of Horus in his many forms.

They visit the Temple of Karnack, walking through the promenade of rams into the Temple of Amon. They wander the ruins, the silence uncanny. No one speaks, perhaps for fear of disturbing the dead, or angering the gods.

They return to the hotel for a late supper and drinks by the pool. A few autograph seekers approach shyly, probably hotel workers Morris surmised. Some guests, American and Russian, recognize Yana and feel compelled to tell her how much they love her movies.

By their third trip, this time to the Abu Simbel Temples, Yana feels like a regular tourist. They tour the massive shrines cut into the cliff, hear the history of Ramesses II who had them built to intimidate the kingdom of Sudan. How it had to be cut up and moved to a higher elevation after the building of the dam. After a short time, it was back to the plane and to their hotel in Cairo.

The next day is different, Morris orders breakfast from room service then he and Yana slip out of the hotel unnoticed. They sit in a small shop a few blocks from the hotel drinking freshly squeezed guava juice. Yana is dressed in another white explorer's outfit and wearing an assortment of bangles, that Morris bought from a bazaar the night before.

Yana senses that his mood has changed. "Are we done with visiting tombs and temples?"

"I'm sure there are plenty more to see, but not today."

"So what are we doing today?"

Before I can answer, two men enter the shop. They are dressed in jeans and tees, but have the look and walk of soldiers.

"Come with us." The taller of the two Egyptians commands.

"Come, Honey, our ride is here," I take Yana's hand and stand up.

"No. Not her," objects the other Egyptian soldier, "we have orders to bring just you."

"She goes, or neither of us goes," I say.

"It's okay," Yana quickly offers, "you boys go have fun. I think I will spend some time at the pool."

"Sorry, Dear," I say to her then turn my attention back to the soldiers, "she goes where I go, are we clear?"

"The General is not going to like this," the tall Egyptian informs me.

The word 'General' causes Yana to roll her eyes and she gives me a look of disgust. I smile sheepishly at her and we follow the two men to a waiting car. We climb in the back. The second Egyptian in the front passenger seat turns to us, "I must search you both."

"Turn around and tell your asshole partner to drive before I change my mind," I direct him.

The first Egyptian jerks the car into gear, toots the horn and cuts into the heavy morning traffic. We've been here ten days so we are already accustomed to the symphonies of car horns playing in the streets. He darts in and out of traffic, cuts across lanes to make a right turn or left. I don't know where he is taking us, but I can tell it is not a direct route, having made three lefts in a row. The little car criss-crosses thoroughfares, flowing wildly from wide to narrow, and small to large, twisting through the city like the Nile. I'm guessing he is making sure we are not followed. People flow, pool, and churn in endless motion to the chaotic beeps of car horns and dialects berating the traffic and the other drivers.

We end up at a restaurant on a bluff across town. A great veil hangs low over the city, rising from the tombs in the City of the Dead. The spirits of eons shroud the land and cover her in history. It is an old building, brick and stone form an oddly shaped archway to the kitchen. We go through the kitchen, through colorful beaded curtains, and into a back storage room. There sits General Ahmed Amoul. Alone.

He immediately rips into the two soldiers in Arabic. They stand stoic at the archway. After the General brush back his thick black hair, the first Egyptian says, for our benefit, "He has been very uncooperative."

General Amoul rises to his feet and extends a hand to Yana. She takes it and he graciously leads her to his seat at the table. He's not a very big man, maybe five-seven at best, and less than 180 pounds. He does however present a much bigger image of himself. His body is straight and sharply defined. His features are keenly placed, eyes and nose just right, a moustache neatly trimmed above his lips, and a rugged clean-shaven face that demands respect. He has a look that tells of a direct line to the Pharaohs of antiquity.

Yana is beaming, radiantly looking up at him.

"Forgive my outburst," he apologizes to her. "But the desert is no place for such a fine lady."

"We've been in the desert for three days, I think we will manage one more, General." I'm starting to think bringing Yana may have been a mistake. Then I hear the hum of a plane, followed by the screams of startled customers. The little plane lands on the table next to her.

The General blurts out more Arabic.

The tall Egyptian responds, "They were very uncooperative."

"So, Mr. Morrison, you have a radio transponder, not very impressive," General Amoul says, taking a seat next to Yana.

I take Yana's hand and hold up her arm with the bangles. "Not a radio, a laser, invisible to the eye. Low power but detectable from space."

"From space?" Both General Amoul and Yana ask simultaneously. Yana can only guess at the implications my statement carries.

"Yes, a satellite tracked our every move, picking up the laser reflection from any shiny object, and when we were stationary, launched the plane from our hotel on a direct course here."

"That is impressive," admits General Amoul.

Yana eyes me suspiciously. And suddenly, she realizes why her dance was worth a billion dollars. She is no stranger to the high price of warfare, or its technology, and she had been with enough power hungry men who tried to impress her with details of their dealings. She just never thought Morris to be one of those types.

"It's one thing to track a signal, of any sort, back to its originator. But how well does your satellite work when it's tracking a foreign target?"

"That is what we are here to find out, isn't it, General?" I respond.

The General politely kisses Yana's hand. "As this little demonstration is over, my man will drop you at your hotel, Madame."

"As I told your men, she goes where I go," I reiterate.

"Surely, you don't want to take her so far into the desert," objects the General.

"We have more sights to see," I insist.

The General's face sours and he visibly disagrees with my decision. He isn't worried about her health or safety, he is concerned with his security; the fewer people involved in our actions today, the better.

But from the look on my face he knows I don't trust him, his men, or this deal. It is nothing personal, just the nature of being an arms dealer. I will not allow Yana to become a bargaining chip in this game should people loyalties shift. And the best way to do that is to keep her by my side.

Yana points to Abu Simbel as the helicopter continues south. The General gladly provides narration to this unique sightseeing tour. At his command, we pass low and close over the temples and monuments in the military helicopter. Occasionally, Gen. Amoul circles his hand above his head and the pilot obeys, flying around a selected site. This is better than the last three days of sightseeing, because although she doesn't see the sites close up, she sees them in the comfort of an air-conditioned ride.

Half an hour after passing Abu Simbel the helicopter sets down on the scorching desert. Once the rotors stop turning, they are once more in dead silence. Even the wind as slight as it is passes by in eerie quietness. There are no trees for it to rustle, the sand is hard and baked; it will take a lot more force than this wind can muster to move it. There are no birds, or animals of any kind to voice protest to the unforgiving heat and relentless sun.

Two minutes outside the helicopter and Yana appears faint. Gen. Amoul hands her a bottle of water and turns to Morris, "This is why I suggested leaving her at the hotel."

"We won't be here long," I say and point to a sand cloud approaching from the north.

It takes some time before the sound of the approaching vehicle reaches us, even longer for the jeep to pull up alongside the helicopter. Two men get out and take two large long cases from the jeep. In each case is a long tube with a handle and a trigger. The men shoulder the weapons.

Yana is puzzled, she looks around but sees no targets.

I ask the General, "How much time?"

"Five minutes," barks Gen. Amoul, all of his charm and culture evaporating in the desert wind. "They are fifty miles northeast. They will be flying five miles from the Sudan boarder."

The two men turn in the direction of the approaching jets.

Yana shields her eyes but still can't see anything.

The two men flip the scope to the side and make adjustments to filters and resolution. "I have one," says one of them. His American accent surprises Yana.

"Mark it," I order.

"Marked!"

"Josef, allow for satellite targeting."

"Done," the second man replies.

"We are too far out for these Stinger missiles to be effective, Mr. Morrison," the General suggests.

"That would be true if the missiles were chasing the targets," I agree. "But the modifications I made allow the missiles to take an intercepting course. The satellite will fire the missiles when the targets are within striking distance."

The two rocket launchers pop out a cloud of white smoke as if commanded by Morris' statement. The rockets ignite fifteen feet in the air and streak away from the group. The rockets never gain altitude as they race across the desert far too fast for their eyes to follow. A glint of metal appears high in the sky and in front of the group. The helicopter's radio comes alive with frantic voices. Two more quick flashes emerge and streak upwards. More commands from harried voices. A puff of black smoke materializes and then another. The radio goes silent as a low rumble echoes across the desert floor.

"My God! Did you just shoot down two Sudanese jets, Morris?" Yana cries out in horror.

"Egyptians," states Gen. Amoul. Seeing the shock on Yana's face, then he adds, "training exercises. They knew to eject."

Yana watches the trails of black smoke stretching to the ground. "Shouldn't there be parachutes?"

"Too far away to see them," I tell her. "Well, General, are you impressed?"

"Very. Very impressive indeed." The General is smiling and shaking my guys' hands.

Yana is about to speak and I shoot her a sharp look. I take her hand. "Then you know what to do next General Amoul."

"Yes, of course. I will fly you back to Cairo now."

"Thanks, but I have made other arrangements," I tell him, "other sites to see. Oh, General, some tombs should never be opened, you understand me."

"Yes, of course. I would not spend much time on the sites around here. There will be patrols," warns the General.

The jeep takes Yana and Morris to the Nile. They make one stop, to drop the two rocket launchers down a dry well in an abandoned town, if you can call a handful of adobe huts alongside a road a town. Yana hasn't spoken a word since Morris silenced her. She is mad and Morris knows the look well. She won't be able to contain herself much longer.

They board a felucca at the river. The helmsman resembles the long banana shaped boat. He is lanky, bony arms and legs, with muscles like steel strands running their length, deep brown skin, old and dry just as the boat he sails. He shows them below deck, moves a bale of cotton and opens a small hatch in the floor, "you go there if trouble comes."

He returns topside and one push on the ten-foot pole puts the cotton-laden boat in the river. Yana watches him dance about in his dingy galabia, his bare feet finding their place and anchoring him as the great triangular sail fills, working the lines and tiller with precision and finesse.

It is much cooler on the water in the shade of the tiny cabin. Several mats on the wooden bench are probably this man's bed, Yana thinks, this boat his only possession. He will lose it all if they are caught on board. The tiny transistor radio, strapped to the ceiling of the cabin, blares an alarming tirade. The announcer is probably warning citizens to be on the lookout for terrorists, traitors, and murders.

Where do monsters come from? What makes a man a monster? These are the questions plaguing Yana's mind as she seeks refuge from the day. *Every man is born with light and darkness in his eyes. They are in equal proportions; he has the propensity to do great things, building; healing; teaching, or to cause suffering; decadence; abomination. The battle of good and evil, as is known, rages in every man, lifelong. However, in some men only the darkness shines from their eyes. Is Morris such a man?*

She can no longer contain her anger, and explodes, "How could you make me a party to such a crime? And don't hand me that bullshit they parachuted safely. That was no training exercise. Those pilots had no idea what was happening. They had no chance to escape. This whole honeymoon has been for what, to make me part of your world of death? Why Morris? I thought you loved me. Why?"

"Because I DO love you. You are not part of this. We went to Russia to see your family and I was not necessarily looking for them to launch the satellites. I could have gotten the Iranians or Pakistanis to do it just as easily. And I didn't bring you along to be a witness or an accomplice. I brought you with me to keep you safe. If you are by my side, I can protect you."

Tears stream down her face, anger tearing her apart. She has loved him for too long without really knowing him. Who is he? What is he? How will she ever know? "Protect me from what? Protect me from whom? The Egyptians... The Russians..."

"Yes," I cross the tiny cabin, wrap my arms around her shoulders, and lock her arms to her sides. "I need to protect you from everyone. In my world, my friends and my enemies are one and the same. These scars I got came from my so-called partners. I'm sorry if I brought you into something you aren't ready for, but the man I was ten years ago, and the man I am today haven't changed. If you want out, if you can't be part of my world, just say so... But do it now, before you get in any deeper."

"Can we PLEASE, just go to Greece and enjoy the sunshine and the beach?"

We are lying on the tarp-covered bales of cotton when we approach Luxor. Little settlements dot the riverbank. Men watch over their livestock, water buffaloes, cows, goats as they drink from the river. Their children, no more than a yard or two away, never deeper than their ankles in the water, splash and scream as children do. Every now and again, we see a man higher on the embankment with a rifle in his arms, ever vigilant. One waves and shouts to the helmsman. He waves and shouts back. It is mid-afternoon.

"Why do they have guns?" asks Yana.

"Crocodiles," replies the helmsman.

Yana pulls her hand out of the water instantly.

"You be pleased to take the lady below," advises the helmsman. "Remember the hatch if you be needing to."

"Crocodiles?" questions Yana, looking at how low the boat keels in the water, the gunnels only a few inches above the surface.

"Patrol boats ahead," warns the helmsman.

I hold Yana's head down as I lead her into the cabin and then below deck. We squeeze past the bales of cotton to the bow, I remove the hatch, and tie a line to one of the sacks of cotton in the middle of the stack.

Yana looks into the black hole. "That is pretty small and wet," she complains.

"You'd be surprised how much can fit into a little wet hole." I joke, trying to erase the fear on her face.

Soon, her fears turn into reality. The boat is bumped and halted. I know two patrol boats have pulled alongside. I lay her in the secret compartment, her head on my balled up shirt for comfort. I climb in on top of her, the hatch resting on my back. I tug the line sharply and toss it out the hole. Sacks of cotton quickly add their weight to my back. I hear voices and boots above my head and gently lower myself down on Yana. There is a small wooden slide above my head and I ease it into place. We lie between two ribs of the boat, 18 inches apart. Yana fits nicely. I have a little less wiggle room.

"You're right, it is pretty small in here," I whisper in her ear. She grunts and shifts, trying to get comfortable. I listen to the muffled voices and count the number of boots onboard. Six men have boarded.

"What's that!" Yana exclaims, trying to keep her voice down.

"What's what?"

"That," she says a little louder, lifts her leg quickly and presses it into my hard-on. "You've got to be kidding me!"

I start biting off the buttons of her blouse and spit them to the side. "Well, if we are gonna die, I want to go out with a bang."

"Die!?"

I lock my lips to her and quell whatever was coming next. "Not if we do this quietly."

I pull her blouse and the rest of her buttons pop off and bounce around in the pitch-blackness. My hands go to slide off her pants and mine at the same time. We are wet and slimy.

"Oh, Morris."

"I know, Baby."

"No. It is nasty in here," she objects.

I kiss her and slide into her, also hearing the voices clearer now. She moans. I push harder, but quietly, burying myself deep in her. There isn't much room to move. But I don't need much. I thrust my pelvis downward and relax. Then thrust downward again, each time sucking her sighs into my mouth. I feel her body relax and give into my wanton power. She accepts each thrust with a soft cry of pleasure. Her voice dies on my lips as her hands squeeze and release my ass in perfect rhythm with me. Her body is soft and malleable in my arms, unconscious to the danger just above our heads. I continue pumping her, listening for the voices to subside, the boots to take their leave, the boat to heave and tilt into the wind again. Then I make use of what little room I have to fuck Yana as hard as I can.

It's hard to tell how much time passes while in the secret compartment but there is enough for two sex sessions. The second takes considerably longer than the first to complete, there is shuffling overhead, followed by a hard thumping on the hatch. I slide the latch back and lift the hatch a bit. The helmsman holds a lamp in one hand and a sack in the other.

"Dry clothes," he says with a big toothy smile. There are a few gaps in his smile. He knows we'd need dry clothes, just never imagined we'd be wearing none at all. After the patrol left, I no longer felt the need to shield Yana with my body and we had shift to a more comfortable side position. It allowed more freedom of movement and unfortunately a better view when the hatch opened.

At nightfall, all the feluccas are docked along the shore. The helmsman anchors alongside two old derelicts for the night, hangs a sail from each boom, and makes a shower stall for Yana and I. I pour fresh water over her head and watch the streams cascade from her peaks into her valleys.

The helmsman gifts Yana one of his daughter's galabias; a fine specimen in black and gold silk with beads and silver coins. We lay on the bales under the star-filled Egyptian sky. I stack the bales around us, concealing the bed from all eyes, except God's.

The helmsman retires to his cabin on hard wood and mats and I convince Yana, that as good as she looks in the galabia, she will look better out of it.

Yana makes the most of the beaches in Naxos, as we spend the summer on the white sands. In the first few weeks, we were an attraction, naturally... the movie star and her mysterious companion. But as the weeks turn to months, we simply become the Americans in the villa by the sea, and after six months, we have been assimilated by the town. We spend the days on the Mediterranean in our twenty-three foot Coronado yacht. While most of the boats are out fishing, we spend our time drinking wine and wreaking havoc with our lack of nautical skills.

However, one skill I have mastered is running the Sea Wolf aground in the soft sand in front of the villa. With most of the bow on the beach and a mooring chain to make sure it stays there, I slowly lower the main sail and lap it over the boom. I leave the top quarter heaved, the gray wolf's head with its blazing red eyes watching over us.

Summer has passed, fall is nearly over too, and the heat of the Mediterranean has cooled. We enjoy warm days and cool evenings. Greece is good for Yana, she is happy, she is content. If she has any worries left, they do not show. But that was until a night broadcast shows a video of the Afghanistan war. It shows a Mujahideen fighter firing a stinger missile. The missile snakes along the rocky mountain terrain then takes a sharp steep climb up to a Russian Mig. The fireball is greeted with jubilant cheers from the freedom fighters.

The newscaster says, "It is the third Russian jet downed in as many weeks. The Afghanis are gaining momentum, thanks to the new breed of American made deadly stinger missiles."

"Isn't that the missile you sold to the Egyptians?" Yana shrieks.

"Most likely," I answer matter-of-fact.

"Did you know the Egyptians were going to give them to the Mujahideen? Did you know when you went to Russia, that you were making them a party to killing Russians."

"I did. They didn't."

Yana studies Morris. A cold lifeless shroud seems to obscure him. He has returned to the man she knew in Miami. The transformation is instantaneous. He is less than human once again.

"I make weapons. I sell weapons. I don't concern myself with who buys them or who uses them. Today, it's the Afghanis, tomorrow the Iraqis, the day after that the

Nigerians, and so on. The nature of women is to bring life into this world. The business of men is to take it out. It is just that simple."

"Have you no heart, no morals?" laments Yana. "How many people must die before you've had your fill? Is Guy part of all of this? Was this part of your deal?"

"Your husband's business is movies and television, that's it. You can go back to him knowing he is not the man I am. But before you go, you should realize that I didn't put those men in their jets, and they in turn were dropping bombs on the Mujahideen. Not that it matters to me. You think I'm killing Russians. No, my dear, I'm saving Russians. This war will go on, no matter how many people die. People are easily replaced. It is the war machines that must be destroyed."

I can see I am not getting through to her. She doesn't understand what war is, not like I do. She knows of soldiers and generals, but I was born into war, I know the logic, what drives it, what gives it life.

"First, kings threw thousands at each other and wars lasted years, decades. Then, they got better machines and more lives were lost. Then they dropped hundreds of bombs to destroy the machines and those that made them. Whole cities, countries were destroyed. And finally, they thought they built the ultimate weapon, one bomb that could annihilate their enemy. However, their enemy could also extinguish them. What is needed is a weapon that is guaranteed to kill the machine every time. You see, it is much harder to replace the machine than the man. Once the Russians realize their war machines are useless, they will pull out. Countless Russians lives will be saved."

"You're no hero, Morris Johnson," says Yana demoralized.

"I never claimed to be one."

Chapter 11

Out of Darkness

Yana changed after hearing of the downed Migs. Her sleep became fitful, she retracted from Morris' embrace slightly, but noticeably. She is in a living nightmare. Guilt eats at her soul for what she believes her part in this business of death. Her radiance has dimmed and Morris knows there is nothing he can do to change what she is going through.

A few weeks pass and he is watching the news when a report of an explosion in an Egyptian's warehouse airs. The report says the warehouse stored diesel fuel, but he knows it did not, Gen. Amoul tried to peek into Pandora's Box. While he is sure the General is safe, someone else under his command paid for his curiosity. Though he isn't sure why the General would disregard his warning, it is disturbing that he has.

The next afternoon, Yana is watching the news when the reporter announces, "Movie mogul, Guy Gordon, died quietly in his sleep at his Bel Air mansion last night. His wife, movie star Yana Kerchovich, could not be reached for comment."

Morris hears her scream. He reaches the lounge in time to see the last of the report on Guy. "I will have the plane ready."

"Why? This whole thing has been a scam from the start anyway. I haven't seen him, or spoken a word to him since the day we were married. Am I now to pretend to play the grieving widow?"

"I'll take care of the arrangements and ready the jet. We will leave within the hour. And I am sorry."

The trip back is solemn. Yana and Morris barely speak. The plane stops in the Cayman Islands to refuel and Morris gets off. Two men take his place, bodyguards. He doesn't elaborate why he thinks she might need them, just that they will be with her night and day. As the plane taxis down the runway, Yana can't help but wonder if Morris will be gone from her life for another ten years. Tears stream down her face.

Hours later, she lands at LAX. Black dress and veiled, she passes through the gauntlet of cameras and reporters, head down, and makes no statement as she climbs into the back of a waiting limo with her two bodyguards. Two other SUVs form a motorcade as they leave the airport. A dozen men in black suits line and block the exit, keeping the reporters from following her. She is driven to the mansion.

The two bodyguards, whom she calls Thug 1 and Thug 2, tell her their names are Arthur Penn and Eli Boston, but apart from that bit of information, they have little else to say. They look more like ex-wrestlers than bodyguards, both six-two black men with brands on their necks and biceps. Yana has seen those types of marks on college football players and other professional athletes, but she knows these two never went to college or played sports.

The lead SUV pulls over at the bottom of the hill leading up to the mansion. The second, continues further and stops somewhere above them. Arthur and Eli setup on the first floor, like they are right at home. The one thing they do confide in her before she goes to bed is that they have known Morris for twenty-five years and are as loyal as hound dogs. Eli, also known as Bone Crusher, says she will be safe, but from what or whom he fails to mention. Yana goes to sleep thinking that Guy did not die quietly in his sleep.

Morris waits on the beach outside Vicky and Derrick's house until dawn. Vicky showered for hours to wash away his blood, but what she can't wash away are the memories, or the pain. Two men entered the house after she left. She looks down and away as she passes them. She doesn't want to know them, they are the cleanup team, and are going to erase any and every trace of her two-year marriage to Derrick, they are going to make sure he will not be found. She gets into the jeep with Morris and drives out of this life and into something completely different, again.

As they fly to New York two days later, she attempts to ask how long had he known. *Did he leave me in the hands of someone who wanted me dead? Or did he come back as soon as he found out?* She wants to ask but is afraid of the answers. She is also afraid of the life he may be into now. Morris looks different, and it isn't from the news that Maria has been kidnapped. He looked that way the night he showed up in her bedroom.

Morris had always kept things to himself and away from her. Even as kids he rarely told her what he was up to. It was always a half answer with him. When she helped him fake his death, he only told her they were going to the Caribbean. She had assumed it was to continue in the drug trafficking business. The business she thought made it necessary for him to fake his death in the first place. But his life, below the surface, is much more complex than cocaine and the mafia. And now, so is hers.

One thing does simplify it for her, once they leave the Caribbean she will again do whatever he wants, and kill without question. Her life is over anyway. She tries to push those nagging questions away and just do what he tells her. His secrets are too much for her to comprehend, and they bring so much pain. She doesn't want to deal with his pain anymore. She can't live with it, or without him.

I am in the basement of the Sons of Italy having lunch. Nicky comes down, "We have a problem. I got a call from Chicago… They are sending some guys out to talk."

"So, what's the problem?"

"They are probably going to want to know where their guys are," Nicky laughs. "You know, those boys you had Vicky blow the brains out of their heads."

"To tell you the truth," I sip the wine, "this stuff sucks. For an Italian you have a horrible taste in wine. Anyway, they are probably coming here for me. I'm sure they are going to try and bug the place."

"Never gonna happen." Nicky takes a drink from the bottle. "This is shit! I'll get you a better bottle. But seriously, I sweep this place three times a day, they'll never bug me."

"Oh… but you are going to let them bug the place this time," I tell him.

"Why?"

"Because we need to know who they are talking to and what they know," I pour a glass from the new bottle Nicky hands me. "The best way to find that out is to let them think they are playing you, when you are actually dealing the cards from the bottom of the deck. How do you think I got the list of agents I gave you? They bugged me. I bugged them..." I take a sip. "This is better."

David Sartori walks into the Sons of Italy and slicks back his black greased hair. His five-foot-four body is top heavy from lifting weights most of his days. He looks around and then motions for another man to come in. Franco Russo is a foot taller and thin, he surveys the club then points to the pool table.

David walks over to the bar, "Hey Doll Baby, give me two whiskeys straight, two bottle beers, and change for the table. Pronto."

Nicky and Morris watch through the priest holes in his office. The two-way glass is hidden under arches of wall-length murals of the Coliseum. There are also black cloth panels that allow them to hear what is said in the bar. Morris whispers, "Here we go. Nice way to disguise your two-way mirror, but why not go with the simple glass?"

"I used to have a plain one, but all these guido bastards spent their time admiring their fucking selves. I could never see anything, the stupid pricks."

"I bet you a C note the big boy just bugged the pool table."

"The quarters, right?" Nicky wagers.

"That's my guess. Do you recognize him?"

"I wouldn't know if I pissed on him before."

"A simple, 'no, I don't', would have sufficed," I joke.

David Sartori leans his back against the bar and grabs Rosalina's arm firmly. "I'm looking for a John Morrison. You know him, Honey?"

Rosalina struggles a little to free herself. "Never heard of him. You a cop?"

"No. No. Friends of his from out of town. He said we should look him up here. Said he hangs out with the fellas here most nights, a medium size nigger," David smiles and holds his hand above his head to give her a general idea of what he is talking about.

"I don't know who you are talking about," Rosalina starts to walk away.

David grabs her wrist again and gives it a painful twist, "How about your husband, Nicky Nails? I'm sure he's around."

Nicky bursts out of his office through the Coliseum gates. "Take your hands off her or lose the arm faccia a cazzo!"

Franco slides his hand into his leather.

David holds up a hand to him, without looking back. "There he is! The Little Godfather. Greetings from Benny. Where are the boys, Nicky?"

"They are straightening out some business down south. Teaching one of my boys the ropes." Nicky looks at Rosalina's wrist. It's red. He backhands David across the face, sending him sliding down the bar.

Franco draws his gun.

Nicky pulls his just as fast and aims it at David's head. "Who the FUCK ARE YOU to come into my place and disrespect my wife?"

"Easy, Franco," David smiles, "Brunello said you were a tough son of a bitch. I was just seeing if you stood up to your rep. I'm here to deliver a message, nothing more."

Morris has seen enough. He takes Vicky out the back door and into the alley.

Vicky walks down the block and sits on the hood of an idling black caddy with four men inside.

The driver taps the horn. "Park your black ass somewhere else, bitch!"

"That's no way to speak to a lady," Vicky replies sweetly. She slides off the hood and walks around the car, her fingers gently running along the body. She goes past the passengers and around the back until she gets to the driver.

He rolls down the window.

"You wouldn't want a girl with a cold bottom sitting in your lap, would you? Nicky sent me to see if you boys were comfortable while your guys are inside talking business. It could be a very cold night."

"That cheap wop sends one girl for four guys," laughs the man riding shotgun. "Go about your business, Sister. We are just fine."

"Really, because I can handle all four of you. I hear you guys from Chicago have very... small... dicks."

The man behind the driver laughs and rolls down the window. "Come here, Baby. Let me show you what Detroit steel feels like."

"I've seen bigger, Cowboy."

"Why don't you grab hold of my bull, it will get bigger. More than enough to fill your smart-ass mouth."

"Hey, close the fucking window, asshole," yells the man riding shotgun, "Bitch, get the fuck out of here."

"What is that fucking smell?" asks the driver.

Morris rolls from under the back of the car, and crawls beneath the car behind it.

Vicky says, "My perfume. Like it? I call it Brimstone and Death."

She takes a step back and throws a lighter into the car. A blue blaze shoots from the air vents and envelop the interior. The men quickly open the doors but a bigger fire rushes in. Vicky keeps retreating from the growing sea of flames pouring out of the gas canister under the car.

"You know I was sent to speak to your friend, the nigg... the, what do you call them here... Moolies?" David wipes the blood from his mouth on the back of his hand. "I hear you guys are all jumping in bed with whatever. I mean, they call this place the Melting Pot, right? That's cool and all, I'm OK with it, but back in Chicago, we like to keep our laundry separated. You know, whites on one side and nigg... black guys on their side of town. And things been going along nicely; they have their thing, we have ours. Then some guys from out of town come around and start messing in places they shouldn't. That's why I'm here to talk to your friend. Mr. Benny heard he may have misplaced something. Something very important to him. He's been looking here, there, and everywhere."

"If you have her..."

"Whoa. Whoa. Hold your horses, cowboy." David takes a step back from Nicky when he seen his nostrils flare and his muscles tighten. "Mr. Benny doesn't know where his lost sheep has gotten to. No, he wants to talk to him and if they work out an agreement, he can pull some strings for the nigg... moolie and find out where his lost sheep might be found."

"If you know where my goddaughter is you'd be better off telling me now." Nicky is eyeing Franco.

"Look, all I was told was that the nigger should meet a man in Grayson Park at 3 am tonight. Alone of course."

"Well, there you go, you went and said it," I say from the gateway door, two guns in my hands, one trained on each man. Franco is frozen and can't take his aim from Nicky. "Relax. You're not the first guy to call me a nigger."

I swing both guns at Franco and fire. He stumbles backwards and falls to the floor. Blood pumps from the two holes in his chest as he struggles to breathe, then dies.

Nicky mocks a shocked tone, "Whadidya do that for?"

"He laughed," I say angrily.

"I think he was laughing with you, not at you," explains Nicky.

"See how misunderstanding can happen?" I tell David, turning my guns on him. "I heard you say Mr. Brunello has my daughter and you're here to return her."

"I didn't say anything of the sort," David bolsters up his courage. "I don't know anything more than what I told you already. I'm of no further use to you here."

"Don't say that, Franco was of no use to me, and look at him now. Hey Nicky, you ever noticed the littlest turds smell the shittiest? You, Shit Sandwich, are more valuable to this deal than you think. And we will see what you really know about my daughter."

"Hey, we didn't come here alone," David pumps up his chest and looks at his watch nonchalantly. "If I don't walk out that door in two minutes..."

Morris walks to the front door and swings it open. "You mean this door."

David is shocked to see his backup car on fire and rolling slowly down the street.

Akilina and Maria are sitting on the bed with the covers over their heads. Akilina whispers, "We are getting out of here tonight."

"Nooo," objects Maria, "we should wait for my father to come for us. You know he will."

"Maria, listen, that man hasn't said anything about a ransom. Just that he wants something your father has. What if he just wants your father? We can't sit here and let him walk into a trap. We are the bait, but we don't have to be."

Maria wipes the tears from her eyes. It is pitch black but Akilina knows she is crying. "Mom always tried to hide the truth from me, but I know Uncle Nicky is in the Mafia. He doesn't try to hide it. The kids at school call me The Mob Princess and Queen of the Gangs."

"Why didn't you say something?"

"What? And have Uncle Nicky break some ten-year-old girl's arm?" Maria's voice stiffens up. "No, it's ok. That stuff doesn't bother me. I don't remember my father; he is just a couple of pictures Mom hangs onto. But if my uncle is a mobster, and my father has been pretending to be dead, he must be into some really bad shit too."

"Maria!" Akilina's voice jumps. "Up until this happened we thought your father was dead. But this man wouldn't go through all this if he didn't know he wasn't. Your father told me once that if we were ever in trouble then we were to get out into the open, and he would find us. I heard companies in South America put radio devices on their executives in case they are adducted. I think he has placed a tracking device on you, or in you. We been here almost a week and I haven't heard any traffic, so I'm guessing we must be in the woods. If we get out of here there should be lots of cover where we can hide until your father locates us."

"But how are we going to get out? The only door is locked from the outside and there are cameras in every room."

"That is going to help us," Akilina says, "I have a plan."

Sgt. Warren picks up the receiver, "My team is in place. Is the Italian ready to go?"

"The bug went live at midnight," says a voice on the line, "haven't picked up much. We haven't heard from Little D or his team."

"They're dead," states Warren matter-of-fact.

"My boys can handle Nails and his darkie."

"You don't know this guy like I do, Mr. B. He's not one to play by any rules."

"Oh yes, now I recall, it was your team that let him ruin our Venezuelan deal," chides Benny Brunello. "Try not to fuck this one up as well."

"Let's not go down that fucking rabbit hole again," barks yet another man on the line. "It's three o'clock and I got confirmation he is on the bench. Send in your man Beniamino."

Sgt. Warren calls out over the phone, "Alpha team, stay on your toes. Close the door after contact is made. Beta, seal the box, no one in or out, check it."

"Check!"

A husky man in an overcoat enters the park. His hands are in his pockets, obviously clutching something. He approaches the figure sitting alone on the park bench under the street lamp. He eyes him suspiciously, the man is wearing a black hooded sweatshirt and sweat pants. His head is drooped down but he appears to be breathing heavy. Arman Borland stops ten feet from the bench, "You Morrison?"

The man on the bench stirs and mumbles. Arman swings a shotgun out of his overcoat, "Look, we just talk. No funny business."

The man on the bench moves oddly but doesn't reveal his face. Arman approaches curiously and puts the barrel of the shotgun under the chin to lift the man's head. "Holy Shit! Little D, what did those bastard do to you?"

Arman looks quickly around the park. It is a small sitting area, two trees on one side and nothing blocking his view. A few parked cars line the streets but there is no one in sight. "This meeting is a bust. They left Little D here tied up. Looks like they gave him the business," Arman speaks into his mike on his lapel.

"Take a seat." Comes an order from David Sartori's sweatshirt.

David's eyes are swollen shut. Dried blood from his nose covers the duct tape over his mouth. There is a wire around his neck running inside the sweatshirt holding his head down. He mumbles again and Arman sits and starts to pull the tape from his mouth.

"Leave the tape. Shit Sandwich talks too much. I want to have a quiet conversation with the guy who took my girl."

Arman slowly unzips the sweatshirt. The wire goes through a small transistor radio to David's belt. There are two pipes taped to a vest with wires running from the transistor radio. More wires run from the pipes around his back. Arman touches the radio carefully.

"Careful," I radio to the man in the overcoat, "Shit Sandwich is wearing the latest style in suicide vests, straight from the Middle East. I have to warn you, these things have a way of going off unexpectedly."

Arman jumps to his feet.

"Don't do that!" I warn. "The radio has a motion detector in it. Once you came within range, you can't leave without setting off the vest. If Shit Sandwich moves too much, Ka-Boom. Get the picture?"

"Yeah," Arman sits back down. "Didn't David tell you we just wanted to talk?"

"Yes he did," I respond, "but I don't want to talk to you. I want to talk to the person holding my daughter. They send you as their messenger. I send Shit Sandwich. Can they hear me or should I turn up the volume?"

"This is Alpha Team Leader, got eyes on the device, low power, they have to be close. A block, maybe two, standing by."

"Alpha team begin a sweep, find them." Commands Sgt. Warren.

"Tell him we can hear him," says the third man on the line.

"They can hear you," answers Arman.

"Oh, it is a THEY. Well, I don't care, if my daughter and her nanny aren't released by first light your two guys will be raining down on the Lower Eastside."

"They say it doesn't matter what happens to me," Arman relays in a shaky voice, "you will do as they say or they'll cut the girls into tiny little pieces."

"OK, now what?" asks Nicky. "You got all this fucking equipment but what are you going to do. I told you, BB wouldn't give a shit about these guys."

"We just need to keep dealing the cards until we have identified everyone at the table," I say. "Start the microwave transmitter."

The third man with Nicky and Morris, Russell Mills, flips a switch and a red light on the panel of equipment starts to flash. "It's live, we can start tracing."

"I still don't get it." Nicky complains.

"It's very simple," I tell him. "The microwave signal is being picked up by Trenchie's microphone in the park and sent to whoever he is talking to. We can pick up the microwave using the satellites we have in orbit. I got boys on the ground in almost every major city to close in on them. We've just got to keep them talking."

"You fucked up my deal before, but I'm willing to forgive and forget if you turn over what you owe me," the voice from the speaker fills the little room.

"See, it won't be hard to keep them on the hook," I say. "They are also trying to locate where we are transmitting from. The difference is, they can't pick up the microwave signal, nor will they be able to find us. We are sending our signal to the van via a laser beam, a direct line of sight, with no interception possible. The van is a dead end."

I hold down the transmitter key, "What deal? How do you figure I owe you shit? If you just tell me who you are, and what you want, we can work a deal. I'm a businessman." Then I ask Russell as he watches the equipment, "any pings yet?"

"Several. They are probably bouncing their signal too. Looking for the strongest spikes, we have one in the city..."

"Of course, and it's probably ours," Nicky blurts out.

"No sir, we are blocking out the park. But it is somewhere in the city, and we are trying to pinpoint the epicenter. We've got a strong response from Chicago's Northside. And a very strong signal from D.C., looks like the Capital building."

"That's the one," I exclaim, "who do we have on the ground around there."

"We have the Waxman, he's working tonight."

"Good. Have him locate and tag the target!"

The speaker comes alive again, "I think you know who this is, and what I want. The deal is simple, you turn over what you had in Colombia and we turn over your daughter."

"Colombia?" I say into the mike, "I don't have any holdings in Colombia. Someone is feeding you a load of shit."

Sgt. Warren says to Alpha Team Leader, "Status."

"We have located a van one block from the park. Strong signal... looks like they are transmitting from there. Permission to engage the target."

"Hell, yeah! Grab those fucking guys now," orders Benny Brunello.

"Remember, we need Morris alive."

"Beta Team, close the circle, Alpha move in," orders Sgt. Warren. He watches the body camera feeds from the four-man attack team as they split into two groups to approach fast and low behind the parked cars.

Morris' man says, "They are going to be on us any minute now. What do you want to do?"

"Keep the trace going for as long you can," I order. "Concentrate on the city, that's where Maria is."

"I brought some ground units online to help with the search but I don't think we will have enough time."

The third floor of the Senate office building is nearly deserted. A few first termers are sleeping in their offices. The janitor, a lanky old man, dark and wrinkled, is spraying waxing solution and sweeping the buffer across the floor. He notices the name on the office door, Kirkpatrick, a two-year senator. The microwave signal is coming from his office. The Waxman takes a small aerosol can off his belt and sprays a good long time through the keyhole. The silent odorless gas fills the outer office. It will slowly work its way into the inner office. Whoever is inside listening to the goings-ons in New York will soon inhale the radioactive marker.

For the next week, wherever Kirkpatrick – or whoever is in that office – goes they won't be alone. The Waxman quickly heads for the elevator with his equipment. There is another signal emanating from the sixth floor in the House offices. He knows he won't have much time before that signal is lost.

He exits the elevator, leaving his equipment by the door. He runs down the hall. The radio receiver in his ear beeps louder and louder as he rounds the corner. Another long dark corridor lies ahead. The Waxman takes out his cleaning rag and walks slowly down the hall. Listening for voices and wiping doorknobs as he goes.

Nicky is watching the men approaching the van through powerful binoculars. "They surrounded the van. One of them is at the back door. Why are we so far away again?"

"You really won't want to be any closer in a few minutes," I tell him. "The laser is beaming the signal to the optic receptor on top of the van. The equipment is changing it to a radio signal and sending that to Shit Sandwich in the park. They won't know where we are."

"I don't know about this plan of yours," Nicky voices his concern as the man in all black fatigues places a small box on the van door and backs away. "I still say we should talk to these guys."

"We will talk to them. Just not to these guys."

"This is Alpha Team Leader," he whispers, "ready to go."

"This is Warren; we need Morris alive… the others are expendable."

"What about the Italian?"

"Fuck him!" yells Brunello. "If you get the opportunity, shoot him in the face."

Alpha Team Leader presses the detonator button in his hand.

Nicky sees a small puff of white smoke rise from the van. Then, a bright explosion lights up the night. A cloud of smoke and flying debris swallows the blocks a mile from Nicky's position in the tenth floor office. He hears the rumble of thunder through the thick glass. He noticed several of the building tops have disappeared in the explosion. A fainter flash from the Grayson Park goes unnoticed.

"Jesus fucking Christ, Morris! How much explosives did you use?"

"The van was packed with it. Enough to vaporize the van and all its equipment. Good luck on them finding out how we operate. And the microwave transmitter on Shit Sandwich is just a memory. Much like Shit Sandwich and the Trench Coat Man."

"Hell, you levelled the whole block."

"Well, now they know we mean business," I say and light up a joint. "Good thing they picked a deserted neighborhood."

"That is great, but how are we going to talk to them now? You think Benny B is going to send any more guys for a meeting? He'll be sending a hit squad," warns Nicky.

"Don't worry about Benny," I hold up the joint for Nicky, "he's just the muscle in this little tea party. The real power lies with the guys in the Capital. We are going to reach out to them, and they are going to want to talk to us, because this is barely a sample of how far I will go to get Maria back."

Nicky, Morris, and Russell watch from the tenth floor window as fire-trucks, police and a dozen other emergency vehicles arrive at the scene. Three buildings have totally collapsed and the rest are burning out of control. The tech begins to pack up the equipment. They know they are going to be there a while.

"Be very careful, MoJo," Nicky says and takes a long hit. "You are starting a war with the United States Government. That can't end well for you."

"Technically, they started a war with me. It won't end well for them. And it's not the whole United States Government," I correct him, "it is at best, a couple of misguided politicians."

Sgt. Warren sits alone in the small control room two storys above the trailer parked on the warehouse floor. He watches as emergency workers dig through the rubble of the lower east side neighborhood. News media is reporting a major gas leak beneath the streets has devastated five blocks in one of the oldest sections in the city. Two blocks completely levelled by a blast ignited by two unidentified persons smoking in a park a block away. In addition to the two bodies that are scattered across the park, they pulled two bodies from the rubble. They are still searching for any others that may have been in the neighborhood at the time of the accident. Sgt. Warren picks up the phone and waits.

A voice answers, "What is it?"

"I told you this guy will not play ball," Sgt. Warren speaks slowly and deliberately, trying to hold in his anger. "I lost eight good men last night. Eight, and there are two more still buried out there, sure as shit they are dead."

"Hey, you've seen battle before. You've lost men. This is no different," the man with the gruff morning voice responds. "You just keep our little package safe and sound and he will play ball. And when the game is over, and he gives us the codes, you can do what you want. To him, the girls, hell, you can fuck his whole family if it makes you happy. But until I get what I'm after, you sit tight, and if it costs a hundred of your men, so be it."

The line goes dead. Warren stares at the trailer in the middle of the empty warehouse. He turns to the video cameras monitoring the girls. He can barely see them. They no longer turn on the lights inside; they have become accustom to the dark. *They are smart. They are plotting an escape attempt. The little girl is too young to have been trained by Morris, but the Russian, she can be a problem. Who am I kidding? This whole operation is one huge cluster fuck waiting to bite me in the ass.*

Chapter 12

Strike One

Benny Brunello is on the phone. "That little piece of shit and his darkie friend think they are real funny, don't they? Your man was right. They are fucking animals. No respect those two."

"Relax. We are going to take care of this…"

"No! I have my own way of teaching that figlio di puttanta a lesson. It is happening right now. The next time Nicky Nails is told to sit down and talk, he fucking better listen." Another phone on his desk rings. "That's my man now, I gotta go." He hits the button on the phone and switches lines. "Yeah."

"We are here!"

"Well, what the fuck are you waiting for? Do it!"

The man in the gray wool coat hangs up the phone on the corner of 86th Street in Bensonhurst, Brooklyn. He joins two others and they cross the street to a private two-story house. A boy and a girl exit the green and white house as the men reach the front door. "Hey Champ, is your daddy home?"

"No mister," says the boy to the man in the gray wool coat. "My Grandpa and Grandma are in the kitchen." The two children run off towards the school bus waiting down the block.

The man in the gray wool coat enters the house followed by a man in a long black leather and another in a short denim jacket. They walk quietly down the hallway to the kitchen.

"What did you forget?" asks the elderly woman at the stove with her back turned to the door.

"Nothing," says the Italian man's deep voice, "we are here to deliver Nicky Nails Rocci a message."

The woman jumps, startled by the stranger's intrusion. Her husband drops his paper on the table and stares doe-eyed at the trio moving around the kitchen, like they are at home. The gray wool coated man pulls out a chair and makes himself comfortable.

"We have no money here," says the white-haired man across the table. His blue eyes lock on the stranger, but he is quite aware of the other two men. "I can take you to the shop and give you what you want."

"Paisano, do I look like a thief?" the man responds, showing off his diamond watch.

"You, you hooligans leave here now," commands the old woman, her Irish accent becoming more pronounced.

"Hey, I didn't take you for a spud poker." The other men chuckle. "Smart move though," he continues, "you get a nice comfortable job with the Boys, and since your kids are half breeds, they don't get a second look from your Mafia boss. Smart."

"Mafia... My husband is a good hardworking man. He owns a jewelry shop in the city. This is a terrible mistake."

"She doesn't know, does she, Antonio? Your husband works for Nicky Nails Rocci. You need to remember that name because we have a message for his boss."

The two men are standing behind Antonio. The black leather coated man pushes the old woman into a chair on the side of the table. She squeals with fear. Antonio starts to get up but is forced back into his chair. The gray wool coated man slowly stands and waves his hands over the table. "Easy guys, no need to upset these nice people. They haven't done anything. What's your name, Honey?"

"Margie."

"Margie... Short for Margaret I bet. Is that coffee hot? It's really cold outside today." The woman tries to get up but the gray wool coated man holds his hand up again. He moves around to the other end of the table and turns the stove on high. "Don't you trouble yourself, Margaret, I got this. You just remember the message. OK?"

The old woman nods nervously. The denim jacket man is standing behind her. The black leather coated man is behind her husband, pulling on his black leather gloves. His knuckles are bulging in the leather already and it is as if he is trying to make them pop through. The coffee kettle whistles loudly.

"You tell Nicky Nails that the next time he is told to sit down and talk, he better fucking sit the fuck down and do what the fuck he is told that fucking little piece of shit motherfucker!"

The man in the black leather coat grabs Antonio by the hair and yanks him backwards. The old man's legs are trapped under the heavy wooden table, keeping him from falling from the chair. His head is tilted so far back his mouth is forced wide open. The gray wool coated man grabs the pot of boiling coffee from the stove and pours the liquid into Antonio mouth.

Antonio screams for a moment as a steady stream of steaming liquid flows down his throat. Then he begins to gurgle on the liquid almost silently, unable to resist the heated flood. Smoke rises from his mouth as he falls to the floor when the black leather coated man releases his hair.

Maria stands ironing a pair of pants in the bedroom while Akilina takes a towel and goes into the bathroom. She turns on the light and starts the shower. She wraps the towel around herself and shimmies out of her pants. The mirror starts to fog up and Akilina pulls open the medicine cabinet to get a razor from the shelf. She steps into the shower and pulls the curtain closed. A second later, her hand drops the blouse and bra on top of the pants and undies already on the floor. Akilina draws the shower curtain back a bit and places her leg on the edge of the tub. She lathers up her slender leg, well aware that the medicine cabinet mirror has her reflection.

Robert Fremont sits up at the monitor. "Hey, finally some action out of that little cunt," he says to Curry.

Curry clicks a knob on his monitor and changes from the bedroom to the bathroom too. "Yeah, that is a tight little ass she got. I bet she never been popped."

"Oh fuck. The fucking mirror is fogging up too much."

"Zoom in, dick," Curry tells his partner, "you can see much better."

"Oh yeah, that's better. Turn around sweetie, give daddy a show. Whadaya think, full bush or landing strip?"

"These Russian chicks like to keep it clean," Curry says with his hand instinctively sliding down his pants. "I bet you a hundred she's completely shaved."

"No way, but you're on. Come on you little whore, turn around." Robert slaps the side of his monitor. "You think she knows we're watching? She knows we're watching. Fucking little cunt."

A red light starts flashing on the table and a loud buzzer rips through the silence of the warehouse. The two men are shocked into action. Robert says, "What the fuck! They set off the fire alarm. What the fuck are they doing in there?"

"It must be the girl," Curry says, "we got to get in there." The two men bolt down the metal stairs to the warehouse floor. Curry grabs a fire extinguisher from the wall. "Hurry, get the fucking door open!"

Robert flings the door open, smoke billows out, and Curry rushes inside. Robert follows him as he sees the flames in the back of the trailer. "The bedroom! Get to the bedroom, quick."

Maria, who is behind a chair in the living room, dashes out the door. She runs two feet and stops, not knowing what to make of her surroundings. She expected to see trees and night sky, but there is nothing. The huge empty warehouse with a metal staircase leading to a metal cage one floor above has her totally confused. The red flashing light inside the cage must be where the monitors are, where they watch them from. The brrrap, brrrap of the alarm buzzer fills her head. Finally, focusing, she spots a door on the wall a few feet from the stairs. She makes a run for it.

Akilina has on a dress she had hidden in the towel. As the second man runs past the bathroom door, she grabbed his ankle and sent him crashing into his partner. They both hit the floor hard and she races down the hallway to the open door. She had told Maria to turn left when she left the trailer and run straight through the woods. To stay clear of roads as the kidnappers might have cars out there to stop traffic, prevent anyone from finding the trailer, and would pick her up in a heartbeat and bring her back.

She was planning to lock the two men in the burning trailer to gain more time, but her escape scheme went up in smoke when she flung herself onto the warehouse floor. Stunned by the unexpected exterior, she lost precious seconds, and forgot to lock the trailer as she stared around the cavernous building. They may have escaped the trailer but they are far from being free. Seeing Maria struggling with the door handle, she yells, "Forget the door. It is locked! Up the stairs, get to the roof."

The girl does as she is told and Akilina finally remembers the trailer door. She turns but for a split second, she sees a fist, then feels the hard ground beneath her back. Blurry-eyed, she manages to espy Maria through the chain link of the control booth. *Run, Baby, keep running.*

"Fuck, the girl is getting away," Curry yells. "Robert, shoot her, quick."

Robert pulls his nine millimeter from his back holster. The buzzer stops as abruptly as the fire had started it. The warehouse echoes with silence for a brief second.

A voice booms through the air. "If you shoot that girl, I'll rip your balls off, one at a time. Am I clear, Mister Fremont?"

"Yes sir!" Everyone recognizes Warren's voice over the loudspeaker.

The young girl stops for a moment outside the control room to get her bearings. Another set of stairs leads up the wall to a small landing, and the roof.

"Maria, I know what you are thinking, that you can make it... But then, what? You can see the monitors. Look, there is nowhere to go."

The monitor changes from the smoke-filled interior of the trailer to a view of the roof. Then it changes to views down the outside of the building, and a few point back at the warehouse. There is naught to see, no other structures for blocks around, nothing but emptiness in the picture. Maria looks down to Akilina, as if to ask, "What now?"

"Robert, take your gun and put it to Akilina's head."

He complies and smiles at Maria.

"Maria, you can continue to the roof, but it is a five-story drop to the pavement, so you probably won't make it. If you take one more step up to the roof, Robert puts a bullet in Akilina's head. She definitely won't make it. Now stop all this foolishness and return to the warehouse floor, before someone gets hurt."

"Maria, keep going." Akilina yells.

"Shut up, bitch!"

"I give the orders here, Mister Curry Ports. Now, go put that fire out."

Maria starts back down the stairs slowly. The smell of smoke is thick in the air. She sits next to Akilina. "There is nothing out there. I'm guessing that door is locked as well."

"Don't worry, it will be OK," Akilina clutches her to her chest and looks around and notices the windows high on the walls near to the roof. She immediately starts working on another plan.

Nicky walks into his office and slams the door shut.

I look up from his desk, "Who pissed in your cereal this morning?"

"THE MOTHER FUCKING F B I." He stands staring down at me. I decide to roll back from the desk and get up. Nicky takes the seat and wearily lays his head on the desk.

"So, you gonna tell me what they wanted? Or do you need to have a good cry first?"

"I'm not in the fucking mood, MoJo. Antonio Giomi is in the hospital. Benny B sent three thugs to serve him his morning coffee. Burned his fucking sarcophagus."

"Esophagus… They burned his esophagus. A sarcophagus is a coffin the Egyptian put their mummies in."

"Yeah? Whatever, Professor. The point is that they did it in front of his wife, with a message for me. The FBI spent all morning crawling up my ass."

"Well, are they gonna find anything?" I ask. "Do you want me to send someone to silence the wife?"

"Hell No! What's the matter with you, MoJo? Have some compassion, the poor bastard will probably never speak again, if he lives. Besides, he's one of the old dogs from Angelo's days and has no direct ties to me now."

"Then why him?" I'm curious.

"To put the Feds on me. Just to fuck with me. I told you we should have talked first, then gone after them." Nicky runs his hands through his hair.

"Grab a drink on the way out, we've got us a road trip," I tell him cheerfully. "I got IDs on our Senator and Congressman."

"We already know Kirkpatrick..."

"You really think these guys would run black-ops out of their own offices? He is obviously fronting. They probably use the Capital because it's nearly impossible to bug. Com'on, let's get going."

On the way out of the Sons of Italy, I point at the cardboard sign standing in the middle of the pool table. It reads in large red letters:

BUG.

KEEP YOUR MOUTH SHUT.

Between the two lines of warning is an object that at a casual glance would appear to be a quarter. A closer look reveals it to be a micro-transmitter. High quality sound pickup, no doubt. "Hey, Paisan, what gives?"

"Just want everyone to be aware," Nicky says after we exit the club. "Some of these guys have short memories and big mouths. How long am I going to have to keep that thing?"

"Not long," I say climbing into the driver's seat of a Mercedes Sport Coupe. "I plan to throw a little party of my own. It will make the other night seem like choir practice."

We are an hour outside of the city before Nicky realizes we are on our way to his father's place. I think he was sleeping most of the time, the FBI obviously kept him awake all night with questions about the attack on the old man. He doesn't look pleased to be going to see Nicolas but plays it off well. "You been missing my mom's veal and penne?"

"Yeah, I could go for some good Italian right now. But your dad is going to give us the skinny on our friends in Washington."

"What does my dad know about Senators and Congressmen?"

"Unlike you, Mr. Rocci and myself, cultivate contacts in the government. We are not afraid of doing business there."

"I'm not afraid," Nicky counters, "cautious. There are more snakes in that pit then even St. Patty can chase out. Oh yeah, how is it working with the good ol' USA? Is it going according to plan, MoJo? Don't think it slipped by me that you weren't the least bit surprised that your trace led to the Halls of Congress. I keep telling you, 'Fuck with the government and you will get FUCKED!'"

Nicky leans his head back and seconds later, he's snoring loudly. I'd rather listen to him snore than listen to his paranoia ranting anyway. *The air is crisp up here, much cooler than the city. It's going to be a cold winter. Can't take that anymore, have to wrap up this business quickly and get out of here.*

We pull up to the house a little before dusk. The sky is a vibrant orange, gray, and pale blue. I exchange pleasantries with Mrs. Rocci and joke with Nicky's brother, Sal. I'm saddened that the man with a steel trap for a mind doesn't remember me. Mrs. Rocci puts a hand on my shoulder and whispers, "It's the medicine. It keeps him calm, but messes with his head."

After veal meatballs and penne, we take a walk out to the barn. The three of us, Nicolas, Nicky, and me go down into a wine cellar under the barn. The place is soundproof to the nth degree. We wouldn't hear the sun exploding down here. No radio either, we are completely cut off. Nicolas is old and slow, but sharp as ever. He pours us wine from a casket and sits at the little table. We take our seats across from him.

"This is what I know," he starts, "Sen. Thomas Carter is the man with his lungs full of shit. He sits on the

Senate Arms Subcommittee. A senior member, he fucking chairs the damn things. Jim Webber is the Representative who chairs the Foreign Relations Subcommittee. Together, they can and do start wars. It was these guys who got the whole War on Drugs thing going too. You know why, don't you, Morris?"

"I found out for sure in Egypt. Seems we, the USA, are losing our grip on Middle Eastern oil. And a bunch of Islamic radicals are making it increasingly difficult for us to do business there."

"Yeah, Webber got into Congress thanks to Brunello. They were going to make a lot of money taking over the Venezuelan oil fields. The War on Drugs was Carter and Webber's plan to destabilize the area. They wanted the Colombians to cross into Venezuela. Then we would send troops to protect them, advisors to guide them, and ultimately, one way or another, replace the Venezuelan government."

"Well, MoJo, you fucked them in the ass on that one," Nicky laughs. "No wonder they grabbed Maria. When you had me advise all the cartels to move their businesses out of the jungles and into the cities, that effectively crushed the War on Drugs effort. They probably want to personally shoot you in the face."

"No, that's not it," his father says. "Brunello holds a grudge; you know how we Italians are; we don't forgive nothing. However, I seriously doubt that Brunello is pulling the strings anymore. But for them to grab your daughter, it has to be something more. Our arms deals, that is bigger than oil. That guidance system you developed, it's worth more than all the oil in Saudi Arabia and Venezuela combined. The ability to strike anybody, anywhere?.. It's, how do you say it... a game changer." Nicolas looks his son in the eyes and all the love drains from his face. His eyes are black lifeless shark's eyes ready to feed. "It's worth a little girl's life, that's for sure. You took care of those two fools?"

"I beat the fucking shit out of them," Nicky says of his father's two men who let Maria and Akilina get kidnapped. "And then I waited for MoJo—"

I cut him off. "He waited for me to arrive so I could see him put one in their heads," I know that's what Nicolas wants to hear. Nicky is afraid his father would place a higher value on the life of his old friends than on his leadership but I know differently.

Nicolas smiles, color returns to his face, and his eyes light up with pride as he reached across the table, and pats Nicky on the cheek. "Good. Good boy. You've got to be fair but firm. If someone fucks up... can't let anything stand in the way of business. You are going to take control of this thing we got. It was always yours to run. These guys have to fear and respect you. But mostly, respect you."

Akilina and Maria sit on the hard concrete of the warehouse floor outside the trailer. The air smells of burnt plastic. Curry stands over them, holding a bag of ice to the small mountain growing on his forehead. He had slammed his head on the fire extinguisher when Akilina tripped them. The girls smile at him, knowing the pain he must be feeling.

"He's here," Robert says, hurrying downstairs to join his partner on the floor.

A second later, the door opens – the same one Maria couldn't get to budge. It slams shut heavy and loud. Sgt. Warren walks up to Curry, grabs the ice from his head, and throws it across the warehouse against the side of the trailer.

"What are they doing on the ground? Get them some chairs. Bring four," he orders. Warren reaches his hand out to Maria. She hesitantly takes it and he pulls her to her feet. He does the same for Akilina. He looks down at Maria. "I'm very disappointed in you. I told you to stay in the trailer. A couple of days and you would go home. Unharmed."

"I don't care what you say," Maria screams. "I want to go home now. I am going to run away. You can't stop me. You can't keep us here! We are going to escape."

"I am even more disappointed in you, Akilina." Warren speaks softly, ignoring the young girl's rage. "I kept you here to help her. I thought you would be sensible and wait patiently to be released. I'm very disappointed. I knew you were planning an escape this whole time. Putting her in danger."

The two men return with four folding metal chairs from the control room. They set them up where Sgt. Warren points. Two on one side of him and the other two across from them. Then he tells all four people to sit down. Akilina and Maria sit side by side facing Curry and Robert. Warren paces back and forth behind the two men.

"Yes, you put her in real danger. You almost got her shot."

"I wasn't going to..."

Warren punches Robert in the face with a left hook he didn't see coming or was prepared to receive. Robert's head and body halfway land in the chair with Curry. Akilina gasps. Maria looks cold and steady at Warren.

"My father isn't coming," Maria says. "You think he's alive, but he is dead."

"I heard from your father two nights ago," Warren smiles. "So he is very much alive. I thought he loved you, at least enough to want to see you freed. But maybe I was wrong." Warren says and watches her squirm just as if he had plunged a knife in her heart, then, he gives it a twist. "But let me worry about convincing your daddy to save you. Here's the thing, these men will do anything I say. But, they are real stupid too. If left to their own plans they would hurt you, or let you hurt yourselves. If they didn't open that door, you would have died in that fire."

"I don't care! I want to go home."

"I DON'T CARE! You GO when I say you GO. This ass... This man almost shot you. Not smart. Curry was supposed to be watching you. Instead, he was watching the beautiful Akilina, and probably jerking off. Then this genius tells my other moronic man here to shoot you. Not smart at all. Robert, shoot Mr. Curry in his head."

Robert Fremont pulls his nine millimeter from his back and fires a contact shot to Curry's head. Curry falls over dead. Akilina and Maria scream as warm blood splashes onto their faces. Warren walks past them and into the trailer. The girls are crying uncontrollably, staring at the body on the floor. They can see the red volcano on the dead man's head, a river of blood running under Curry's head.

Robert shushes them and says, "It's going to be alright. It's over now."

"Not quite." Warren grabs Akilina's long blonde hair and pulls her head against his thigh. He places the iron to her cheek and her skin sizzles immediately.

Three seconds lapse before the pain registers in Akilina's brain. She screams.

Maria jumps from the chair.

"Sit down!"

Maria stands spellbound, then her eyes dart everywhere. She wants to run. But she also wants to go to Akilina, who is slumped over in her chair, a patch of her face pulled away and hanging. She is too close to Warren and the skin-stained iron. Maria looks to Robert for help, her eyes begging him to shoot their jailer.

Robert gazes into her eyes and feels the pain, which is racing through her mind and body. He knows what she is asking him to do. His nine millimeter is still in his hand, dangling at his side. He drops his gaze.

"Sit down!" Warren commands and she obeys. "I have orders not to harm you. But no one cares what happens to this BITCH here, understand? This was strike one. You don't want to go for strike two. Trust me. Now go back in the trailer and BEHAVE. And Akilina, I don't think these guys will be looking at you the same way anymore."

Maria helps Akilina to her feet. She can barely move, except for holding a flap of skin carefully against her face. She is on fire. They slowly walk into the trailer.

Sgt. Warren turns to Robert Fremont, "Get the first aid kit and see what you can do with her face. Knock her out, she'll be better for it. And lucky for you that fire didn't compromise the structural integrity of that trailer, or you'd be lying next to that asshole. After they are locked in, call for a cleanup crew."

"What about Maria?"

"What about her? I didn't touch her. She'll be fine."

As I'm leaving the barn, I notice all the empty chicken coops. "What happened to all of Sal's chickens?"

"Sal," Nicolas says as if he just swallowed acid. "Found him in here one night just snapping their necks, laughing and singing. That's when we put him on the medicine."

"Sorry I asked."

"Well, what can you do? It is what it is," he says with no emotion at all. "Hey, before you go off and do something crazier than you already have, you make sure you find your little girl. Don't think they won't hurt her..."

"I have people searching night and day, we'll find her soon," my voice lacks confidence.

"You've been looking where she might be found. Have you thought of looking where she won't be found?"

We just stare at him blankly.

"They know you have a chip in her. Back in the old days, before you were born, Nicky, I was looking for this snitch. A real wop. A piece of work this prick, gambler and loser, wife beater and whore chaser, drinker and talker. I looked everywhere, bars; after-hours; floating games; whorehouses. Nothing... Know where I found him?"

We both shake our heads.

"In a fucking rectory, the guinea fuck was using his brother's identity to hide out in a fucking church of all places. Well, good thing he was in a church because I introduced him to God Almighty in person."

Just before we climb in the car to drive back to the city, Sal hugs me and whispers, "My brother from another mother... we gonna do super-secret family business, right?"

I smile, "You know it."

The drive back is half-quiet and half arguing. Nicky keeps flipping back and forth about not being included in the arms deals with his father, even though we all know he would never want to be involved anyway. I keep bring up the fact he is getting his cut so what is his problem.

"It would have been good to know," he complains. "Here I am thinking you're just running around the world with your Russian piece, fucking like rabbits in spring, and the whole time you and my Dad are working some really fucked up backroom deals. It would have been nice to know... That's all. And another thing, maybe, I would have known to pay more attention to certain situations..."

"Fuck, Nails, give it a rest! You hate the government. You would have blown every deal out the water."

We arrive at the Sons of Italy as the sun is on the rise.

Russell is waiting at the bar, "There's been a blip. Not long enough to get a fix on, but it looks like it is somewhere in Queens. Around the same area we picked up the trace the other night. We have doubled the guys combing through the neighborhoods."

"I've got another plan I want you to implement immediately," I tell Russell.

Head of the Government

Chapter 13

Backroom Black Deals

Senator James Harris is sitting in his office reading the New York Times. There is a five-page spread on the failing infrastructure that led to the catastrophic losses in New York's lower east side neighborhood. The pictures are particularly disturbing. They remind him of his time in Nam. The buildings look like they have been bombed, not the result of a gas line rupture under the street as being reported. For one, the crater in the middle of the street is blown-in, as if the blast occurred above ground. The buildings too, there is a definite radial signature that suggests the damage initiated somewhere in the street, not below it.

He knows a cover up when he sees one. But something this big, he would have thought that he would have heard echoes and whispers in the halls by now. Someone does not pull an attack on New York City and no one has anything to say about it. He sits on both the Foreign Relations and the Arms Control Subcommittees, and this has to be tied to one or both of them. *America is picking up enemies faster than flies on shit. The Middle East, South America, not to mention her old favorites, The Soviet Union and China. Although the last two seem a bit farfetched to pull something like this. Way too much collateral damage for them to be involved. The blowback from this is going to be costly to whoever is behind it.*

The phone rings once then his secretary's silky smooth voice floats through his mind, "Senator Harris, there is a gentleman here to see you, he doesn't have an appointment but says he is an old war buddy of yours. A Mr. Charlie Johnson."

The senator jumps up quickly and pulls the drapes closed. "Send him in. And Barbara, I am not in for anyone one else. Clear?"

"Yes sir."

The five-five Puerto Rican with long flowing black curls swings open the door. She is there alone in a short plaid skirt and black low cut blouse. James Harris looks past her half expecting to see the ghost of his long dead friend behind her. He waits for several seconds then says, "Morris, get the hell in here already."

The secretary looks oddly at him and then at Morris, who is peeping around the door like a little kid. The office is dim with the windows covered. She walks across the room and turns on the lamps in each corner of the office. She patrols the entire perimeter of the room lightening it up as much as possible. Then she closes the door, giving them one more inquisitive look.

"I see you still like the spicy dishes," I say and drop down onto the soft leather couch. "I bet you two really worked this thing out."

"Morris, are you crazy? You've lost your mind. What are you doing here?" James is shaking nervously, as if my dead brother is paying him the visit. "What if someone sees you here? Then what?"

"Little Miss Chiquita Banana wouldn't know who I was if you didn't call me by my real name."

"Oh, yeah, getting a visit from my friend who's been dead… What? Twenty years! That won't raise any questions." He grabs the newspaper off his desk, walks over, and drops it in my lap. "I suppose your resurrection has caused this."

"There have been some very bad things happening, especially in New York." I stand and throw my arms around his neck. He hooks an arm around mine and squeezes. "It has been a long time since the South Bronx. You look good as a senator. I bet you will look great as the President."

"You smoked so much shit your brains are shot," he laughs and pushes me away. "That will be the day a Black Man sits in the White House. Hell, wasn't long ago they shot one guy just for coming to town. But really, what is this all about. What the hell happened in New York?"

"Sit down. It's a long story and you are right in the middle of it." He sits next to me on the couch and I go through the whole thing, starting with Vicky. He, of course, never believed we were dead. I tell him how Sen. Carter and Rep. Webber tried to set her up to be killed and make it look like the Colombians, just so he would vote to send troops into Colombia and eventually Venezuela. He isn't as surprised as I thought he would be. He thanks me for keeping her safe. I give him the lowdown on the stinger missiles, my deal with the Russians, and the explosion in the Egyptian warehouse; when someone undoubtedly tried to open one. "I warned them not to go looking for things that didn't concern them." This does cause him concern. Then I finish with Yana's husband, his untimely death, and Maria's kidnapping days later. "They are trying to strong arm their way into the business. Your partners are a piece of work. They think they are too big to fall."

"Carter has been in office for twenty-five years," James informs me, "If there are any skeletons in his closet they have turned to dust. Webber has been here a little longer than I have, and there have always been questions about his loyalties. Inside the loop, he has been able to keep them to a minimum, a questionable vote here and there to help his district. But that's Washington, the only thing that raises an eyebrow is sex and sports."

Sen. Harris goes to the bar and pours two drinks then presses the intercom and tells Barbara to order lunch for them. He returns to the couch, handing over one of the vodkas. "I owe you for Vicky, what can I do to help?"

"I need to know what dogs are on whose leash. We know Tom Green orchestrated the kidnapping, but who is he working for? Brunello? Carter? And if he is not holding her, then who is?"

"I don't know about Green, but after your disappearance in South America, Sen. Carter pushed through funding for a paramilitary unit operating out of his home state of Texas. You know, black ops like the work you were doing. They are called the Black Scorpions; most are ex-Nam guys. They have people in the CIA, FBI, probably the NSA too. If you know for a fact that Green made the grab, then I put money on him being a Black Scorpion too."

"Yeah, they sound like the kind of people who would kidnap a ten-year-old," I say throwing down my drink in one gulp. "Find out who is running the operation in New York. But be careful, don't let Carter and Webber know you are onto their games."

Harris rattles his ice, "I know who has Maria. You know him too. A guy named Sgt. Warren. Does a bloody eagle tattoo with a sword bring back any memories?"

I nod, remembering the helicopter ride into the jungle.

"He's Carter's big dog. His name came across my desk a couple of times, and I started seeing him around every now and then after you went missing. Usually runs security for Carter and his cronies. He wouldn't trust this to anyone else."

Barbara brings in lunch and several messages, a couple from Webber's pals.

He tells Barbara to inform all other callers that he has gone to New York to assess the gas line explosion. We spend the rest of the afternoon going over old times, as friends do. When Barbara leaves at five o'clock, she tells him that Senator Carter called twice with an urgent request for him to call back.

She says, "Goodnight Senator, and I'll be in early tomorrow to clear your calendar for the next few days. Goodbye Mr. Johnson, it was nice meeting you."

"Goodbye Beautiful, and if anyone should ever ask, we never met. I was never here."

Senator James Harris nods his affirmation.

She gives the two men a nod and leaves.

"Are you sure you're not hitting that?"

The phone rings once and Sgt. Warren snatches it up, "It's about time you return my call. There has been a development."

"What kind of development?" asks Senator Carter. "The girl is all right... Not a scratch, I told you..."

"Yeah, yeah I know. The little princess is fine. They tried to escape, broke out of isolation but not the containment zone."

"Are you sure?"

"Of course, or we'd be up to our eyeballs in jiggers and coonass." His Cajun accent slips out and hangs on each word. "We need to knock those two fillies out for the duration. I told you we should have kept them under from the start."

"Look," the Senator yells into the phone, "I'm not taking a chance that one of you swamp-rat morons overdoses that girl before we get the deal done. How fucking hard can it be to keep a ten-year-old and her goddamn nursemaid locked up? She isn't Bonnie Parker."

"She is not your innocent little prep school darling sitting next to your grandson," Warren is back to his sophisticated demeanor, "she has been raised by gangsters and mobsters all her life. She's probably well on her way to becoming Ma Barker. I've looked into those eyes; she has her daddy's killer blood flowing in her." He pauses for effect and starts again as Carter tries to speak. "Speaking of which, how do you intend to get Morris to turn over his information? May I suggest we send him the babysitter all chopped up and gift wrapped?"

"And if he doesn't respond?" Carter is exasperated, "then what? Where do we go from there? Mr. B has turned up the heat on his friend the wop. The FBI is crawling all over him like ants at a Fourth of July picnic. He'll convince his friend to make a deal."

"Well, just so you know, I had to punish that little hottie. It should keep them in line, but you'd better hurry it up. The longer you take, the greater the likelihood of him finding the girl and then your leverage will be gone."

"I'll worry about that," says the Senator, "you just make sure she isn't harmed. And no drugs. Clear?"

"Yeah, clear," says Sgt. Warren, "you underestimated him once and he destroyed the whole South American campaign by himself. If I was you, I wouldn't make the same mistake twice."

Carter slams his fist down on the desk, "And who screwed that one up?"

"You. He was supposed to be a thousand miles away. Imagine my surprise when he jumped on that bird and started chatting me up. At least I proved Bulletproof Morris Johnson wasn't all that bulletproof." Warren slams down the phone.

"You hear all that?" the Senator says to Webber who has been on mute the whole time.

"I caught it. He's not happy being a babysitter," Webber replies. "And I don't think he's any good at it. Torture and murder are his strong suits. Why did you pick him for this job?"

"He sees it as a chance to redeem himself, but what we really need is someone we can toss to the bear we poked. You know Morris isn't going to be satisfied just getting his daughter back safe and sound, he's going to want revenge. So who better than the guy who put three bullets in him? The Sergeant will make a good sacrificial lamb. One Morris can't pass up."

Rep. Webber runs one hand through his thinning hair then shifts his girth in the office chair, which whines in protest. "I don't know. Double crossing Warren could be more dangerous than grabbing this guy's daughter. I wouldn't want either of them on my ass."

"The way I picture it going down is," Carter says, "The bear and the wolf fight to the death. We walk away clean."

Senator Harris is at the site of the explosion at first light. There is police tape starting on the block where the crater is and stretches all the way back to the park, then down the street and back up to the other end of the block. The news crews have been camped at the perimeter of the four-block disaster zone since the first night. They descend upon him like locusts.

"Senator, is Washington providing any funds to aid in the cleanup?"

"Senator Harris, what is your office doing to bring charges against those responsible for this tragedy? People have died here, someone must pay!"

"Mr. Harris, what have you to say about the rumors going around that this was no accident, but a coordinated attack on the city by an organized group bent—"

"There are always rumors and conspiracy theories when something as devastating as this has occurred," Sen. Harris calmly faces down the man with the mini-recorder in hand. Flashbulbs pop incessantly. He holds up his hand to cut off any more questions, and states, "I am here to assess the damage. My office and the proper authorities will work together in an orderly fashion to ascertain the facts and bring them to the public. We will launch a thorough study of New York's infrastructures to assure the citizens of this great city that they are safe. What I need from you is to refrain from treating rumors and accusations as truths and facts. Report what is given to you from reputable sources. Thank you, my office will put out a statement by the end of the day."

The senator walks quickly away from the news hungry crowd. He is flanked by his aides, some Con Edison engineers, the Police Chief, Fire Chief, and the Mayor. He notices men in white overalls everywhere, combing through the debris. When he reaches the edge of the fourteen-foot-deep crater, an FBI agent stops him. "You can go down the ladder but don't touch anything," says Agent Peppers, "this is an active crime scene."

"A crime scene? For a gas explosion?"

"This was no gas line explosion," he reports. "I haven't seen damage like this since I was an A-6 Intruder Bomber pilot in Vietnam turning villages into lakes. This hole was caused by at least five hundred pounds of high explosives, maybe more. The gas line was rupture as a result of the explosion. I have men collecting every scrap of evidence, looking for parts of the detonators, but it doesn't look promising."

"Someone at the line said this was an organized attack," Harris probes for clues as to how much the FBI knows.

"Crackpots," Peppers dismisses. "We went over the building records in this area, nothing here worth blowing up, at least not on the surface. Just a block of old garment factories. I got a team looking into the history though, never know what could be hiding in the weeds. I'm thinking maybe they made the bomb here and were moving it when it went off. Remember, don't touch anything down there."

"Don't worry, I have seen enough," he answers. And heard enough also, they have no clue as to what went on here. *Whatever you were trying to hide, Morris, you did a great job of it. But I'm damned if you didn't raise a lot of eyebrows with this one.*

James Harris is in his Harlem office preparing a statement for the evening news. The FBI want him to stick to the gas line explosion story and give him some bogus facts to back it up. He is not to mention the van, which they surmise is what the bomb was in from a part of an axle they found in the hole. The official body count remains at four, and the derelicts in the park are taking the blame for causing the blast. Peppers did however confide in him that from the teeth and hair samples recovered, and there isn't much to go on, they think that six or perhaps as many as ten people perished.

He can't say why they were there, or why the two men were shredded in the park. The park is of particular interest to them because it is covered in buckshot. Cars and some of the buildings had been hit. As for the two men, they found pieces of them for blocks around. They recovered teeth and portions of their bodies no bigger than quarters on rooftops blocks away. Seems they rained down on the neighborhood.

Harris' secretary buzzes him, and says Senator Carter is on the line again. He's not sure what he wants, but he can't keep dodging him. *I wonder if he knows how bad it is to piss off my friend.* "Hello Carter, what can I do for you? And make it short, I'm trying to put together a press release for the six o'clock news."

"Oh yes, terrible thing," Carter jumps in with both feet, "Good thing that gas line ruptured in the middle of the night. Had it happened during the day, there would be countless deaths you'd have to deal with."

If he didn't know better, he would swear Carter set off the explosion. "Well, one death is one too many."

"Yes, of course. That is why I'm calling you. An incident like this can have a very negative impact on your career. If you don't get out in front and handle it right, before you know it, people are pinning this on you."

"What do you mean pinning this on me?" Harris takes exception to the remark, the way it was delivered, and isn't afraid to show it. He's been in Congress long enough now not to let Carter bully him. And he is more than angry about Vicky, but he can't let on he knows anything about that. "This is an unfortunate accident but these things happen. My office is going to make sure the right steps are taken to rectify the situation."

"Good, because sometimes these things have a way of becoming personal." Carter says smoothly. "I'm at the Waldorf. Maybe we can get together tonight and talk man to man. Make sure this story doesn't spiral into some kind of family affair that would reflect badly on everyone involved."

"I'm not following, what do you think is going on here?" Harris tries to get the senator to reveal his hand.

"Better we talk in person and private," Carter says like an old cowboy gambler and cuts off the conversation with the cold click.

Before James can hang up the phone, the secretary is in his ear, "Senator, there is a young woman here, says it's about a contribution to your campaign, a Mrs. Maria Delitanni."

"Sure, send her in," James says, not sure who will walk through his door this time. His jaw drops and his heart explodes in his chest. His eyes well up, giving him blurry vision the moment the young woman steps in his office.

"Hello, James." That is all Vicky can get out before tears start rolling down her face.

James almost falls over the edge of his desk trying to get to her. He throws his arms around her and holds on forever, tears freely flowing from his eyes. Neither can stop them. Neither can let the other go. He rocks her side to side, squeezing her ever tighter, until he realizes she is barely breathing. "This has to be a dream."

"More like a nightmare is what my life is now."

"I'll kill Morris!"

"No," Vicky objects and grabs him again, "He has been… good to me. I chose this life and he has done everything to keep me safe. Make me happy. He sent me here to let you know that he has a plan to get me out of this life and back with you. For good."

James backs her up and looks her over. She looks well, and thankfully, there is not a scratch on her. She has dyed her hair a deep copper gold but other than that, she looks the same as she did ten years ago. A deeper look into her eyes reveals the pain that a ten-year nightmare undoubtedly has left on her soul. He finally says, "I know about Maria."

"I know you do. I can't use my real name, and he didn't give you my alias. Said you would know what was up if I used his daughter's name."

"And he doesn't think a black woman with and Italian name would be suspicious?"

"Not in New York. Your secretary did give me a funny look, but probably not because of the name. I don't think she believes I'm a campaign contributor." She opens his jacket. "You lost weight, brother."

"My life has been hectic over the years. Washington is a rough town." He walks over to his desk and turns a picture around. It's of her in high school, maybe junior year. "I don't think Vie believed any of your story."

"Oh my God! This was so stupid of me," Vicky stares at the office door, expecting a flood of cops, reporters, or his secretary at the very least, to bust in yelling liar. "This is bad. Morris said he would arrange a better meeting, but I insisted. I should go…"

"Calm down. Relax. Don't you recognize Miss Viola from across the street? Hell, she was your babysitter for years. And she's been with me since my first term. She often wondered when you would make it back home."

"So that's Viola Campbell! The lady with the drunk for a husband."

"Yes. He's dead now." James says sadly. "He was a nice guy when he wasn't drunk. Some people have really hard lives." James presses the intercom button. "Vie come—"

"No…"

The door flies open before either of them can finish a sentence. Viola sweeps Vicky up in her arms and squeezes her into her massive bosoms. Again, Vicky is struggling to breathe. "Maria whoever," the two-hundred plus pound Jamaican woman cackles. "Like I wouldn't pick ya out in the dark with me eyes closed. Look at ya. You look like you haven't eaten decent since you had me peas and rice. I cried the loudest and the longest at your funeral, dear."

"I'm sorry about all that."

"Nonsense, me knew you weren't dead. I cried because you run off with that rag-a-muffin no account Morris Johnson. You were always running after that boy.

Him a bundle of trouble and then some. I know, I married one just like him."

"Oh, I'm sorry about your husband."

"I'm not," she laughs and flashes a big gapped tooth gold-filled smile to hide what she really feels. "So, is that no account Morris Johnson dead?"

Vicky doesn't answer. Viola sweeps her up again, swinging her like a ragdoll. "It's ok, honey, him not really a bad boy. Like me Henri, trouble is just drawn to him. And like Henri, they always find a way out of it."

Viola insists that Vicky go to Brooklyn with her for a Jamaican feast. James pushes her out of the door saying he will lock up. He is smiling from ear to ear as the two women exit the outer office. He finishes the press report and faxed it to his press agent just in time for the evening news. *What a pack of lies, but it is what they want. Truthfully, it is better for the public. Viola is right about Morris, trouble always finds him, and that is bad for trouble, because he's the one person you don't try to find. Carter was talking some crap about family affairs. He has no idea he is messing with the wrong man's family.*

James decides to blow off Carter and has his driver take him to his apartment on Central Park West. *Let that sonofabitch sit and stew in his own shit for a while longer. Try to kill my sister, you fucking prick. I haven't put my foot in someone's ass in a long time. Lucky, I don't go there and blow your fucking brains out.*

Morris shows up at the senator's Westside apartment building with a load of newspapers in a canvas shoulder bag. The doorman gives him a hard look, "Where is Joey? The regular paperboy?"

"Got some school thing going on, entrance exams or something, I'm running his route and two others." I say.

"You're a little old to be a paperboy, aren't you?" Asks the white-haired doorman with a face like leather.

"Tell me about it," I sigh, "I did this shit ten years ago for three years. When I moved inside the distribution center, I swore I'd never pick up this bag again. Fuck, it's even heavier than I remember. Well, what you're going to do? Tell the kid he can't go to college?"

"Yeah. The service elevators are down the hall and to the right. Do me a favor and don't hold the door open with the bag. It makes the alarm go off at the desk."

"No problem, boss. I'm probably the only one using it at this time in the morning anyway."

"Hey," the old man stops me again. "And no throwing the papers against the doors. The tenants call me and complain."

"Boss, I got a mean slider, leaves the paper an inch from the door. No one hears a footstep in the hall." I disappear down the hall and deliver all the papers before I get to James' apartment. *I don't want the kid to lose his job.*

"What the fuck are you doing here, Morris?"

"How did your meeting with Vicky go? Is she here?"

"It went well. And no, she went home with Mrs. Campbell."

"Oh. How is the old Voodoo Queen, and her husband?"

"Good and dead, she speaks highly of you," he says walking to the kitchen.

"You know, that crazy old woman threw a meat clever at my head once."

"Well, shows how much she liked you," James laughs. "If she didn't, she would have split your head open. Don't you ever sleep?"

"No." I open the fridge, there's nothing in there. "That's sad." I close the door. "Have you talked to your buddies yet? I know they are real anxious to have a sit-down with you. Especially since the last one blew up in their faces."

"Carter has been trying to get at me," he says with an acid tone, "but I haven't been in the right frame of mind. After what you told me, I might rip his fucking head off."

"Go for it."

"I can't. Not anymore, those days are behind me. And what was with that explosion, everyone says it was way more destructive than necessary."

"Of course it was," I am very quick to the point now. "When you meet with these motherfuckers, tell them if I don't get my girl back pronto, it won't be a deserted street in New York next time. It will be a very crowded street in Washington. And a much bigger bomb."

"You can't be serious," James cautions, "you do something like that and they will hunt you to the ends of the Earth. And not just you, Maria, Vicky, Liz, anybody and everybody you care about will pay."

"They already took Maria," I shoot back. "You just let them know, I'm ready for a war."

"You can't win."

"Haven't you learned anything," I poke him in the chest. "You don't have to win a war, just make it too costly for the other guy to fight. Just let them know I have nothing left to lose."

Senator James Harris returns to Washington that same morning. He doesn't say goodbye to Vicky, but does leave a letter for her on Vie's desk, no name on it, naturally. Morris told him that he was getting Vicky a new identity, and in a few days, she will be free from this life. He never intended for her to go into this thing with him, but once she was in, he couldn't let her walk away until he knew she would be safe. James thanked him profusely.

He doesn't meet with Senator Carter, despite two more calls to his apartment and the New York office. He'll deal with him when he's ready. He imagines they want him to be the go between for them. Makes sense, at least Morris won't kill him. And he'll do it to save his friend's life because Morris will never back down. He also knows Morris has no conscience, has been a warlord all his life, it is what he's good at. And for all he knows, Morris has an army primed and ready to fight.

He will be the go between, not because he wants to be, but because if he doesn't do it, Morris will burn America to the ground. He hopes for all their sakes, Maria is safe and unharmed.

Chapter 14

Scum Floats

Yana hears a car go by, followed by the roar of motorcycles a moment later. She frowns and sighs exasperatedly, "How long is Morris going to keep this up?"

"Morris is just making sure you have nothing to fear," replies Thug 1.

"Ah, you call him Morris," Yana says, "You knew him back in the day, before he disappeared and came back as John Morrison."

Arthur Penn hesitates, not sure he should confirm her suspicions, but the stern look he receives from Yana forces his compliance. "Yeah, we grew up in the South Bronx together. He was an Original Sinner and I was a Slum Slayer. We fought a war and his gang won. We kept our territory and colors but became an extension of the Original Sinners. That was the way he did things, assimilated his enemies into his organization."

"What happens if you don't want to be assimilated?"

"Then there was annihilation," answers Thug 1. "He beheaded our gang leader and ran several others through the heart with a sword until he came to me. I agreed to join forces and that was that. We didn't have to split our business or anything with his gang, just had to fight for him when called upon. I later learned this was how the Roman Empire spread its power. He unified most of the gangs of the South Bronx, or wiped them out. Eli, Thug 2, came along much later. The bikers work for Morris, I'm sure to stay alive. He said no one approaches this place, and no one will."

"What is he so afraid of? My husband died of a heart attack, he was old."

Thug 1 is careful how he phrases his next sentence. He is more afraid of Morris than Yana. "From what I heard, your husband went from being a movie giant worth a couple of millions in the porn world. no offense..."

"It's okay."

"To a billionaire in the telecommunication industry. Makes you a target in anybody's eyes," he continues. "Morris doesn't believe in accidents, coincidences, or bad luck. He believes in murder."

Yana looks out the window as four bikers roar past the property. They are beyond the hedges and security walls out of sight from the house itself. No one could reach the house without being intercepted by them and it's possible these two guys alone can take out an army all by themselves. Knowing what she does about Morris' Middle East dealings she is sure Guy's death was not a factor of his age, but his unfortunate dealings with Morris. Morris isn't paranoid, he is cautious. As he told her, "My friends are my enemies and my enemies are monsters."

Guy was a very organized man, who kept files of everything he did. Yana started going through his office and computer, looking for anything that would prove his death was a natural one. She didn't want to believe it could have been caused by something they had done and she is fairly certain Morris wouldn't have shared any of the military capabilities of the satellites with him. All his letters dealt with programming and scheduling, exactly what she expected to find. There is however an inordinate amount between him and Hefner over broadcasting rights, but that was the crux of his business. There are only a few letters between him and Morris, mainly about putting pressure on the Russians to launch the satellites. Guy really wanted the Russians to do the job. She is glad there is no mention of her dance in any of Morris' correspondences. Not that she expected him to say anything, in fact, he didn't mention her at all, not once.

His computer files are in the same meticulous order and she has no trouble guessing his password, 'Yana_My_1_Love'. It was how he always addressed her. There is nothing to find either; definitely nothing that would be worth killing him for. She does find a doctor's appointment in his calendar. His annual check-up had been two months ago. She calls the doctor, he gives her his condolences then assures her Guy had a clean bill of health. He also tells her that when he heard of Guy's death, he ran all the test again, trying to see if he had missed something. He hadn't, "Guy should have lived another twenty years, easily", his words. The only thing he can think of is a fall or something that caused an embolism that went to his heart. A freak occurrence, but plausible in a man his age.

So it was murder. But who? And what did they have to gain? He knew nothing of the true nature of the communications business. If she hadn't been present at the downing of the Egyptian jets and only seen the news broadcast from Afghanistan, she would also know as much as Guy did about all of this. The motorcycles roar past the house again and it dawns on her. 'They', whomever they are, killed Guy to get to her. It's her connection to Morris they are after. He kept her by his side because she was the only leverage they could have on him. At least that's what she had thought, but sitting in the house now, under guard, she sees they had found another pressure point to push. But if they thought pulling him away from her was going to leave her vulnerable then they didn't know Morris at all. In Europe, there was him and a handful of men to overcome, here in California... she is surrounded by an army who most likely have sworn a death oath to protect her. Poor Guy, his death was a useless act perpetrated by some desperate monsters.

Russell Mills and two Original Sinners enter the Sons of Italy looking for Morris. Joe Castor and two other mobsters stop them and pat them down. It is a wasted effort, as they are all armed and refuse to surrender their weapons. "Come on, you fucking moolies, you ain't getting in that office until you give up your pieces!"

"You know MoJo and your boss, Nicky Nails, called us to meet them here. And they know we don't go anywhere unless we are strapped."

Nicky and Morris come out of the office to break up the impending shootout. They quieten the group and usher them into the office.

"Did you idiots forget about the bug on the pool table?" Nicky asks after he slams the office door shut.

"And what's the matter with you guys, using my name in here," admonishes Morris. "Russell, you know better, we need to keep everything on the QT."

"It's not like those Greaseballs in Chicago don't know you are here," retorts Russell.

"Hey!" Joe steps up to Russell's face.

"What, you can call me a Moolie, but you're offended by the name Greaseball?" Russell bumps chests with Joe Castor.

"Hey, MoJo, should I settle this for them?" Nicky says. "I'll pop a cap in both your asses. And I dare you to bleed on my floor!"

"Damn," MoJo laughs, "That's some harsh shit!"

The two men step back and then go to opposite sides of the office. Nicky returns to the chair behind his desk.

MoJo takes control of the meeting. "OK, now that we all have our dicks back in our pants, let me tell you why we are here. Russell, you and the boys have been cruising the neighborhoods for two weeks looking for a signal from Maria's transponder."

"Except for that one short blip the other day in Queens, we've come up empty."

"It has been pointed out to me that we are going about this all wrong. Apparently, they know about the transponder, so the logical thing to do, is to have her in a shielded location. Instead of looking for where she is, Russell, you and the boys will start looking for where she is not." All the men look at him as if he has gone insane. "Are any of you familiar with the theory of black holes? No? Let me give you the short version. It's an area in space where gravity is so strong not even light can escape. Which means you cannot see it. So the only way to detect it is to look for an area where there is no light."

"Ah! A black hole," says Russell, "We look for a place where the radio signal is blocked."

"Exactly. You ride in pairs, one car transmitting a high frequency signal, the other receiving it. Every place the signal is blocked you alert Joe and his guys."

"Why? Why don't we just move in?" objects Russell.

Morris places a hand on his shoulder. "I believe they are holding her in a neighborhood where you will be easily spotted. This is why you boys need to play nice together. Joe, I'm going to need your men on the streets looking for men with an eagle tat on their arms. It has been two weeks, I'm sure they must have gone to a store for cigarettes, coffee, TP. Turn the streets over until we find an exact location, an eagle clutching a sword tattoo won't go unnoticed. Now, do you see why I told you no tattoos years ago, Mr. Mills?"

Russell's mind goes back to a summer eve just after he was given control of the Original Sinners. They had a fight with two other gangs in Van Courtland Park in the north Bronx. All three suffered severe injuries before realizing they were already in league with each other. Russell gathered the members together and was about to tattoo a halo pierced by two red horns – the Original Sinners' emblem – on his shoulder, and the rest were going to follow him. That's when MoJo walked in. Like the devil himself, he always seemed to know when he was needed.

"If you ink your arm, I'll cut it off," I bark and everyone froze.

"You are going to cut the tattoo off my arm?"

"No, I'm going to cut your arm off your body."

The guy puts down his needles and moves away.

I look around the room. "Do you know what is the first thing cops ask when you are arrested? For those of you who have not yet had that pleasure, they ask if you have any tattoos or identifying marks. If you say yes, they enter that into your record. Let's say a tough guy like you."

I hold Russell's arm up. "Has a Tweedy Bird on his arm. Know what the police put down? 'tattoo: bird'. Any time they are looking for a gang banger with a bird tattoo, any kind of bird tattoo, your name is going to come up. Do you want that?"

"We almost killed each other in the park tonight," Russell yanks his arm away. "How are we supposed to tell friend from foe?"

"Maybe you should hold a nice social. I little dance in the school gym or something… get to know one another on a real deep level." Morris laughs. "Seriously. You guys are into colors and that whole bullshit, make a patch and put it on your jacket. At least if the cops are after you, you can take the fucking jacket off, Asshole."

Russell says defiantly, "What's to stop some asshole from sewing on a patch and saying they are part of the gang?"

"Nothing. But if they are wearing the patch they'd better step up when called on, or you cut them down. That's gang loyalty. Besides, do you know the real reason you should never mark your skin?" Everyone looks at him for the answer. "The Jews say you can't get into Heaven with any marks on your body. Do you want to go to Heaven when you die?"

After Morris leaves, the banger who was going to do the tattoos approaches Russell and says, "Does he think a tattoo is really going to make a difference in his afterlife? I can't even count how many people he has killed so far."

Russell and his guys leave the office.

Morris turns to Nicky, "Just a moment. Before we go out there and do this thing, I have something to tell you."

"Now what?"

"You know the story of Judas, right?"

Nicky nods his head and shoots me a look of 'please don't', which I ignore.

"Well, then you know that when he hanged himself he bled black blood."

Nicky's eyes double in size, "What the hell are you talking about? I've been to Catholic school just like you, and I never once heard any priest, brother, or monk say something crazy like that. But I've seen enough guys die to know if there was a puddle, it was shit. So here's a piece of advice for you, order light for your last supper."

"Think of it," I tell him, shrugging off the sarcasm. "God knows everything. Jesus is God. He knew Judas was going to betray Him. So why did he pick Judas as one of his apostles?" Nicky and Joe just stare at me. "He needed a killer with black blood to make His plan work. One day, you may need a friend like Judas or to be Judas. Now, let's go put on a show."

As we walk out the office, Joe says, "One minute, Boss, I almost forgot some urgent family matter I need to tell you."

Nicky looks at him sternly, but doesn't budge. "Oh, what the fuck! Mo... go grab a drink, I'll be out in a minute. You can wait a couple of minutes, can't you?"

I nod and smile at Joe. I know the important family matter he needs to discuss.

Nicky slams the door, drawing the girls' attention. The Sons of Italy is mostly empty these days. To be on the safe side, Nicky had his capos meeting elsewhere. Only wannabes and the uninformed local boys hang out here now, and without any real suits around, they come in less frequently too. *It always amazes me how so many people want to be around powerful and dangerous people, like they are expecting one of us to pull out and shoot the person standing next to them a million times. And then offer them the Swiss cheese's position in the gang. If it ever happened, they would shit themselves and die on the spot. But that's what they hang around to see.*

"Well, Joe, what the fuck is on your mind?"

"You don't think Morris was threatening you just now?" Joe says. "I'm not just your Consigliere, I am here to protect you too. I think he is warning you to do what he says or else."

"Hahaha, is that what's on your mind? Morris and me, we go way back, my friend and you don't know him like I do. MoJo doesn't make threats or give warnings. If he meant to kill you, you would be the first and last to know. I'm not sure what the fuck he is talking about all the time, but he means me no harm. But if I had to guess what he was talking about just now, I'd say he was telling us to prepare for war... A very ugly war."

Joe gets excited, "That's what I'm talking about. Think of it... You are about to take a seat on the board and here comes your old friend Morris, who wants to drag you into a war with the Feds. Something like that will surely end your chances of getting that seat. Maybe he kidnapped his own daughter to derail you."

"That's crazy," Nicky fires back. He is also on the verge of violence. The two other capos give the two men a lot of room as the office seems to shrink around them. "We know Tom Green took her, either under orders from his Chicago bosses or his Washington ones, or both of them together. My father told me this a long time ago, 'before you make a move ask yourself... What do I get out of it? If it's not worth the risk don't bother.' So answer me… What does Morris get out of blocking me from sitting on the board?" Joe doesn't answer. "Well?"

"Maybe he wants complete control of New York. If you are on the board, that will never happen. Or perhaps it is not Morris directly, it could be someone in his gangs trying to get him and even you out of the way. I'm just saying, keep your eyes open, Boss. Don't let friendship blind you. We can't afford a war with the Feds, not now… not ever."

"This is going to be some deal we have to work out," Nicky smiles a twisted grin and pats Joe on the shoulder. "You don't trust our Black partners. I have to make a deal with the Feds, who I trust as far as I can throw'em. And Morris doesn't trust anyone, especially when it comes to his family. This is going to be one fucked up deal we are about to get into."

The office doors open and Nicky exits alone. I look for blood on his hands and smile.

He takes a seat across the table and grabs a drink. "What?"

"I was expecting at least some bloody knuckles."

"Oh, that. It was nothing serious," Nicky says dismissively, "just some girl trouble. One of them may be falling in love with a john, giving out discounts. Hey, talking about girl trouble, you believe what your guys reported?"

"Hell, yeah," I exclaim, "They know I'll be madder if they lie, rather than just saying nothing yet. They said they are a day or two away from zeroing in on the location, then that's a fact."

"OK. Then what are your plans," Nicky takes another drink and looks at the pool table.

I shake my head and smile. *He's a terrible poker player.* "I have two teams ready to go. The first will take down the exterior forces, and at the same time, the second will breach the interior holding place and take out anybody there. These guys are the best. I personally handpicked them. Two minutes in and out and we will have her."

"I know you've been in this game a long time, MoJo, but sometimes the obvious move is not the best. There is one problem with your plan..." I start to defend my position but can't even get a word out. "The one problem is all they need is one man, with one gun, in one room with your daughter. You may be bulletproof, Morris, but you are not faster than one. If you go in shooting, you'll be rescuing a corpse... I know what you're thinking... They are probably under orders not to harm her under any circumstances, but knowing your... how should I put this? Extreme behavior. Hell, it is legendary. Whoever is tasked with holding your daughter is most likely planning on putting a bullet in her head, then one in his own. Orders or no orders. I'm sure he'll rather face the Devil in Hell then the one here on Earth."

"So what am I supposed to do? Get on a bullhorn and say, 'Bring the girl out and all is forgiven?' Then we all sit around and sing Kumbaya or some shit!"

"No. Hear me out," Nicky tries to calm me down. "That little block party you threw in Manhattan the other night got their attention. They don't want a war."

"How do you know?" I shout impatiently.

"Because they only poured hot coffee down my guy's throat," Nicky crosses himself, thanking God. "If they really wanted a war, they would have lit this place up by now. Everybody has anted up in this game, now it is time to play our cards. I suggest you release the girl Fed as a sign that you are willing to make a deal, and I'll make sure they release your girl in turn. Then we can sit down to serious negotiations."

"You think that will work?"

"Sure, somebody made a real poor decision and they know it by now. The thing to do is for everyone to make the right decision and get this thing on the right track. You're a businessman, right? Then let's get down to business. No more blood, no more bombs, just dollars and sense."

"If you think you can set it up, go ahead." I hold up my empty glass and Rosalie starts over with the vodka.

"I have a couple of guys from Chicago working on a deal in Miami. I'll have them contact their guy in the FBI, he works for Chicago, but they don't know it. He can be the go-between." Nicky holds his glass up as Rosalie fills it. Then he grabs her ass, "Boss' privileges'. Nobody else better try that."

"I still know how to break fingers, you know." Rosalie smiles and fills my glass. "You need to call Yana. She worries about you."

I nod dutifully. I down the drink and get up. Grab Rosa around the waist and squeeze her ass, then kiss her cheek.

"Hey!" Yells Nicky. "Where's the talk about breaking his fingers?"

"He has nice hands." She laughs and leaves.

"If Vicky wasn't over there looking for a reason to drill my skull, I'd clip you right now."

I smile at Nicky and say softly but loud enough to be picked up by the bug, "You won't have to worry about her much longer. In fact, I need you to take care of her. She's done all she can for us. I don't need her around anymore. Make sure no one can ID her."

"What? Hell no! So, this is what all that talk about Judas was leading to," Nicky is furious but tries to keep his voice down as not to let Vicky hear us. "What the fuck is wrong with you, MoJo?"

"With me! What's with you! Just do it!" I counter. I know the bug may pick up this conversation too and reply in his ear, "I need you to get Vicky a new identity so she can get out of this life. She needs to reconnect with her brother, so the ID has to be flawless. Pass any security check she may encounter. What the hell did you think I wanted you to do?"

"Kill her," Nicky whispers with his hand over his mouth. "You really got to work on your choice of words, Morris."

I laugh. Mission accomplished. I put the glass back over the bug.

He looks at me with a touch of anger in his eyes. "I think you do this shit to me on purpose. Don't mention any of this to Vicky. I don't want her to get the wrong idea. You know how she feels."

"Yeah, and she has been meaner than a two-headed viper," I joke. "You couldn't kill Vicky anyway. She would take you apart before you knew what was happening. To tell you the truth, I don't think I could take her either, especially not after Derrick. But she needs out of this life. And you need a vacation. Like, I'd kill my best and oldest friend."

Nicky grabs my hand as I start to leave. "Where are you going?"

"Have to see to the girl and make arrangements for plan B. You know... Just in case."

Nicky drinks his vodka, stands up, and throws his arms around me. "You should go out the front. The boys are still in the back talking things over. Watch your back."

The morning news is ablaze with a story out of Miami Beach. Six men were found dead, execution style in a hotel room. The Dade County police chief is doing all he can, not to call it a murder for hire, or anything that will resonate with the drug wars which plagued the area a couple of years ago. He is refusing to confirm the men are of Italian nationality, but one news station out of Chicago has flashed the mug shot of Tony "The Plummer" Richards as among the men in the room. The reporter says, "He is known as 'The Plummer' because he was reputed to use a large pipe wrench to beat his victims to death. But it looks like someone has finally pulled the plug on Tony's criminal affairs. Both his and his associates' careers have gone down the drain here in Miami."

As the television plays out the dramatic scene from sunny Florida, Morris, Nicky, and their technician are in the basement listening to wire taps out of Washington and Chicago. The Don is trying to convince the Senator that he had nothing to do with the hit in Miami, and at the same time accusing his partners of the deed. The one question each wants answered is, 'Who is Tom Green really working for?'

After a two-hour verbal meltdown, they hang up. Morris continues listening in on the Don lines and as he hoped the Don places a call to Mississippi, a small spit on the map deep in gator country. It is a short conversation.

"Is he there?"

"No. I haven't seen him in days," informs the unidentified recipient. "Any message?"

"You don't say a fucking word! Call the minute he shows up. Capisci?" Don Brunello throws the phone against the brick wall, shattering it.

"Address?" I ask.

"Got it right here," answers my guy, "the satellite pinned it down to within a quarter of a mile."

"Well, I'm off to go pay our friend Tom a visit. Anything in particular you'd like me to tell him?"

"Just, I hope Hell is a twenty-four hours a day ass fucking," Nicky sneers. "Do you think he's there?"

"Oh, he's there all right. I just have to beat the Don's men there because he didn't believe that lying piece of shit that answered the phone either."

"He might run," Nicky worries.

"He would if he was smart," I concede, "But I'll bet that asshole sits right there thinking he can kill anyone that comes a-calling. We will just see about that, won't we." As I am heading into the tunnel, I turn back to Nicky. "You let me know when the boys find Maria. I'll come right back."

"Of course. We won't make a move without you. And I'll stay on top of our friends in Washington, they sound a bit desperate now. Have fun!"

"Oh, you know I will."

Chapter 15

Through the Eyes of God

A red Cadillac pulls into a gas station in Bayou Pierre, Mississippi and the driver immediately lays on the horn. The young man in coveralls sits on the porch and waits for the horn to stop blowing. He looks at them and goes back to his newspaper.

The driver starts on the horn again and his passenger smacks his hands from the wheel. "Look, it's hot, sticky, and we are fucking lost. Piss this guy off and we will never find Grant's cabin." The passenger gets out and walks over to the porch. He loosens his tie and unbuttons his jacket. "Look, friend, I'm sorry about my buddy but we've been driving up and down these roads for hours and we are lost."

"Y'all don't say."

"Can you get us some gas and directions to 37-24 Jackson Road?"

"Jackson Road, huh?" The young man stands up, looks past the man in the suit, walks over to the car, and studies the other three. He is followed by the suited man. "Jackson Road is way deep in the bayou. What would you city boys want to be doing out there? Plan on doing some gator hunting?" He starts pumping gas.

"We are supposed to meet our guide out there," says the man in the suit. "He's going take us on a hunt. Supposed to be quite the experience."

The young man shuts off the pump. "Well, I don't know what you are paying this guy but he's a lousy guide if he didn't meet you somewhere and bring you out to Jackson Road himself. It's going to be dark soon and you will never find it in the dark."

"Hey, yokel," yells the driver, "I think we can follow simple directions."

"Obviously, ya can't if you all's are already lost." He spits on the ground to show how he feels about the name yokel.

The suited man hands him a small wad of twenties, "You're right, but if you can just mark the route on the map we have—"

"Sorry, I can't. Because Jackson Road ain't on any map. But if you are desperate to get there... go straight down this road and cross the Big Bayou Pierre Bridge. You are going to come to a fork in the road and take the left. A couple of miles you will come to the Steel Gator Bridge... Cross it and drive a half mile then take the dirt road on the right. That's Jackson Road. Of course, if you take the wrong road or miss a single curve on any of these roads out here, you will end up in the bayou. And the gators will be hunting you."

"Is there someplace around here to stay the night?" asks the man in the suit.

"Back up the road a few miles, the big white house is a boarding house."

The four men get four rooms on the second floor of the four-story old Colonial. There are eight bedrooms and one bathroom on each floor, and all are empty except the ones on the first floor where the owner's family lives. They attempt to get the four men to talk about their upcoming hunting trip, as it is nearly the end of the hunting season, which is why the place is empty. The men say very little, except to admit they have never hunted gators.

After the father and the two boys tell them how gators have turned over boats, the driver pulls out his .45 and says, "I was told this is the best equipment for hunting gators."

"Yep, that's what I use. I hope you have a rifle too," says the dad. "You don't want to wait for the gator to be in the boat to shoot it." After dinner, he takes the men into the parlor for whiskey, and to show off his 32-foot gator. "Took six hours to get'im to the surface and for me to get one shot with my Smitty.45. Be ready for a real fight."

"We are," says the driver.

Following the drinks, the men go to their rooms and check their equipment. Each has a high-powered scoped rifle, handguns, and camouflaged waders.

The driver says, "Looks like there is only one road in and out. We block the road with the caddie and walk in. Drop whoever is there."

"We three will go in," says the suited man. "You stay with the car, just in case he gets past us. We need to get there at first light."

"Why?" asks one of the other gunmen.

"Gators are cold blooded. I don't want to be walking around out there once they start moving around."

The men leave before dawn and follow the gas station attendant's directions carefully. Once they turn onto the dirt road, they cut the lights and start driving slowly. They nearly go into the bayou at several turns, as the road is especially narrow. They stop when they see a ramshackle wooden house among the trees. It is put together with planks and has a single window on each side, no glass.

There is a front door and a back door that show sunlight straight through. They can't see any movement inside the one room shack, but as they approach with rifles trained on the door and windows, a gator slides into the murky water as they pass. One of the gunmen drops to one knee and takes aim at the door.

The other two continue on to the cabin from either side. The leader slides under the window, the other gets ready to kick the door in. He raises his foot, kicks the door, and falls flat on his face. A large red spot moves down the center of his back. The leader jumps up, spins around the side of the cabin, and yells, "Ambush."

A piece of wood above his head brakes from the cabin. Then another a bit lower and to the left rips away. He ducks then fires a few shots into the trees. The other man follows suit and lights up the treetops. They hear the sound of a zipline and turns to fire in its direction. A couple of shots fly back and forth and the man on the zipline hits the ground with a thud. The leader approaches carefully. The other man keeps his gun pointed at him. Suited Man flips the poncho covered body over. "Damn it! It's not him."

A motor erupts in the rustic morning air. The men look around and see a boat halfway across the river. Tom is making his escape while his friend gave him cover. They fire at the boat and riddle it with bullets. The boat runs aground on the other side of the river.

"Let's go!"

Suited Man grabs his partner's arm. "Are you kidding? That's alligator infested water."

They see a black figure crawl from the water several feet away from the boat then running up the embankment and disappearing over the top. A shot blows the top of suited man's partner's head off.

He hears a car engine start in the distance. "Damn it." He runs back up the road. "Let's go. Let's go. Tom is getting away."

"What happened out there?" asks the driver.

"Sniper, decoy motorboat, skin diver suit... he's getting away."

The driver tries to back up as fast as he can then roars up the road, trying to catch up to Tom. His driving skills kick in and even though they slide left and right on the dirt road, he can see the dust cloud ahead. Suited Man takes aim with his rifle and fires a single shot.

Tom's rear window shatters but it doesn't seem to bother him. He speeds up, trying his best to stay on the narrow road and out of the line of fire. He swings down the embankment and roars along the river's edge. Another bullet shatters the side window behind his head... The caddie is gaining on him. He rips across the road, around the bend to his left and heads for the bridge before him. It's his escape plan. He holds a radio in one hand and floors the gas pedal. There's nothing to it, just a straight run to the red rusty bridge, which he wired with dynamite. He drops down in the seat as bullets shatter more glass, mirrors, and punch holes through the seats. He is seconds away from freedom.

"Aim for the tires, you moron," says the driver as he floors the caddie.

Tom's Mustang hits the bridge, leaps into the air and crashes back onto the metal grating. Halfway to freedom... He holds up the radio and prepares to press the detonator button. Both ends of the bridge explode, twisting and folding around the Mustang. Then the whole structure rolls over and crashes upside down in the water.

The caddie driver slams on the brakes but the vehicle slides in a cloud of red dust and dives into the metal structure in the water. The caddie slices down the middle and the right side peels back to the trunk, its two occupants finished.

Morris goes into the shallow river in a skin diver's suit. He quickly maneuvers through the wreckage to the Mustang, straps an oxygen mask on Tom's face, and turns the pressure up high. The air forces its way into his lungs and he coughs and spit blood into the mask. Morris pulls Tom to the shore, cuffs his hands behind him and drags him to his car. Tom is hurting but awake.

Morris throws him into the trunk, looks down at him, and says. "That was a great escape plan you had. Nice use of explosives, excellent placement, made for the perfect trap. I am so glad you didn't die; we are going to have such fun."

Tom's brain pounds inside his skull. Sights and sounds swirling around come into focus and then fade out again. His head wobbles as he tries to lift it, feeling like a tombstone is dangling from his forehead. Sunlight stabs him in the eyes. Bird and insect sounds fill his ears. Finally, he says, "Now what?"

"Ah, you're awake," I respond. "I was afraid you weren't going to make it. It was touch and go there for a while. But I knew you were a fighter."

"Where are you? I can't see you." Tom struggles but his arms and legs are strapped tight at the wrists and ankles. "Where am I?"

I walk around in front of him and hold up a mirror — the kind women carry in their purses to apply makeup. His face is ashen and he tries to twist himself free of the cross-like structure he is bound to. I let him struggle for a while, suspended a couple of inches off the ground. His arms are tied to the top crossbar and his legs spread and tied to the bottom one by shoelace leather strips. The four-by-four wooden crossbars are mounted to a center beam and staked into the ground. It looks like a double cross. Tom isn't going anywhere and he knows it, but still he tries.

Finally, the coarse wood scrapes against his naked body enough to start small trickles of blood running down his back. The leather ties also cut into his wrists and ankles, producing a rhythmic dripping of blood. He grimaces one last time then falls still. "Hey, I know what you want."

"No you don't. Not yet."

"Yes. Yes, I do." Desperation drives his voice a pitch higher. "I know who has your daughter. I know where she is being held."

I laugh and walk behind him.

He strains to turn his head.

"Relax. The game is about to begin and I don't want you to miss any of it." I wheel a full-length mirror in front of him. "You took my daughter, handed her over to the Sergeant, but you don't know where they are holding her."

"Yes…" Tom screams out. "I do. I do know where they took her."

"You're lying," I say softly, "they wouldn't have told you that part of the plan. They knew you would end up here in this situation, and try to bargain the information for your life. Or at the very least I'd rip it out of you before you breathe your last. No. You have no information I need."

"Sure I do," he answers much calmer, "and I know you want what I know about the people who are behind her kidnapping. Or else why would you go through all this trouble to capture me? If you just wanted me dead, you would have killed me by now."

I walk behind him again and return with an operating room cart. It gleams in the morning sun. I see Tom's eyes turn to slits, trying to identify the objects on the trays. "Who said I wanted to kill you, Tom? Or should I rather call you Franco? Your dear ole granddad, he wanted you dead. Maybe your bosses in the Black Scorpions want to silence you. Although, you know the way they operate, any information you had on them went up in smoke when that bridge blew up. I have other things in mind."

A cloud casts a shadow on the cart and Tom sees various knives, meat hooks, and pliers. He shakes uncontrollably and his voice trembles as he asks the question he doesn't want the answer to. "What are you going to do with those things?"

I pick up a large bowie knife and let it sway in circles as the handle rolls through my fingers. For such a heavy blade, it moves fluidly through the air, inches from his abdomen.

His breathing quickens rapidly and his muscles tighten with fear.

I smile. "When I was a boy, my father used to tell my brother and me to behave, or he'd skin us alive. We would laugh and joke about it when he couldn't hear us. Then one day we went hunting with the old man. We didn't hit anything but he nailed a fox, a rabbit, and a squirrel." I ran the blade up the center of his body, leaving a minuscule red line behind. It didn't actually cut him, just gave him a razor burn. He is breathing heavy hot wet air on my face.

"He tied the fox to a tree, its front legs above its head and its hind legs down. Then he took a knife similar to this one and sliced that fox from head to crotch. He slid his fingers carefully into the little cut, gripped a handful of fur..."

Tom looks away, afraid of making eye contact, as if my memories are playing vividly in them.

I yell, "And ripped that thing open."

Tom Green stops breathing. Several seconds pass before I feel the life return to his body.

"Oh, good. For a moment, I thought I scared you to death. That wouldn't have been any fun. But I'm sure you have seen worse. Done worse too. No?" I wait, looking him directly in the eyes.

No answer. His breathing is shallow, as if he is trying to hide from me.

"Do you know what I thought at that moment?" I wait.

Tom finally shakes his head sheepishly.

I tell him. "I was glad that fox was already dead. After my dad finished pulling the skin off that fox, he tied the rabbit to the tree and handed me the knife. My brother was supposed to be next but he was busy puking out his guts." I dig the tip of the bowie knife into his chin bone. "You know now, you're not going to be as lucky as that fox, rabbit, or squirrel was."

Sam Black hears about the bridge explosion on the morning news. Already en route to Mississippi, he realizes Morris has beaten him there. He is not sure what he can find at the cabin but having travelled thus far, he hopes some kind of evidence was left behind. He is in luck, the local police bypass the shack in the bayou and the fresh bullet holes confirm that someone, but probably Tom Green has been there. Blood on the ground means others were there too. Of course, the alligators left no trace of who or how many. They also cleaned out the caddie and mustang at the bridge. There is nothing at either scene to suggest Tom Green made it out the bayou alive, but he knows Morris.

"Sheriff Cole, I'm Special Agent Sam Black, FBI. I'm going to need your assistance in locating this man." He hands the Natchez man a drawing of Morris. Then he passes him a picture of Tom, "I believe he abducted Special Agent Tom Green."

The sheriff's dark brow creases with six new lines at Tom's picture. "Special Agent, you say. Was he undercover?"

"I'm not at liberty to discuss what he was working on."

"Of course," replies Sheriff Cole in a tone that conveys disbelief. "Your Special Agent has been hanging around some very bad people for quite some time. Bikers and truckers we have been after for drugs, arms, and a host of other crimes up and down the Mississippi. I knew him as John Dolby, and most people called him JD. If he is FBI, he did an excellent job of hiding it. Never seen the other guy, you got a name for him?"

"He goes by John Morrison. Although, his real name is Morris Johnson. He's a real killer."

"Then what makes you think Green is alive?" the Indian sheriff eases off, "from the looks of this bridge I don't think he was trying to take him alive."

"Morris is a psycho. He wants him dead alright, but not all at once, and not right away."

"Well, there are no tire tracks on the other side of the bridge," informs Sheriff Cole. "He's smart enough to know if you want to leave the bayou without being followed, you go by water. I'll put out an APB for the both of them, and set some checkpoints on the roads. But it has been hours since this bridge was blown up, I feel your guys are long gone or in the belly of the gators."

"Why did it take so long for you to come investigate this explosion?"

"Are you kidding?" Cole is offended. "This far out in the bayou? An explosion out here usually means a shine or meth lab, not high on my give a shit list. Some gator hunters radioed in the bridge was out, and that is what got me out here. We will do what we can to find your guys, but don't count on a good outcome."

"OK. You ready to party?" I ask.

"Fuck you!"

"That's the spirit." I trail the knife down Tom's torso, slicing him from chest to groin. I can see the pain in his eyes, but not that bad yet. "I bet that feels like one bad paper cut."

Tom says nothing. He is channelling his pain into hate, I can see it in his eyes. I smile as I wiggle my fingers into the oozing slit. The warmth of his blood feels good on my fingertips. As my fingers inch under his skin, sweat beads form on his face. He fights to remain silent, but loses it as I ball up his chest in my hands and yank it away.

"Aaaiyee!" Drowns out the sound of ripping flesh. Tom's head drops into my bloody sticky hands. That scream takes all the energy from him. I lift his head so he can see the skin on his chest flap loosely in the mirror, the blood flowing slowly out and down his body.

"That was a good start. You held up well." I grab the left flap of skin with both hands and swiftly snatch it all the way to his side. The scream this time is of pure agony. "Now that was a bad one. I'll give it to you."

Tom's chest is on fire, his eyes blurry with tears. He looks into the mirror at his wet red muscles heaving, not much blood but plenty of pain. Tom can't stand it anymore and his eyes close.

I take a bucket of swamp water and throw it with force onto Tom Green's chest. The murky water rushes up, driving his head back and causing him to gag. Eyes snap open as the blood on his chest slows to a trickle. "Com'on! You can take more than that. I'll tell you what, you pick the next spot. I can do your face or your *you-know-what*."

Sheriff Cole comes out of his office and takes a hard look at Sam. "I just had a long and interesting call from your New York office. Do you know what they told me?"

"What? Put me in cuffs and send me back home."

"Close." Cole laughs, "Put the cuffs on and keep you here. They said you were suspended. Now, you are fired. You really rub people the wrong way."

"Did the Director tell you why?" Sam is nonchalantly drinking a coffee.

"Oh yes!" Cole is excited to answer, "You lost your team. Aiding and abetting a criminal. Flagrant disregard of your orders. Should I go on?"

"No. So, now what?" Sam asks the old Indian defiantly.

"Unless you want to join my department, you better find one of your guys alive." Cole brushes his thick black hair back and pulls his straw cowboy hat down over it. "I have hunters searching the waterways. But there are a million places they could hold up in. I think we need to get out there before it gets dark."

The two men join another two deputies in a Coast Guard RHI docked in the back of the office. One of the deputies stands at the fifty-caliber machinegun on the aluminium hulled inflatable.

"You explained to these guys we need to take Morris alive, right?"

"We will try, but we want to come out of this alive too."

The sounds of birds, insects, and gators barking fill the twilight. Tom's moans are low wallows of pain and despair. I had stripped away the skin from his head, chest, arms, and legs, and the slightest of breezes causes a new wave of pain. Flies and mosquitoes are feasting on him now. His body slumped and I used two extra chords to support him at the shoulders. He has a narrow strip of skin down the center of his back where the main beam is. And the final strip, I am preparing to remove from his crotch.

"Hey, Tom! You'll be glad to know we are almost done here. I saved the best for last..." There is a dull hazy look in his eyes. He is tired. He has been through eight hours of cutting and pulling, ripping and drenching. "Naturally, I could have done it all in under an hour but we were having such a good time, don't you think? All the yelling and screaming, I never felt so alive. How about you?"

His head rolls in a slow circle, I don't think he is responding to me. It's probably the insects burrowing into his muscles that cause the occasional spasm. I continue,

"You know, as uncomfortable as you may be right now, you are going to live. I have no intention of killing you today. When your friends find you, I assume you have a friend, there will be that pile of skin they can sew back on. Now, instead of the slice and rip method I've been using all day, I'm going to peel your little pecker like a banana."

I take the scalpel and go from his abdomen down the center of his shaft. If he had had any strength at all, he would have screamed the loudest at that moment. But the body can only hold so much energy and Tom has used all of his up. I carefully maneuver the blade beneath the skin, lifting it away from one side then the other. It hangs like an old rag from his balls. I grip it firmly and with one good tug he is completely skinless, except for the strip down his back, and his testicles dangling beneath him.

I peel off the bloody surgical gloves and throw them into the metal drum. I toss all the knives and instruments in there too. Next, my blood-splattered clothes go in, all of them. I get dressed in a fresh pair of jeans and a shirt, new sneakers too. Then I pour a couple of quarts of hydrochloric acid into the drum. "Well my friend, there you have it. Skinned alive, it ain't no joke. By now, the sheriff's office should have received a map marking this very location, so I'll be leaving you. I'm sure they will find you by morning and you will have quite the story to tell."

I climb into the skiff and motor slowly and quietly into the gathering darkness. One last look back and Tom reminds me of the Michael Angelo drawing of man.

A young black boy about twelve is sitting on the steps of the sheriff's office.

"Marcus, what are you doing out this late?"

"I have a message for the FBI."

Sam looks the boy over, "Who told you I was with the FBI? Was it this man?"

The boy looks at the sketch and nods. "He said to give you this." He reaches into his pocket, stands up and starts to pull something out.

Sam jumps back off the steps and draws his 9mm.

Cole immediately shields the boy with his body. "Are you insane, man?"

"You don't know this guy."

"But I know this boy." Cole takes the wadded up paper from the boy's fist and sends the frighten child home. He opens the paper, "It's a map."

Sam holsters his gun and looks at the paper, "No markings. It could be anywhere."

"I know this place," says the sheriff, "it's deep in the swamp. We busted a country caine factory there a couple years back."

"A what?"

"A methamphetamine lab, or, the poor man's cocaine. I told you your boy was mixed up in some bad shit," Cole and Sam go into the office. "It's going to take a few hours to get there so we will leave as soon as the boat is gassed up." Cole turns and rubs his smooth dark face around his mouth.

"What? Really, how could I know if Morris paid that kid to shoot me or what? In a world full of monsters, he's fucking Godzilla and King Kong rolled into one."

"No, it's not that," Cole exhales heavily. "I've been investigating your guy Green and his friends for a couple of years. I believe they have been running a disposal service in the bayou. You know what I mean."

Sam shakes his head, having no clue what the sheriff is talking about.

"A couple of years ago some hunters brought in gators with human body parts in their guts."

"And that's a big deal? They are alligators," Sam responds naïvely, "I'm sure they must get a hold of a person now and again."

"Not really, you have to trip over one in the dark to get bit. Gators and crocs don't hunt people, they rarely come in contact with them. And when they do, the people come out on top. Besides, the limbs we recovered were severed, not bitten off. I suspect they slipped up and were fed to the gators during hunting season. I had an eye on them ever since."

It's Sam's turn to wipe the sweat from his face and open up with how and why he is there. "I know a little about that, I suppose. Green's associate is allegedly running a disposal service for the mob. Green was here laying low after a job he did in New York. But he's probably been working with him a whole lot longer."

"Are you telling me your Special Agent is working for the Mafia?"

"More like he was in the Mafia before he became an FBI agent," Sam admits. "Morris Johnson kidnapped my team and forced me to track Green down for him."

"Ergo, the aiding and abetting charges."

"Yes, but what I can't figure out is how Morris beat me down here."

Cole thinks for a second. "Let me see your piece."

Sam ejects the magazine and the round in the chamber. He sticks out the butt of his 9mm but Cole takes the magazine instead. He flips the bullets off the magazine until he gets to the last one. He bounces it around in his hand for a minute then drops it in Sam's hand. "You've been carrying around a tracking device, probably picks up sound too. He knows every place you've gone, listened in on every word said."

One of the deputies comes in the back door, "We're all gassed up."

"Let's go," says Cole. "We got to beat the sunrise and the gators. Alligators don't attack people, but they don't pass up a free meal either."

Sam reloads his gun and throws the bug off the dock as he climbs onto the orange and black Rigid Hull Inflatable.

Cole can see the anger cutting deep into Sam's face, "Let's go get that sonovabitch." They look at each other for reassurance, but they know Morris Johnson is long gone.

They approach the tributary with sirens blaring and flashing lights. Two more boats are close behind and police cars' lights can be see darting between the trees, no need for stealth this morning. The boat coasts to a stop just as the hard aluminium hull cuts into the soft sandy shore. The four men stand horrified.

Three alligators had climbed out of the swamp, drawn by the scent of blood. The sun has been up for an hour and the bayou is alive. Two small gators, no more than five feet head to tail, are gulping down strips of flesh from a pile, the other, is making its way towards the bloody crucified man. Cole draws and shoots the large gator. The two deputies emerge from their shock-induced paralysis and kill the two smaller ones. Splashing from beyond the trees means others decide to go elsewhere for a free meal.

The sheriff jumps from the boat, followed by Sam then the deputy driving the boat. The other deputy stays on the 50-caliber machinegun and sweeps the area continuously.

"Cut him down!" Orders the sheriff.

One deputy pulls a knife, the other leaves his gun and spreads a blanket at the foot of the cross.

As the two men cut the last bond and lower the body towards the blanket, they hear a ripping and popping sound. Three fishhooks had been imbedded in Tom's back and tore the last shreds of skin from his back. Blood spurts from his back and a low alien groan escapes his lipless mouth. The two officers drop him on the blanket. A renewed wave of disgust overtakes the four.

"This is more than insanity," Cole declares, "What in God's name did you people do to this Morris Johnson feller?"

"He believes Green kidnapped his daughter." Sam says and stands over the body. The three holes in his back mean Tom's spinal cord has also been severed. He is alive, but from this day forward, he'll be a peeled vegetable. Sam aims and shoots him in the back of his head. "He was like this when we got here."

Chapter 16

Cerberus

Rep. Webber crashes through Thomas Carter's outer office like a bull in a china shop. His hands flailing as he chases the senator's aides from the office. "Get outta here! Go get a coffee or something. I need to talk to your boss, alone and in private, woman."

Senator Carter leans to his right and makes eye contact with his secretary. He presses the intercom button with his left, "Gertrude, dear, show the Congressman in and try Senator Harris' office again. Thanks, sweetie."

"Go right in," Gertrude commands, never looking up from the work on her desk.

Jim Webber slams the heavy oak and frosted glass door shut behind him.

"Whoa, cowboy! Easy on the fixings. That door came all the way from my favorite watering hole in Abilene. Did I ever tell you that the people of Abilene were so happy when I won my first senate seat they tore that door off my then headquarters and told me to take it with me? To this day, that saloon has only one door. Ha Ha. It never closes."

"Yeah. Like a dozen times a year since the first day I met you," Webber retorts. "Have you seen the news out of Mississippi?"

"Of course I have," Carter smiles, "Boy, you are going to give yourself another heart attack."

"Do you think he talked?"

Thomas Carter throws a large manila envelope at Webber's chest, it hits the floor, spreading its contents at his feet. "Look at those pictures. The poor bastard told him everything he ever knew. But that changes nothing."

Webber is quickly sweeping the gory glossies back into their container, unable to stomach the sight.

Carter nudges him with his cowboy boot and grabs his Stetson, "Get yourself a drink, man. We are going to pay a visit to Senator Harris. It is time to bring this boy to Jesus!"

Webber doesn't have time to get a drink, as Carter heads straight out of his office. Everyone in the halls clears the way for the six-one Texan. He walks with a purposeful stride that demands respect. Webber, a short and paunchy figure, makes the pair look like Don Quixote and Sanchez when they are together. Webber always walks in double steps to keep up with the slimmer, quicker senator. "How do you know he is there? He hasn't returned any of our calls."

"He's been in his office for two days now. I had my men watching him." Carter stops abruptly at Harris' door. He knocks lightly, waits a few seconds then lets himself in. "Barbara, dear girl, let the senator know we are here. Then make yourself scarce."

The inner office door swings open quickly, Harris nods assent and the young woman gathers her things and leaves. As she passes by the two men, she locks eyes on Carter.

Two men enter behind her and walk around the offices with antennas attached to metering devices. They announce, "the place is clean."

"Can never be too careful, the Russians," Carter says. "Webber, get yourself that drink. You look overdone." He walks into the inner office and positions himself on the sofa. He throws his left ankle on his knee and begins to polish the side of his boot with a linen handkerchief while waiting for Harris to return to his desk. Webber manages to get in the door as he begins, "Your boy has been running around stirring up trouble everywhere. It is time to put this foolishness to rest. All we want to do is sit down and negotiate a business deal with him. All this killing and destruction is counterproductive."

"You should have thought about that before you had his daughter snatched." Harris' anger is written on his face and reverberates in his voice.

"Ok, it's time for a Come to Jesus meeting, I see." Carter says as his smile turns to a sneer. "Let me turn over my hand, as we say back in the saloon. Morris Johnson probably told you I tried to have your sister killed. The dead sister, whose name you used to get into this office. It's true. I don't know if you really believed she was dead or if you knew she was working with Morris and his dope-dealing partners, but I've been grooming you from day one to take part in the Grand Plan. You, my friend, was dragging your feet." Carter's eyes are locked on James Harris as if he's expecting him to draw.

Harris too feels as if the Senator is about to go for his hip, like in an old western movie.

"You needed a push and I figured you were sincere about your stand on drugs. At least publicly, and if your sister was killed in Colombia you would finally vote to send in the troops. The Colombians would flee into Venezuela and we would follow. But your friend Morris screwed that up for us. And not because he was doing some kind of heroics to save your sister. Or because he was trying to keep the big bad United States out of South America. He knew that with troops on the ground his little cash cow was going to go belly up along with the rest of them."

"So you are trying to tell me you wanted to kill my sister to stop the flow of cocaine into this country?" James' words climb the scale.

"Hell No! The war on drugs, that's the President's spin. You've been in the committees long enough to know, he's the face of the Government. He tells the people what they want to hear, what is popular. I am the voice of God. When the people are praying in church Sunday mornings, it is my voice that answers those prayers."

"You are fucking nuts!"

"Oh really? The people are complaining about gas prices. It's too high. Those ungrateful camel-humpers have us by the balls. And let me tell you, it is going to get worse. We are losing our hold on the Middle East. Isn't that right, Jim? You know it is. You're in the Foreign Relations meetings, those religious radicals are going to cut off our supply. The only way to keep the oil flowing is by war. And it won't be a pretty one either. It will be our God versus their God."

"What's the matter," chides Harris, "not up to the task, old man?"

"Don't worry, we are going to win that battle. But I learned a long time ago, to always keep looking for another source of water when you are thirsty. Venezuela has just as much oil as the Middle East, and with them we won't have to worry about Jihads and Crusades." Carter stops his tirade for a moment. The smile returns to his face. "As much as Morris fucked things up down south, he came up with something more precious than oil. He developed a weapon that can turn a handful of men into a fighting force, rivalling thousands. He developed it while working for us in South America, so I believe it's ours. He obviously wanted us to know about it, that's why he downed the fighter jets in Egypt and been testing it out on Russian Migs in Afghanistan. And that is why we are here today."

Harris sighs heavily, the senator's speech has bogged down his mind. "So you thought the best way to get this man to the bargaining table was to kidnap his daughter? That is so... Twisted. And I thought Morris was a madman."

"He is," confirms Carter. "You have seen how some of his business dealings have gone in Colombia. A whole villa slaughtered, countless people executed if they didn't go his way. Weren't you a member of that gang, the Original Sinners? I believe he got all new members after he slaughtered all his friends. Lucky you were safe in Vietnam back then, or you wouldn't be here now, I'd bet. Grabbing his daughter wasn't my idea, it was only meant to get him to come to New York and talk. This mess would be over by now if he did. He dragged it out these three weeks, looking for revenge."

Carter almost sounds genuine, but it's more likely he's lying through that phony smile he flashes so easy. "So I guess you are expecting me to get Morris to make a weapons deal with you. Or you'll what? Kill my sister?"

"No, of course not." The words drip from Carter's lips like honey, thick and sweet, "She is much more effective alive. Just think… what all those people in New York will say when they hear she's been alive all this time. And with just the right spin, you, my dear boy, will be looking at treason for that bombing in New York, the kidnapping of FBI agents, and his latest - the killing of another FBI agent. With your sister and her boyfriend alive, you can go to jail forever. So you tell Morris, we will meet him anywhere he wants, but it has to be within the next twenty-four hours."

Carter tucks his shine rag back into his boot, he had been working on the one side the whole time. He stands and walks pass Webber as if he is invisible.

In the hall, Webber grabs his arm, "don't you think meeting with him face to face is dangerous?"

"That is why I am going without you. I don't want you to piss your pant when Morris starts talking," Carter tells him. "I don't want you to cream in them either."

Late afternoon, Webber bursts into Carter's office for the second time that day. "Things are looking up. I just heard from Chicago, someone in Little Caesar's camp has defected."

"What? One of Rocci's boys turned on him? Sounds like a setup."

"It was one of the old boys, a Lucerella man. They were okay with Papa Rocci running things, but Junior brings too much dark meat to the table… if you know what I mean. Anyway, he said looks like Morris' boys are gearing up for something big. He delivered quite an arsenal of assault rifles and the likes. He gave us the address and said the kidnapped agents are there too."

Webber is overly enthusiastic about the news. Carter is not. "He says if we take out Morris' army then he can take on Nicky Nails Rocci."

"OK. Who is this defector?"

"Nicky's second in charge. And if we take out Morris' New York gang, then he will be more inclined to make a deal."

"It is worth a shot and we'll get the FBI on it. After all, it is their agents. But we have to make sure Morris is in the clear when they strike. I don't want some cock-eyed gunslinger killing our goose before he tells us how he lays those golden eggs."

"Absolutely," agrees Webber, "he spends most of his time in Rocci's place." Rep. Webber is more interested in stopping Nicky from taking control of the New York mob than stopping anything Morris has in mind. With Nicky out of the way, he will have both New York and Chicago under his belt and boast a power base that will keep him in office for quite some time. Without Morris' gangs, Nicky is vulnerable to an internal power struggle. "We should make a move tonight, before they can do whatever it is they are planning."

"I agree," the senator says quickly, "and I'll have Warren send in some Black Scorpion guys as SWAT agents, just to be on the safe side. We don't know what Morris peeled out of Green before he killed him. Not that he knew much more about the operation past the kidnapping."

7:00 pm and Senator Carter sits alone in his office with a drink in his hand. It's his fourth whiskey, and he's sipping it slowly, savoring the flavor as much as the burn in his throat. He called Sgt. Warren and told him to put together at least four teams of Scorpions to assault Morris' gang headquarters.

Warren disagreed vehemently with the plan, as he said, "You are going to attack someone with tactics he devised, that's like trying to catch a shark by jumping in the water with gaping wounds."

He's still considering those words when the phone rings. It's what he has been waiting for. "Hello, Senator Harris, what do you have for me?"

"Tomorrow, at sunrise, be on the steps of the Lincoln Memorial."

Carter can hear the animosity in the senator's voice. "Did he say to show up alone? I won't do that."

"I don't think he cares one way or the other. And neither do I." Harris hangs up without another word.

Carter drains his glass then refills it. He picks up the handset again, dials New York, and doesn't wait for acknowledgement. "You have a team in place for me? I'll be meeting your friend at sunrise."

"I'm a little busy now," answers Sgt. Warren in a surly tone, "You know, planning this nightmare of yours. I have guys meeting you at your office in about an hour, they will be with you from here on out. The teams are ready to roll; I have to go now."

Chapter 17

When Cries The Moon

Akilina has been keeping track of the time according to when food is brought to them. Since their escape attempt three days ago, they have been under constant surveillance. The lights in the trailer no longer go off, the refrigerator and stove have been disabled, and she knows the cameras in each corner of the room monitor and record their every move. They talk only in whispers into each other's ears, and only under a blanket. The same man delivers their meals. The same meal every time, a baloney sandwich and a box of milk, like the one would get in school.

She judges how late in the day it is by the beard growing on his rugged face. His coarse blonde hair and dark blue eyes lead her to surmise he is from Eastern Europe. Although he never speaks to them, she feels he is there to interpret anything she may say in Russian to Maria. Their last meal was around lunchtime, as his face has the slightest hint of hair on it. Now, he enters with the plain brown bag and a darker streak of brown running down his cheeks and under the chin. It must be around six in the evening.

Akilina stands like a stone looking in the mirror, touching the still swollen burn on her face, her hand gently caressing the blackening triangle on her cheek. The scar is going to be permanent.

The East European watches her intently then leaves the bag on the table behind her. He can see her eyes seem lost to his presence, only focusing on her own reflection and the side of her face.

"She is freaking out," the blond says to his partner when he returns to the monitor room.

"Yo man, the Sarge cooked that babe's face," replies the other guard in a thick Spanish accent. "You no mess with a woman's looks like that, Chica is going to be messed up in the head for the rest of her life."

"Okreni je, ona će biti u redu," his Serbian slips out.

"¿Qué es eso?"

"I said, I'd put a pillow over her face and you would fuck her," he laughs.

"Yeah, you got that right! But I wouldn't let her blow me, I like stroking my women's faces and hair while they do it. Let's them know how much I love what she is doing. That face would just freak me out." The Puerto Rican guard leans back in his chair and grabs his dick. "At least those two ain't giving us any trouble. The Sarge scared the shit out of them!"

Three hours later and the two captives have not yet touched their food. Akilina had eventually left her spot before the mirror and gone into the bathroom. She bends over the tub and started the water.

The two guards perk up as the girls have only taken one shower since they took over guard duty. They get in the shower fully clothed and come out from behind the curtains fully dressed when done. The two men look at each other. A bath? This is something new.

Akilina sits on the edge of the tub swishing her hand mindlessly back and forth in the water as it fills up. The water is warm. She glances up at the camera in the corner. The bathroom is the only room that only has one camera monitoring it and therefore doesn't give the men a view from every angle like the other rooms in the trailer. Akilina has her back to them. She turns for a moment, looks directly at them, and calls out, "Maria would you come here dear?"

"In a moment, Lina," Maria replies from the bedroom.

The men's eyes swing to another monitor with four pictures of the girl wrapped in the blanket on the bed. She is completely under the heavy blanket as it is the only way to block out the light. She throws it off and bounces from the bed. They follow her down the narrow hall on the next monitor and into the bathroom.

"What are you doing, Lina?"

"We are getting out of here," says Akilina in a cold and inhuman voice.

"No. No more escapes," objects Maria, "it won't be safe."

"Oh, we are not leaving here, alive." Akilina grabs the girl's arm and twists, flipping her head first into the bathtub.

The two men watch in shock for a moment, as the girl's legs and arms flail wildly on the screen. Manuel is the first out of his chair. "Dios mio! The bitch has lost her mind."

Rollo, the big Serb is first out the door. He clears three stairs at a time then jumps the last of the iron steps to the warehouse floor. He grabs the keychain from around his neck and fumbles with the lock.

Manuel is right behind him, "Come on man. We got to get in there. The Sarge will kill us if that girl dies."

"Hey, you are supposed to stay at the monitors!"

"Fuck that! Open the door man, before we are too late!"

The two men burst into the trailer and down the narrow passage to the bathroom. Rollo slips on the wet floor and goes down hard on his back at Akilina's feet. Manuel stumbles over him and grabs Maria by the shoulders, pulling her from the tub.

Maria reels around with a jagged black plastic comb in her hand. Half the teeth have been broken off and she chewed the end down to a point. She strikes Manuel in the side of the neck and as she pulls back the weapon, blood gushes across the tiny bathroom. But he's trying to maintain a grip on the wet girl, and doesn't feel the pain as she stabs him a second and third time in the throat. It is then he realizes the tub is less than half-full and it it's his blood that is turning it red. Maria shoves him against the wall, trying to untangle her feet and run at the same time. A hand, Rollo's hand, has a tight grip on her left ankle.

Akilina snatches the bloody comb from Maria's hand in mid swing, and drops her knees onto Rollo's stomach. He barely flinches from the blow as he holds tight onto the girl's leg. In the twisting mass of blood, water and bodies he lies exposed to the savage fury of Akilina's attack. With both hands cupped around the makeshift knife, she gouges at his face and neck. One blow spears an eye, another goes through the side of his cheek, the same place where her face had been burnt. A couple of blows scrape his forehead, doing little damage, before the final hit pierces his windpipe. Rollo gasps loudly and spits a large volume of blood in Akilina face, blinding her.

Maria stumbles from the bathroom covered in blood. She reaches the trailer door and is thankful the door didn't close and lock. The men, in their rush to get in, had left the key in the lock and the chain hanging from it got caught between the door and the jamb. Maria swings the door wildly and runs across the warehouse floor.

Akilina runs out of the trailer, appropriates herself of the keys, runs towards a small door in the corner, and calls out to Maria.

But Maria keeps running up the steps towards the roof. It's the only way out she knows of.

Akilina calls her back as she frantically tries the guards' keys in the lock. There are only three on the chain and none open the door. It dawns on her, the guards are locked in too.

Maria reaches the roof door and discovers it is padlocked. She kicks and throws herself against it.

Akilina catches up to her and says, "let me try these keys."

Surprisingly, one works and the two walk out onto the roof. They start looking around for a ladder that will lead down to the ground but see nothing along the roof. Akilina looks around, trying to get her bearings, it is night and the skyline around them is empty. They are in a desolate part of town, the nearby buildings have long been decimated by fires. The nearest structure that shows any signs of life is two blocks away. They see a flicker of light, moments later they hear a metallic ping behind them then another flash of a camera taking a picture and the same pinging sound. When the third flash goes off, the brick on the edge of the roof in front of them explodes and spray red granules, Akilina drags Maria down and back into the warehouse.

She knows it wasn't photos but gunfire that caused the tiny flickers of lights. The sound of bullets continues as the metal door lights up with holes. Akilina says, "there are three keys, we must find what door the last one opens. Quickly!"

Russell Mills opens Nicky's office and sticks his head in, "we got a strong ping from Maria's transponder. She's in Queens, on 32nd Ave in the Linden Hill section, near the river."

"I want teams to close off that section. No one goes in or out," orders Nicky immediately.

"That's going to be hard to do. There is Northern Blvd., Linden Place, College Point Blvd., and the two highways, the Van Wyck and Whitestone Expressway."

"Also, get some robots in the air," I order, "do we know exactly where on 32nd Ave she is being held?"

"It's an industrial site, factories and warehouses," informs Mills. He is motioning to guys in the club. "I already have a call into our people in Queens."

Nicky picks up the phone and dials. "Hey, I need a couple of work crews to shut down traffic on all major roads in the Linden Hill neighborhood around 32nd. ...I don't care how you do it. Dig up the streets for all I care. I need traffic to come to halt out there." He hangs up the phone. "That ought to buy us some time, but we got to get moving, we're going to have a hard time getting into the neighborhood ourselves in a few minutes."

Three carloads of Black gangsters and Italian mobsters pull out of the street around the corner from the Sons of Italy.

Morris and Nicky are in the lead car, an unmarked detective car with lights and sirens wailing. The other two are also from the Bronx Task Force on Gangs. They are heading straight across the Bronx to the Whitestone Expressway, the quickest route to Queens. They have gone only a few block when they hear on the radio that a truck has jumped the divider on the highway in Queens, shutting down traffic in both directions. A minute later, another reports a pile up on the Van Wyck Expressway.

"I hope we are not tipping our hand. Don't want the Black Scorpions to know we are coming," says Nicky.

"Oh, they know we are coming," I answer with a widening grin.

"Hey, I forgot to ask. How was your trip down south?"

"Very gratifying. Almost therapeutic," I say as I check my 9mm. We whip around the tollbooths and head out onto the bridge.

The phone rings in Carter's office, he answers.

"I don't have a lot of time, but you may want to delay your meeting tomorrow. The girls have been very naughty again. This time they broke containment."

"What! How the hell does this keep happening?" yells Carter.

"I told you she is not some little girl who sits at home playing with Ken and Barbie dolls," Warren scolds the senator, "and her nanny is a well-trained fighter too. They were not just going to sit still and wait to be rescued. But don't worry, I'm going to take care of the situation now. Just a warning though, she may be free by morning."

"Why don't you move them to another location?"

"I don't have the manpower for that as they are already en route to tonight's festivities. And it's too risky now anyway. This area will be crawling with niggers and greaseballs real soon." Warren hangs up the phone. He nods to three large bodybuilder-type black men and follows them out of the building.

The small door in the sidewall of the warehouse opens. Sgt. Warren walks in, follow by his three henchmen. He yells, "Where the hell are you bitches?"

One man goes into the trailer, another behind it. The third goes up the stairs to the control room.

"They are in here," the third man yells to the sergeant.

The door is locked and the women huddle in the corner under the desk. Warren and the other two men stand outside the wire mesh walls.

"Do you think I don't have a key? Come out now," Warren demands.

They remain clutched to each other.

The first man unlocks the cage, grabs Akilina by an ankle and drags her out and down the stairs. The second grabs Maria by the arm and she flails helplessly against him.

"Careful with her, she is a delicate bloody flower." Warren says as she is being brought down. He takes Maria by the arm and lifts her up to his face. "You only needed to behave yourself one more day. Why couldn't you trust me?"

Akilina screams and kicks wildly on the warehouse floor.

Warren holds Maria with one arm around her neck. She squirms and struggles to breathe. "You two behave like animals! You killed two of my men. Now, I kill your bitch and you get to watch as my dogs tear her apart."

As the three men surround Akilina, she looks insignificant in their midst. One grabs her by a shoulder and lifts her half off the floor before he yanks her blouse and the bloody garment rips away, as he drops her hard back onto the cement. Another grabs one leg and pulls her pants from her in a single move. Akilina balls into the fetal position, trying to shield her nearly naked body. Red blood streaks end at her black bra and panties, and her white skin grows paler.

Maria struggles to get her words out, "No, please don't. She is a virgin."

"Well boys, you heard the young lady. This is her first time," Warren's voice is hot in Maria's ear. "Make it a good one. And make it quick, we don't have all night."

Maria tries to turn her head as the first man dives onto Akilina, his hands forcing her legs apart. Warren tightens his chokehold on the girl. She can't move but she closes her eyes painfully tight. His breath is burns her neck as Akilina's screams pierce her ears.

The first man had forced his way into the petite body. Then he rolled over onto his back with her trapped against him by his huge hands on her ass. She feels her insides being torn apart by his massive size, his nails digging into her cheeks, pulling her apart. Seconds later, shock shoots through her as the second man penetrates her from behind. Her scream is immediately choked back by the third massive cock filling her mouth, as he pulls her head up and backwards by her hair.

"I hope you are getting all of this. It called three the hard way," Warren sneers.

Akilina can barely feel anything but fire as the three men relentlessly violate her body. Her inability to breathe causes her to thankfully pass out.

Warren sees her body go limp. After a few more minutes he laughs, "I think you men have fucked that little bitch until she is well done. We need to get on the road now."

Warren drops Maria to the floor. The two men stand and the third bench presses Akilina like he is lifting weights. Then he tosses her up and to the side, letting her body smack back down like a discarded ragdoll. She lands in a twisted heap and doesn't move. Maria hears their odious laughter as the four walk out the door. She crawls to Akilina, and cries out in anguish as she cradles her head. Blood pours profusely down Akilina's legs and she is barely breathing. Her breath wanes as Maria rocks her helplessly on the cold hard cement floor.

🔫🔫🔫

"Midnight Fury... Midnight Fury... This is Eagle's Nest, do you read?" The radio in the car suddenly comes alive.

I nod to Russell Mills in the front passenger seat and he hands me the radio's mike. "We got you. What's up?"

"We got a location on your package. One of the remote planes just spotted four men leaving a warehouse on 32nd Avenue and Downing Street in a black van hauling ass for the highway."

"Good, track them, but don't get too close," I warn. "Have to make sure the girls aren't hurt."

"I don't think the girls are with them. Video only shows the men leaving the warehouse. The girls must still be inside."

"Take them out!" I order. "They are not to get away. Understand me?"

"We copy," the voice replies with confidence, "we have two fast attack vehicle heading north on College Point Boulevard about to make contact."

"We are heading to the warehouse. Keep me informed."

The black van makes a hard right onto College Point Boulevard.

"The highway is jam-packed."

"I can see that," says Sgt. Warren to the driver. He also sees a Ford Mustang coming up fast in the side mirror. "Shit! We've been made. Take the service road until we get ahead of the traffic."

Before the driver can make the turn, bullets rattle off the back door of the van. The driver floors the gas and the van careens downs the narrow street. Sgt. Warren doesn't have to order the other two men into action. They open the panels under their seats and pull out assault rifles. Another dimpling on the back of the van lets them know the Mustang is not far behind.

The dull black Mustang is half a block behind its target. The passenger has his M16 on a mount outside his window, its muzzle forward of the car's windshield. He fires another short burst into the back of the van.

The driver yells, "the van is probably armored, aim lower... Take out the tires."

A panel pops open on each side, near the rear of the van. Bullets shower the front of the car with orange streamers. They bounce off the bulletproof glass, leaving large white spots. A second barrage follows immediately, punching through some areas in the windshield, to be repelled by a second thicker sheet of Plexiglass inside.

A supped up Grand Fury swings in front of the Mustang. Two men in the back seat stick Uzis out and open fire. They riddle the right side and back of the van with a steady drumming of bullets. The van swerves wildly, slamming off parked cars. As it crosses an intersection, unaware drivers are caught in the crossfire. The van smashes through.

The Fury follows the path cleared by the van. The Mustang swings into oncoming traffic, which is crashing to the side of the road to avoid the approaching hailstorm. They spray the street and bottom of the van. The two cars are gaining on the heavily armored van.

The Kevlar lining in the van panelling keeps the bullets from piercing the hull. However, the bullets cause large pox marks all over the back of it. "We can't take much more of this, Sarge. Those cars must be carrying some heavy plating of their own. It is the only reason they haven't overtaken us."

"OK, what say we break out the big boy toys. Show these guys what a real kick in the ass feels like."

The two men swing their guns around to their backs and pull out two bazookas from the weapons hold. "We're not going to be able to get a shot at them without opening the back doors," reports the man who sodomized Akilina, "are you sure you want to risk it?" Another rattle of gunfire punctuates his words.

"You're not aiming for the cars. Quick, pull under the highway," Warren orders the driver and he obeys. Underneath the expressway is a parking lot, full of cars, which stretch for blocks. It is a single lane with cars slanting into their path.

Warren sees both cars behind them in what's left of the side mirror. "Can you see the support to the highway overhead? On the count of three, take them out."

Another round of gunfire hits the van, and this time, punching holes in several places. The two men spring to the backdoors. They don't wait for a three count.

The Grand Fury driver sees the van doors fly open and flames exploding inside the dark hull. The boom shatters windows on cars and buildings along the street, and a riotous cacophony of explosions and crashes play out in their wake. A large slab of the road above crushes the Fury flat. The Mustang, only seconds behind, right angles to the left, slamming into cars and the falling concrete. Vehicles appear out of nowhere and nose dive into balls of fire. The Mustang's driver and gunner are decapitated by the shielding, which was mounted on the dashboard moments before. The gun re-loader in the back seat is badly hurt but not dead. He crawls and reaches through the mangled carnage to take the radio's mike. "Wolf One and Two are down. The prey has escaped. Cannot confirm any dead. Over and out."

We reach the warehouse just as the radio message comes in. It isn't hard to find, the only building on the street not burned to the ground. Our car stops in front of the garage door. The second car pulls in alongside of us. The third turns down the alleyway to the back of the building. I get out and start to the side. Noticing the cameras mounted at each corner of the roof, I pointed them out to Nicky. I reach the corner and see the small steel door. I turn back to Mills and Nicky's men, who are donning bulletproof vests. "What the fuck are you doing?"

Mills is the only one who has the guts to answer, "There could be some more guys inside, or the place may be wired to explode."

"Get your stupid asses over here," I fume, "the way those guys left out of here, they had no intentions of coming back. And I doubt anyone would be stupid enough to wait around to be gunned down. Now get over here with a crowbar and get this door open. And don't worry, I'm going in alone."

It takes less than a minute to pry the lock back, but it is long enough to fill my mind with all sorts of horrors that await me on the other side; my daughter hanging from the rafters, or bound and shot through the temple. But as I step inside the bright cavernous warehouse, the sight fills me with more pain than has ever been levied against my body before. It stops my heart.

I don't know how I get to Maria. I am just there, on the floor, holding her head to my chest. Her breathless sobs continuing as they had for God knows how long. One of Nicky's men covers Akilina's body with his coat. We all know what took place here.

Nicky gives orders to his men and mine, telling them he wants to know about everyone who has been in the place. "If they had a pizza delivered, I want to talk to the delivery boy."

"He said you wouldn't come," Maria moans in my ear as I lift her up in my arms.

"But I did come for you. I am here."

"But not in time!" she screams.

One of Nicky's guys approaches with a hypodermic needle, "it's a sedative. She's in shock and needs this for the pain."

"No! She can't run from the pain. She can't hide from it. The pain will make her strong. She will have to accept it and grow from it. Feed on it."

"He said all they wanted to do was talk to you, and we could go home," she wails and kicks in my arms.

It had been so long since I've last seen her. She is still mostly arms and legs, but now almost as tall as me. Her eyes are red from crying, red from anger, red with hatred. They burn for the man who has taken Akilina away from her. They burn for me. Her nails dig into my neck, and I let her do her worst. Pour her pain into me. I carry her to the car. "If all he wanted was to talk to me, he wouldn't have taken you and Lina. He lied to you. He could have just called if all he wanted was to talk."

"I told him you were dead," she sobs less, "told him you've been dead for years. He knew you weren't. Where have you been?"

"I was in my grave. I crawled out the day he took you."

Nicky opens the front door and pops his head in.

Maria is against the far door, clutching her knees to her chest. I am trying to sit next to her but she shrinks away into the seat.

"This thing started years ago. Your dad has been through Hell, Little Girl. He had to stay away to keep people like this man from getting to you. He did his best but he did not fail..."

"I promise," I interrupt Nicky, "this man and everyone who had a hand in this, will pay. They will suffer ten times, no, a thousand times more than you and Lina have. I will never stop. They will find no mercy."

Russell Mills comes to the car window, "where are you going to be?"

"I'm taking Maria to her mother. You need to go back to the Bronx and finish preparations for our block party," I tell him.

"Do you think they are still coming? Now that you got your daughter back, what could they possibly gain?"

"They are arrogant. This is far from being over. I want you to make sure no matter how many they send, no matter what they bring with them, that anyone entering our house never leaves. Come morning, what has happened here will never be ventured again."

As we pull away from the warehouse, Nicky turns back to us, "Maria, what say you? We stop somewhere nice so you can get cleaned up before you see your Mom. You know she will kill your Old Uncle Nicky if I bring you home looking like this."

She nods.

Nicky smiles warmly at her and slips me the black case with the sedative in it. He whispers to me, "for later. She is gonna need it."

Sam Black catches the news coverage of the Queens' highway collapse in JFK and is prepared for one hell of a traffic jam home. He arrives home a little before midnight. As soon as he flips on the light in his apartment, the phone rings. Sam is startled by the sudden noise but knows who is calling. He toys with the notion of just letting it ring, the image of Tom still fresh in his mind. Once he starts counting, he gets to twenty rings before he grabs the receiver, "What the hell do you want? Do you still have me bugged?"

"Of course not," I reply. "Those things are expensive and they don't work well once you throw them in the river. I just have someone watching your apartment. Welcome back."

"The Manhattan bombing, the bridge in Mississippi, the highway in Queens... Morris, when is all this going to end?" He sounds really concerned, and very tired.

"Hey, the Queens thing wasn't me," I correct him quickly. "But that is the reason for my call. Tom was very forthright and cleared your guys of any involvement in this whole nasty affair. And true to my word, your team will be released in the morning."

"Am I supposed to say thank you?" he replies warily.

"Well, here's the thing..." I wait a moment for his question, but he never asks what, so I continue, "Your people, the FBI, are being setup. They are about to walk into a trap. I know because I set it up, but these other guys... you know who I'm referring to, told your bosses your team is being held in my gang's hangout in the South Bronx. Nothing could be further from the truth."

"Well, if it wasn't true why did you say it?" Sam is either too tired or Morris is talking in circles.

"Because I really want the other guys, but at the time I didn't know if the FBI was part of this bloody mess or not. Now that I know, I'm giving you the chance to be a hero. Go to your bosses and convince them not to take part in the raid."

Sam thinks it through. For some reason he feels Morris is telling the truth. He doesn't want to harm the FBI, but he is going to unleash Hell on everybody else. His remark about the bloody mess resonates with him. "The thing in Queens, is Maria alright?"

"As well as can be expected, considering the last three weeks, and the people she was with. Thanks for asking. I would love to keep this up but you don't have much time."

"Wait!" Sam yells in panic, "How am I supposed to convince them our agents aren't in the building in the South Bronx?"

"You've had a stellar career up until this point, tell them to trust you," I laugh, "if that fails, check your mailbox."

There's a click and dial tone in Sam's ear. He goes downstairs to the mailboxes in the lobby. His is full with bills and other junk mailings and one plain white envelope, that looks like a greeting card. He opens it and there are five pictures of his team. They look doped up. As he studies the pictures, he sees a small television in the background with the Queens highway story being reported. *Ok, so they were taken tonight.* Then he realizes what the pictures really show. He races back upstairs to the phone.

He calls his boss, "Cox, you have to order the team to stand down tonight."

"Sam, is that you? Where are you?" asks the Assistant Director of the New York office.

"I'm here, in New York. At my apartment, I have proof you are being lead into a trap."

"Really, proof from whom? The criminals you been working for?" answers Joe Cox in his usual acid tone. "I thought I gave that hick sheriff orders to lock you up and throw away the key. Can't anybody in this Goddamn country follow simple orders?"

"Tom Green did, but I don't think he was ever following our orders. That's why the sheriff found it very difficult to keep me there. Look, I have proof my team is nowhere near the South Bronx Slayers' headquarters. It doesn't matter where or how I got it, just that I have it. And if you don't at least take a look at it, you'll get a lot of good agents killed for nothing. And you will have made the worst decision of your career."

"You better get here quick. The ATF, NYPD, and SWAT teams are about ready to roll. I organized this thing tonight. I had a tip from a good informant that says your team is in the building. It is your word against hers and I can't call it off without real hard evidence."

Chapter 18

Scarecrow Plantation

Sam arrives at Fort Apache, the Police department's 41st Precinct in the heart of the South Bronx. He quietly takes a position behind A.D. Cox and listens to a young white-haired man in full SWAT gear.

"This plan was put together hastily so SWAT teams will take the lead, all other departments will give support as needed. This building on Longwood Avenue is a massive target. It is a double apartment building surrounding a large courtyard between Beck Street on the south side and Kelly Street to the north. The main entrance is on Longwood, there, the main stairs lead up to the doors in the middle of the conjoined buildings, and there are additional side doors to each building on Beck and Kelly streets, as well as rear exits to the alley. As everyone here knows, this is a major gang territory, the South Bronx Slayers have an estimated hundred plus members. Many of those members call this building their home. SWAT Teams One, Two, and Three will be ten men ground assault forces, they will enter the build once the two helicopter teams land on the roof and repel to the third floor where the hostages are being held. We believe they are in the interior apartments facing the courtyard."

"I believe you're wrong," interrupts Sam.

"Who the hell are you?" the white-haired Nickleson asks impolitely.

"He's one of my agents," Cox intercedes. "I think he has new intel on the situation," he says to the group of fifty law enforcement officers. Then he turns to Sam and in a half whisper everyone can hear says, "this better be good."

Sam tosses the Polaroid photographs onto the planning table before the group. "Take a good look at these pictures. I received them from Morr… an informant I fully trust."

"These are your kidnapped agents." states Nickleson, passing the pictures to Cox.

"Yes, they are, and these were taken just hours ago. See on the television, they are reporting on the highway collapse in Queens." Sam waits for the leaders of the ATF and NYPD to examine the photos. "I'm sure you had this building under surveillance all day."

The police chief speaks up, "We have men across the street in the high school and several others in apartments on Beck and Kelly."

"And has anybody come or gone from the building this evening?"

"Just a few known gang members…"

"Make your case Sam, we don't have all night," Cox rebukes him angrily.

"In fact, the helis are inbound, you have five minutes, probably less," Nickleson says curtly.

"Ok, so here it is," Sam says confidently, "did anyone notice what was outside the windows in each picture? I did. It's a nice view of the Brooklyn Bridge. Take a good look because here's the thing… You can't see the Brooklyn Bridge from here. Maybe from the rooftop… But I truly doubt it."

Each of the department heads grabs one picture and studies it again, except for Nickleson. He says, "the pictures are fakes. Probably a backdrop to fool us into calling off the raid."

"Only thing is, my guy said they don't want you to call off the raid," Sam tells him. "He just wanted me to get the FBI to back off."

"That's absurd," Cox is offended.

"Well, we have an overwhelming force here," offers Nickleson, "they are trying to better the odds. Or get us to call off the raid completely. But we're not falling for it. Three minutes to roll."

"He didn't want you to call off the raid. In fact, he was fairly certain you wouldn't." Sam turns directly to A.D. Cox and whispers, "he said he knows the FBI had nothing to do with his daughter's kidnapping. So he's offering you a get out of jail free card. These other men, I'm not sure how they fit into his plans, but this is a trap for them." Then Sam speaks up so everyone can hear him. "These guys are waiting for you inside those buildings. They are well armed and looking to kill. My team is not in there, so there is nothing to gain here."

Then the top agent from the Bureau of Alcohol, Tobacco, and Firearms speaks up. "whether we rescue your agents or not, they still have a large cache of weapons we need get off the streets. We are going in."

Two helicopters hover high above the massive gray brick apartment buildings of 725-727 Longwood Avenue. They are too high to be heard on the ground below, but that is about to change. The pilot radios, "Beginning our descent, all units move in."

They drop quickly, within twenty yards of the rooftops. Five ropes fling from each side of the helicopters and SWAT forces rapidly slither onto the roofs. Just as fast as the helicopters take their positions, three armored vehicles of the SWAT forces roar out of the police station garage and down the three streets to the building. Nickleson is amazed that the gang had set up its headquarters so close to the station, almost as if they are daring the police to do something. Well, tonight they anted up. Each vehicle jumps the curb, screeches to a halt, and headlights illuminate the three entrances.

The ten manned teams charge the double glass doors. Gang members scramble inside, locking the heavy iron and thick glass doors behind them. They scatter across the voluminous foyer and up the four staircases. The SWAT teams set small explosive charges on the doors, seconds later the glass shatters and the metal frames twisted open. The three teams enter the building quickly but cautiously expecting gunfire at any moment.

The two teams on the roof send five men each, repelling down the side of the building and the other five rip the metal door open and proceed down the stairs. They move in single file, compact guns at the ready. The five man teams smash through the courtyard windows on the third floor. Three end up in one apartment, two in the other in the two conjoined buildings.

Dozens of police and ATF cars surround the buildings and eight FBI trucks, two at each corner, cordon off the blocks. The FBI trucks light up the streets brighter than a noon summer day. The building is iridescent in the powerful spotlights. The helicopters retreat up into the sky, focusing their beams from above. The scene has fallen into a graveyard quiet.

The radio squeaks in the SWAT members' ears, "assault team alpha, we are in the south east apartment, no sign of the hostages, securing the premises."

"Team Beta, south west apartment all clear."

"Roger that," acknowledges Nickleson on the stairway between the first and second floor.

"Charlie Team has nothing in the north east apartment of 727."

"We are clear here too. Delta team is preparing to egress from north west apartment. We are going across the hall to apartment D."

"Stay sharp," warns Nickleson as he hears a tone of frustration in the last message. He is in the west stairway of building 727, the back stairs, underneath Delta team. He motions his men forward up the steps to the second landing.

Delta and Charlie teams exit the apartment and approach the other two doors on the third floor. It's dark, the light bulbs are broken, and the place smells of piss. Then strobe lights ignite the tight square hallway and the spray of blood and bullets awoke chaos within the confines of the massive gray building. The teams hear the machinegun fire which drives the four attack squads backward into the empty apartments. The muffled gunfire is heard in the streets around the buildings, as a prelude to the bullets pouring out the windows from the second, third, and fourth floors. Bullets rain down on the police forces as a maelstrom suddenly sprang forth from the darkness within. The radios become an unintelligible clamor, as everyone tries to report what everybody already knows. They are under attack.

"Move in! Move in! All Teams converge on the third floor," Nickleson brakes through with his orders. But his team makes it no further than the second floor as the hallway is crisscross with bullets fired from gun ports cut into the four doors, each porthole at a different height and the gun barrels sweep back and forth. Several of his men are riddled with bullets and the others take hits pulling them back to safety. The radio reports come in a disorderly fashion from the SWAT teams. The three floors are death traps. One man from Beta team throws a hand grenade against the opposite door blowing it open, but the gunfire continues spraying at an angle up and down the hallway.

Nickleson finally gives the order to fall back. He reports the building is empty except for the dozen gang members who run inside and are probably operating the guns by remote control. The men in the street have reached the same conclusion as the pattern of gunfire doesn't target anything in particular, but is designed to make approaching the building impossible. Cops hunker down behind the armored vehicle see Nickleson and his men running through the foyer before gunfire erupts and cuts them down.

Men from the three forces make a heroic dash into the building under bulletproof riot shields to rescue the trapped officers. Twenty to thirty men survive the gauntlet and entered the building. Some stop in the foyer to block the bullets while their comrades toss grenades at the doors. The explosions disable the automatic weapons or redirect them to a useless pattern. Others race into the stairwells to reach the upper levels.

Within seconds of the second wave of officers' attacks, a series of explosions, much louder than the percussion grenades used by the officers, rock the building. The stairwells collapse in a blinding debris laden cloud that billows out into the street and from the doors on the roof. From the helicopters the pilots report the partial cave in of the rooftops. The pilots remain on site but little can be done as the roof is now on fire.

More thunderous noise rolls into the street as those still outside see giant metal doors swing down over the entrances, effectively sealing the building like a tomb. So massive are the doors they knock bricks out from the façade of the buildings. The spotlights on the first floor windows reveal they have also been sealed by metal plates. Sam, Cox, and the other law enforcement leaders listen back at Fort Apache how those inside are trapped and at the mercy of whoever is in control.

It is nearing dawn and Cox has listen to and vetoed every plan of rescue put forth by his counterparts. The Special Weapons and Tactical Team has come from D.C. with a hundred men and a plan to rescue his agents. It is obvious they are driving the bus and everyone else is just along for the ride. At the last minute, Cox orders his fifty agents to set up an outer perimeter and stop anyone escaping from the scene. Some of them are taken by surprise when the shooting starts, but most are out of the direct line of fire. And while a hundred other officers, including the rest of the SWAT Team, storm the building, Cox's men hunker down. Out of all those officers from ATF, NYPD, and SWAT his is the only team left.

"This is no longer a rescue mission," argues Cox, "it's a recovery mission. The explosion that took out the third floor corner of 725 made that clear." It had been the second massive explosion of the night; debris flew in every direction from the windows. The gaping hole on the side of the building providing clear access for the fire department to douse the flames from a safe distance. After an explosion of that magnitude Cox expects to recover bodies in the street, he is surprised there are none.

Now as the sun is just below the horizon, he says, "we can use the SWAT armored vehicle to ram those buildings and gain access. They are pre-World War II construction, just brick and mortar, should be easy enough."

The others complain and argue with him for withholding his plan but he has no intentions of sending his men into that Hell Hole. The breech goes smoothly and his men swarm the ground flood, climbing a mountain of debris that is the guts of the building in the center. Cox joins the team with Sam, and looking over the destruction, he can't help but think, *this is overkill.*

Cox can't put his finger on it, but the scene troubles him. There is something missing. After climbing a fire ladder brought inside to reach the upper floors, it hit him. *There are no bodies. Where are all the officers that entered this God forsaken place?* No one is finding anyone buried in the tons of rumble. There is no one in the gutted apartments. Fresh blood spatters everywhere, but that is it.

Cox gets his answer as radio reports start coming in with first light. On rooftops, all-round the South Bronx, bodies in bloody tattered uniforms are hanging. Crucified!

The reports don't last long, only a few managed to get out, before someone in the government, the NSA most likely, put out a gag order. All helicopters are banned from the skies above the South Bronx.

Cox is livid, "Your man Morris had gone too far! I swear! If it takes the rest of my life, we will hunt the bastard down. I don't care where in the world he goes, we will be there, to bring him to justice, or send him back to Hell." He grabs Sam Black by the arm, "And I'm starting with you! You are going to tell me every word he uttered, every place he's been, every twitch he made. Then we are going to pull in every gang banger in this country. If two people are walking down the street, wearing the same color shirt, they belong to me. Am I fucking CLEAR?"

A steady chorus of "Yes Sir" echoes in the devastation surrounding Sam. The eyes of his once trusted colleagues upon him feel sickening. *Morris, you better keep your word and release my team.*

Three black limos pull up to the steps of the Lincoln Memorial. A combined twelve men get out of the first and last car. Several run up the steps of the Memorial, others fan out across the site. They sweep every corner, trashcan, look in every door, and after a ten-minute extensive search, turn up nothing, the lead agent radios, "all clear."

Sen. Carter walks up the stairs and stands at the foot of the Monument. He's looking around as he has done the past two mornings he came for his meeting, only to leave half an hour later. Then a side door opens just a crack. The two Secret Service agents see it and place themselves in front of the senator.

"What are you waiting for... an engraved invite?" I call out from the darkness. "Get in here." The two agents start towards me. "Are you kidding me? Just the Senator, this room is a fucking broom closet."

Sen. Carter pushes past the agents, "it will be alright. He's not here to kill me."

"I wouldn't bet on that Senator," I say seriously. The senator keeps walking and when he gets to the door, I open it all the way. Everybody sees I'm alone.

"You were supposed to be here two days ago. I know your people are notorious for being late... But two days."

"I had to tie up some loose ends. You know how messy that can be."

"How come my men couldn't find you in here? Not a single hiding place that I can see." Sen. Carter is poking his head into every corner.

"Maybe, because I wasn't hiding. You wanted a meeting, and paid a heavy price to get a one on one. You want to state your business so I can get on with killing you?" I square up to the man who is six inches taller and much more muscular.

"Oh, you're not going to kill me," Carter says confidently. "I am here because you developed a satellite based missile guidance system. And then you sold it to the Goddamn Russian!"

I laugh and drop my back against the wall. "I didn't sell it to the Russian. If I did, you think they shoot down their own planes with it? They don't even know they have it."

"Well, I am going to make sure they never find out!" The senator now steps up to me.

"Careful Senator, you don't want what happened in New York to happen here," I push back in the cramped space.

"You think what you did in New York scares me?" Carter bellows, "I sent more men to their death over breakfast. You blew up a building or two, I bombed entire cities and villages back to the stone age. All I care about is what's good for the USA, and to that end I won't let you leave here without giving it to me."

"You don't have anything I want anymore. I don't know what you're planning but I have my daughter back. If you ever think of going after my family again, I'll make it rain blood in every city in America. Starting in Texas."

"First of all, let's get one thing straight," Carter starts, "I didn't order anyone to kidnap your daughter." My look tells him I got the truth from Tom Green, but he continues with his version. "I told my man to get you here and that was the method he chose. Now, I know you are looking for the man, I've seen how you get your kicks. You'll be searching for years and never find him. But I can tell you when and where he will be. That's the deal."

"That's some crummy deal. You give me some guy; I am supposed to turn over a billion-dollar business."

"No, you keep your assets. You just deal exclusively with us." The senator smiles his signature smile. That 'I got you' look.

Man, I hate this guy. "Let me tell you a little story, Senator. There is a farmer. He plants a large field of corn. As the corn grows, here come the crows. First, the farmer goes out with his shotgun and BAM! He kills a few and the rest fly away. The next day, the crows return so the farmer puts up a scarecrow. He looks out his window the next morning, no crows. Happily, he goes to tend his farm and finds the crows had just moved a safe distance from the scarecrow. So, he puts up another one, then another, yet another. With each one he puts up, the crows are forced to move closer and closer to the scarecrows. And each scarecrow protects less and less corn."

"What are you trying to tell me? Am I the farmer or the crows?"

"I don't know. Are you trying to get into my field of business? Maybe you should be asking, why doesn't the farmer just give a shotgun to the scarecrow. You tell me where and when to deliver the guidance system and we will see what kind of business we can do."

Sam Black spends two days in debriefings. He tells and retells his story, both orally and in writing, continuously going over every detail of the past three weeks. It is simultaneously a debriefing and an interrogation. But each time he relives those days, he recalls with more clarity the events. And he is tested relentlessly, is he a criminal, accomplice, or an ally to his team?

His team was found in Central Park, the morning after the South Bronx raid, and have been in a detoxification unit in Belleview Hospital ever since. The four men and one woman can't give any indication as to where they were held, except one, they were in an opium den. They were locked in separate rooms, food was supplied regularly through a sliding opening at the bottom of the door, and the sweet smell of opium funnelled through the vents. At times, the smoke was so heavy it clouded the rooms. It didn't take long for the agents to become stoned and remain that way.

Sam goes to the hospital as soon as he is released from FBI Headquarters, against orders. He meets with each of his team separately and alone. First, is Benjamin. "On the day you were taken, did they say anything about Dean? Give you any reason or indication why they killed him?"

"None sir," he answers sadly. They had all been debriefed and he knew Dean Jones was executed. "I didn't see it happen. We were grabbed from behind and chloroformed. I didn't know if any of the team was alive or dead."

Robert and Pierre didn't see the truck that t-boned them. The crash was so violent it knocked them unconscious. Robert woke up the next day in the room. The windows were blacked out, but he knew it was daylight outside. Metal bars made it impossible to break the windows and the constant exposure to the opium sapped his will to escape.

Pierre didn't know how long he was out for, he was driving and took the worst of the crash. His head was bandage, as it is now. He thought he heard voices, very faint through the vents. They were foreign, maybe Chinese, maybe Spanish. He couldn't be sure; he wasn't sure if he heard them at all. He was in and out of consciousness a lot of the time.

"I am sorry, so sorry we failed you," Jonathan says then breaks down in tears.

"No. You didn't fail me," Sam takes his hand across the little table in his hospital room. They sit in two overly plush chairs by the window. Jonathan looks down, unable to make eye contact. Sam looks tired. "It is I that should be sorry. And I am. I put you into a situation you were not trained for, or ready for."

"But I'll do better the next time," Jonathan says excitedly. "You just have to request me on your team. I want to be on the task force to go after that black bastard! You can get me back in the bureau."

"I can't. I'm out."

"What? No way. They can't fire you over this..."

"Hey, it's ok," Sam tries to calm the young man down. "Nobody got fired. Not me, not you. I retired. I have been at this for too long, and let this thing with Morris Johnson get to me. I got careless and it cost one in our team his life."

"But you can't just walk away. They are forming a task force. You are my only hope of staying in the bureau," he pleads. "The psych says I have an addictive personality. I'll never get over the effects of the opium. Even now, I can still smell it. I still want it. And I want to get Morris Johnson for doing this to me."

Sam shakes his head wearily, "listen to me good. I have been obsessed with capturing this guy ever since the Raven Social Club Shootings and the bloody aftermath that followed. One thing I've learned over the years; revenge never satisfies the soul." Jonathan looks on the verge of tears again. "Look, they should have never told you about the task force. And if you are done with this job, consider yourself lucky. This job will suck you dry."

He finally meets Cathy. She too is surprised he is leaving. She also says the only thing that made the whole damn thing worthwhile. She asks, "did we get the girl back? What happened to Maria?"

"He assured me she is safely back with her mother. Somewhere where they will not be found."

"Well, then I guess our job was a success. You accomplished what you told Elizabeth you would do, return her daughter to her. You should feel good about that."

I sail a small twenty-five-foot Coronado yacht into the Chesapeake Bay, drop the bow and aft anchors then drop the sails.

Russell Mills pulls alongside in a Hunter Cruiser. "You sure the Coast Guard is not going to investigate this boat?"

"It will be fine here. It's sitting in Thimble Shoals, a prime fishing area with its anchor lights on, nothing unusual about that. Besides, it won't be here for long," I assure him as I climb onboard the Hunter.

"I still think we should sail it further up the bay, that navy base is really close. You are begging for trouble here," Russell warns.

"It is because the navy base is here that we are here." We reach the dock of a little house in Norfolk, Virginia. The bay windows give a spectacular view of the Chesapeake Bay.

Nicky is waiting for us inside. Rose, Honey, Yana, and Svetlana – Akilina's big sister are sitting on the couch with drinks in hand.

"It is all set. Won't be long now."

"You trust that scumbag senator gave up his top dog?" asks Nicky.

"No, but it was either Warren or his ass next," I tell them. "He's kinda big on self-preservation. But just to be sure, I have independent confirmation coming in."

"I can't believe you think killing this guy will make up for Akilina. That we would be okay with doing business with the man at the other end of the leash," Yana's rebuttal is sharp.

"It is not okay, but it is necessary," I counter her argument. "I have learned the way to lose a war is to fight it on too many fronts. So we take the victory where we can and fight the bigger battle when we are in a better position."

"What better position? Being in an exclusive deal with your worst enemy," Nicky jumps in on the girls' behalf. "You know damn well he is going to try take you out as soon as he gets control of the companies that manufacture the guidance controls."

"First, you know there are no exclusive businesses in the arms business. We sell to the USA, they sell to everybody else, we make a ton of money. I'm ok with that. Second, Senator Carter will be dead long before he can get his hands on anything. We put down his dog tonight and then we put down the rest of them." The phone on the wall rings once. Everybody looks to it, as I answer, then say, "Ok, it's a go."

I hold up a remote control unit and the room turns to the large window. Night has fallen and drops of rain dot the window, producing a Christmas tree effect. *How appropriate, this is the week before Christmas.* I hand the remote control to Maria, who has been sitting quietly on the loveseat next to Elizabeth. "You do the honors."

Elizabeth looks angrily at me, but says nothing. Maria mashes the red button as hard as she can. A split-second later, the little white sailboat bobbing in the bay is swallowed up by a bright white cloud. A white streak leaves the cloud and disappears into the night. The multicolor lights on the bay twinkle on, oblivious to what just happened. The cars on the bridge flow unknowingly to their destinations. The naval base across the bay, carry on with business as usual. The green and red lights on the various boats do not alter course. The only difference is that the little white Coronado sailboat has disappeared beneath the waves as the steam cloud dissipates.

"Was that it? Now what?" The questions are the only time Maria has spoken. She said nothing on the flight to Norfolk; eight hours in the jet and not a single word. The once exuberant and inquisitive girl was transformed in that warehouse weeks ago. I hope that pushing that button will be a step on the road back, but I doubt it.

"It is roughly two hundred miles to Washington, D.C. and the missile is travelling greater than Mach 1, so in about fifteen minutes, Warren and his entire Black Scorpions Squadron are going to be toast."

The missile's flat black body races above the bay at just under one hundred feet. The satellite picks a course that avoids any aircraft, changing the missile's trajectory three times along the way. It flies undetected past civilian and military radars, even those designed to detect missiles heading towards the Capital.

Carter sits in his office, wondering if he will see anything before the missile hits its target.

He picks up the phone and starts to dial Warren's number in his headquarters at 20th St NW and L St NW, but hangs up before spinning the dial on the last number. It isn't his conscience that is troubling him. He knows Warren can read him like a book. First, he called him back to Washington, then, also ordered his men in from the field to take stock after the South Bronx fiasco, and now a mysterious call in the night... If he spooks him and the attack fails, Morris might take the call as a double cross. He looks out his window, this affair will be over soon.

The missile shoots straight up over the Capital. It climbs to five-thousand-feet and flips over, diving on its target in the city. Ordinarily, the missile would have hit its target flying in low and level, but the building at 20th and L is just a front. The Black Scorpions headquarters are several stories below ground. Setting the missile to dive straight down on the building will make it crash through the three-story building and plunge into its subterranean structure.

A sonic boom rattles the windows all around D.C. and the force of the missile's impact causes the building to collapse in behind it. The hardened steel nose of the missile burrows deep below ground before the warhead explodes. The small entry hole and the collapsed bricks that fill it before the warhead goes off traps and intensify the explosion. Washington, D.C. feels like it has been hit by an earthquake.

Carter's glass rocks loudly on his desk then a plume of fire lights up the night. A widening circle of flames and smoke spread outwards along 20th St NW. The surrounding buildings fall like dominoes into the expanding pit of flames as the ground gives way to multiples eruptions. The Black Scorpions Squad undoubtedly had a large store of powerful weapons in their headquarters. Within minutes, the devastation to Washington's West End section is unimaginable. Five blocks of homes and people are simply gone. Another dozen blocks around the area is on fire. *This must be what Nero saw. Morris Johnson, this was unnecessary. You must go.* Carter drinks his whiskey in one shot.

Within minutes of the missile strike, Maria is watching fire-trucks and ambulances rushing to the scene. Only from helicopters can she see the extent of the damage inflicted, the newscasters on the ground are continuously being pushed back by the flames. It goes on all night. Very late, when everyone else has fallen asleep, Maria leans her head against me. She hasn't touch me since I carried her from the warehouse.

"He must be dead, right?" She asks softly.

"Yes. I made sure of that."

"Then how come I don't feel like he is?"

"In time you will," I say and brush her hair back. "And I will get the rest of them for you."

Senators Carter and Harris are among the dozen lawmakers, NSA and FBI directors, and other cabinet officials the President calls together to combat what he terms, "domestic terrorists." Although the events of the past few months are covered up as unfortunate accidents brought on by extreme cold, those in the government know they are not gas explosions. New York and Washington have been attacked, and the one name that surfaced is John Morrison. Although no real motive for the attacks are given, he is the country's top fugitive, wanted dead or alive.

Carter and Harris also head up the acquisition of new technologies from several companies on satellites photography, laser imaging, and high frequency telecommunications. All of which lead to the development of the Navy's newest weapon, a Tomahawk missile. It is able to skim along the water's surface and strike targets with pinpoint accuracy. The Army and Air Force aren't far behind in the deployment of their own versions of the Cruise Missile.

These new weapons can be the turning point in any battle. They are worth billions to Yana, Elizabeth, and Vicky – who has once again changed her identity, now to the widow of a Midwestern businessman – who hold controlling interests in the parent companies. Carter and Harris are working together on a number of projects.

The months after Washington's West End explosion turns out to be not a good time for Rep. Webber. He is under investigation for corruption and racketeering, which seems to have exploded when a dead girl is found at his winter retreat. She died of an overdose and was then tied to a Chicago mobster. A paper trail of payoffs and kickbacks runs through the dead girl's bank account to Webber's and back to his business dealings with the mobster.

One night, just days before he is to testify before a House Ethics Committee, Webber goes home to his Chicago estate. Sure he knew the girl, knew she was a gift from his friends in Chicago, but the money and business contracts are a setup. He also knows he is screwed. As he sits in the dark house alone – his wife moved out after the news broke, his colleagues avoided any contacts – he drinks himself into a stupor.

He hears a faint click in the darkness. He looks around with squinted eyes and blurred vision, "who's there? What do you want?"

"It's Justice. I'm here for retribution."

A quick muzzle flash illuminates the room and the sound of the .22 Cal barely reaches the street. The Congressman is found dead two days later when he fails to appear before the Committee. A gun lies on the floor beneath his fingers, an obvious suicide, his admission of guilt.

Senator Carter takes the news of Webber's death in his stride. He never liked the man and felt that someday he would have to get rid of him. Lucky for him, Webber did it himself. He was sloppy, and let people get too close. Carter keeps everyone at a safe distance, just close enough so he can keep an eye on them. But as grateful as he is for Webber's removal, he feels the whole affair is Morris' doing, or his friend Nicky Nails.

Nicky is now the head of the New York Mafia. Carter surmised, that as a peace offering from Chicago, they served Webber's head on the veritable platter. He was a weight around everyone's neck, it's good he's gone. Carter's ruminations are suddenly interrupted.

Driving through open country in Texas, and no one else on the road, he spots something strange in his rear view mirror. Long and narrow, white and silver, flying behind him. Carter presses on the gas and pulls away from the object. But when he looks again it has cut the distance in half. He floors the gas pedal.

The Cadillac roars down the road leaving a cloud of dust that hides the rocket from him. He knows he can't out run it and veers off the highway. The car bounces and bucks like the horses he tamed as a boy on the ranch. He can't see the rocket but can't chance it finding him either. He swerves hard again to the left, thinking he'll need to abandon the car soon.

Then he sees the flaming spike out of the driver's side window. He's surprised, it's much smaller than he imagined, two feet, maybe three at most. Before he can make another maneuver, it slams into his tire. The car immediately noses down into the dirt and begins flipping end over end, rolling and throwing parts into the air. The car ends its journey upside down. Every inch of it dented.

The senator is strapped in and bleeding from his forehead, nose, and mouth. The shattered glass has striped him with blood and the crash broken his arm in two places and his kneecap is shot. He's in pain but alive. Then he sees a pair of boots outside his window. "NOOOO. PLEEEASE."

"It is much too late for that."

He watches as the boots move around the car. He struggles with the seatbelt, trying to free himself before the gunshot he knows is coming will ring out. The boots disappear and he sighs in relief, but moments later, he smells gasoline on the warm gentle breeze.

The highway patrol finds the senator's car the following morning. The report reads that he was drinking and racing through the countryside when he flipped his car. A discarded broken bottle of whiskey proof of his foolhardiness. The crash didn't kill him. The ensuing fire turned the car into an oven and roasted him.

The task force on domestic terrorism is called into the President's War Room the morning of July 1st, 1984, two years after the attacks in New York and Washington. They are quickly briefed of the situation unfolding in the Greek isles. Jacques Françoise, aka John Morrison, aka Morris Johnson has been located on a small isle south of Andros by the CIA.

"The island is inhabited by Mr. Johnson and his family and staff," the President informs the group of twelve, which includes Senator Harris, his chief advisor on foreign relations. "And by staff I mean thugs and criminals. I have been given absolute assurances that his daughter is away at a boarding school in France. We have a navy destroyer with a SEAL team ten miles from the area ready to deploy and take this man into custody, or take him out. The Greeks are giving us clear authority to put boots on their soil and take Mr. Johnson. What are your positions on this action?"

The vote goes around the room and each person in turn gives their approval. Then it came to Sen. James Harris, the last man to the President's left. He says. "You got re-elected on the promise of bringing terrorists to justice, both domestic and foreign, I don't think you can pass up the opportunity to bring this man down."

"Good, I'm glad to hear you say that." The fact that Morris and Harris grew up in the same neighborhood is no secret, their ties to each other well known. Harris had also come out in private meetings with his colleagues as blaming Morris Johnson for the death of his sister. It was the main reason Carter had recommended him to the President. "Give the order Admiral Thompson, to commence Operation Spearfish."

The operation called for two teams of SEALs to land quietly on the tiny island and neutralize the guards, before attacking the main house. Non-lethal force was to be used against the women known to be with Morris: an American, a Russian, and a Venezuelan; while he was to be subdued by any means necessary. The teams prepared to launch in the fast attack inflatables.

Captain Charles enters the bridge of the HMS Bulldog and receives a casual salute from his officers. "Reports," he orders.

"That Argentinean Cruiser is still mirroring our course fifty kilometers off our port," replies his security officer.

"As long as they keep their distance we won't worry about them," Capt. Charles says, "no one wants to relive that whole Falklands mess anyway."

Before any of his officers can agree with the captain, one of the six missile launchers on the portside of the ship roars its disagreement. The huge metal trapezoidal container that housed a dozen cruise missiles releases one in a burst of flames and smoke. The missile drops a few feet above the water surface and rips away from the aircraft carrier.

Captain Charles grabs the microphone, "What the bloody hell is going on down there? Who fucking fired that missile?"

An officer from the fire control room responds immediately, "it launched on its own. A malfunction of some kind. We have no keys in the board. I repeat we did not fire that Tomahawk."

"Override now!" screams the captain. "Self-destruct. Destroy that missile."

"We are trying, but she's not responding to any commands," the voice from the speaker is equally frantic. "Self-destruct sequence not registering. We can't alter her course. My God! We have impact."

The captain looks to the west and sees a black cloud rising. The type of ship the Tomahawk struck will not be able to survive. It will be gone beneath the waves in a matter of minutes, long before he can attempt a rescue of her crew. He picks up a red phone on his command console, "get me Naval Affairs on the line. We have a big problem on our hands." Before anyone on the other end of the secure line can answer he commands his bridge crew, "get those damn Tomahawks out of those tubes."

Phones in the war room start lighting up all along the table from the head of the Joint Chief of Staff all the way around to Senator Harris and then finally the President's. The room is hushed as the President listens intently to the Prime Minister of Britain. After a few "I understand" and some assurances that his administration will "get to the bottom of it" he hangs up. A few moments pass as the other phones are all hung up. Each person ending their conversation with their counterpart in the British government.

"Recall the SEALs," the President says softly.

"What? Why?" objects the Admiral.

"We will never have a better time to do this," FBI Director Cox concurs.

"Nancy is the one who believes in psychics, karma, and all that mumble jumble. I believe in cause and effect. This Morris Johnson... he had a hand in the development of these missiles. The minute we try to move against him, one of them goes off the reservation. Gentlemen, this is no coincidence, or a case of bad timing. It is a warning to back off. This time, it was the Brits firing on the Argentineans. In five minutes, it could be an American vessel firing on the Russians or Chinese. Hell, what if one of our battle groups launches on another? We are about to be pulled into the center of an international firestorm, I don't intend to throw more gasoline on it. Recall your teams Admiral Thompson, this is a fight we cannot win. Not today."

THE END

About The Author

A native New Yorker, born and raised in the Bronx, James L Hill spent his adolescence years in Fort Apache, the South Bronx 41st precinct during the 60's, during a time when you needed to have a gang to go to the store. Raised on blues, soul, and rock and roll gave him the heart of a flower child. Educated by the turmoil of Vietnam, Civil Rights, and the Sexual Revolution produced a gladiator. Realizing the precariousness of life gave him an adventurous outlook and willingness to try anything once, and if it did not kill him, maybe twice.

12 years of Catholic education and a couple of years in college spread between wild drug induce euphoric years, which did not kill him, gave James an unique moral compass that swings in any direction it wants. A scientific mind and a spirit that believes nothing is impossible if you want it bad enough guides his writings. He enjoys traveling to new places and seeing what life has to offer.

James began writing short stories and poetry back in his early years. In his twenties moved on to novels. He worked in the financial industry and later got a degree in computer programming, his other love. James has a successful career as a software engineer designing, developing and maintaining systems for the government and the private sector. He has been programming for nearly forty years in various languages.

After years in the computer world he returned to his first love, unleashing the characters in his head. Still a hopeless insomniac, he feels free to pound out plots. James L Hill is a prolific storyteller writing crime stories, fantasies, and science fiction, with a slant on the dark side of life.

The next step on his journey naturally led to the business of publishing. He started RockHill Publishing LLC not only to produce his own work, but to give others access to the literary world. His computer background and experiences in word processing gives him insight into what it takes to publish good books.

The Killer series is an adult crime novel centered around the life of Bulletproof Morris 'Mojo' Johnson. *Killer With A Heart* introduces us to the young gangsters and mobsters in the conflicting worlds of Organized Crime.

Killer With Three Heads has the boys from the Bronx return as international criminals and more deadly than ever.

The Emerald Lady is a pirate/mermaid adventure/love story set in the Golden Age of Pirate and the first novel in the fantasy Gemstone Series.

Pegasus: A Journey To New Eden, his science fictions deal with the emotional effects of technology, and answers the question, "How do I feel about nuclear war?"

Killer With Black Blood
Chapter 1
A Home in Hell

Nicky exits the Long Island mansion and quickly turns up his collar against the harsh March wind. A scowl carves his face but not from the cold outside; bitterness eats through his soul this morning. He pulls the door to the Cadillac with enough force to almost unhinge it.

He dives into the back seat to the cheerful voice of his driver Rocky, "Good morning, Boss! Looks like plenty of sunshine today, a great day for a ride. Don't ya think?"

"Who the fuck asked for a fucking weather report," snarls Nicky. "Drive the Goddamn fucking car. I want to get Sal and get this Goddamn thing over with. Fucking great day for a Mother Fucking drive. Are you shitting me?"

"Well, I say you just found out somebody been kicking your dog. But I know you don't have dog, not as a pet anyway. So, what got your nuts all twisted this morning, you miserable fuck," Pauley says, shifting in the back seat next to Nicky. He gives a nod and wink to the young driver through the rear-view mirror and the car speeds up the driveway.

"I just got the final bill on the thing," Nicky throws his hands up, "fucking crooks, every goddamn one of them. Three fucking mil, can you believe that!"

"I've seen it," Pauley says in his serene voice and opens the bar built into the back of the driver's seat. He shuffles the two .45 automatics aside and takes out two glasses. "Here, hold these."

"I don't want a drink!"

"Well, I do. It's fucking early. So, hold the fucking glasses and stop being a prick."

"Uncle Pauley, stop trying to treat me like a kid. I ain't no kid anymore!"

"Then stop acting like one," Pauley's face is hard now. His snow-white hair barely covers his head, which is why he always wears his fedora, except in the car. He pours two stiff drinks and takes back one glass. "Look, you did a good thing. Italian marble all the way, not that cheap façade stuff. It is going to make Sal happy. You know he's fucking miserable in that fucking nut house."

"I know." Nicky shoots down the drink and holds his glass up for another pour of Absolut. "But what am I supposed to do with him now? It's been six months and not a word about it. Somebody got to him…"

"You know that's crazy," Pauley sips his drink like a gentleman, "I've known you boys all your life, nobody could talk to Sal but you and your father. And Sal never left the farmhouse except for his doctor's visits. And I was with him for most of those. And your father or mother, it's just impossible…"

"That's why he's at St. Joseph Hospital. And let me tell you, those fucking guys…" Nicky shoots down his second drink, as if forgetting he is holding it. He shudders and blows hard as this shot burns more than the first. "…no one can spend the money like the Catholics. I'll give you that."

"I did like you asked and checked out the doctor. He was handpicked by your father," Pauley sounds apologetic. He wants to tell Nicky something good, but this is not going to make him feel any better. "The doctor is clean. Has more money than God, so no one could have paid him off. No evidence of coercion either. He said it could have been the medication. Maybe they gave him too much, or Sal stopped taking it, you remember the chickens. There is just no way of knowing what was going on inside Sal's head."

The rest of the short drive out to St. Joseph is quiet. The hospital complex is about ten miles from Angelo's mansion, which Nicky now occupies fulltime since Elizabeth and Maria moved to the Greek Islands with MoJo. It has always been the seat of power for the Family; even when his father ran things they would meet out on the Island, not at the farm upstate. When he took over from his dad everyone knew he would run things from there.

The car turns up the driveway of St. Joseph, each of the white-brick buildings separated by immaculate green lawns the size of a football field. They pass three edifices, before turning down another driveway towards the biggest of the buildings. It's five stories high, made from massively large granite stones, and the only one in the complex surrounded by a six-foot tall iron fence. The black rods come straight up out of the ground, too close together to get an arm through. Every window has the same black iron rods.

The place looked more like a prison than a hospital, and it had been a military prison during the Civil War. In the mid-nineteen-hundreds the Jesuits bought it and added two more buildings. Now, there were five, thanks to Nicky's generosity.

Nicky laughs. "Is it just me or does this place get bigger each time we come here?"

"We haven't been here in what... a month? But I would say so. You want I could come in with you?"

"No, I'm gonna talk to the fucking priest for a minute before Sal comes down."

The gate rolls back slowly as something that size would, and the black caddy with blacked-out windows drives straight to the front door. A very old priest, Fr. Sheridan, steps out of a crack in the huge oak doors.

Rocky, the driver, says, "you think the old guy has the cojones to open that door? Or are there like a dozen old guys back there with him?"

They laugh.

As Nicky is exiting the car, Pauley grabs his arm, "I have to tell you something later. Don't let me forget. It's important."

"Tell me now."

"No, it can wait. Just don't let me forget. You know how us old guys are," he looks in the rear-view with a twisted grin.

"I was talking about you, Mr. Pauley," Rocky says with a slight shrill in his voice, "I know who got the balls for anything."

"Relax, kid. Maybe one day, when you are ready to become a man, I'll let you borrow them."

Nicky laughs, "You should be thankful your momma sucks good head. Marrone!" He takes the stairs quickly, shakes the priest's hand, and disappears into the hospital.

They walk down the marbled hall, their footsteps echoing loudly in the spacious interior. It is dark with drapes and tapestries. Pictures of Jesuits hanging everywhere, a few are smiling, very few. He hates this place. From the prison look to the austerity of the atmosphere within, it embodies everything he hates about his religion. Putting Sal in here was a bad thing to do, but he felt if anyone could get through to him, these priests could. They reach the office and he takes a seat. "So, tell me, Father, has he said anything about what happened. You know, has he made his confession."

"Confession?" the old priest leans back in his high-back chair covered in plush red velvet. "He was very agitated this month. With you not coming for your weekly outing. He doesn't confess to anything per se, but he does... and again he got extremely emotional when you didn't show for the second weekend in a row. He started talking about killing bananas and Old Joe. Ah, I don't know how to put this, so here's the thing. He wasn't involved in any other killings…"

"Hey, I'm not interested in any other killings!" Nicky explodes. "I brought him to you so you can get the truth out of him about one thing, and that's it. Youse guys have been taking my money for years and now you want to get all holier than thou on me?"

"Mr. Rocci, this place may look like a medieval castle," Fr. Sheridan says firmly but calmly, "but we don't practice any inquisition tactics here. We don't do exorcisms or any magical spells. The priests here are trained psychologist, not mind readers. Let me give you a little advice."

Nicky squirms in his plush chair and sinks a little deeper. He has hated the clergy for as long as he can remember. He felt the sting of his mother's slap on the back of his neck when they were called into the office for something or other. He pretended to listen.

"There are three people you should never lie to," cautions the priest. "Your lawyer because he holds your freedom. Your doctor because he holds your life. And your priest because he holds you for eternity. We might be better able to help your brother and get you the answers you seek if we knew more about what went on at the farm. What Sal was exposed to and what was kept hidden. Think about it. I'll have Sal brought down."

Sal sits between Nicky and Pauley and asks every five minutes where they are going.

Nicky hasn't said a word since leaving St. Joseph.

As they cross the Throgs Neck Bridge, Sal squeals, "You are taking me home to Mommy and Daddy!"

Pauley looks at Nicky and shrugs.

Nicky shakes his head slowly, "Sal, you know where we are going. But I have a big surprise. I built Mom and Dad a house just like the farmhouse."

The car pulls into St. Peter's Cemetery.

Sal starts rocking and bouncing in the back of the car. "No. No. No. Nicky you are supposed to take me to Mommy and Daddy. Not here. Mommy and Daddy are in Heaven. Daddy said you will take me to Heaven with them. I've been good. I've been a good boy, Nicky. I promise." He starts to cry.

"Well, there go three million dollars down the drain," Nicky says angrily. "Get the fuck out the car, Sal. Let's go look at this fucking mausoleum I built for you."

They walk up the hill; a hard climb as the path is steep to the marble farmhouse at the top. Nicky had to buy all the grave sites around his family plot to build the mausoleum. He remembers the picture on the office wall of St. Peter, maybe a hundred years or more in the past. Then, the view from the cemetery was of apple blossoms, white trees, and quaint little homes spread out across the valley. Now, the view is blocked on three sides by high-rise building towers fifteen stories. The only clear view is a sliver of the river to the north.

Although no one has been buried in the graves around his family plot in more than a century, they still charged him over a million dollars to buy the land. And of course, he could not move the grave, there had to be a small plaque in the ground alongside the mausoleum with the name of those it covered up, state law. The last time Nicky had been here it was to bury some uncle or aunt he barely knew, years before he had to bury him mother and father last winter.

"NO. NO. NO. I DON'T WANT TO BE HERE. DADDY SAID I WOULD GO TO HEAVEN WITH HIM AND MOMMY. HE PROMISED ME. I'VE BEEN A GOOD BOY." Sal gets hyper, turning in circles not knowing where to go.

Nicky grabs his arm and gives him a yank, then places both hands on his shoulders, "I don't know what you're talking about, Sal. You can't go to heaven if you're still alive. And even when you do, God knows you'll be the only one in this family to make it in, I sure as hell won't bet on Papa being there. Mom, yeah, she'll be there. But if you see Dad, you took the wrong elevator."

Sal pulls away, standing in front of the marble structure mumbling incoherently.

"What are you saying? Look, why don't we go inside. You can see Mom and Dad's caskets. Maybe say a little prayer. Tell them YOU ARE SORRY FOR SMOTHERING THEM... YOU FUCKING RETARD."

"Mommy said you are not supposed to call me that," Sal says. "Father Sheridan said God knows everything. The why and the how, He forgives all that we do."

Well, thank you, Father Sheridan. At least you are not just taking my money and fucking me up the ass.

Sal drops to his knees in front of the mausoleum door.

Nicky yells, "If you're crying I'm gonna kick your ass!"

Sal falls face down on the mount.

Nicky sees a wide blood spot on the back of his head. Then, nothing.

"So, what do you think?"

Pauley lights a cigar, "What do I think about what, Rocky?"

"Think Nicky is going to off his brother? I mean, the word is Sal killed his parents," Rocky remarks. "Nicky seems to be on the edge of crazy."

"Shut the fuck up! Are you fucking crazy?" Pauley, about to take a swing at him, notices Sal and Nicky lying in front of the marble farmhouse. He starts running up the hill, dodging headstones as he goes.

Rocky takes the path, and being younger, beats him to Sal's side.

Pauley arrives a second later and quickly accesses the situation, "Leave him! Sal is dead. Help me get Nicky to the car."

Rocky grabs Nicky under the arms and carefully pulls him into the back seat.

Pauley takes off his own jacket and shirt. "Here! Use my shirt and keep pressure on the wound. I'll drive." He floors the gas pedal and the caddy roars through the cemetery.

He hits the street heading for Our Lady of Mercy Hospital, not far in the northern section of the Bronx. The car weaves in and out of traffic, blowing through red lights. His experience as a get-away driver kicks in, and four cop cars fail to stop him until he's at the hospital's emergency entrance.

The police look in the back seat and run inside to get help.

A doctor throws up his hands and stops Pauley from entering, "Sir, you have to ditch the cigar."

Pauley looks at his right hand, where the fat stogie is lodged between his index and pointer fingers still smoldering. He tosses the cigar into the street and follows Rocky, the doctors, and Nicky with his fedora neatly on his head.

Two police officers, one on each side of him, are shouting questions at him.